THE SPIRIT GATE STOOD SIX TIMES THE HEIGHT OF A MAN

Its bars must have been driven deep in the riverbed itself, into the water far below the choppy water. Where the shore reared up, the gate was fitted into a wall: featureless, towering undulant up the banks, extending undiminished into the forest. Thunder roared and rippled toward us. Over the gate danced lightning.

At that flashing signal the rain stopped. But the sound remained, redoubled. With querulous protest, the lower half of the iron gate split, each section retreating into its wall of stone.

Chayin, with a grunt, ran. Sereth, motioning me before him, followed. I stumbled in the gaseous mist, broke my fall with outstretched hands.

"Come on," urged Sereth. "Look!"

I looked. And saw. And heard: the great gate, mysteriously as it had opened, had begun to close. We ran for it.

My numbed fingers grasped the slow-closing iron bars. I grabbed the lattice of body-thick, slimy iron and pulled myself through. The gate's sides rejoined, to present once more an impenetrable barrier.

"Estri, did you [...]
Chayin, touching [...]

"No. I was going [...]

"If you did not, [...]
did?"

Also by Janet Morris

THE GOLDEN SWORD
HIGH COUCH OF SILISTRA

THE CARNELIAN THRONE

JANET MORRIS

science fiction BAEN BOOKS

THE CARNELIAN THRONE

A Baen Book

Baen Enterprises
8-10 W. 36th Street
New York, N.Y. 10018

First Baen printing, March 1985

ISBN: 0-671-55936-2

Cover art by Victoria Poyser

Printed in the United States of America

Distributed by
SIMON & SCHUSTER
MASS MERCHANDISE SALES COMPANY
1230 Avenue of the Americas
New York, N.Y. 10020

to Perry Knowlton

Contents

I.	*The Spirit Gate*	1
II.	*Deilcrit*	21
III.	*Of Whelts and Wehrs and Imca-Sorr-Aat*	51
IV.	*The Eye of Mnemaat*	77
V.	*Stepsisters' Embrace*	124
VI.	*Nothrace by Night*	162
VII.	*The Bowels of Dey-Ceilneeth*	200
VIII.	*The Carnelian Throne*	239
IX.	*Gardens of Othdaliee*	263
X.	*Imca-Sorr-Aat*	270
	Estri's Epilogue	296
	Glossary	299

1

The Spirit Gate

"Gate!" he bellowed over the storm, his dripping lips at my ear. The deluge had made us sparing of words. Under leathers soaked to thrice their weight, I shivered in spasms. Arms clutched to my sides, I stared into the rain. The driven sheets slashed me for my audacity. Lightning flared, illuminating the riverbank white. A moment later, the bright noise cracked through my head. The hillock trembled.

Over the gate danced the lightning. Its crackling fingers quested down thick-crossed slabs of iron, seared flesh. Emblazoned as they tumbled were those six-legged amphibians, their streamered tails lashing, scaled, fangful heads thrown back in dismay. I saw their afterimage: beryl and cinnabar, aglow upon the storm. Then their charred remains splashed into oblivion, spun away on the fast current.

"Down!" One man shouted, the other shoved me, and as I staggered to kneel in the sedges, the god that washed this land shook it, grumbling. I crouched on my hands and knees on the bucking sod, between them. Little protection could they offer up against shaking earth and searing sky, not even for themselves, without divorcing themselves

from the reality they had come here to explore.
And that they would not do.

Somewhere far off the weather struck earth again.
We knelt on a fast-declining shore. On our right
and left, steeps ascended, cresting in a plume of
dense rain forest. In that moment of illumination
the whole river valley and the gate set into the
river stood bared of shadow. Six times the height
of a man was that gate. Its bars must have been
driven deep in the riverbed itself, into the rock far
below the choppy water. Where the shore reared
up, the gate was fitted into a wall: featureless,
towering undulant up the banks, extending undiminished into the forest. For a swath about its
base the earth was black and devoid of vegetation.

"Did you see that?" I yelled into the wind, which,
like a hymn to power in its last stanza, trailed off
to a murmur as the rains recommenced.

"Higher ground, before any of those six-legged
toothfulnesses decide to take a stroll!" His roar
echoing in the abating gale's last howls, the cahndor
of Nemar lifted me bodily to my feet. The other
man shaded his eyes with his hand and peered up
into the enshrouded sky before he abandoned his
squat. He has borne many names, before that time
and since: we will call him Sereth.

"Chayin, I would take a closer look," Sereth
called, wiping his streaming brow. Chayin rendi
Inekte, cahndor of Nemar, co-cahndor of the Taken
Lands, Chosen Son of Tar-Kesa, and in his own
right a god, ceased dragging me across the suck
and slide of the sedges. The nictitating membranes
snapped full over his black eyes. For a silent moment the gazes of the two men locked, and the
worth of a thousand words was exchanged therein.
Then Chayin nodded and propelled me toward the
gate. Or to where it must be, beyond the sheeting
rain, white as if boiled, through which little could

be seen for farther than a man might extend his hand.

Sereth dropped back behind, blade drawn, sidling through the grass with his eyes turned riverward, that he might see a slither, a shifting of reeds, a muck-covered, armored snout before its owner could make a strike.

We had seen few of them, these legged ones. We had seen their larger cousins, who have no legs, in the open seas to the north. They were much the same; irridescent scales striped their lengths; their wide-hinged jaws, fringed round with glowing streamers ever-changing in hue and deadly with poisonous barbs, boasted two rows of blade-sharp teeth; their eyes were bilious, side-set under protrusions of bone. One of them could doubtless shred a woman-sized carcass free from flesh in less time than it takes to realize dreaming in sleep.

Though some might say I am sufficient protection unto myself, I was glad of Sereth's sword behind me, and Chayin's upon my left, on that shore. I squinted into the rain, straining for sight of the sun. Somewhere, unvanquished, it lurked behind the black-bellied clouds that had come so fast down from the north to envelop us. Beneath my booted feet, the reeds gave way. I lurched, gasped, sank ankle-deep into the mush.

Chayin whirled. Then, chuckling, he offered out his free hand. I took it—his, deep, rich brown, surrounded mine, copper with a muted tinge of light—and he pulled me from the slurping sink. Sereth, brows down-drawn, stepped with care.

Once again the angered giant hurled firebolt to earth. At that flashing signal the rain stopped, asudden as if the lightning's heat had razed all moisture from the land. The sedges began to steam, throwing off their putrid perfume.

The sound came, slowly growing, ineluctable as

an injured limb reporting its message. Renewed, thunder roared and rippled toward us, borne on a wind that bent the reeds whooshing flat. Before that wind the clouds took flight. But the sound remained, redoubled. Above the gate, daysky crawled shakily upward as the thunder, disheartened, slunk away before the other sound: It pealed like some mountainous bird screeching to its mate: It made a chalybeate taste come into the mouth, and water into the eyes. Might the earth's bowels scream that shrilly? If the continents sob as they pulverize each other beneath the sea, might such a sound be their dirge? It sanded nerve and quickened blood, and stopped us each in our tracks.

Searching amid the mists for its source, I made it out, even as Sereth's eyes sought Chayin's for confirmation. Ahead, swathed in dusky green shadows, the gate continued to draw itself back. With querulous protest, the lower half of that iron lattice split, each section retreating into its wall of stone.

Chayin, with a grunt, ran. Sereth, motioning me before him, followed. High reeds jabbed us. I stumbled in the gaseous mist, broke my fall with outstretched hands. My palms, when I raised them, came away speckled with burrs. Chayin gained the water's edge. Sereth, his hand at the small of my back, urged me silently.

Running, I scraped the burrs off onto my tunic. Harsh in my ears, my breathing and the break and hiss of the marsh grass beat time to my stride, as did the ever-welling clouds of insects released by the storm's retreat. A flying thing as large as my hand, vermilion and gold with great staring eyes upon its wings, hovered before us. An eager ray of sun struck it, bejeweled it, passed on. The ground under my feet had spongy strength. Sereth loped easily at my side, accommodating his pace to mine.

"Move!" implored Chayin, half-blended into the dark brown, towering wall before him. So skillfully joined were those blocks that there was no shadow of stone upon stone. Nor did mortar show between them. As we quit the last of the rushes a silver-winged bird screeched and burst upward, scolding, its curved cobalt beak open wide.

"Kreeshkree!" it accused, diving so low I shielded my eyes. A wingtip brushed my temple. "Kreeshkree! Breet, breet iyl!" it blared, whirling in midair to hover above my head.

In a single motion, Sereth pushed me aside and struck out at it as it dived. His blade flickered. The bird ("*Kreesh . . .*") dropped to the ground, its severed head covered by the plummeting body where it fell into a bier of red flowers.

"Come on," urged Sereth. "Look!"

And I looked. And saw. And heard: the great gate, mysteriously as it had opened, had begun to close. Vibration and rumble grew loud, then unbearable. We ran for it. Chayin hesitated, poised in the crural water of the wall's lee edge, imploring, body tensed to spring.

"Go on," urged Sereth. In a handful of bounds, the cahndor had disappeared between the gate's drawn-back portals.

Over the cinder swath that paralleled the wall's extent, we ran. Sliding down the bankside, over the wall's plinth, we splashed into the water. In moments I was hip-deep, slogging with sinking feet through the sediment. As we assayed the crossing, the screeching noise began once more: the gate, in stately approach, paced us, drawing us with it toward the river's center.

Sereth's needless, urgent demand for speed ripped through my mind even as my numbed fingers grasped the slow-closing iron bars. I grabbed the lattice of body-thick, slimy iron and pulled myself through. The wail of metal was deafening. I stood, frozen, gaping at the gate while its sides rejoined, to present once more an impenetrable barrier.

Sereth pushed me ungently toward the shore. I stumbled, and cursed him as, thoroughly soaked, I waded to the bank. He himself stood up to his hips in the water, oblivious of danger, bow and blade held high, staring with narrowed eyes at the gate. It was silent, suddenly. No longer did the screams of tortured metal ride the wind. The air was still. The water, earlier dark and gray, shone warm with the reds of day's end. The sky was fired green, cloudless.

It was Chayin who called him out from before that gate of iron, latticed like some giant's garden trellis. He came, shaking his head, taking short backward glimpses. He joined me where I stood on the plinth and ran his hand over the groove where gate met brown stone, then over the woven iron bars, through which nothing larger than a hand might pass. There was no sign now that the gate had ever opened (save that we were now within whatever this barrier had been constructed to protect), nor that it might ever do so again.

With a toss of his head Sereth sheathed his blade, shouldered the bow, and aided me up the bank to where Chayin sat amid a puff of dark-capped weeds on a hillock.

My feet sloshed and squished in boots filled with silt and water. I sat beside Chayin and emptied them, tearing up handfuls of grass with which to scour the muddied leather clean. In the puddle I poured out from my left boot onto the ground, a tiny, red-striped fish flopped, wriggled, then lay still. A tremor, then many, coursed over my flesh.

The wall, dour, devoid of feature but for its gate, dwarfed all else. On this inner side, extending from its base three man-lengths outward, the turf was blackened, free of weed or twig. Everywhere else, the shore was wildly fertile. From the dappled forest, gibbering, trilling, came the sunset songs of unnamed beasts. Mewling, snorting trebles mixed with deeper, hissing growls as the rain forest reaffirmed its celebration of life. But the wall spoke not of life. In the blackened, time-and-again-singed earth were set iron stakes. Not more than a pace apart, as high as my knee, they flowered the scathed earth. Like the armies of Chayin's Nemar formed up for review did the black-iron sentinels flank the sheer brown wall. As far as my eyes could see ran that wall, and the blackened earth, and the sharp, pointed iron stakes.

"Iron rusts," observed Chayin as I pulled from my boots the last of the muddied, sharp-edged gray grass.

"The sun sets," I snapped, and winced as a thorned weed made its sovereignty clear to my right thigh. Carefully I disengaged it from my flesh and continued what I had started—the working of wet, muddy feet into wet, muddy boots.

Sereth, who had been doing likewise, gave the task up as a bad job. Wriggling his toes, he leaned back on his elbows and stretched, grinning at me with that sly, under-the-brows demeanor that has ever boded ill for the universe at large, and for me, especially, has come to signify his readiness to collect that tribute which he chooses to call humor. I bristled, like the countless women before me subject to the tax imposed by such a man.

"I would not, if I were you."

"Would not what?" he inquired innocently, while hiding his smile with a hand rubbed across his jaw.

I did not answer, but turned to Chayin, who raised up both palms toward me and cringed theatrically.

"I was only going to say that it seems we have found some sign of man," spoke Séreth, not to be denied. We had wagered upon this point.

"Not living man. That," said I, sweeping my hand over gate and wall, "could well be an artifact left from before the rebuilding." It was a half-hearted objection, even to my own ears.

"Iron rusts," said Chayin again.

"And it is getting dark. I am wet. I am cold. I want a fire." I sighed. "And something to eat—you promised me a local meal." I had grounds for complaint on that score: we had been eating the ship's stores far too long. Three days past we found this river's mouth and sailed the Aknet up it, as far as Chayin had deemed safe. There we left her, and her crew, making a twenty-one-day rendezvous. If we did not by then reappear, they were on their own. And the ship's commander had not been happy; but what objections he voiced had only been wasted breath. These two men, who between them reigned over all Silistra, listened no more to their shipmaster than they had to me. It had made me feel, somehow, less useless when they heeded not the sage council of Neshub, the ship commander. Though I agreed with him, in substance, I was pleased when they ignored his demands that we take an armed party—he was a man, one they respected, and their heedlessness in his case made stinging their heedlessness in mine. It was not that they ignored my advice because I was a woman, but that they ignored all advice that did not agree with their plans. And what were those plans? In sum, they were simple; self-indulgent, if any stranger had been present who might have dared judge them: we had no purpose there, at that time, other than hunting.

Sereth, with a squint at the sky, notched into his bow one of the arrows he had demanded I fletch.

"If your arrow flies, you will have the game meal you crave," he grunted, rising.

"Straight," Chayin amended. My first attempts had evinced a marked rightward propensity. Sereth, soundless, slipped into shadowed trees.

I peered around me, taking stock. The shore on this side of the gate rose less steeply. The marsh and riverbed knew no boundaries, but entwined each other's domains. Just north of us, the shore was treed to the waterline and beyond with white-barked giants (which we would come to call memnis) whose leaves depended in places to trail along the river's surface. The bend along which we had come, the bend that had revealed the gate, continued its twisting course northward.

"Estri, did you open the gate?" asked Chayin, touching my shoulder.

"No. I was going to ask you." I turned from the river view.

"Sereth surely did not." No, Sereth would not have set his will to opening the gate. We had pacted with him to refrain from such activities, that we might calm ourselves and the time around us. Nothing was known of this place upon whose banks we sat. Perhaps there was nothing to know here. It would have suited me, had such been the case.

"If you did not," Chayin pursued it, stretching out on his side, "and I did not, and Sereth did not, then who did?"

"I told you: the wall is doubtless left from before the rebuilding. The lightning hit some old mechanism."

"Conveniently, just as we happened to be passing by?"

"Coincidence?" I offered.

"Even you know better than that, by now."

"Make a fire," I suggested. "No fire, no portentous discussions."

"Without skills? In this all pervasive dampness?" he objected, but rose up with mutters about women on hunting trips and stalked about in the bushes. I turned away, surreptitiously seeking with mind for intelligence secreted near the gate. I found none who might have triggered its opening.

Chayin's voice, out of the rustling leaves, was determined: "Iron rusts. Those stakes are in good shape. That ground is kept cleared."

I suppressed a guilty start, momentarily sure that he had caught me seeking—a thing Sereth had forbidden. But Chayin, grunting and cursing as he sought materials for fire in the sopping wood, had not noticed. I watched him, pensive. It was he whose aegis had underwritten this trip. It was he whose couch-mate, Liuma, had been slain by those we hunted. Or would hunt, when spring thaws made the northern rivers navigable. This plausible excuse served us, each one for our own purpose. True, we all hunted here: peace, and nature, and a respite from our concerns. We had left, each of us, all that we had so recently acquired. Or tried to: what we had lost could not be regained, and what responsibilities we fled trailed determinedly at our heels. As in the mythical book of prophecy to which Chayin felt us bound, we had sailed an ocean, bearing with us a sword which might—or might not—be Se'keroth, Sword of Severance, and the material sign of that long-prophesied age, the coming of the divinity of man. Sereth subscribed not at all to that belief. So he said, now, though it had been he who first voiced the possibility. I was uncommitted. Or rather I did not want to be convinced, yet half believed. If the sword that Sereth had acquired with his accession to Silistra's rule *was* Se'keroth, the blade would be quenched in ice. Until that time, I withheld both support and censure. In this place, I thought, looking around me, ice might be hard to find.

But then, dry wood should have been hard to find.

Chayin unburdened his arms and arranged brush and branch to his satisfaction. He lit it with a flint device, and not his mind, bending low to the piled tinder. Though Sereth was not here to see, Chayin honored his will. I might not have been so patient. It was the third try with the sparking wheel that caught. He blew into cupped hands, cajoling the spark.

By the time I knelt at his side, the spark, judiciously nursed, had become a flame. Chayin sat back, staring into the fire.

"I am very sure that we are being watched, and not by any artifact. Sit still! You might sense it." Casually, he met my eyes.

"He asked me to forgo such things," I reminded him, unable to resist. "And you also."

"So scrupulous? This is no time for it. He asked, yes. Whenever possible, and if we met no men, and not to any extent that might endanger our lives. We are about to meet men." Out of his loam-dark face the fire shone back at me, red-gold, from enlarged pupils.

It was then that Sereth, with no more sound than a gust of wind between the trees, emerged from the swamp. Over his shoulder were two red-furred, motionless animals, tied together by the tails at his shoulder. Their black muzzles dangled around his knees. Their staring eyes, even in death, were gentle.

"Local meal," he announced, dropping the two warm carcasses in my lap. "Your arrows are improving."

I stroked the soft fur of my dinner-to-be. Then I thanked it for its flesh and took my knife to it.

"What did you see?" Chayin demanded.

"Plants and animals with which I am not familiar. No men. But man-sign," added Sereth, taking one of the carcasses into his own lap.

"It has come to me that we are being observed. What think you?" growled Chayin, scratching beneath his tunic.

"I am sure of it," said Sereth quietly, and nothing more until the little animal lay gutted and skinned before him. Then: "There is a path, very straight, wide, well-tended. It runs northwest from the wall, just beyond those trees." He rose, scrutinized my novice's butchering, and went to cut a spit pole.

By the time the meat spattered above Chayin's fire, the constellations were beginning to poke their way through the haze. Sereth had helped me with my preparation of the meat; patient, soft-voiced as always when concerned with what he termed "life-skills." The more deeply I had involved myself, during that long sea voyage, with affairs of mind, the more insistent he had become that I take instruction from him in weaponry, in survival on land and sea, in hunters' lore. I knew, by then, more than I wished of butchering and the catching of fish; and less than I had hoped of what lay in his heart. Of his turmoil, I had been instructed only by omission: he never spoke of it.

"Why do you think it is that none of these plants and animals are known to you?" I asked him.

"Because I have never been here before," he answered, hacking off our dinner's left hind leg. "Chayin, take what you will." He who hunts eats first of the kill. They observed the old rules ever more closely, with fervor. Perhaps with desperation:

that which is invulnerable is unnatural, and though they were not truly immortal, nor as yet all-powerful, they were no longer, even in their own eyes, "normal" men. This deeply troubled them, those reluctant gods. As it had troubled me when I first discovered what latitude I might exercise in this that we call life. So I said not a word while the cahndor and Sereth ripped bites from a steaming joint of the nameless meat, but waited until they were satisfied that no immediate symptoms of illness developed. For only a quick poison, one that could strike in an instant, and catch the victim unawares, could incapacitate such strengths as we now possessed. Between thoughts, must a crippling blow be landed on an intelligence so highly skilled. I waited, hardly tense, sure in my capacity to intervene should the beast-flesh prove deadly. But it did not, and soon I was crunching happily the crisped outer flesh of Sereth's kill. The meat did hold one surprise, however: it was neither gamy nor tough, but sweet and rich. Even as I thought it, Sereth spoke:

"We may well be expected to pay for this meal when we come upon the owner of this preserve."

"Why wait?" mumbled Chayin around a mouthful. He gestured with a greasy forefinger. "Our observer still lurks. Let us go greet him. Perhaps we could take a live pair home, and breed up a herd ourselves."

About us, the insect shrills grew strident and rhythmic. I put down the meat and lay back, stretching full-length on the alien grass. My mind, denied the search of the woods for which it clamored, peopled the forest's orchestra, gave the nascent choir a sinister aspect as it wailed low, ululent homage to the darkness. From all around us, even echoing back from the river's far bank, waxed that numinous evening chant. I liked the sound of it not at all.

Further disquieted, I twisted around to face the gate. Thereupon danced a soft nimbus, surely marsh gas rising. Over the stakes it flowed, maggot-white, sentient. I pulled at the clammy straps of my stiffening leathers, shivering, and shifted my gaze back to the fire.

But the foreboding, the ineffable hostility I sensed from the encroaching wilderness, would not be dispersed by that reassuring crackle. Its heat did not warm me, its light could not chase from my flesh the touch of a hundred hidden eyes. Sereth's fingers enclosed mine where I fumbled with my tunic's closures. He shook his head. I let my hand fall away, and shrugged. Chayin leaned forward, stirred the branches. A knot popped, showering sparks. Somewhere inland, a beast roared. It was a roar of rage and vengeance, hovering long in the air before it tapered to a growl indistinguishable from the forest's deep-throated mutter.

"Sereth, free me from my vow—let me seek the sense of this place." My voice, calm, unwavering, did not betray me. The principle on which he had based his decision of noninterference was right. The decision, I had long felt, was wrong.

"Not yet. I would explore Khys's—*this* land for what it is, not what I might assume it is, or want it to be." I did not miss the stumble of his tongue over his predecessor's name. It was Khys's work here that he would explore. And alter, if he could. Khys, the last dharen, or ruler, of Silistra, had spent long periods absent from his capital. None knew where, in those days. He had made quite certain that his successor would undertake this journey to the east, to this shore so long isolate from our own culture. And, despite himself, the inheritor had come to take stock of what had been left to him.

"Chayin, let us toss for watch," suggested Sereth, his head slightly cocked, closing indisputably the subject I had broached. A second roar, fainter than the first, echoed to us from the far bank.

"I will take it. Sleep is not within my reach," offered Chayin. Sereth grinned, shrugged, sought my side. Before he lay down to sleep, he spent a while staring around him, though it was mind and not eye that could penetrate the mist and darkness and denude them of their menace. But he would not do that. Finally he blew a sharp breath through his teeth and stretched out on the damp ground. I fit myself to him, my head resting on his arm.

"If those roars get close, wake me," he rumbled. Chayin chuckled. Sereth's sleep is light as an insect's wing. The familiar smell of his leathers, as I pressed my face to them, almost masked the rank, salt-laden river odor. Almost, I could mistake the river sound for his pulse. Almost, I could quiet the whispers my mind spoke, the oddly framed thoughts that touched mine, timid, and withdrew.

I twitched and tossed beside him, sleepless, until he growled and pushed up on one elbow. Chayin, ministering to his fire, hummed softly under his breath.

"What troubles you, ci'ves?" Sereth whispered, using the lover's name he had given me, that of a pet kept as talisman in the hills where he was born. In his tone was no annoyance that my restlessness chased sleep from him.

I thought about it, seeking proper words. I did not find them. At the river, he had sought Chayin's counsel without words. When he sought me that way, I would give him what he asked. Now, he was not ready to hear me. So I said instead: "Hard ground, a number of itching bites, and the scratch on my thigh."

I put my arms around his neck and pulled him down beside me, willing my body still. It would not be I who mouthed portents. They were surely as clear to Sereth as to Chayin or myself. It would not be I who broke my word, and searched owkahen, the time-coming-to-be, accepting and rejecting and thereby conditioning what might, in these lands, occur.

Sereth sought respite from just such manipulations of time by mind, at least long enough to determine what forces were at work here. And why, by his predecessor's will, enforced for countless generations, this land had been a shore of which nothing was known, of which none were empowered to speak. By my side lay he who might, if he wished, call himself dharen. The dharen before him had forbidden all commerce between this land and the one from which we had come. The impression had been fostered in the minds of the people of Silistra that nothing had survived the holocaust, on this farther shore. Even in the "autonomous" southlands ruled over by cahndors such as Chayin, none had disobeyed that injunction; or if any had, in silent defiance of the law, made the journey, they had not returned to speak the tale; or had, returning, kept silent.

As I have said, Sereth might have called himself dharen of Silistra. At that time he was not yet willing to do so: he did not wish to bear that burden.

I was—a number of things. Once, keepress of the premier Well on Silistra, with seven thousand people under my care. Later, with Chayin, I held a high commission and for a time served as regent in his southern principality. At still a later time, I was dhareness to Silistra's ruler, when Khys held the title. With all else, I passed into Sereth's hands at his predecessor's demise—a place I had long coveted. I might have called myself dhareness yet or chosen among certain other dignities which were mine by right. My left breast hosts a spiral symbol that twinkles as if bejeweled. It eloquently bespeaks my Shaper heritage; would that it did not. I could rid myself of it, but that *I* will not do.

Chayin, least changed of us up until that time, sought not forgetfulness, nor was his name abrasive to his own ears. Raised from childhood to believe in his personal divinity, he alone was not compromised in spirit by the affairs of the preceding years. And yet, he had turned away from those lands over which he ruled rightfully by blood and birth and effort. He, as Sereth, for the moment sought no reign over men. He, as I, had looked upon the burdens of his heritage and shuddered. With Sereth, he shared in love as fully as I; and between Chayin and myself, first cousins, there existed a long-standing intimacy. Let no one tell you that such a relationship is easy; and likewise, let none demean it. For the three of us, upon any one commission, are as close to a surety as exists in this ever-changing universe. And that—the realization of the possibilities in our merged skills—more than even the multifaceted affection we shared, entitled us in our own sight to this reconnaissance of an unknown land. We had come, two men and a woman, each divested by their own will of all but each other and those skills we had given so much to acquire, to explore the potentials inherent in our triune nature. Or so I saw it.

But Sereth, giving scant explanation, would not allow us their use. I sighed, and burrowed closer. I would try. I understood his thought. But even Chayin chafed under Sereth's constraint.

It was not far to my father's house, I thought in the dream, just as the trees bowed down to make of my path a darkened tunnel, and from the tunnel's end came light and a great roaring. I turned and ran, but my feet, after the second step, would not be raised up from the soil. Struggling, I fell to the ground. Up through wave after wave of dizziness rose my body. Sitting upright, hand to my forehead, roars louder in my ears, I made at first no sense of it.

Then the shadows that danced in the low-burning firelight took form. My ears sorted sounds. The sounds became voices: Sereth's, Chayin's. The flamelight flickered off their blades, and out from the eyes of the thing that roared.

Its pale paw flashed out, claws extended.

"Estri, stay back!"

I stopped, not recollecting how I had come there, past the fire, to where they held the wounded thing at bay.

Its huge jaws gnawed its own chest, where a dark wound gleamed wetly. It half-lay, haunches bunched, yet unable to spring. Again it struck; a sideswipe at Chayin; near-miss with that massive paw. He vaulted backward in clumsy retreat. Sereth, at the beast's far side, darted in to divert it. His blade raised over his head, he brought the full force of that honed edge down upon the creature's extended neck. Still reaching for Chayin was that immense, clawed forepaw as the roaring head struck the turf. The beast convulsed, rolling over, legs thrashing the air. Its final shudder, explosive, rent the air. Then, limp, it rolled to one side and came to rest, right-side-up, its dead eyes reflecting in the firelight. The fanged jaws were closed. Its tongue, half-severed, flapped weakly, then lay quiet between knife-long, gory teeth.

I backed away, staring at that head; at the great, furred body, no longer even twitching, pale like some mist-spawned apparition in the firelight.

Sereth's hand touched my arm. "Estri, look at me."

I tore my attention from the wedge-shaped head, from the dark-tufted ears. Our eyes met. The thing on the grass closely resembled our western hulions, but one somehow wingless and stunted. Hulions have great intelligence. I would rather kill a man than one of those beasts. Sereth knew. . . .

"It is dead," I said dumbly.

"It came at us as a predator," he said, staring into me intently, his grip tightening. When my tremors ceased, he released me, crouching to wipe his blade clean in the grass.

Chayin, limping slightly, slowly circled the corpse. When he reached us, he said: "Had Sereth not awakened when he did, it would likely be me lying there."

"And it might have been my sudden movement that precipitated its attack." Sereth, in his turn, examined the pale, furred form. When he had finished, he gave equal scrutiny to the stars before he spoke.

"Let us build up the fire. It may be a long night. Estri, stay in the light."

Chayin set about his search for more fuel. I, equally obedient, walked over to the fire's edge, my fingers worrying the thick braid of my hair, wondering if the furred beast was the largest predator in this land's chain; and, if not, what might prey upon it.

When the flames burned high, Chayin sought the dead beast. By its tail, he dragged it into the firelight.

"What are you doing?" Sereth demanded, judiciously poking at the smoking branches.

"I thought I might skin it. Such a beast has never been seen in Nemar."

"Think about it later," Sereth said sharply. His countenance, grotesqued by the flame's dance, was severe. The light poured molten down the scar that furrowed the left side of his face from cheekbone to jaw. Later I asked him, but he would admit to no foreknowledge come upon him then, though his eyes met mine and held them a long time.

II

Deilcrit

He crouched amid the sedges, in the tufted reeds
that banked the salt river. He wept, leaning against
the root of one of the great trees where it reared
up, entwining its brothers before diving deep. His
clenched fist pummeled the fahrass bush which
concealed him. The silvered balls of its fruit plummeted downward, plunking in rapid succession
upon the pool's surface around his calves, pelting
his arms and shoulders. Stepsisters, most called
them. He paid them no mind; it was not their
touch, but their taste that killed. He brushed them
from his hair, then again buried his head in his
arms that he might not see the corpse of the sacred ptaiss glowing whitely in the firelight.

Within the comfort of his arms' shelter, he prayed.
He did not know what to do. First, seeing them, he
had been consumed with fear for his mind. Then
for his life. And then, when they had not detected
him, he had waited. A man does not hurry to his
death. He had been content to sit, then to crouch,
finally to stand erect in the shore pool, watching.
His spear lay close at hand, propped against the
menmis tree's white bark, forgotten. Or rather:
useless. His hand, feeling for it, grasped the familiar polished wood. Without raising his head, he

curled his fingers around the shaft. His terror, by this means, was somewhat eased. The spear was a trusted tool, a remnant of his well-ordered world. He blanked his mind.

"What, what, what?" he sang to himself under his breath. He had been sent to clear the Spirit Gate of the hated guerm; the lightning had done it for him.

He had been late. He had not hurried. It is a risky business, keeping guerm from surmounting the gate and infesting the Isanisa River. He had not been afraid, then. Now, tears welled up in his eyes. He shook them fiercely away, averting his head from the fire, and those who fed it, and the slain ptaiss, Aama. Though he looked into darkness, he saw, with the clarity of long familiarity, all that grew on the Isanisa's shores. As a man facing conscription might walk one last time around his holdings in silent farewell, so did the young man, in his memory, walk the twists and turns of Benegua. Benegua, Land of the Spirit Gate; of the Wall of Mnemaat, the unseen; of the sacred ptaiss; she was all the young man had ever known.

In the dark, by his leg, something glided along the pool's still surface, the barely perceptible ripples of its passing lapping against his flesh. He waited, unmoving, for the swampsnake to pass on. Red-headed, perhaps, and deadly; or green-and-black-patterned, and holding within its fangs the most beneficent of drugs. With the back of his mind, he followed the snake's progress, his trained ears noting the reeds' rustle as it slithered away.

Wide-eyed, staring at nothing, housed in the emptiness that attends the shedding of tears, he waited. What would they want him to do?

Old Parpis—he would have known. The ache of throat that always accompanied his thoughts of the old man, now dead, did not dissuade him: A ptaiss was slain. A shiver of loss cooled his skin. He thought abstractly that if he did not soon quit the pool, he would catch the ague.

"Now, boy," Parpis would have said, "fear gets you naught but frightened." The young man swallowed, with difficulty. Parpis had taught him all he knew of ptaiss, and guerm, and Mnemaat's service.

"Deilcrit," Parpis used to say, before the young man had been entitled to the "iyl" before his name, "tend the ptaiss and spit the guerm, and the world will take care of itself." It was Parpis who had taught him to dress an injured paw, to strip the white bark of the memnis and extract the healing fluids therefrom. But never had Parpis said to him, his wizened old face screwed up, his long teeth flashing: "Deilcrit, if the Spirit Gate opens, if lightning chars the guerm to ash, if three walk, fearless, the risen Isanisa and set a fire upon her banks, here is what you do . . . it is a simple matter." To Parpis, even the most complex matters had been simple. But Parpis was dead of age and wisdom, and Deilcrit was iyl-Deilcrit, and upon the western shore of the Isanisa sacrilege had been heaped atop sacrilege: two quenels had been butchered and eaten; and the ptaiss Aama, heavy with child, lay lifeless by her murderers' fire. And he had stood by, helpless, afrighted, witness.

He was no familiar of cowardice. He had not feared, sojourning alone for the first time, to attend to the guerm that dependably, at the moon's absence, assaulted the Spirit Gate. He loosed his aching fingers from the spear's shaft, flexed them, let them curl once more around its comforting strength. He took a deep breath, and then another, forcing his constricted chest to take in air, his head to turn, his eyes to rest upon the abomination flame-lit on the bank.

Then he picked up the spear and stepped out of the pool into the thicket. Water ran from his laced boots. As he waited for it to drain, so he might be silent in his approach, he studied them. He had no clear idea of what he would do; only that he must do something. They were three, large and oddly dressed. For a moment he wondered wildly if they might be guerm, taken man-form, come to avenge themselves on Benegua.

He dropped to his knees. Not guermgods, surely, but perhaps gods, come to punish him, to show him unfit to bear the "iyl" before his name, to unmask him, pretender to Mnemaat's service. He had had thoughts of the high priestess again, only the night before. Dream-thoughts, but thoughts, nevertheless, and as such evil. Retribution? He had never heard of offended deities acting so fast, or on such a scale. His fingers digging into the spongy grass, he knelt there, staring through the leaves. What he saw then, he could not believe. It stopped the prayer in his mind as if it had never been.

Hardly knowing what he did, as if it were some other hurtling through the bush, he ran, crouched, spear slippery in his sweating hands. The darkest, largest intruder looked up from the unspeakable atrocity he was committing with his knife on the ptaiss' corpse.

Deilcrit froze in the rustling brush, suddenly conscious of the tiny stabs of jicekak brambles caught in his clothing. The dark face remained fixed in his direction; white teeth flashed as he spoke a meaningless garble of sound. The other male, a bit smaller, a trifle lighter of skin, answered the first in kind, rising. Unerring, the paler one walked toward the thicket in which Deilcrit crouched.

Time distended: in slow motion, the female drew

a blade and joined the dark one in armed approach. The weapons gleamed cold and alien in the fire's light, as bronze or iron had never gleamed. The one who stalked him, too, had such a knife.

Deilcrit made no noise with which he might betray his position. He ceased breathing. His pulse thumped, strangling, in his throat. Along the spear, his fingers spread, tensed, burned. The readiness ran tingling up his arm. Painstakingly, silent and slow, he rose up amid the jicekak, uncaring of the thorns raking his cheek. If he lived, he would find time to dress the itching scratches. Soundless, he maneuvered the spear, his forearm aching with restraint. Teeth locked, Deilcrit waited, setting and resetting his grip on the spear's shaft.

The foremost intruder was close. His leathers, much-used, were strangely cut, matched, once opulent. About his waist was a belt from which unfamiliar shapes and a scabbard, too long for a knife and too short for a sword, depended. On his legs were boots that reached to his thighs.

Now, surely!

The ptaiss murderer closed, inexorable, as if Deilcrit stood in the open, in clearest day. He thrust his arm, decided, forward. But his fingers could not release the shaft. The cast, aborted, marked his position beyond hope of escape. He stood gasping, rock-still, feeling the slide of the shaft in his slippery palms.

The man, close enough now to be completely enshadowed, stopped. He tossed his head, and spoke in some unintelligible tongue, staring directly, it seemed, at Deilcrit's benumbed form. Again that man-likeness spoke to him where he hid in the thicket. Deilcrit's guts turned so violently that it was all he could do to keep his hold on the spear. With a great effort of will, he kept his body from doubling over and tumbling to the ground.

Then, without thought other than the shame upon him, and the ending death would put to his pretenses and his cowardice, he stepped from the brush.

The creature before him showed no surprise.

Deilcrit, having fought evil and the spirit temptations all of his life, laid down his spear. It was a simple thing. He pried his fingers from the shaft and it fell on the ground between them. That the message be more clear, he followed it, his head pressed to the rank, salty earth. For a moment, he had met those eyes. There had been no fear, no mortality therein. Freed now of hope, of regret, Deilcrit awaited death.

He heard the others join the one before whom he knelt. Under his left knee was a stone. It pressed against the nerves there. The red light of his inner lids turned grainy.

The three spoke together. Then it seemed to him that his spirit was lifted gently from his body; that it was examined, considered. It felt odd, being relieved of spirit. A cool touch washed over his empty place, where spirit had been, as cool as the grass and earth beneath him. A final shiver of horror shook his frame, for it came to him that even death might be denied him, that he might be forced to live on, denuded of selfhood, servant to whatever force held him entrapped. He sent a plea to Mnemaat the Unseen that he might be allowed to give up his life rather than become some mindless tool of sinister purpose.

Then a voice spoke to him in Beneguan.

"We will not harm you," said the voice, male and low. He heard it again, and the second time the words made sense, poking their meaning out through the unfamiliar accent like quenel their black noses through the foliage at feeding time. Then the sense was gone, as the voice spoke to its companions. The female said a thing, of which he caught only the tone: concern and relief.

Deilcrit ached to move. He could not. Grass rustled as the spear was removed from beside him.

"Can you understand me?" came the male voice once more, slow and distinct. "Get up!"

He raised his head slightly, enough to see their booted feet—and between them, the fire that defiled the bank and warmed the ptaiss' corpse.

A hand touched his shoulder. Without volition, his flesh quivered beneath it. "Can you understand me?"

"Yes," came the admission through his gritted teeth. The touch withdrew.

"Stand up. Now!"

Without warning, he was standing, not recollecting how he had come erect.

His hand clutched his empty scabbard, forgetful. The knife was lost somewhere along the Isanisa, lost when he had fallen, rolling heedless down the bank with the screams of the opening Spirit Gate in his ears.

The speaker raised his weapon away from his body. The woman stared at him levelly, through eyes the color of smelting copper. In the shadows, they shone bright, like the night-stalking eyes of the ptaiss. The male spoke sharply to her. She retreated slowly toward the fire. No mortal womb had spawned those eyes, nor skin that glowed like marsh gas.

Only then did he notice the dark one, hovering behind his male companion. By the sheathing of his blade, the movement of his form through the night as he turned away to purposefully approach the fire and the slaughtered ptaiss, was Deilcrit suddenly conscious of his retreating presence.

"No!" It came out of him an inarticulate sob,

tremulous and hoarse. Leaping wide of the lighter man, he sprinted toward the ptaiss.

He heard them shouting in his own language as he bounded the hillock. Cutting through the edges of his fire itself, he cursed his slowness, his cowardice. His feet, among the live coals, blistered through his rude boots.

But he reached her before her defiler. Aama, of the silvery, softest fur, whose breath smelled of new morning and whose black-tufted ears had always been the first to hear him. She would hear no more. How vulnerable is the desolated body in death. How empty he felt, kneeling beside her. Her eyes reproached him. Did they follow? He touched her muzzle, lifted her head in his arms. Then he saw, holding the inert weight against his chest, the extent of her wounds. Above him, far off, he heard their footsteps. Their shadows crowded out the firelight. He buried his face in the ptaiss' fur, to smell one last time of her. The hair, loosed in death, came away under his hands. She was still warm. Once more he conjured up life in her. Then he laid her head back gently upon the ground. His hands, surely his face, were covered with blood and fur. He tried to close her eyes. She would not allow it, but stared mournfully.

The intruders were talking. He heard it as the buzzing of insects, far off. By the ptaiss' belly lay the knife the dark one had used to loosen her hide from her flesh. He snatched it up, fingers clumsy on its hilt. Then, taking a deep breath, he straddled her swollen belly, leaning down.

If it could be, he would ask nothing else, as long as he lived.

As he cut her, deep, he prayed that they would not obstruct him. Then he totally forgot them. He was with Parpis. It was not he, but Parpis who made the incision, sure and true, who endured the

gush of blood and fluid from her ravaged belly,
and the smell of preborn life. His eyes watched his
hands, sunk up to the elbows inside her; but it was
his fingers which saw. What he touched in that
hot, yielding darkness, moved. He recited the laws
beneath his breath, but he did not know it. He
knew bone sliding in its membranous sac; then the
beslimed head, then the forequarters—and the
cord. The cord, once grasped, must be held firmly
between the fingers, whispered the shade of Parpis
in his ear. But alone, he had not enough hands, not
for keeping the head down and the cord pressed
and . . . A third hand reached, beside his, attending
the umbilical. Both his own hands freed, he pulled
forth the slippery form. He knew that the other cut
the bond between dead and living, even as the
hindquarters and tail appeared.

With his fingers and his lips and tongue, he
cleared the mucus from the ptaissling's eyes and
nostrils. As he did so, it mewled. Other hands were
upon it. He paid them no mind. He stroked its
matted fur with handfuls of grass. It kicked a leg
weakly. Its black muzzle sniffed, coughed, began a
blind searching. He lifted its quaking warmth in
his arms, pulled it across his kneeling body. He
pressed its head against Aama's cooling teat, aware
of the futility in what he did. He turned, then, to
see if the miracle could be repeated.

The lighter of the two men, arms bloody to the
elbows, knelt so close to him that their knees
touched. He could hear the smacks of the ptaissling's lips, suckling Aama's fast-cooling milk.

The man, as if Deilcrit's question had been spoken aloud, shook his head, spreading his arms wide.
They were awful in the firelight. He again shook
his head, and Deilcrit understood that Aama's
womb held no more miracles.

Halfheartedly he sluiced the blood and mucus

from his own forearms and turned away. The ptaissling pumped Aama, making little frustrated sounds. How much milk can come from a lifeless breast? He did not know, but sense told him: little. He leaned over it, guiding the searching mouth to Aama's second udder. He blinked back tears. In the firelight, the little one gleamed black. And huge. A young male, overyoung, perhaps too young to survive this untimely introduction into life. He stroked it, not wanting more than its warmth and to feel the life coursing in it.

He shifted, ripping up more grass with which to dry its matted fur. It shivered. He murmured to it. Was it for this his life had been spared? He crouched down over the shaking form, trying to warm it with his body.

He did not notice the woman until she was on her hands and knees at his side, holding out the garment she had worn. He was too stunned to even avert his eyes. He took from her the damp, supple leather, and with it rubbed the remaining placenta from the ptaissling. Once more he moved its suckling head, to the third of Aama's teats.

It was then that the man's hand came down upon his shoulder, digging, insistent. Man? Not man. He pushed them from his mind. They had murdered Aama, yet one had helped him save her only child. What, what, what?

"Who are you?" said the creature, murderer and midwife both. His head, of its own accord, raised up to meet that fearsome, scarred countenance. He wondered what kind of spirit could be so marked, and what adversary might have inflicted those wounds. Then all rational thought stopped for him. His eyes, once in the grasp of the other's, were entrapped. He could not look away. The power of the being was too great. His hand sought the newborn's head, rested there.

"Come into the light," the man-fleshed spirit ordered, lifting him up with a grip that dug like iron into his arm. The eyes holding him narrowed.

"The ptaissling," he pleaded. "Do not kill it . . . you will not kill it?" He knew that he weaved in the man-spirit's grip, and that his voice trembled. The bloody hand holding him did not relax. "Please, the ptaissling . . ."

"I will watch it," said the woman, low, hovering close. Or at least she seemed to say that. Unhanding him, the man-form, with flicks of his gleaming knife, repeated his order. Even as the blade disappeared in its scabbard, Deilcrit, like one in a dream, complied. His feet were uncertain on the hillock's slope. Weight upon them caused pain, pain caused dizziness, dislocation, disregard of all else. He stumbled through a tuft and found himself leaning upon the other for support.

Dazzled, this close to the firelight, detached from the blaze of his blistered feet by the cocoon of returning fright, he stopped, blinking, at the other's command. His eyes strayed to the disemboweled ptaiss, to the woman-form, and to the black shadow of the ptaissling.

"Look at me."

With a strangled sob, he did so, turning to his tormentor, submitting once again to that gaze which turned bones to powder, muscle to jelly, mind to prayer. Slowly the man wiped his arms of Aama's blood. Then he nodded at Deilcrit, and smiled, and indicated that he should sit.

He collapsed on the ground, as if the other's will had been all that held him upright. He heard a voice, and knew it his: reciting the laws from rote in the old tongue.

"Stop," said the man-form. "I cannot understand that."

Deilcrit stared. Cannot? If not from the lawgivers, then whence?

"Who are you?" demanded his inquisitor.

He wanted to answer. He meant to answer. He said: "If you have taken life from the sacred ptaiss, will you not take mine also?"

The spirit did not take his life, but grinned, revealing white teeth that flashed in the firelight. Then he shaded his eyes with his hand.

"What do you call this place?"

"Benegua," mumbled Deilcrit, startled. Across the fire, the woman-form ministered to the ptaissling. If she intended it harm, he could not help it.

"And this language?"

"Beneguan," he answered, fear rising to lock his jaw in ice and turn the sweat cold as it rolled down his brow. How can language be spoken by one who has no name for it? he wondered dully.

"We have come here from Fai Teraer-Moyhe," explained the man-form. Upon hearing that, he understood. Deilcrit, wailing, struck his forehead repeatedly upon the grass. From the Dark Land. . . . Tears of repentance flooded him. Not once had he failed, but endlessly. Aama died. He would die. The ptaissling would die. All of Benegua might be carried off to eternal penance, because he had not fled with word. Over his own moans, he heard nothing. Not until the avenging spirit dressed as a man touched him did he realize that it desired to further enlighten him.

"Be at ease," the man-form said. "We have no quarrel with you."

Could a man be so simply absolved of misdeeds in their sight? He did not think so. A torrent of guilt burst within him, until dammed back by the thought of the ptaissling. Then he raised his head. Stilling his body's tremors, he faced the spirit of Fai Teraer-Moyhe.

"Sereth," called the woman, from the ptaissling's side. "You will kill him with fright." At her first word, Deilcrit leaped to his feet, filled with concern for the newborn. Even before the hand reached out to stop him, he sank back down. The spirit nodded approvingly, manlike. Once more he tried to fit the man-mold over this being, that his terror be eased. No amount of trying allowed him this grace; what sat before him could not be a man. Even if from its own mouth had not come the name of the Abode of the Dead, the other-worldliness of his interrogator's very frame would have made the distinction clear. Men did not carry themselves with such lordly bearing, nor did they wear such garments. Nor carry such weapons. Nor speak so to women. But none had ever lived to tell what Fai Teraer-Moyhe spawned.

"Will I?" demanded the spirit. "Will you die of fright?"

Deilcrit looked at the ground. "My life is yours," he whispered.

"I have not asked for it," said the spirit. "I am Sereth." And he held out his hand.

Deilcrit looked at the hand, brown and sinewey and mottled with Aama's blood. It hovered in his field of vision, palm turned toward him. Then he bent his head and kissed it. From under his lips it was jerked away.

He raised his eyes, once more braving that terrible scourged visage.

"What is your name?" the spirit Sereth asked.

"Iyl-Deilcrit," he said, not vainglorious, but in admission.

"And what do you do, iyl-Deilcrit?"

"I tend the ptaiss, and spit the guerm," he replied through unwieldy lips. Now it would come, whatever judgment the spirit had thus far held in abeyance. He straightened his shoulders. When it did not come, when those eyes compelled his to speak, he repeated what he had said, adding: "Let me do so," and ripped his glance from the other by an effort which left him breathing hard.

"Get up, then. I would keep no man from his calling," said the grinning spirit Sereth, rising.

Dazed, he followed suit, moving slowly so that his legs' tremors would not throw him to the ground.

"That is Chayin," said Sereth, pointing out the dark one who squatted near the ptaissling's head. "And Estri." The woman-spirit smiled over her shoulder and turned back to the newborn ptaiss. Her naked back gleamed in the firelight, as if it bore a fire of its own. "They accompanied me from Fai Teraer-Moyhe, and before that, across the western sea." Deilcrit could not suppress his shudder.

The dark man had something in his hands. Deilcrit could just make it out as it flew through the air: the spear, suddenly launched at him, sideways.

Automatic, was the reaching. Then Deilcrit leaned upon the spear he had caught, like an old man on his staff. He was relieved that they were not *of* Fai Teraer-Moyhe. But all knew that there was nothing of man across the western sea. Ever more man-seeming, they were. But man could not have entered Benegua through the Spirit Gate. At least, he did not think so. What, then? The night hovered heavy, misting. No stars could be seen, just the dully glowing clouds. He shivered. If Parpis leaned upon this spear, he thought, what? The shade of Parpis, this time, remained silent.

His eyes fell upon the ptaissling. He would have to find milk for it. Where? He shook his head, and leaned it against the cool bronze of the spear's head. His cheek itched with the nagging pulse of the jicekak poison, and he angled the metal out of contact with his scratches.

The one called Sereth spoke: "How long were you watching us, and why?"

His voice snapped Deilcrit's head around. His body followed. Disoriented, he almost fell. Grasping the spear in both hands, he regarded his inquisitor. If it had not been somehow useless against them, he was sure that they would not have given it back. The act magnified his helplessness. As a man rousted out of bed in the middle of the night, hustled off by taciturn soldiers, might desperately construct excuses for some misdeed unknown to him, so did Deilcrit seek some answer that might please these who had entered through the Spirit Gate. But he found none.

"I tend the ptaiss," he mumbled at last. "And spit the guerm."

But the spirit Sereth was not sated.

Writhing as if in physical pain, he fought the impulse to bolt: he could not leave the ptaissling.

Sereth fastened him still with eyes that pulled the words from his mouth: "The ptaiss . . . what you did . . . I saw it all," he blurted out. "I did not know what to do. Aama was great with child. This was her first bearing." The words, slow starting, poured out of him, uncheckable. "I was long at her side, soothing her ill temper. I was late to the Gate. . . .

"Listen, you can hear them. They mourn. All of Wehrdom mourns, by now."

At his words the woman spun around, regarding him across the slain ptaiss. From the forest's depths, even from the far shore, came the wails of grieving ptaiss. He stared at her openly. And slowly, feeling with his spear behind him, he backed away.

Sereth stood unmoving, silent, hands at his hips as Deilcrit retreated.

The shifting wind brought their scents clear to him; their flesh smelled of strange food and sweat.

"Kreeshkree, kreesh; breet iylbreet," came the cry from above their heads, intrusive. The woman looked anxiously above, then down, then sought Sereth and touched his arm. It was hard to think of her as a spirit; her life flowed too full. Her presence made Sereth loom larger, if possible more forbidding. "Let him be until morning," she said.

"He might not be here in the morning."

"Let me try," she spoke again, softly. She was naked to the waist. Sereth grunted, and shrugged. Then retreated, ever so slightly.

"Deilcrit, will you stay the night with us?"

Deilcrit laid down the spear and looked at it. Then he crouched beside it in the grass, swallowed hard, and said: "Command me, Most High," while thinking how unfair it was of them to use Woman's Word to imprison him. Something many-legged crawled up his hand. He shook it off without notice, his eyes fastened on her as she approached. In some unfathomable way, she brought the flames' light with her. He pondered this, for she stood with the fire at her back, and he could imagine no other source whence light might be reflected by her skin. Thus he neglected suitable obeisance. And his body, as she came closer, waxed audacious, presenting him with one extreme reaction after another. He tore his attention from her, setting it instead upon the dark one, Chayin, by the slain ptaiss' head, and on the ptaissling, shadow turned sentient clambering at her belly.

"What is this Wehrdom? And what did you see that so affrighted you? And speak to me of the ptaiss, and why they are sacred," she commanded him.

Deilcrit nodded dumbly. Miserable in realization of his insufficiency, he studied the grass, and her booted feet. "It is not me you want, Most High. I am low in Mnemaat's service. Only the first ten parables are known to me. And I am no wehr—none but the initiated could speak to you of the Way. Ptaiss, I know . . ." He trailed off, spreading his hands wide.

She took no notice that he looked upon her breasts, but smiled encouragingly. "Tell me," she insisted, "what you saw."

Deilcrit shivered. She would have from his own mouth his death sentence. He sensed it. And then there would be none to care for the ptaissling. But she knelt down on the grass opposite him, and his resistance was dissolved by her proximity. Unable to stop either his staring or his words, he did as she bid him: "I saw the Spirit Gate, upon which the guerm climbed, struck by lightning. I saw you enter through it. I saw you build a fire. I saw you eat of the flesh of quenel, long denied to man. I saw you strike dead a ptaiss, a thing that no man could do, which no man has ever done. What more?" Then he lowered his head, waiting. When death did not come, he raised it. "Most High, what are you?"

She blew a breath, soft and hissing, through her teeth.

The ptaissling, at that moment, began to whimper. Its cries tore at his heart. In this world into which it had come, those needs for which it moaned could never be filled. "The ptaissling, may I see to it?" The audacity escaped his lips before thought could intervene. "I ask you, in Mnemaat's name, to allow me."

In the ensuing silence, his restraint dissolved with the newborn's ever-more-urgent cries. Finally, while he crouched ready to spring for his charge and the forest's safety, she spoke:

"Do as you will, iyl-Deilcrit."

He sprang like a loosed arrow to the ptaissling's side.

"Be assured that your god is not defiled by what we have done." Her words trailed after him, wrapped in a humor that appalled him.

His hands around the ptaissling's head, he pulled its mouth from Aama's depleted udder. Then, only, he looked over his shoulder at her. Out from her flesh gleamed starlight, a patch of it. He had not imagined it. It winked there, uncanny, embellishing her left breast. The ptaissling whimpered more insistently. He squeezed the last drops of milk onto his fingers and let the searching mouth suck them clean. Its teeth, tiny yet sharp, nipped impatiently.

"Estri," snapped Sereth, and a great deal more in their alien tongue as he led her forcibly into the shadows. Deilcrit's hand sought the ptaissling's pounding heart as it butted its unseeing face against his leg. The Most High's voice, low and musical, made short, conciliatory answers to the other's anger. He had never even imagined such a state of affairs: she did not curse, nor abrade, nor turn Sereth's form to stone, but accepted meekly whatever chastisement was in progress. Even with her body stiffened by the manform's rough treatment, the grace of her was astounding. He dragged his gaze away, discomfited at all that he saw. Her image danced before his eyes, though he looked upon the black-furred newborn, huddling against him for warmth. He lay down and curled his body around it, pulling it to him, away from the cold corpse of its mother. The ptaissling snuffled its way up to his chest, pushing its wet nose into his armpit. Its body was quivering. He drew up his knees so that they touched its hindquarters, and threw his arm over it. Even early-born, it was large. On its feet it would stand as high as his thigh. A flicker of pride in Aama's child came and went, and in its wake a sharper awareness of his irrevocable loss. He crooned to the orphan, forgetting all else in that moment of shared grief.

From beside Aama's head, the dark one, Chayin, chuckled and crawled toward him. He tensed, and the ptaissling mewled. He racked his brain to match that name with a god from Benegua's pantheon, but his limited schooling provided no correlation. The unfamiliar deity squatted near, staring. He felt compelled to stare back.

"She affected me that way, the first time," Chayin said, the whites of his eyes bright.

"Thus it always is, with those that cannot be had. How else?"

"That one," assured the dark tempter, "can be had."

Deilcrit sat up. The ptaissling sobbed softly. His hands balled into fists. He said nothing. But he felt those eyes, somehow inside of him, weighing his most incriminating thoughts, that licentious evil he ever strove to suppress but which bubbled unimpeded up from the depths of his sullied soul. If only Aama's corpse did not lie here . . . He wondered, wildly, why this had happened to him. There were others upon whom life lay easier, others who found no torture in the laws. Like the lightning assaulting the Spirit Gate, it struck him: it was for precisely that reason he had been chosen. What profit to them, if man not be weak? He put his head in his hands, pressing his palms against his eyelids. The ptaissling climbed onto his lap and buried its face between his crossed legs.

He heard the rustle of Chayin's movement, just before the hand came down on the crown of his head.

"Do not fear so," advised the dark one awkwardly. "Questions beginning with 'why' have no true answers. It is not likely to be as bad as you make it, unless you make it that way. I will help you dispose of the ptaiss. I would not have sought to make a trophy pelt of her, had I known. I regret your loss. Must you inform someone?"

Deilcrit, his head still bowed, pressed his palms more firmly against his lids. He nodded.

"I will go, also, and speak for you. You will be back, doing whatever you do, before you know it."

Deilcrit, without raising his head, shook it. Beyond doubt, he knew that it could not be true. He was not the same. Nothing was the same. Nothing would ever be the same again.

"By the Wing of Uritheria," exploded the dark one. "A man fully grown, in good health . . . What has you huddled up like some infant, shivering? I have said that I will help you." The hand upon his head, with a desultory shake, withdrew. "I have promised you protection, to the extent that I am able, in this land, to give it. Though I am as yet unknown here, I assure you that you have received no small gift! Whatever befalls, in your need call my name. I will hear you. When you are ready, we will see to the ptaiss."

Upon those amazing statements, the dark one rose up and joined his companions.

Deilcrit, staring after, wondered with what he had just pacted. A part of his mind noted the ptaissling, sleeping on his lap; and the ptaiss sounds, coming ever closer, in the forest beyond. His ears heard, also, the discussion, incomprehensible but for its heat, occurring by the fire. He slid his legs out from under the newborn, drew up his knees. Over them he crossed his arms and on his crossed arms he rested his chin. He hardly knew that he did these things. The ptaissling muttered but did not wake. He regarded it freed of emotion. Could he chance its life upon a night hunt? Could he flee with it, despite his vow? The last thing he wanted was to stay near Them. What was to be done with Aama's corpse? He could not just leave it. What would he do if he could not find a surrogate mother? He tried to recapture some shadow of Parpis' wisdom. He recollected only what the dark one said. As a man, lost beyond hope of returning home, stands at a fork in the road, undecided, waiting for an omen to make his choice for him, so stood Deilcrit before the task of assigning sense and value to what had occurred. He had come too far, he knew, to turn back. As fearful as he was of the wrath of Mahrlys-iis-Vahais, twice that fearful was he of those ranged around the fire, those who could lift the thoughts from his mind and the will from his limbs. Now the dark one had so much as designated him a servant. So conscripted, whether for good or evil, into the designs of Mnemaat the Unseen, could he do other than obey? A strangely replete surrender came over him. Buoyed by its strength, he got to his feet. Slowly he approached them, his eyes fixed on the ground, to do as the dark one had bid him, and attend the body of Aama. Then, for better or worse, he would lead them to Mahrlys: Mahrlys, whose body tortured his dreams incessantly; and whose eyes, though often upon him, had never seen him. She would see him, soon enough.

Just before he reached them, he turned about once more to reassure himself that the ptaissling slept. Wings fluttered above his head.

Automatically, he reached out his arm.

"Kreesh," said the whelt, flapping wildly, its claws fastening around his wrist.

"Kreesh," he whispered back to it, bringing his wrist slowly toward his chest. The whelt, cobalt crest raised, humped its wings up and sidled to his shoulder, where it perched, silver beak clacking.

"Kreesh, breet," said the bird dejectedly, and rubbed its head against his. The fire crackled. The whelt started, half-spread its wings, and shifted from foot to foot.

"Ssh, ssh," he soothed, reaching up to smooth its crest. The whelt shivered, stretching out its neck until one green eye was level with his. The eye blinked.

Among the strange ones, all converse had ceased. The woman half-hid behind the lighter man, staring.

Self-consciously, he further quieted the whelt, whose talons still twitched and trembled. A big bird, this; not the whelt he had expected, nor any of his. His questing fingers found its banded right leg, traced there the sign of the Vahais, Benegua's high council.

"Go on," he advised softly. "Why get involved?" The whelt, as he, knew better. But it only cocked its head.

"Breet, iis," he accused it. It ruffled its feathers, shifting its weight from leg to leg. "Go on," he advised, pushing his wrist insistently against its chest.

Again it stretched its neck and rubbed its head against his cheek. The jicekak scrapes, irritated, began itching. The woman hesitantly approached. He closed his eyes and took the whelt's message. Here was his omen, come unasked. Mahrlys' face hovered before him, and from her mouth came the words of death and waiting. Of death, the whelt was better informed than he: ptaiss, quenel, and whelt. *Whelt*?

With a disparaging screech, the whelt took sudden flight from his shoulder, talons digging, wings battering his head. Reflexively, he ducked down and away. It climbed the air, screeching, wingtips nearly brushing the woman's face. She screamed, and threw herself to the ground. The men rushed to her aid, but the whelt was gone, heavenward, safe from their blades.

None of his would have behaved so, he thought, fingering his punctured shoulder. Under his tunic, the clawed flesh throbbed wetly.

He brought his fingers to his lips, licked the blood. She rose up, slapping ashes from her hands, and stood there, at arm's length, her whole body an eloquent demand for explanation.

He raised his head high, under that scrutiny, then grinned uncertainly.

"Whelt. One of Mahrlys-iis-Vahais'." His whole body turned hot, as if the fire had caught his flesh. He could not look away, but he could think of nothing to say to her. He merely stared back, with every pore of his body. He was dimly aware that the dark one shed his outer garment and then his inner, and replaced the outer alone. The inner layer he offered up to her. She, hardly seeming to notice, took it and slipped it over her head.

Deilcrit breathed a sigh of relief.

Then she said: "You are hurt," and he wondered whether anything mortal could have voice so soft, as she rolled up the dark sleeves and pulled her thick braid over her shoulder. "Take that off, and I will dress it."

She was pointing at him. He backed away, shaking his head, toward the ptaissling, surreptitiously chancing a glance at her companions. They leaned close together, talking quietly. Thus he stumbled over his own spear. Glad for the respite from her flame-colored eyes and his confusion, he reached down to retrieve it. He dared not do what she asked. And yet he dared not disobey her. Miserably he retreated into the cloaking dark beyond the fire's circle.

"Iyl-Deilcrit"—she laughed, following him—"stop and let me see to your wound."

He stopped, in the blessed shadows, and leaned his forehead against the flare of the spear's head. His eyes strayed to the ptaissling. He could just make it out. There was no question, now of escape: by way of whelt, that had been forbidden him. Waiting, he could endure. But the deaths to be met by more of the same . . .

At her touch, he jumped as if scalded. It was all he had conjured it to be, that touch. Hopeless, at her repeated command, he fumbled at the strap tied about his waist, fingers plucking clumsily at the knotted, damp-swollen cord.

"Here," she murmured, "let me do it." He stood, not daring to breathe. When the knot was freed, the belt, with its pouch and scabbard, fell to the ground.

"Well?" she urged, smiling. He was glad he could not see the starlight on her breast through the fine cloth. He peered over her head, at the two lounging in the fire's glow. Then he stopped thinking, in response to her stamped foot, and pulled the tunic upward quickly, before he could turn and run. And if he ran, he would have Mahrlys to face. . . .

His chin caught in the headhole. He struggled with it. When he could once again see, she was searching something from the wide belt she wore. Naked but for a strip of cloth—and it old and threadbare—wound around his loins, he crossed his arms over his chest and squatted down. Not ever had he been naked before a woman. He hoped that the whelt was gone, and not spying on him from the trees.

She, too, crouched in the grass, palm outstretched. Her eyes appraised every inch of him, calmly. The tiny smile upon her face fanned bright.

Ptaissling or no ptaissling, Mahrlys' whelt's orders not-withstanding, he almost ran, then. At length, he crouched before her like a man set to jump, palms flat to the ground between his feet, weight well forward.

Never afterward, though often he tried to recall the truth, could he determine if her touch alone had healed him or if the sticky brown substance she applied to the trough the whelt had dug in his shoulder provided the cure. Her palm's proximity caused his flesh to turn cold, then so hotly cold he flinched. Then the touch was gone. And back a second time, smoothing the sharp-smelling gel into the wound. At that moment, he paid the healing process little mind: her gaze had found what he had hoped that she would not see. But when she raised her face there was no censure, no fury in it. She merely stretched toward him and repeated the same procedure on his right cheek. As the evil-smelling unguent began stinging, he tried not to flinch, but his flesh trembled under her hand. He studied the ground, biting his lip, so desperately did he want to look at her.

"I have found another scratch," she said, touching him upon the belly. He groaned softly. "What did this?" she asked, as if she had not heard.

"Jicekak," he answered, first knowing he did so when the sound surprised him. She stared intently at his scratched cheek, nodding. Then she leaned closer. Her thinly clad breast brushed his arm.

"Please, Most High," he begged, holding the surging inside him. His fingers ached in their trenches newly dug among the weeds.

"Does it hurt so much?"

"Yes," he admitted, very low. He longed to touch that strange, glowing skin, unwind the thick braid of copper hair.

She sat back, inspecting him critically. "Let me see the back of you. Go on, turn around."

He was glad to do so, that he could not see her.

"Who is Mahrlys-iis-Vahais?" she asked, her strong fingers rubbing salve into his back.

"Mahrlys," he repeated, pulling away from her. If Mahrlys knew that he had been naked before this creature, messenger of Mnemaat or no, the iis' retribution would be terrible. But he remembered the slain quenel and ptaiss, and the whelt's message, and he realized that no worse could befall him.

"Mahrlys-iss-Vahais rules Benegua," he said simply, when she asked again. "Please, do not amuse yourself with me. It is not permitted." His voice even to his own ears, came thick and hoarse. Her hands turned to soothing, to kneading the thrice-knotted muscles of his back. "Most High," he moaned, driven to desperation. "No!"

"Turn around." And when he did not: "Now! Face me!"

Slowly, he obeyed. Her face was unreadable, eyes half-closed.

Implacable, she reached out a hand to him. He squeezed his own eyes shut, kept them shut, but he knew what he did. He simply could do no different.

When it was done, when he had committed the final, most heinous sacrilege, he groaned softly and pried his lids apart. His fingers, digging into her arms, would not at once heed his command that they release her.

He allowed himself the further iniquity of appreciating her, as he waited for death to come. He had earned it.

She rolled aside, and he felt her finger run the length of his transgression. Pulling her legs under her, she put her finger to her lips and licked it, her eyes huge over her hand. Then she laughed and scrambled to her feet. He followed suit, naked, his belongings forgotten in the grass.

"Most High, who are you?" he asked, taking her

proffered hand. Behind her back, the two firelit figures hovered, blades drawn, at either edge of the blaze, stone-still, listening.

"Estri," she replied firmly. "But that is not what you meant. Chayin once observed that we are more than men, yet less than gods, and sometimes used by the latter to mold the former. Will that do?" She smiled, touched his lips.

Deilcrit, then, heard what softly rising sounds had so concerned Sereth and Chayin. He pushed her toward them awkwardly, unable to answer her bright smile. From behind her he said, "In that case, you three may yet survive." He could feel the breeze of them, the restless air that always accompanied the gathering of wehrs in numbers.

"What do you mean?" she demanded, then stopped dead so that he stumbled into her. This time, it was she who gripped his shoulders.

"That I did not tell you all that the whelt told me. I was forbidden to. But I cannot . . . What we have done . . . Most High, forgive me, but I am trying to tell you that the whelt told me to await the wehrs' justice, to keep you here. Wehrs' justice is that of death. Can you not hear them? See?" And he pointed to where pair upon pair of glowing eyes bestarred the forest's blackness from ground to treetops.

"Deilcrit . . ." With a shudder she released him, whirled, and scrambled up the hillock in a dash that ended her in Sereth's arms, babbling urgently.

He turned his eyes from their frantic embrace, and sought the ptaissling, who slumbered fitfully now that ptaiss-mutter filled the air. He had to pass by the dark one, Chayin, to get there.

That one fixed him with a piercing glare, half-pitying, half-contemptuous, and spat in Deilcrit's direction.

"Well, will you fight, ungrateful whelp? Or will

you meet your death like you have spent your life, cowering before gods and spirits and even dumb beasts?''

Deilcrit, his face buried in the ptaissling's neck, felt at last the first spray of horror cool his skin. The wave surged close behind. A shuddering racked him. When it was gone, he pushed the youngling away, and uncurled himself to stand straight before the glowering Chayin, in whose unwavering extended grasp was a white-bladed knife.

A ptaiss roared, a cough answered, and a high-pitched cry silenced both.

"I cannot lift weapons against the ptaiss," Deilcrit got out. "It is not . . . not possible. Please . . ." His arms, of their own accord, stretched out to encompass the fire, the clearing, the denser shadows of forest cushioning the moonless night. "I cannot."

Chayin, with a shrug, flipped the knife and cast it between Deilcrit's feet. Then he turned his back and joined his companions.

Silently the three walked to a stretch of level ground, and there, halfway between fire and slope, formed a triangle, back to back. Their alien weapons gleamed. Sereth spoke tersely, very low, and Chayin grunted an assent. And then they stood like statues, unmoving, for an instant.

Even as Deilcrit bent to still the ptaissling's sudden bleat, even as the knife jumped of its own accord into his fist and every vestige of his composure fled, the black forest exploded. Into the light leaped and bounded and flapped the wehrs. Ptaiss predominated, and their roars, deafening, were only a background for more terrible cries. A wall of diverse creatures erupted out of the dark.

Deilcrit had no time to survey them, only a moment for the incredulity of their numbers to sink in, and then a spirit-white ptaiss was upon him. Blindly, his face contorted so that his teeth lay bare, screaming without knowing that he did, Deilcrit stabbed about him. No law, no question of submission stayed his furious thrusts, though he had knelt a hundred times while the wehrs passed ravening among the folk of Benegua, striking dead whom they chose. This time his palms lay not on the ground with his forehead upon them: In one fist he grasped a ptaiss' ear, in the other the blade that tore again and again into the beast's belly. The claws of one forepaw raked the ground by his head as the awful weight bore him down; its mates sank deep into his right shoulder and scraped bone. Up into its vitals, again and again, did Deilcrit plunge his weapon. His grip on the beast's ear slipped, and the slavering jaws thrust toward him, drenching his face in drool and spittle.

With all his strength, he thrust his free arm down the ptaiss' throat, gouging the soft palate with his nails. Halting momentarily in surprise, the suddenly choking creature arched its back, threw its head up, and Deilcrit's knife hand was no longer skewered to the ground by the claws in his shoulder. He thrust the knife upward, deep into the ptaiss' jugular, even as those hideous jaws closed upon his elbow, and the ptaiss' frenzied convulsions snapped him up into the air. He had only enough time to drop the blade and hug the beast's neck as it reared up, shaking its head. Gorge rose in its throat, spilled from its mouth, but the ptaiss would not release Deilcrit's arm, now torn half from its socket. For a moment, swinging free of the ground, the whole clearing was revealed to him:

Sereth, Chayin, and Estri, still back to back, stood amid a growing circle of corpses, over which new assailants vaulted. He saw the wing-flutter of an ossasim, its manlike body strewn uppermost on the pile. Then, as a screaming ptaiss launched itself over the barrier, Estri uttered a hoarse cry, she and Sereth both threw their weapons—he at the ptaiss and she at a tusked, long-bodied campt—and the three joined hands. Then they were gone. The campt, with a roar of pain, fell aspraddle where they had just stood, and Deilcrit's vision went red with pain as the ptaiss jerked him to the ground. His lungs emptied, his head struck a stone. And while he hung limply, gasping, the ptaiss, fangs locked around the limb choking it, blood spurting from the gaping slash in its neck, snapped Deilcrit first to the right, then to the left. Then, with a growl and a bound, it dashed him to the grass, raking his torso with its hind talons. He did not even feel the creature's grip go slack as it collapsed on top of him, nor its huge heart pumping out a final jet of blood that spilled over his face, into his ears, and from there trickled down upon the sedge grass.

III

Of Whelts and Wehrs
and Imca-Sorr-Aat

I crouched in the sand, gulping great chunks of air out of the moonless night. I had brought us into time-space a trifle high, and we had fallen a short distance to land in a tangle. I was not displeased—dragging the both of them, the cahndor a dead-weight, and Sereth so much heavier that it seemed as if I attempted to pull the whole congruence plane out with me onto the sand of the bayshore—I counted myself fortunate to have emerged at all. That I had brought them both through on my power alone was near miraculous. But desperation is an inspiring instructor, and a propitiously timed obviation of space had seemed our only alternative to an eventual death atop a mountain of suicidally ferocious animals.

Chayin's voice, cursing monotonously in his native tongue, was the first sound I heard over my own pumping lungs. Then, as I struggled to my feet and brushed the sand away, I saw Sereth.

He stood at the water's edge, facing out to sea. Chayin, hunkered down nearby, stared straight at the sand between his feet, still excoriating in Parset.

It was not until I saw the severed hand, badly chewed and bearing a ring about one swollen finger, that I understood. Then I cursed myself for a fool and joined Sereth where he stood looking out at the empty sea.

"Do you think you miscalculated? Are we at the right point in space, but the wrong one in time?" he asked, his eyes never leaving the water, voice so soft it might have been the lapping of an articulate wave against the shore.

"I am afraid," said I, "that you overestimate me. I hardly calculate."

"Estri . . ." Even softer.

"No, then. I do not think so. There is no moon. What chance there is that I might have accidentally landed us here on another moonless night during which a severed hand wearing a Parset ring exactly like Neshub's found its way to the shore—that chance is far less than the obvious: the ship is gone, and Chayin has lost at least one of his crew."

He did not acknowledge me, and after a time I said that perhaps the crew had mutinied, killed Neshub, and cast off for Menetph, far across the sea.

In answer, he took my arm and pointed, and I saw what nestled against the jetty's rocks, and looked away. I had no desire to closely examine those misshapen hulks and shattered timbers.

I shook his hand off and retreated up the beach, until I found a spot free from growths and shadows, where I could not be stealthed upon.

"Come away from there," I cautioned Sereth, who had not moved. "The wehrs . . ." And the speaking of that word reminded me of Deilcrit. I saw him as I had last seen him, prostrate, while the ptaiss . . . I covered my eyes with my palms, but it did not help.

"Estri," said Chayin in my ear, "do you think you could return us to Port Astrin?"

I nodded. "It is no harder than was returning

here. There is no distance, just the procedures of entry and exit, and a choosing, in that cold place." I shivered, recollecting the shriveling agony of the procession of matter through the congruences. "But give me some time. And let the sun be risen. Then I will be stronger."

A shadow fell that was not material, and I looked up to see Sereth, all the heavens' fury in his crossed arms and forward-jutting hips. "So, we must simply stay alive until sunrising. With one sword and two knives between us. Then we will meekly turn our backs on fifty dead men, a gutted vessel, the criminals we came to this land seeking, and slink home by the aegis of Estri's skills, to sit and chitter and get fat and lazy ruling our various holdings, secure in the knowledge that should we ever again find ourselves in difficulties, we need but call Estri and she will remove us from the scene."

Chayin stiffly rose up, kicking me roughly from his path. Standing opposite Sereth, he growled, "A man must know when to cut his losses."

I scrambled to my feet and insinuated myself between them. Sereth shoved me aside.

"Do not speak to me of what men must do. You are overqualified. Both of you"—and he inclined his head at me, that there might be no mistaking my inclusion in Sereth's "you"—"would do well to keep silent in that regard. Shapers' blood makes for too many disparities. Flee! What of Se'keroth, and your much-vaunted 'age of the divinity of man'? For that matter, what of your vow to that pitiful savage?"

Chayin had no answer. He merely stared at Sereth's empty scabbard.

"Call my name and I will aid you," mimicked Sereth savagely. "A god who can offer his followers so little might have trouble retaining them."

"I did not realize," said the cahndor, "that you had lost Se'keroth in the fray."

At that, Sereth wheeled around and strode into the surf. Knee-deep in the shallows' froth, he stripped off the chased scabbard and threw it, belt and all, out to sea. The spinning sheath flew thrice the distance of a man's normal cast and was lost in the darkness.

"That," called Sereth, "is what care I have for Se'keroth." Beside me, I heard Chayin's harsh indrawn breath. "And for all of Khys's manipulations, and your cursed attempts to follow in his stead." A waterspout rose in the sea, born of Sereth's rage.

Chayin put his arm around my waist and drew me close.

"I cannot believe," I whispered through my shock, "that he is saying these things to us." My internals felt as though someone had just removed them, and my empty carcass was only momentarily capable of sustaining the fiction of life.

"Be quiet," Chayin advised. "It will pass. He is distraught. This has been long coming. There *are* differences . . ." And he trailed off, as Sereth approached. But I did not miss the unsteadiness in the cahndor's voice.

We three stood facing each other, only breathing, a long time. I spent that time bewailing, in my mind, the impossibility of ever foreseeing what this man, whom I loved as much as my next breath, would have me do.

"This serves no one," said Sereth at last, quietly, but without that deadly edge to his tone. Almost shyly he reached out his hand. I took it: It was clammy.

"Sereth, did you mean to start that turbulence?"

"No."

His reply was almost inaudible. I longed to comfort him, but I had no comfort to give. The bridling of such strengths as he had so recently acquired is an intimate undertaking, different for each. But I understood why he had, of late, so strictly controlled both his temper, which had never been placid, and those of his new skills which dealt with the direct application of mental force.

Chayin, grunting, unhanded me, squatted down, and craned his neck toward the sky.

"What is it?" Sereth, suddenly cautious, pulled me down to the sand.

"I heard something, something large flying, perhaps even circling overhead. But I cannot see it. And my sensing gives me a presence, though what kind, I do not know."

"Estri, what *are* the chances of your successfully obviating space again this night?" Sereth asked, squinting into the starry evening.

I thought about it. The obviation of space is a painful, draining, and ever-uncertain undertaking. Once I was caught for three days in the congruences. I shuddered. "Not good. Especially with you both as passive companions. If you two tried, perhaps—"

"I have tried," Chayin cut me off. "With no great success. This is something I know: a time comes when such skills will be within my reach. And this is another thing I know: that time is not yet." He paused, rubbed his right shoulder, and continued in a ruminative growl, "You, yourself, have told me that such feats remain the most precipitous of all that you attempt. The chance of hindrance by our efforts to help is too great to ignore." He looked at me questioningly. I kept silent.

"But you could do it," pressed Sereth, "if you had to."

I sighed. "I can try, if I have to, though if it is a choice between dying under the teeth and claws of ptaiss and wehrs, or dying lost between the moments in the domain of eternity, I should rather it be the ptaiss."

"Then let us hope," said Sereth gently, "that you do not have to try. But we must agree: if an insurmountable attack comes, from the forest, from the sea behind, that is what we will do. My bow, quiver, and"—Sereth shifted, looking pointedly at Chayin—"Se'keroth, and Estri's blade lie in that clearing. There also are a number of dead creatures who possibly could have been dealt with more humanely. Do either of you have any ideas . . . ?" And he broke off, and half-rose, staring upward, then around him at the ground.

"What are you looking for?"

"A good-sized rock. Chayin, I think I see your winged creature."

"What would you do?" demanded the cahndor, also suddenly searching rocks along the beach. Then he cursed, stiffened, and peered out into the sea, which was no longer still.

"Estri, watch those guerm, and be ready to get us back to camp if we need you." Like a spring-loaded bolt, he was gone from where his words rode the air; an eyeblink later, a star-frosted shadow holding a naked blade loomed atop a jumble of rocks fallen sideward from the jetty, cutting off my view of the shore.

Above my head I could just make out the star-shine on something large that soared in slow circles. Its shape was not as easy to define as its mind-touch, which I had felt before, ever so softly, when first we entered Benegua.

"Sereth," I called, as the first of the guerm waddled, deceptively quick, out of the surf. Behind it rose another streamered snout, and another, and I knew we could not hack them all apart, one by one, even with three swords.

"What, ci'ves?" Sereth said from directly behind me. I jumped, then replied: "I am going to bring down the winged thing for you. If I am right, the guerm will—"

"Do not explain. Do what you can do." And with that he left me, bearing an armful of fist-sized rocks, to join Chayin where he awaited the guerm.

It was not until I had seen two of the six-legged amphibians disemboweled that I managed to gather sufficient concentration. Then I merged with the thing in the sky. Its thoughts were soft and layered, like a million far-off voices speaking at once, and as it became aware of me it showed no fear. Only my sense of numbers diminished. As I struggled to reach a mind with which to reason, a great horde fled me, leaving only a tentative intelligence within that body whose every wing flap was now so much a part of me that my shoulders ached.

"Come down. Cease this senseless war, be—" Then something that knew no words jumped ravening from behind the clouds of animating hosts that seemed to dwell in that single brain, and I screamed aloud and found myself flat on my back, my hands to my pulsing temples. One quick glance at the shore told me I had no more time, that by my clemency I might have lost us all our lives. Then, coldly, with no thought of anything but destruction, I constructed a turbulence of my own. Wide, I built it, and long, so that it formed a contracting sphere that showed as fire clouds in the otherwise clear night. Tighter and tighter I forced the sphere, and I could hear the thing within it scream, as the buffeting storm tongues threw it about like an autumn leaf. Screwing my eyes shut against the glare, I willed the lightning-charged ball to spin ever faster; to shrink ever smaller. A bolt shot through the clouds, then another, and I cursed, ceased struggling to bring the whirlwind to earth. Rather, I dispersed it, and as the turbulence turned

to mist and the fire of the electrically charged air abated, a form plummeted downward, limbs askew, wings inert and wrapped around its body.

It fell with a thud between me and the two men, and lay still, one wing jutting into the air.

Pulling damp hair from my brow, I ran toward the shore and the streamered guerm which rode the incoming tide like a living band of froth across the bay. The main body of the school was perhaps twenty man's lengths out to sea. The forerunners, living and dead, littered the surf. In the shallows, Sereth and Chayin were but darker shadows from which came an occasional grunt or a syllable of warning, punctuated by Chayin's thwacking blade and the splash of rocks and the thrash of silent-dying guerm.

While I squinted past them into the moonless dark, the luminescent band of froth which was in reality uncountable surfacing guerm became a dotted line. Then that line seemed to shudder, then surge raggedly into a circle which immediately exploded into a thrashing mass of individuals who turned upon one another in the overly close waters. Moment by moment, the disintegration of the school, now denied the organizational mind of the winged thing which had deployed them, became more pronounced.

Sereth, with a satisfied grunt, threw one last missile into the midst of three guerm that were greedily gorging themselves on their dismembered fellows. Then he clapped Chayin on the back, and the cahndor's laughter rang out over the still night as they approached.

I nodded to myself, pleased that my desperate experiment had worked. But I wondered, as I turned to the winged corpse, whether even this evidence would be adequate to support my conclusions, should I dare present them. I need not have worried on that score. On another, I was disastrously wrong:

The grayish, winged, manlike creature was no corpse. It lived, after a fall that shattered half the bones in its body; lived after the application of such force as might have sufficed to end ten men.

I knelt beside it, awestruck, and as I did so, fear rode up from the abyss to possess me. Not that small fear, a mere breeze, that whispers at the back of one's mind and conjures specters; but that overwash of howling gale force that cripples so that all that remains is a deaf-mute, empty of thought, trapped nonvolitional in a body seeking to prepare itself for suspended animation. Looking down at that gray chest, fine-furred and slabbed with muscle, I could not believe that the chest rose and fell, though with every respiration, blood that glinted black in the evening monochrome trickled from between two crushed ribs. Its right arm was thrown back, twisted at an unlikely angle, or so I thought until Sereth, his hand on its right wing, which jutted almost straight up into the air, murmured, "Look at this."

He spread the pinion wide. That arm and the soft-furred, membranous wing comprised one limb, inseparable. The very human-looking arm formed the main strut of the wing: six-digited hands with webbed, clawed fingers fringed by delicate wing edges tipped it; six massive fleshy vessels, each as thick as a human wrist, ran diagonals from shoulder, elbow, mid- and forearm to wingtip, branching repeatedly. Even while Sereth held the arm high, the vessels became visibly less tumescent as blood seeped out of the creature and its strength failed. When Sereth dropped the arm, to the eye no wing rested there, but two soft drapes of gray-furred skin that hung like some doubled cloak from the creature's arm and shoulder.

"Chayin, give Estri your sword." And to my horrified shudder, Sereth added: "Long ago I told you that in future you must dispatch your own wounded. Is there not even that much mercy in you, Shapers' spawn? The thing suffers."

With downcast eyes I took the weapon from Chayin, but as I bent close, debating whether to slit its throat, lop head from shoulders, or simply drive the sword point into its heart, the creature stirred, and fixed upon me its yellow-eyed stare, and its words stayed my hand:

"Woman, wild or no, you should know better than to lift arms against a representative of Wehrdom! Imca-Sorr-Aat's curse upon you! Upon all your heads, it is levied." The voice was a soughing wind. It came from everywhere, so ubiquitous that I thought for a moment that my mind alone had heard, for its cartilaginous mouth had not opened. Solicitous, I dropped the sword and raised up its head. From that crushed skull out onto my hand oozed spongy, viscous pulp.

One look at Sereth and Chayin proved that they also heard the winged wehr, and even while its brains and blood ran down my arm, the thing recommenced its speech:

"There is no escape! Though you roam the earth entire, the creatures of land and air and sea will follow to exact their vengeance. You have defiled the river, you have laid about you with all the wantonness of your kind. He who eats our flesh will in his own turn be eaten; he who has slaughtered ptaiss will end under their claws.

"But you"—and the creature lifted its mashed skull from my palm, and thrust its gory head so close I could smell the stink of death on its breath— "you have murdered not one wehr-master, but two, and for your crimes, Mahrlys-iis-Vahais' justice would be too merciful. It is Imca-Sorr-Aat himself

who will exact from you the price of . . ." Abruptly
the creature sagged in my arms. Then, in a racking
spasm that spewed blood and bile over us both, it
succumbed to its fate.

I laid the corpse back on the sand and made a
desultory attempt to sluice the foul death fluids
from my breasts and arms.

"Well," said Chayin, wrinkling up his nose in
distaste and lifting me bodily from the corpse's
side, "let us get you cleaned up. You may be
accursed, but you need not smell like it." And he
gave me a broad grin, whose like I had seen before,
too often.

I twisted in his grasp to confront Sereth, just
quitting the wehr-master's side.

"You are well pleased, are you not?" I accused
him.

"I must admit that events have taken an intrigu-
ing turn," he said, tossing his head. His temper,
so vile earlier, was not at all in evidence. Even the
night's mask could not hide the deepened channel
where the scar on his cheek brushed his mouth. He
was eager, now that the enemy had declared
himself, for the battle to be joined.

"And I would add"—Chayin chortled—"that my
mind is greatly eased by the revelation that there
exists here more than a handful of bronze-age
primitives, affrighted of their own shadows huddled in the ruins of their ancestors' prehistoric
technocracy."

"Thank you, Oh Stoth adept," I jibed, as I
splashed water over my beslimed self, keeping a
careful eye out for straggling guerm who might be
dining in the shallows.

"Perhaps it was only boredom that you sought
to vanquish here, Estri, but it was knowledge of
what has so long lain unknowable that called me
out from the desert," retorted the cahndor.

"And what of the M'ksakkans that murdered the mother of your son?" I demanded.

The cahndor snorted. "They did me a great service in that. I will admit that the gesture of pursuit needed to be made. But may I also point out this: considering that the denizens of this land seem to be actively at war with man, little chance would a handful of comfort-bred off-worlders, weaponless, ignorant of wilderness skills, have had. No, when the wehrs first attacked us, I had to face the fact that searching out M'ksakkan bones would be merely an exercise in tracking. But no matter, we have something infinitely more stimulating to do, and, I would predict, more demanding. After all, we cannot just go home and wait for the curse to strike. My sleep would be marred beyond repair. And I hate, above all things, waiting."

"Indeed," joined in Sereth as I made my way out of the surf, "in such engagements it is better to take the offensive. It might serve us to pool our suppositions with an eye toward determining what weapons we could most profitably bring to bear." Both Chayin and I knew what arsenal Sereth proposed to inventory.

"And then? Surely neither of you believe in this . . . this Imca-Sorr-Aat's curse?"

Sereth snorted softly. Chayin chuckled aloud, and recalled a time he had said to me that every curse ever written had been laid upon his head.

"And then," Sereth replied, "we will collect our belongings from the clearing, and travel the road I saw among the trees. At the end of it, I suspect we will find Mahrlys-iis-Vahais, whose control of these wehrs is far less ephemeral than any curse, and from him exact either a suitable vessel and crew to replace that which his wehrs destroyed, or sufficient satisfaction to convince us to return home without a ship. But"—and here he leaned forward,

his eyes narrowed, and his voice knifed the night—
"I am not going to be frightened away, or driven
away, by either his curses or his wehrs."

"But you are willing to risk being carried away,"
I spat back.

"Estri," opined Chayin, "Sereth is right. Neither
of us could turn our backs on such an open chal-
lenge and retain any semblance of self-respect. And
if we did flee, who is to say that one morning we
might not wake up with all of Wehrdom encamped
upon our doorstep? They know we are here. Doubtless they have some glimmering as to whence we
have come. And it is Mahrlys-iis-Vahais that has
threatened *us*, wherever we are. Better here, I say,
than in Menetph, or Astria, or at the Lake of Horns.
And that reminds me ..." He turned to Sereth.
"Before the guerm attack, you accused me of
cowardice."

Sereth started to make some excuse, but Chayin
would not allow it: "Let me finish. When I asked
Estri if she could get us home, it was because I
had not, in all the probability scans I made for our
immediate future, seen a single path which led us
home from this bayshore, and it occurred to me
that the reason I had not seen it so was because it
was not possible. Now I realize that although it is
possible, even then it was highly unlikely. Though
the question may presently seem academic, the
procedure is pertinent, even critical: There are a
number of alternatives in the sort that deserve our
attention. Now, Ebvrasea, speak your say." It was
by an old nomer, one which Sereth acquired while
afoul of the law on the other side of this world—
our world—that Chayin called him.

Sereth smiled, and tousled the cahndor's black
curls. "I regret, then, that I falsely accused you.
What do you see in the sort?"

Chayin frowned. "As always, it is more what I

do not see, than what I do. . . . Estri will support me in the statement that when involved with a future in which no constants are known, it is very difficult to read any coherent pattern. When first we arrived here, I saw a number of futures in which were a youngish, roughly dressed man whom I think now was Deilcrit. At any rate, if aforehand there were differences between Deilcrit and the young male in my foresight, those differences have evaporated. Wait."

Sereth sat back.

"I still see a number of futures, viable derivatives of this moment, with a Deilcrit very stubbornly existing therein."

"In other words, he is not dead?"

"Either that, or a very lively shade. Are you not pleased?" Chayin demanded, when I showed no reaction. I shrugged, shielded, and kept silent.

"Next time, I will ask for a synopsis," Sereth snapped.

"That is a synopsis. Go down that road, and you will find not only Mahrlys-iis-Vahais, but Estri's magnificent savage as well."

"You have greatly eased my mind," said Sereth dryly. "Now that the worst of my fears have been allayed, may I feel free to call on you for counsel as to what owkahen holds when the need strikes me? Good. And will you also, occasionally, update my awareness when you feel you have something I should know?"

"I would have, in any—"

"That is enough on that subject. Estri, you look like you have something to say."

"I do. The wehrs are a community of minds. I felt minds in great numbers when I touched the thoughts of the wehr-master. The community, as I conceive it, spans species lines, which is why

Deilcrit referred to the conglomerate of species that attacked us as wehrs."

"I had gathered that. Even the guerm, I suppose, are wehrs."

"But you have not realized the importance of it. That thing, the wehr-master, should have been dead when it hit the ground. I poured enough force into that turbulence to lay flat ten of Chayin's Parsets." I was leaning forward, recalling my fear when I had realized how resilient the wehr-master was.

"That makes good sense. If a hundred minds are linked together, and one applies force sufficient to destroy ten, then the hundred minds spread and share that force among their ranks, so that no one entity receives more than a hundredth of that force," reasoned Chayin.

"It is Mahrlys who controls the wehrs, through those winged wehr-masters," Sereth reminded us. "One does not count on matching strength with each foot soldier, but seeks to debilitate the chain of command, as did Estri."

"Why, then, did we not witness the same effect when Estri killed the other winged one in the ptaiss battle?" Chayin pondered.

"Perhaps there was more than one of them," I hazarded.

"Or perhaps if we had tarried longer, we would have seen it. That was as close as I would like to come."

"I was meaning to ask you," Chayin picked up the thread, "what possessed you two to cast your weapons like that?"

I opened my mouth to protest, but Sereth was faster.

"When three people join hands, only one has his right hand free. And if I had not *thrown* my blade, the ptaiss would have been impaled on it just at the moment Estri pulled us into the congruence. I did not want to take a chance on dragging a wounded beast with us out of time, nor could I ignore the fact that if I did not stop its charge, I would have ended there under its claws."

"I, too, found myself facing such a choice. And lest we all face it again, let us set about considering what weapons your excellencies would judge meet in dealing with our foes," I urged, unable to keep either the sarcasm or the concern I felt from sharpening my words. Almost, then, I succumbed and spoke my mind; but Chayin jumped eagerly into the breach before Sereth could retort, and his proposition of a neutral barrier, a sort of perimeter to keep us isolate, took long enough to explain that I had time to regain my composure. Still, Sereth's harsh words and Deilcrit's plight rang in my ears and danced before my eyes, and I was little aid to them in their planning.

At length we had compiled a list which included a method for reintroducing any given signal into the mind-matrix of the wehr system in such a way as to promulgate a disabling feedback; a group of contingency choices based upon the utilization of the most fruitful alternatives available from the probability sort—the propinquitous futures produced by the present moment; an arsenal of turbulence techniques effective against a conglomerate attack. These last Sereth strictly regulated as to what was and was not fit: For the dispatch of men in strength we could employ naught but flesh-lock— the removal of a body's control from its owner— and weapons of the most mundane materiality, these to be physically wielded.

Through it all I managed to keep silent, passive. Let Sereth handicap us in whatever ways eased his ulcerated sense of propriety: it mattered not to me. I had no great trepidation as to how we might fare among the wehrs or the Beneguans; Imca-Sorr-Aat's curse troubled not one whit my mind: I was resigned; I knew the signs; by now, how not?

Entrapment is only a state of mind. They, the cahndor and the dharen, felt not entrapped. They were better than I at self-deception, and it served them both well. They spoke of burying the fragments of the Aknet's crew, or firing the few pitiful remains, and I knew it to be Sereth's way of closing the discussion. He looked curiously at me, and then melted into the dark.

I smelled my father's breath on the land, and the legacy of Sereth's predecessor, Khys, was a tight and obdurate band around my throat. We had come hunting a few off-worlders, for sport, for peace and recreation: I had never believed that. From the start I had been suspicious, for I had read extensively in Khys's writings, and I knew Sereth. And Chayin. And Estrazi, my father, I knew him, also. He had promised me certain things: rest, respite. But there is no fitness of Shapers' scales that I can comprehend, and Estrazi, like Khys, twists truth and in his hands half-truth often takes double seeming. The Spirit Gate had opened at lightning's stroke; we had, in the normal course of our camp-making, committed importunate acts against the fitness known in this land. By the time the fire was crackling, it was already too late. And I had not been unaware. I never am, in retrospect. Instead I am calm and thoughtless of consequences, but sure in the singleness of owkahen's purpose. Wehrs? Doubtless we could successfully confront them; and wehr-masters; and Mahrlys-iis-Vahais. It was not these things that had kept me presenting an enquieted facade before my companions, for in lucid moments even I can take comfort in the fact that though the tasks and trials we create for ourselves are oft strenuous and even grueling, purpose is served thereby, greater than ours, underlying all our free will and choice.

No, it was not Benegua, the Wall of Mnemaat, which would soon again enwrap us in others' dilemmas, nor what I had gleaned from Deilcrit's memories of the exigencies before us in this most singular land, but Deilcrit himself, lying, if Chayin's foresight was accurate, wounded yet alive among the carnage we had wrought at the campsite which concerned me. To him, in my sight, we each owed a debt. Yet Sereth's sharp tone at Chayin's revelation, his immediate change of subject, had made me quite sure of his feelings. And now he fussed among the disemboweled. He would not hasten to reclaim the blades that glittered by the dying embers at our camp within the Wall of Mnemaat, not with the wounded boy there. This I knew surer than my name, yet I did not understand. His displeasure at my mode of interrogation of the youth came back to me.

And another thought, fast upon the heels of that one—a thought that seemed meaningless at the time and preceeded Chayin's appearance out of the dark by an eye-blink. Once, long ago, when I came to Sereth on Chayin's arm, Sereth had said to me: *"Two men can share anything but the love of a woman."* His face in that moment, his voice on that night, burned so brightly as to obscure my vision. And then another moment, seemingly unrelated: another speaking: the cahndor himself. Then another instance of my past experience burst in on me in a new and unsuspected sequence, as is often the way with the sorting talent, and I was shown, in a final avalanche of apprehension, one last moment: my father, Estrazi. Then that sorting-of-what-is took wings, and it was the future which Sereth and Chayin and I would build in this land that unfurled in flashes of tableau whose context and cast remained obscure. But the meaning was not obscure. Oh, no, the meaning was bright and clear and shivered before me in those colors only the prescient mind's palette can conjure, and I heard my throat sigh a groaning sound and became aware of my hands, balled into fists, supporting my crouched weight, and the cahndor's presence close by.

"What did you see?" And a rustle as he crouched. Raising my head, I peered through shadow at shadow.

Sereth's dire olden words threatened to tumble from my mouth. But I withheld them, peering toward the scant pile of remains, shoreward, where he yet gathered minute fragments of the Aknet's dead. He had snarled at Chayin, called him no judge of what men must do. And me, he had condemned. . . . So I answered Chayin another answer, no less true, from my revelation, that I might not make more real what I most feared.

"My father said to me, when I asked him to release us all on our own recognizance . . ." I stumbled, wondering how to phrase this hurtful thing which Chayin must know to make use of what I had seen. I leaned close, peering into the crimson reflection from his eyes' pupils. "When I asked him to sanction my union with Sereth, to grant us his grace, he said he would as soon not call upon us. But he also said: 'There is no real respite. Your own natures will preclude it.' "

Chayin grimaced, a quick flashing in the dark as my eyes drew more from its depths. I heard two stones click as he shifted.

"Your Shaper father's way with words is legend," he said quietly, not amused at his own joke. Moderation of tone in the cahndor is a portentous omen.

"Come and give silence to my dead. You may not, cannot, do what you intend."

"It is my choice," I snapped, straightening abruptly, chagrined that he had so easily divined my intent. Shields up, mind inviolate, I awaited his retort.

It was slow coming, and when it did, it raised my hackles and set me irrevocably upon that path I had so recently glimpsed:

"What is choice? We freely choose to do exactly what owkahen dictates."

"Am I a schoolgirl in need of lessons? Mi'ysten spawn, you badly underestimate your cousin." That propinquity to which I referred was Chayin's father's, who in turn was son of my father's brother. Both races, the Mi'ysten and the Shapers themselves, progenitors of solar systems, of galaxies, of universes and all they contain, command powers that in the time-space universes make them gods. And so had they been to millions of millions of lesser beings, for a duration of aeons. And we, Chayin and I who were their children in flesh as well as spirit, had inherited from our paternities some few slivers of those abilities. Sereth, too, had come upon the skills of his inheritance: though it was an inheritance diverse from ours, he had acquired its bequests in a similar fashion.

"Estri, never will I underestimate you." I could see now the smile that pulled at Chayin's full lower lip. And I shivered, and rubbed my palms along my arms. "Come and give silence to my dead. I assure you, I am not wrong."

He reached out, I shook him off. "Not wrong in what, cahndor? You give nothing, and expect all in return. What right have you to even conjecture over my activities? Or to judge them. I will go where I will and you *may not* stop me." So soft I spoke to him, he knew that I did not jest. A contest between us two might rip the veils asunder, erode the very fabric of reality. He well knew it. Thus sobered, perhaps pained (for I could not read him—his skills there exceed mine), he still did not go and join Sereth, who must by now be in the formalized grieving aspect, cross-legged, head bowed before the remains of the slain. Or so I thought then.

"I need not try to stop you. Owkahen will!" Chayin retorted: "Two things, dhareness, and I will depart to my duty. First: You *may* not. Sereth will not allow it. You have seen him. Do not provoke the ebvrasea in its nest. It is night. At night he will soar, and hunt. His belly is empty."

I spat a word I had learned among the crew on the Aknet's decks.

"Estri, you have seen! He grows stranger and stranger, while the weight of Silistra upon his shoulders grows ever more great. Of more importance than any one life is the good that could be done upon all Silistra by the consolidation of the northern and southern holdings. And yet reality grows ever more singular for him: more and more he is one and we two another. So many have given so much that this alliance be made, and it seems that at its very inception it will be blighted by doubt and fear.

"What he said to me, to us: it is not untrue. You and I have the Shapers within us. We see the results of the action at hand. And from the emotions of a specific moment, we must often seem removed, cruel, calculating. You thought nothing of sending hundreds to their deaths when you battled my father; nor of putting the helsar plague upon the land—yes, so do some now call those devices of nature which open a man to the power he shares with his universe. I must seem to him little better—I do not flinch at what actions my preference for certain futures demand of me in the ever-mutable present. And we see no harm, no acts lacking in fitness, in what we do. But he does. He takes chaldra very seriously; he *is* the law. Think back. And think of what he is: painstakingly bred mongrel; the descendant of all Silistra, the quintessence of racial mixing. Yet he is trapped by the very society designed to emancipate him: these same self-strengths that drove him, that enabled him to become what he is, to possess you and freedom from the servitude he so despised appall him. He has broken laws that he himself created. And he fears his own nature. In us he sees something he conceives as a lack of compassion, a coldness, an inhumanity that his mind cannot accept, because it senses in itself the like. He—"

"Chayin," I interrupted. "He is more a killer than either of us. And genetic mixes like his produce atavists, not moralists. I studied him. You know him. He is not one to blanch at the sight of blood, nor to turn from necessities by reason of qualms." I objected, but I recollected Sereth, leaning over a wounded girl in the battle that had won him the dharen's sword. And a thousand other occasions on which he took extensive care as to the welfare of those he had caused to become unfortunates. "I fail to see what bearing this has on my tending Deilcrit's wounds," I said at last.

"Estri, do not defend yourself to me. Who is more bloodied among us, is it? There is blood aplenty to go around. Or guilt, if any of us should choose to drag so weighty a stone into owkahen's raging torrent. And as for Deilcrit, I have told you: he will live to embroil himself so deeply in our affairs that even you will be sated. I have seen it."

"And of course I am not strong enough to bear whatever foreknowledge your forereading has bequeathed you. You have done ill before with such—"

"Have I? I have done what has been needed, as have you. I say to you this: do not do *more* than is needed. And I am telling you, Sereth will kill you both if you evince inordinate interest in this jungle boy. After what he has been through to claim you and his regency, he will cede neither one light."

I sat very still, abashed, frightened. Chayin was incensed, and his thick voice shook with his attempts to keep it to a whisper: "He should not have to. He and I should be sufficient, if one man is not."

"You dare speak so to me?"

"I dare what pleases me. Take heed, Estri. You have suffered before by reason of wisdom you would not hear. Be moderate. Be loving. Be a consolation unto him in this need. He has seen your father, Estri. He has heard from Estrazi's own lips that he has been manipulated. His hatred for serving another's purpose knows no limits. You cannot take the chance of straying to the wrong side of the boundary that defines his sense of fitness; it is clear, stringently defined, and he will kill you if you cross it."

I said nothing. This was not the first time Chayin had warned me of Sereth. Though the best of us all at forereading the time-coming-to-be from the probabilities owkahen presents to the sorting mind, when concerned with Sereth, he was consistently inaccurate. As, I am afraid, was I.

"And now I will tell you why you *cannot* blithely obviate space, work your healing on this Deilcrit, and return by the same method." Then he pointed, his arm a dark shadow against the gray of the sky, and said: "The sun is coming up. Therefore, we have lost at least a quarter of the night, perhaps four enths. Therefore, to paraphrase your father: the time precludes it."

I groaned, and slapped my thigh so hard it stung.

But Chayin was inexorable: "In getting here, a good portion of the night's duration slipped from our grasp, unlived. Deilcrit lived those hours, as did all others in sequential time. But we did not. The last time you obviated space, what was it— three days? And the next—you do not know how long you might languish between the moments. You cannot control the effect. How long might it be for us, for Deilcrit, while you spend an eyeblink shunting the nonsequential circuits? It could be a day, or ten, or a full pass of the moon that goes by. Then what might lurk in the clearing you seek? When might you set foot there? Making your way back here to us: how long for that? When you arrive here, subjectively passing a heartbeat's time, might it not be three days, or thrice that, or a season that has passed for us? What would you expect us to do? Wait here until you return at some unspecifiable date? If something went wrong, we would have no way of knowing short of fore-reading, which would be difficult in the extreme under such conditions. And as for concealing this misplaced mercy from Sereth—"

"*Stop!*" I cursed my arrogance, my stupidity, my shortsightedness. Once having conceived the plan, while Chayin first informed us that Deilcrit lived, I had been so busy keeping traces of my intent from my mind that I had not come to grips with the practicalities. Obviation of space is a little like setting up consonance with a congruence plane: one exits sequentiality, which then contracts, becoming so vague and dreamlike that any entrance into it is a good entrance. Or had been, so far, for me, novice in the extreme. It was possible that I could make a perfect transition, obviate space between the moments, and lose only a breath's worth of sequential time, but it was not likely. I knew it

to be true: Chayin was right: I had not yet per-
fected my skill.

"Your will is my life." I sighed bitterly.

His fingers brushed my cheek, traced my lips.
"Estri, it could yet go as I long ago conceived it. If
all else fails, know that between us there can never
be misunderstandings such as even now bar us
both from him. And know too that Nemar and the
Taken Lands have not forgotten you. My people
would welcome you with arms outstretched."

Not until then did I take my eyes from his and
see Sereth, staring down on us, limned in the first
cloud-split, bloody rays of sun's raising.

Chayin followed my stricken gaze, and after a
moment of dumb silence, scrambled to his feet.
They stood that way, taking each other's measure
anew, while the leaden-clouded sky absorbed the
cinnabar light of dawn and then slowly greened as
the mists of night took flight.

It seemed to me that they might have stood that
way, opposed and immobile, forever. With constricted heart, I insinuated myself between them,
pressed myself against Sereth. After a time, his
arm went around my waist and we sought our
duty before Chayin's Parset dead.

But there were no words. Not from any of us.
Aghast at what might be the consequences of our
importunate speech, neither Chayin nor I ventured
to break peace before him; and he, in whom silence bespeaks rage beyond expression and volatil-
ity in the proximity of which even my father might
tread with care, let us suffer therein.

So discomfited, seated before the pitiful remains
of the Aknet's crew—a paltry pile scarce the height
of my calf containing barely enough chunks of
meat and limb to construct a single man—I could
not give our dead the enquieted mind which is
their due honorific. No, my thoughts would not be

still, but rather raged futile threats and impotent denouncements at the time:

Owkahen, thy jest does not amuse me. I will have this man if I must remake the whole nature of time to find us together therein. And if I cannot find it, I will *construct* a moment in which we may live untroubled that life I can conceive but cannot see.

So overweening did I dare to be in the face of eternity's wellspring.

Chayin had made his position clear: He would let Sereth slay me, if it came to that: as always, as it had been from the days when we first met, from the beginning. He considered the Silistran alliance more valuable than any life; his inferno-forged trust with Sereth most sacred: worth any price even if that price was my own continued existence. So did I.

Sometimes, when my mind aches and I am weary, I wonder if any of us will ever learn.

IV

The Eye of Mnemaat

The cessation of pain was all the luxury in the universe: Deilcrit sought it. And in the blackness behind closed lids, he found that the pain had an ebb, and a flow; and holding his breath through the dizzying combers of agony, he found comfort in the receding of sensation that followed every torturous thrill which racked him. In those moments, he exhaled, and each exhalation brought him a whisper of consciousness more. He extracted his body's assessment of its condition from the red-gold nausea that hung like an undulant curtain between him and his selfness: he was alive, and he hurt. The contours of his wound were for a time his total being; his reality a depth and breadth of scourged flesh, of scratched bone and severed nerve. The jagged hole was a mountain range in which he wandered like some zealous surveyor whose stomach lurched each time he raised his eyes and regarded the vastness of this valley torn from his muscles' contours.

Eventually, as one in mourning overlong, he recollected his identity, his name, his position in time and space, and how he had come to the pain.

Then he reclaimed the rest of his body, which by reason of painlessness seemed at first nonexistent, then wizened, then only numb and clumsy. Then he began to sort out the lesser discomforts of bruised flesh, torn muscle, scratched skin, and the nausea receded. He slipped from under the ptaiss' foreleg—*that ptaiss he had slain*!

Very slowly, eyes yet closed, he gathered his remembrances about him and with his good arm pushed himself to a sitting position.

The world wheeled and he swallowed jet after jet of hot water thrown up by his stomach, but he opened his eyes to the new day.

It was a long while before he dared shift his gaze from the patch of bare ground beside his thigh, and regard the wound.

He thought, by then, he could be dispassionate. He knew the extent of his left arm's damage, knew when and how it had occurred, how long it had lain open to the air. But he then saw the bone gleaming dully back at him from above his elbow, and the cavernous hole from which lumps of bloody flesh hung trembling in a pool of viscous white and yellow secretions whose edges were crusted with dried blood. The pool's surface was dotted with floating bits of dirt, grass, and tiny insects whose lucent wings fluttered tremulously with each shiver of his flesh. He retched.

He did not again win the battle for consciousness until the sun was high, and then remained as he had wakened, slumped in a tangle, his head pressed to the earth, consumed with the ineffable sadness we feel when we find ourselves wounded; a sadness not for the self but for the mangled, recontoured limb. It is the body's emotion, deeper than a mother's grief for the stillborn, and it racks the strongest as completely as the coward. In its grip he was a child.

As a child he looked around him, accepting the death strewn about with no understanding. There was a long-bodied sorrel campt staring unblinking at him, its broken tusk of no more moment to its owner. Atop its snakelike back sprawled an ossasim: a wehr-master with wings cut to streamers. The significance of this was lost upon him.

He collected two thoughts: the pouch about his waist held a needle, and line used for fishing. He would ... But it lay not about his waist, and he recalled when he had dropped it. The second thought was the proximity of a memnis tree, and for that he would need a knife. He had had one ... So the two thoughts became four, and the four cubed, and he began to crawl in ever-widening circles about the clearing, detouring carefully around the slain.

It was the knife he found first, but he did not stop: he was afraid that if he halted he would not move again. So he crawled farther, noting on his infinitely slow journey every detail of what lay in the clearing, as is the way of the mind when it is threatened with extinction. So he noted the great green-metaled sword, and the smaller one gleaming clear as mountain water, though he could place no value upon them. Still, he had not looked upon his left arm, nor did he until he held the precious pouch and struggled with the shaking fingers of his right hand and his teeth to extract the bone needle and the fishing twine from within.

Threading the needle was harder. His eyes jumped in his skull, and one hand was not sufficient, and he ended with the needle stuck into the sod, he lying with his cheek to the ground and his hand propped on a flat rock, that he might drive the crimped twine through the needle's eye.

When this was done, he muttered the Law of Nature's Compassion under his breath and began sewing up as best he could the hand's breadth hole above his elbow.

Have you ever done this? Sewing one's own wound is different from seeing it done: as dissimilar as the sight of one's own lesion from that of another's.

The punctures were not painful—his flesh was already giving its all in pain, could not add more. But the tying of the knots, the pulling tight of the twine which he accomplished by holding one end in his teeth, broke a cold sweat onto his brow. Each time he pulled the flesh together, saw the twine protruding from his skin, he was forced to stop, to wait until his stomach ceased bucking. When finally all but the round center (and this concerned him: a round wound is the hardest healing) had been sewn together with the irregular stitching of an apprentice seamstress, he sank back on the ground and let the fit of shivering consume him.

The work he had done danced before his eyes, the black twine a crazy quilt, a barbaric road map of what had occurred. After a time he forced himself to assess it, its irregular contours, its length and breadth. He knew the scar would look ill, that the flesh would heal with all the humps and bumps it now displayed, but it was an intellectual knowledge. He uttered an animal growl and levered himself up, first securing the knife in his too-small sheath, and sought the memnis tree on the clearing's far side.

When he gained it, he scored the white bark deeply with the white-bladed knife Chayin had given him to fight wehrs, the knife he had employed to murder a ptaiss. At that thought, he muttered harshly again, and drove the knife more strongly into the memnis' bark. Then he peeled the oblong section of bark from the tree and repeated the process on the moist, greenish inner bark. This oblong strip of sticky fiber he wrapped around the wound, binding it there with the remains of his twine.

Then, with a sigh of satisfaction, he gave up consciousness once more.

The next waking was easier: the memnis was about its work. He dared a testing of his left hand. The fingers moved, if stiffly. The lances of agony that ran from fingertip to shoulder when he moved them cheered him. He had been afraid the hand would remain numb, the fingers useless.

He attempted a squat. Though he swayed, he held it. Using the memnis for support, he attained his feet. Then he leaned his head against the velvety bark and laughed, a slow-starting chuckle that grew until it racked him with shudders that threatened to throw him to the ground. When the laughter ceased, he was much shaken by its visit, not understanding why it had come. He would not understand for a very long time.

Then he shied away from even the direct consequences before him. He would do something, but he was not yet ready to determine what. He sought a blank mind, that comfort he had obtained so dear and which had served him all his life. He could not regain it. So he settled for a simulation, and did small things: he took steps; he sought the two swords he had marked in his crawl about the clearing. The white blade was lodged in the campt's breastbone and when he had finally tugged it free he was dizzied, panting, ravenously hungry.

And what his mind told him to do affronted his Beneguan soul. So he locked his soul in a hastily constructed cage in the back of his mind and slit the campt's belly and ate of what was within.

Almost, he could not retain it, but at length he wiped the blood from his mouth and set about finding a way to carry the two weapons of strange metal with him.

At last he lurched into the forest thickets, scorning the path and the flesh-scraping jicekak that raked him as he pushed ever deeper. He had bound the two blades together with the placenta-stiffened hide which had been the spirit-woman Estri's tunic. This, with a cord he had scavenged from the intruders' camp, he had fashioned into a rude scabbard. Of what else lay there, he took nothing: their food was not recognizable to him as such, and their various garments were either too small, too large, or too alien. The bow and arrows were splintered, useless.

And he was anxious to quit the clearing. The bushes rustled with life. He heard low growls and the pad of feet and the passage of great bodies through the trees. But no vengeance descended on him from out of the forest. He was breathing easier, and hurting more with the ebb of anesthetizing fear, when the whelt suddenly darted down from somewhere in the laced labyrinths of the wood's leafy roof. Twittering softly, it hovered before his face.

"Leave me be, whelt."

The great-winged whelt pummeled the air, slowly retreating before him. Its size and banded leg showed it to be the one which had earlier given him Mahrlys' message. He batted his good hand at it, but it only twittered. The air from its wings brushed his face.

"Whelt, go away. I must find some vabillia root—if I do not, I will die. I have neither the time nor the strength to be a problem. Spying upon me will be fruitless."

He stumbled over a protruding root somewhere in the knee-deep brush he trod. When he righted himself, the azure and indigo wings still beat an arm's length before his eyes. He well knew whelts, and they no more flew backward than they twittered softly, delicately attentive before one's face. And, too, this was Mahrlys' creature: no whelt of such grandeur inhabited the seaward forest. The band proclaiming this winked balefully at him.

For a while he plowed onward, the whelt ever before. Thrice he stopped, leaning faint against tree trunks, and the whelt each time alighted on the closest bough, twittering. On the last of these occasions, it reached its head down toward him, long neck stretching, silver neckband ruffed.

"Whelt, I can take no message. My mind is fogged. Whelt—"

But its cheek brushed his, and a thousand pairs of eyes regarded him down an endless arch of tunnels, and from those depths came the compassionate murmur of thrice a thousand voices. . . .

He gasped and pulled away, pressing his throbbing head against the moss that cushioned the tree's crook. No message from Mahrlys had he received. He struggled briefly with the complexity of the experience, then recoiled from it: the whelt's name was something close to Kirelli and through Kirelli Deilcrit had glimpsed something of Wehrdom: No man meets Wehrdom face to face and survives! Unless . . .

He heaved a sigh: he seemed very much alive. Once, while a young boy, he had seen a whelt kill a youth with whom he had only moments before been playing at bonethrow. The whelt had descended in a thunder of wings and rushed at the boy, fastened its claws into the child's eye sockets. It had been a terrifying death to witness, and this whelt's odd behavior had minded him of it.

He heaved himself away from the tree to speak to it.

There was no whelt upon the branch.

He clutched the tree, and his head spun. Could it be that no whelt had ever been there?

He staggered, half-running, half-stumbling through the brush. He pushed himself, purposefully unthinking of anything else, until he reached the spring by whose rocky basin grew the vabillia, and behind which lay a small cave, hardly longer than his body and so low and shallow that it would hold him like a cocoon. There he scrabbled among the stones until the yellowish, conical root was torn loose from the water-washed rocks to which it clung.

It took time to peel off the woody outer bark, to separate the meat from the spiny central core. Then he chewed the bitter pulp until it was dry of juice, carefully saving the masticated, fibrous remains. If he lived the night, he would try to redress his wound with it. If not, his sleep would be euphoric. . . .

As the drug reached its downey fingers into his brain, he took the green-bladed sword from its makeshift sheath and cut brush, which he arranged on the ledge before the shallow cave until the whole of the shelf was blanketed. Then he crawled within the rustling sentinel he had created, vabillia pulp in hand, sure that nothing could come upon him in the night without him hearing its approach. Nothing but a whelt. And assuming that the drug did not send him to that sleep from which no creature wakens. Vabillia, most efficacious and poisonous of all Benegua's pharmacology, was so potent as to be used only when there was nothing else. . . .

Crouched panting at the cave's mouth, he surveyed his work. He grunted, and took one last look around him into the waning day. No whelt.

Feeling cheered, he knelt and lowered himself lengthwise into the cave, truly little more than a crevice. He had remembered it larger: or had he been smaller then? Carefully he eased within, back to the wall, left side uppermost. He had made certain that the softest, leafiest branches were those closest to the cave, and as he dragged the cuttings toward the cave mouth, covering himself to the neck, he had one clear moment of elation, of triumph. Then the vabillia took true hold on him and he barely had time to drag close the final, hairy-petaled branch and twist himself comfortable before sleep took him. Thus he missed the sunset through the glade's latticed branches, and the whelt's return.

He would have sworn to a thousand years between that taking and his next wakefulness; he had dreams enough for that many years. Epic dreams, dreams in which he wielded the baleful green-metaled sword against an endless multitude that would not remain dead, though their blood spouted until it became a rushing river that engulfed him. He was swimming for shore against the current when he woke.

To find the whelt peering patiently down at him from the branches of a memnis that grew at the pool's edge. Beneath the branch, piled neatly on an arching root, was an assortment of fruit.

He did not immediately do more than ascertain this, through the hairy-petaled cuttings that protected his face. Unmoving, he was free of pain. (The dull ache of flesh pressed the night long against cold stone was hardly worth counting.) So, there was a whelt out there. A flare of resentment rose in him, then subsided. He put the thought of it away, turned to his body's needs.

He pushed back the brush and rolled from the shallow cave, each movement teaching him new parameters of pain. His whole left side seemed afire. The bands of muscle about his chest screamed their definition. He could not straighten his left shoulder, and the agony of his left arm swinging was such that he had no alternative but to hold it steady with his right hand. Thus he ended scattering the brush with his feet. Kneeling to drink was an absorbingly complex affair, whose strategem was not wholly successful: he moaned and rocked back and forth on his knees, fighting dizziness. But at length he had drunk and relieved himself, and even rubbed water over his begrimed face.

"Whelt," he grunted as he eased his blistered booted feet into the pool. "You will have to come to me."

"Kreesh," answered the whelt, and came, swooping upon the way to snatch a ripe peona melon from the pile at the memnis' foot.

Deilcrit started to shake his head, gasped in pain, and turned cautiously to face the whelt that alighted at his side.

He looked from it, to the glossy black oval of the peona, then back.

"Kirelli," he ventued, trying what he thought to be the whelt's name for the first time. "You are a wehr, are you not?"

The green eyes regarded him soberly, unblinking.

"What does Wehrdom want with me?"

The whelt pushed the melon toward him, butting it with his cruelly curved beak. Then it stretched out its neck, as if with a message.

"No!" he exploded, throwing himself backward, forgetful of his wound.

It was a time before the pain left and vision returned. The soft sobbing sound he had been hearing ceased when he realized his own throat was its source.

The whelt was perched upon the melon, wings half-unfurled.

He pushed himself up awkwardly. "Go away. Wehr! I . . ."

And the soft touch within his mind stopped him

witless. Not all whelts are wehrs. Nor are all of any species. Not until Wehrdom scythes through the forest, leaving all manner of beast dead in its wake, is it known which are wehrs and which are not. Then ptaiss turns upon ptaiss and campt upon campt, and all the wehr beasts drink the forest's blood. And when it is over, and the forest is calm once more, they graze and nest and burrow beside their prey of only days before. Those wehrs that are known are shown deference in the way of their species, according to the members' society. In man, as in beast, the wehr rules. And it is either death to taste of Wehrdom, or something most unthinkable, more awesome perhaps than death itself: Wehrs speak only to other wehrs and their chosen. This latter possibility was one of which he strove not to think at all.

"Wehr, I will be certainly dead by morning. Go tell your mistress—"

The whelt let out an ear-splitting squawk and humped its wings.

"Pardon," he said automatically. "I assumed . . . You do wear Mahrlys' band." Most whelts are not wehrs at all; these can still carry such a picture as messaging requires. None of his whelts had ever been wehrs. He supposed dully that wehrs, even be they whelts, might well be touchy as to rank. But he knew nothing of Wehrdom. He said this.

The whelt responded by hopping off the melon, neck extended. It did a wing-flapping dance in his direction. This time he had not the will to avoid it. And then he understood more than he cared to of Wehrdom. Kirelli, prince of wehrs, had chosen him. Against all odds and until his death (privately Deilcrit thought that this would not be too long, so the whelt princeling risked little), Kirelli would succor and protect him: he was wehr-chosen. He interpreted this from a flood of flashing pictures awash in his mind, from the touch of myriad other minds behind the whelt's, minds that sent homage and welcome incomprehensible to him. So spake the whelt? In substance, though Deilcrit saw and felt emotion with the seeing, rather than hearing language. And then he did hear language, perfect, multitonal, a liquid sound that seemed to come from the exact center of the back of his head: "Allow me to guide you; when that is past, to accompany you; when that time too is gone, to follow. And but recall, in future, that I was first to aid you."

Deilcrit awkwardly dragged his feet from the pool, thinking that he would not much longer recall anything. "Let me be," he mumbled blurrily, and heard: "I will."

The wehr Kirelli seldom again spoke to him in this fashion, and for a time he tried to believe he had imagined the incident; he was too much a Beneguan to think otherwise, to repudiate all he had been. He would not believe until it was forced on him, much later. He said: "Let me be, whelt!"

Accepting the command, the wehr burst into flight and alighted on that same tree branch where Deilcrit had first seen him waiting.

Somewhere within him he was glad that the wehr was not going to kill him. But it had not told him why it was not going to kill him, and this bothered him: he had killed a number of wehrs. Surely Wehrdom would strike him down, not just, as was so obviously the case here, monitor him until his death. So he spoke to himself, insistent, as if no wehr had just proclaimed fealty.

He decided to eat the fruit, and ignore the whelt. After he had eaten the fruit he began to wonder what he would do if he lived. First he considered living the day, then the night, then what he might do if indeed he survived the wehrs and his wound.

He tossed off the whelt's presence: he had always had a way with whelts.

He found it relatively easy to edge his way around the bank to the pile of fruit on the memnis' root. When he had eaten his fill, he slept. He admitted to himself, just before dreams took him, as he shifted the makeshift scabbard tied around his waist and gently positioned his left arm with his right, that the whelt was a wehr. The wehr might be lying. Then he thought that it did not really matter, unless he awoke. His last thought, that of having been unable all day to walk more than a few steps at a time without rest, led him into dreams of interminable trekking.

When he seized consciousness once more, the rain was falling, the midday sky sagging with its weight. Through the gentle screen of the steady drizzle he could see only a short distance, but he saw well enough to know that there was no whelt, wehr or otherwise. He rubbed his forehead. Even slick with rain, he could feel his fever. He pushed himself to a sitting position, and with the strangers' knife slit the twine around his memnis-bandaged arm, peeled back the softened bark very slowly, biting his lip until it bled. At last, with a rip that took half the new scab away with the bark, he stripped it off, washed the wound, and examined it.

His critical facility knew that the wound in its present state would drain. But he was shivering uncontrollably when he finished.

He retrieved the masticated vabillia from his cave, applied it to the round hole in the wound's center, cut new memnis bark, and repeated the binding process. He did it more to keep moving, to still his teeth from chattering, to gather his wits, than for hygiene. It was, in the end, a sloppier bandage than the first. He shrugged, and winced.

Whelt, no whelt, he cared not. No more than he cared about those creatures whose weapons he bore upon his person. He would live if he kept moving, this he knew. And he *would* live. He would seek out Mahrlys on his own, and she would see the artifacts he carried, and listen, and perhaps give him answers for these events and seemings that taxed his mind. The wound was real enough, and the food he ate. And if the whelt that was a wehr had not really spoken to him, then at least it had not clawed out his eyes. Nor had any other in the night.

He threw down the last rind of the whelt's gift, and looked once full around the clearing, that he might spy Kirelli in hiding. Though he barked in pleasure when he determined that no whelt spied on him, it was a false pleasure, and he heard it so. Disappointed, he rose up and moved from the dappled surface of the pool. Without a backward glance, faster than was prudent, he set off down a slight trail he followed without thought, from long familiarity. The whelt's disappearance followed after him; its image cawed derisively; he had believed, he had wanted to believe, that he was wehr-chosen. He had taken up arms against them, and now he wanted absolution. A great host of fears dogged his steps, spreading wide and closing like pincers about him in the rain-misted thickets. Somehow, the exertion upstepped his disquiet and he fled a phantom Wehrdom through the greenlit wood, until, lungs pumping, he stumbled once too often.

It was where the trail intersected the Dey-Ceilneeth road that he stumbled. He knelt there a long time, gaining breath, supported on his good arm, his bad one hanging limp.

It was a sound that forewarned him. He raised his head and peered into the abating sun-dazzled drizzle, down the rainbow-arched way that stretched

wide and straight deep into the bowels of Dey-
Ceilneeth. He could have risen. He could conceiva-
bly have staggered an hour or so more through the
worsening tangle, or fled back the way he had
come.

They approached slowly, with infinite majesty
over the steaming turves of the great way: a multitude of ptaiss, milk-white, churning. Or so it seemed
at first, until his vision focused. Then he simply
sat in the middle of the road with his left hand in
his lap and waited.

Toward him came a score of ptaiss, flowing like
a single drop of water down the road's middle. In
their center, robed in white, walked a tall figure
with long, loose hair black as midnight.

His head lowered, he awaited the priestess of
Mnemaat.

Waiting, he became aware that he could not
have run farther. He began to doubt whether or
not he could run at all. By the time he could pick
out the ptaiss coughs, pad-clicks, low growls from
the sounds around him, he was concentrating on
maintaining a sitting position. His body was free
from pain, but numb.

He heard: "Rise up."

He did that, without distress. Without any feeling.
He stood as if on another's feet. He focused his
eyes on her face, which loomed close, much closer
than the ground, much more comforting. Her eyes
were green, and all colors danced therein. They widened when she spoke:

"Feeling better, my fallen iyl? I would venture
to hope so."

His peripheral vision was aware of the ptaiss
parting, of her stepping down the aisle they made,
ever closer, but his direct sight was only of her
eyes, whose size did not vary even as she approached.

Somehow, his consternation never reached his

nervous system. He viewed it from a distance, coldly; as he noted the whelt which somehow swooped into his sight, its green eyes becoming one with the woman's face, until it was a great whelt's visage that stared at him, looming ever closer upon a woman's body robed in white. He recorded this occult event without bias, sparing it no emotion.

"Come, then, we will help you. When justice is desired by all, it is quickly done." And he took her arm and she assisted him, softly but with infinite strength. He saw that the ptaiss closed around them. Their backs swayed rhythmically on all sides. He felt no surprise, not in that or in the fact that he was able to keep the pace the priestess set: when he faltered she would lay her hands upon him and his legs would lighten, his left arm would issue only muted screams, his mind would float above, alert, impassive. And he would walk on.

She fed him and watered him and allowed him to look upon her without her robe. She tended his wound, and the line of her long throat, swooping, gilded his sleep. The ptaiss hunted and she fed him from their kill, tiny strips of raw meat daintily carved. She boiled herbs in an empty gourd over a rock that seemed to heat at her low command. She touched his forehead in the night and laid soothing cloths upon it. In the morning the ptaiss would form once more around them and she would touch him lightly and they would go on. And she would smile sometimes; but not until the third day did she again speak.

"Deilcrit," she murmured, "whatever possessed you not to die?"

"Ipheri?" he managed, for he did not know her name, and that honorific would do for the iis herself.

"Try not to be afraid. In Dey-Ceilneeth, I will not be with you. If you waste your energy in fear, you will heal slowly, and all will be held up just that much more."

Just then the whelt alighted between them, and her face paled, and her eyes widened until they consumed the sky.

But the whelt beat its wings and screeched its war cry, and seemed almost to dive at her. There was a blur of arms and wings, and the whelt shot into the treetops.

The priestess's white robe was torn at the seam where sleeve met shoulder. The shoulder, striped with a thin red line, held his eyes. He felt, as before with his fear, only a distant, intellectual realization that something was amiss.

"So, you are other than you appear. Let me apologize," she whispered.

His arm suddenly began to broadcast its protests, his feet were their own bed of hot coals, his stomach turned to eating itself.

She traced the scratch with her forefinger. The nail was long, shapely.

"Deilcrit, ignorance is your only salvation. *Be* ignorant. If you are any part of this incursion, even my pity will be insufficient to the plight that must befall you in recompense. Be, by all means, a foolish adolescent, made iyl too soon by circumstance...." She seemed to want to say more.

He peered attentively at her, waiting.

"Call that whelt," she commanded, and before he realized it, he had done so.

It screeched from its perch, but did not move.

"It will not come."

"Because of me. Yet it seems to have answered you. How can you, a guerm-tender, command such a creature?"

He realized then, what she was saying, and bent his head. For a long time he was alone with his pain.

When she chose, she lifted it once more from him.

In the exquisite cessation of discomfort, she asked him for the alien swords he wore about his waist. He would have given her anything, his heart, his life, whatever she asked. He plucked ineffectually at the hastily tied thong, and she slid toward him, and with her own tiny dagger slit the cord. He did not then think to wonder why she did not just take them. Instead, he wondered at the fragrance of her hair. He looked upon the part in her hair, lost in the sheen of the thick smooth strands.

But when the weight was gone from about his waist, when she stepped back from him with a tiny smile of triumph lighting her lips, he was distantly aware that something was very wrong, that more had transpired here than he understood, or would have agreed to had he been . . . otherwise. Then he came to it, what he had known but could not feel: that he was in some odd way entrapped; that he must remember this above all things. He wished to feel determination, felt instead confused.

Having acquired the swords, she retreated to the side of one of the larger ptaiss, curling up against the prostrate beast's belly. Her robe fell in folds around her, riding the line of her turned hip.

He thought fiercely that she had not totally bested him, that he had retained the knife, also of the strange metal. But a part of him dryly bespoke the truth: she did not want the knife. He knew he was going to go to her, but had no idea what he was going to do. He never did recall it. She did not wish him to recall it. Nor, which is more to the point, did she wish him to forget it: he recalled rising, his detached concern for his arm as he knelt before her—then nothing but a sense of shame, an uneasy wondering, and an indebtedness that crouched in his very soul.

He dared not ask her what it was that he had done, nor even make an excuse. Her eyes, when later she looked at him, were those of one who has paid a costly price and been cheated, one whose trust has been betrayed.

She wore the scabbard he had made from Estri's tunic around her supple waist. His eyes were often upon it in the long days of forced march to which she put them.

It was as if the privilege of hearing her voice would be ever denied him, though he might accompany her and look upon her as he wished, provided he himself did not speak. And this he did, because it occurred to him, because it was a way of retaining his selfdom, because he knew that he was prejudged: "fallen iyl," she had called him. Whatever he did now could bring upon him no more execrable fate than that which already awaited: he enjoyed the blessing of the condemned: freedom from care.

It was the day upon which she removed his stitches, by his reckoning sixteen days from that rainy midday she had found him in the road, that they entered the maze around Dey-Ceilneeth.

Now, Dey-Ceilneeth is the seat of Law in Benegua; the Temple of Mnemaat, home of His Eye and Mouth; and, by these necessities, the abode of women only: no man enters Dey-Ceilneeth unaccompanied and emerges. From these labyrinthine paths, tortuous beyond mortal comprehension, grown up from Benegua's most poisonous hedges so long ago that the maze reaches skyward, tall as any deep-forest giants, there is no escape but for the initiate.

He caught himself holding tight to her robe, that he not find himself suddenly alone and helpless among the flesh-eating telsodas that framed the maze's outer corridors. As tightly fitted as a wall of stone, trimmed perpendicular to the ground for twice his height, the pink-petaled mouths on their thorny stems smacked a thousand lips together as they passed. The sound sighed around them in the dappled light, filtered down toward them from the canopy that grew untrimmed above their heads.

Dangling blossoms writhed from that vaulted ceiling of branches, sometimes idly, sometimes striking with such a force that branches rattled about them, but they always fell short.

Even knowing this, even beside the priestess, in the midst of the tightly packed ptaiss, he ducked reflexively each time the hungry telsodas sought him.

Once he caught her face from the corner of his eye, freed, as he had never before managed to see it, from the veil her eyes threw out. She was most certainly laughing at him. This caused him to stiffen, and when they passed through one of a myriad identical breaks in the telsoda hedge to be confronted by two green-patterned serpents of nightmare proportions, he steeled himself to stride unconcerned between those rewound coils, the thinnest of which was the width of his waist, that slithered restless upon his right and his left.

Putting one foot mechanically before the other, eyes on the ground, he strode right into her, for she had stopped.

Dry-mouthed, trembling with each gust of wind that rattled the fahrass berries of the second hedge, he stared openmouthed as the ptaiss split asunder and she walked down the aisle they made directly toward the right-hand serpent's coils.

The musky smell of them was intolerable to his instinct-frayed nerves. He found himself pressed closely between two restless ptaiss, leaning upon them for support.

She stood wraithlike before the viper, whose

wedge-shaped head swayed and descended until it was at a level with her own. Its twin, across the path, hissed and flickered its black tongue.

She laid her hand on the sinuous neck, and laughed, a low, throaty sound. Then the berceide of the second hedge, for such is the name of the great green snakes that guard Benegua's sanctum, began a long series of cadenced hisses and odd sibilances which the priestess answered in kind. When their cheeks touched (if such a viper, with head long as a man's torso, can be said to have a cheek), he cried out, so clearly did his mind's eye see those coils unreel, whip around the gauze-robed figure, so slight and full of life, and squeeze that life out onto the grass.

But nothing untoward occurred, unless it was that the priestess spoke at length to the berceide in its own sibilant tongue, turned her back, and rejoined him in the midst of the ptaiss.

"All is in readiness for you," she said to him, and the satisfaction that rode her voice was dire with its foreshadowings. He tried to retreat from her, but the ptaiss against which he had been leaning stood firm. No longer did he feel the detachment which had thus far cushioned his response to all things as they occurred.

"That is right," she said sweetly. "I have no longer the need to render you tractable by artificial means: you cannot now do otherwise than follow me. You cannot find your way back to the forest, not from within the second hedge."

The berceides, both with heads resting on their coils, regarded the ptaiss and what stood within patiently, ophidian eyes unblinking.

"No, I cannot. I could not have, in any case," some part of him said. "And since you have won, since I am your prisoner, why do you still hide your face? What difference if the captive sees the face of his captor?"

"You have been seeing my face, in your dreams if nowhere else, a long time, impertinent one. Dare your posture that you know me not?"

She stripped off the ensorcelment that had thus far masked all but her eyes in a soft haze of light, and he went to his knees among the ptaiss before her.

"Ipheri, forgive me. I—"

"Forgive you? Hardly. But you bear no additional stigma for what has passed between us; all of this"—and she waved her hand, as if to encompass not only the space around them, but the time he had spent in her presence—"is of my design."

It was then that the whelt, Kirelli, swooped from nowhere, screeching, toward Mahrlys' head. A ptaiss leaped, jaws snapping, claw rending the air. But the whelt was gone into the thick-leaved fahrass above their heads.

"For that," she hissed, "you will suffer. For the loss of Kirelli, I will have full recompense. Now, move!"

He scrambled to his feet, full of remonstrations unspoken: he had not sought the whelt, nor lost her anything by his will. Or he thought he had not. Once he started to speak, but she silenced him angrily and he followed, meek, silent, through the seven concentric mazes that remained between them and the inner chasm.

Before this, in spite of himself, he halted. It was a sight he had never expected to see, nor did he covet its rarity. A great distance below, white water churned and spat and growled. Across the gorge lay Dey-Ceilneeth herself, scintillant and megalithic, like some gemstone wrapped in foliage. But he was not awed that he stood before the hallowed retreat, not while he faced the chasm and the swaying, lacy bridge that spanned it.

The ptaiss, with uncanny precision, parted, and, taking his hand, she drew him onto the pale lattice that spanned the precipitous drop. He stood with one foot upon the woven bridge, one upon the solid sod. At her urging he shook his head.

"I can force you," she reminded him, and at his back he heard a growl, and felt a subtle push. There was a stanchion every dozen steps, through which stout rope was threaded. He closed his right fist over these and focused his gaze upon Mahrlys' white-robed figure before him. It retreated. He followed, not daring to look down, where the white water could be seen between the knotted netting of pale rope. He concentrated on trying to determine of what the ropes were woven, and on Mahrlys-iis-Vahais, moving surefootedly before him. Somewhere about the middle of the expanse, when a cruel gust shook the bridge swaying, he used his left hand. He did not realize it until he took a step onto solid ground, until he with an effort of will pried his fingers from the guide ropes. Then he grinned, and flexed each finger in turn, and performed a number of testings upon the limb. Except for a not-unexpected stiffness, and an aching reminder of what work still proceeded within the bandage of memnis, the arm worked perfectly. A great weight lifted from him. He turned and stared ruminatively at the ptaiss, across the chasm. They were restless, full of coughs and growls; in short: ptaisslike. As he watched, the group dispersed, some heading back into jicekak of the innermost maze, some leaping the crevice with little concern, some wandering along its length.

"Deilcrit," called the priestess, and it was then that he was struck by her beauty. Earlier, when she stripped off her veil of light, it had been her revealed identity that had dropped him to his knees. Before that, it had been her numinous presence and those very veils that had kept him awed, cowed, unthinking—that and her desire. But he recalled her without her robes. He almost recollected what had passed between them that night. He had had proscribed knowledge of this woman standing before him, of that he was sure. And be she Mahrlys-iis-Vahais or no, she had known him—had tended his wounds, had fed him.

He did not understand the promise made him by Kirelli the wehr; he did not understand her fury concerning the bird's actions; nor why the wehrs had not killed him when he had raised arms against their kind; or even what significance was to be put upon the swords she now bore slung about her robe and those who had once worn them.

But he did know that she had wanted him, and the swords. That she had wanted him alive and that she had felt the need to obtain his permission before taking the artifacts from him—this he knew. And it was not lost on him that whatever else might be said about Kirelli the whelt, he was an emissary of Wehrdom, and no small force to have upon one's side; Mahrlys was incensed at having "lost" him. He wondered what she would think if she knew what the power that called itself Chayin had promised him. Perhaps he would try speaking that one's name, as he had been counseled, should his need grow great. And then he remembered the whelt, spying upon him from the trees, and wagered within himself as to whether Mahrlys did in truth already know. Since the wager turned out not in his favor, he determined to keep his own counsel, and to hold these truths, his only possible weapons, sacrosanct against any interrogation. He did not realize how difficult this would come to be.

But he realized her beauty; and he had climbed up out of the pit of hopelessness with his assessment of his position.

He reached out and touched her, drew her to him. Her openhanded slap sent his head snapping to one side, but he did not release her.

"There are no ptaiss here to protect you," he said, looking down into her revealed face, contorted with a fury that swelled her lips and colored her flaring cheekbones.

"It will take me but a moment to call one," she grated through bared, even teeth, "and then I will have wasted near twenty days in the outer forest and you will be the corpse you should have been the night the wehrs raged. Take your hands from me, guerm-tender!"

Hurt rather than frightened, he did so. She was so tiny: her arms so slight, his hands closed around them; her waist so slim the thong he had worn wrapped twice around her. And yet she commanded him, and he obeyed.

He looked at her, then at his hands, then measured his desire, then wondered how this could be. He could take her, throw her to the grass, have her before any ptaiss might intervene. He gauged her labored breathing, the rise and fall of her breasts through the thin robe, and knew that this was so, that she herself recognized this truth.

"Please, guerm-tender, do your iis a service; save yourself for the ajudication. Your crimes are far too momentous to be dealt with summarily in the open air. It is the bowels of Dey-Ceilneeth that must receive your repentance, extract from you their due. I have brought you this far. Proceed the rest of the way under your own will, or die here, now."

"You cannot make me," he said, referring equally to both alternatives she offered.

"You speak truth, yet you do not even know what you know," she snapped, backing slowly away from him, her eyes fastened on his.

Oblivious to all else, he followed.

So intent on her was he that he did not see the shadows, manlike, flitting at the edge of his vision; nor the net, until it fell upon him from midair and he fell, thrashing, tangled in its weight.

The four ossasim followed the net to earth, alighting easily, spaced around their quarry. Even before their wings grew limp they had gathered up the net, and him within it, helpless, his weight on his left arm, the arm, twisted under him, blazing with pain.

He was twirled and turned in the net until it became a shroud binding him round, preventing any movement. Then three of the red-eyed, gray-furred wehr-masters held him in midair, while the fourth pressed a cloyingly scented cloth to his mouth and nose. He struggled hopelessly, until he could not, until pink stars consumed his vision.

The last thing his struggling showed him was her face, green eyes huge, peering through the tough netting.

"Poor Deilcrit," she murmured. "There is no place for such as you in the world. None at all."

And he thought that she kissed his forehead, or was about to, as he spun into the drug's domain.

The guards in the subterranean prison were pleasant to him, in that they did not abuse him, or any of the others in the straw-strewn cage. But then, they were not men, nor women, nor any creature he had ever seen. Some said that they were offspring of ossasim and Beneguan females, and mules as a consequence of this. They could have been, he supposed, given their lightly furred flesh and their horny, lipless jaws; but something told him that more could come from the mating of ossasim and

woman than these. Privately, he judged them
ossasim females, a position for which there were
no other contenders, and reasoned that though it
seemed the flat-breasted things were sexless, to an
ossasim they might be ultimately enticing, with
some other way of procreating than through the
orifice women use. They did not abuse him, and he
did not question them. After his initial fright, when
one of the red-eyed things appeared, characteristi-
cally suddenly, through his prison's door, he took
little note of them. They were another feature of
his new existence to which he simply adjusted.

He was not fettered, he was not stripped, he was
not starved. He was free to walk the extent of his
rocky prison with its one mirrorlike wall of glazed,
fused black rock. This one wall was smooth as
glass, and perfectly regular. All the rest of the
cavern was a gentle circling of seamless, irregular
limestone. The door slid back from the featureless
middle of the black wall, and when it was closed
there was no sign as to exactly where on the wall
it might have been. In the cavern's roof were two
barred openings, to which no man could climb.
There was no reason to restrain any of them within
the cave; its security was unbreachable.

So believed the nine others who shared the straw
with him, two of whom had been here so long that
they had the teeth of their youth carefully stashed
in pockets in the rock. These two were naked.
Their garments had rotted from their bodies. They
did not recall their own names, most times, and
only twice while he was incarcerated there did he
hear them speak at all: one gave a long indecipherable monologue and his companion answered.

There was a man with a broken arm that had
healed badly, and who was blind. He was taken
away not long after Deilcrit arrived, and did not
return. That made one less sharing the food.

This pleased the three young men who doled out the portions, those who slept beneath the openings to the sky, until the next feeding. Then they themselves were taken away.

The two old men could not truly feed themselves. The three remaining younger prisoners waited calmly for their portions to be dealt out to them, long after it was clear to Deilcrit that the men who had doled out the food would not return. Speech was rare in the cavern: but for the two old seniles, Deilcrit had not heard any prisoner speak in more than monosyllables in all the time he had been immured.

First, he got up and went and stood over the cooling gruel that a brown-furred arm had thrust within the cavern. Then he went for the hundredth time and tried to discern the seam of the door that lay directly behind the tray. When he had satisfied himself that all eyes were on him, he went and crouched down before the three prisoners who sat together.

"Should I feed them?" he asked, pointing to the two elders who huddled together.

One of the three men blinked. They were all black-haired, full-bearded, of indeterminate age. They still wore remnants of their clothing, and by it Deilcrit determined that one had been a gatherer and one a weaver and one bore a craft device which was strange but for its class. It was to this last, he who had blinked, he whose craft badge still dangled from a woven jerkin that had once marked him as a deep-forest dweller, a far-ranging taker of risks, that Deilcrit spoke.

"Those men are not coming back, we have to feed ourselves. Shall I do it?" Softly but insistently he sought the other's attention.

The man, whose eyes seemed wholly black, blinked again. He clawed the tangles from his brow and said: "If you will, lad. . . . I . . ." Then he stopped, and smiled hesitantly, proud of himself. "I will help you." The man had come a long way, up from some private world. "I am Laonan."

Deilcrit touched fingertips with the craftsman, Laonan, while the other two black-haired men stirred and muttered and the seniles began a senseless cackling that rose hysterically and then faded into sobs.

Motioning Deilcrit to proceed with silence, the lank-haired Laonan scrambled over to the tray and began with quick, economical movements to dole the food out into bowls.

"You are right," he whispered as Deilcrit squatted to assist him, "they will not be back. Only six bowls. Sssh!" This as Deilcrit began to question him eagerly.

"Do not disturb the old ones. I will talk with you later. Over there." And it seemed that Laonan stared in wonder, sighting down his own pointing hand to the other side of the cavern. Then, that same incredulity in his eyes, he clapped Deilcrit hard on the left shoulder, grinning.

A rainbow built of pain bedazzled him, and when it was gone, so was the man Laonan, scuffling, bowls in hand, across the straw toward the two seniles, mewling with impatience.

"Nothing wrong with their noses," Laonan puffed, returning to where Deilcrit had appropriated a portion of gruel for himself. Laonan moved to take bowls to the two remaining black-haired men, those with whom he had been sitting.

"No," ordered Deilcrit. "If they would eat, let them get their own food. They are men, are they not?"

Laonan, startled, froze with one thumb in the steaming gruel. Then, slowly, he raised it to his mouth and sucked it clean. "As you wish." He shrugged, sweeping up the bowl.

Then, for the first time, he straightened to his full height and headed for the empty nook of rock he had earlier designated as the spot for their conversation.

Deilcrit, bemused, followed suit.

By the time the two had licked their bowls clean and put them beside them on the straw, the black-haired men were beside the tray.

Shaking his head, Deilcrit turned from their crouched forms.

"How long have you been here?" he demanded of Laonan.

"How long? How long is long? You tell me, boy. I have been here since Mahrlys-iis-Vahais' accession."

Deilcrit let that sink in a moment.

"Twelve years."

"Is that all? Feels more like twenty."

"And they?" pointing to the two sitting cross-legged by the tray.

"They were taken with me. My fault, really. We were running contraband between here and Aehre proper."

"What is contraband?"

Laonan snorted. "Any trade is contraband, by Wehrdom's standard. Weaponry, to be specific. They were glad enough to get it in Aehre, lest they go the same way as Nothrace. I was off to Kanoss with sulfur from Aehre.... Eh, boy, did it happen?"

"What?"

"Did the Byeks reach an agreement? Is it Aehre-Kanoss or two foredoomed states? Or, in point of fact, does either of them exist now? Has Wehrdom eaten all without the Wall?"

"I have no idea," he admitted. "I was an outforest

iyl: I tend ptaiss and keep the guerm out of the river, and the rest is none of my concern. Or was."

"Something's your concern, something that shouldn't have been, else you wouldn't have ended here."

"That seems to be the case," Deilcrit conceded. "Though I am not clear on what it was exactly that I did. . . ."

Laonan guffawed, and the seniles whined and threw their arms about one another. "Come, now, boy—what is your name, by the by?"

"Deilcrit." He stumbled over it, almost adding his hard-won honorific. Hard-won and easily lost.

"Well, Deilcrit, you must know what you did that was wrong. Nobody is casually incarcerated in Dey-Ceilneeth. You must have done something?"

"I did a number of things, I suppose." The grin would not be forced back. "But which one got me here, I can not ascertain. I am surely guilty of heresy, blasphemy, unclean acts of any sort you might care to name."

"Sounds like you had a real good time. Care to tell me about it?"

When he had finished, the moon spilled through the ventilators. Rubbing his beard, then scratching, then worrying with both hands a foody tangle, Laonan sat staring into his empty bowl. Sometime during the evening, the two youngish black-haired prisoners had crept up to within ear-shot. Now they ventured close, and took the bowls from the conversants, and put them upon the tray near the door.

At this, Laonan put his fingers to his lips and gestured at Deilcrit to take up his old solitary corner. Seeing this done, Laonan joined his two companions in their previous, passive aspect.

It was not long until the glossy wall opened and the brown-furred creature that guarded the catacombs entered, glared around, and backed hastily from the cell with the tray.

He would have risen. A glance at Laonan's cautionary face persuaded him otherwise, and he sat, head bowed, until he heard a scuffle, and Laonan slid along the wall to his side.

"I still am not sure that they cannot see through that," he confided, indicating the black, glossy wall.

"And if they do, what will they see? And what have you to lose that is not lost already?"

"While I am alive, boy, I have something to lose." And he thrust his face close to Deilcrit. "Are you a wehr?"

"I . . . I do not know. I do not think so."

"It seems that you do think so, when you talk about what happened in the forest."

"No," said Deilcrit, turning a glance of naked helplessness upon the man, "I do not think so. I fear so. What is it, to be a wehr? And what am I, that such a thing could happen to me? And if it is so, why must I die for it? What sense is there in a gift that exacts death as its consequence? And anyway, I am but wehr-chosen."

"And what *that* is, is a matter of interpretation. Deilcrit, I cannot answer you as to what a wehr is. But let me point out that Mahrlys-iis-Vahais herself is a wehr. And all but two of the rulers of Aehre-Kanoss, at least when I was abroad in the land, were wehrs. Wehrs are on the whole very successful individuals and do not as a rule die on acquiring whatever it is that makes them wehrs. It seems to me that a lot of effort has been put into seeing that you do not die. Mahrlys and her wehrs have some use for you. Or maybe just the wehrs do. . . . Did you know that Mahrlys is part ossasim?"

"That cannot be."

Laonan shrugged. "It is."

"You are very knowledgeable for a man with a

trader's badge who has been locked below the ground in this hole for a dozen years," he said, suddenly suspicious.

"I have had . . . ah . . . certain other functions for which trading suits as an excuse, at certain times and for the right individuals. Things change slowly in the lands of Aehre-Kanoss. Deilcrit, what I really—"

And it was at that moment that Kirelli squeezed his way through the bars to swoop in ever-narrowing circles around the confines of the cave.

"Kirelli," Deilcrit hissed, knowing that the moment had been lost, and whatever Laonan was going to say would not for a long while be said. But then, in mid-curse, he looked at Laonan's face and the surprise thereupon was answer enough to allay his worst suspicion: this man was no wehr, planted here to drag out what secrets he might hold all unsuspecting. Such a one would be neither shocked nor affrighted at Kirelli's presence.

A thrill of pride buoyed him as the whelt stalked about the straw and clacked its viciously curved silver beak. The little old men in the cave's rear whined like babies, and the black-haired pair made themselves small against the rock. Laonan, beside him, was stiff and still as a corpse. Though full of words of wisdom, when confronted with an agitated whelt he was timid as any Beneguan.

"Sit up, man," Deilcrit advised him, before his companion melted into that submissive posture his look-alikes had already taken, forehead on palms, hands pressed to the straw. "You too," he called to the other men. "Sit up. The whelt seeks me. Do not be afraid."

The only trouble was that, before all these witnesses, he could not very well shirk from receiving the whelt's message.

With a sigh, he extended his good arm. An explosion of wings, and the whelt rode his shoulder, its head pressed to his own.

From it he received a picture of the whelt, and himself, and a dark-haired man, standing with a woman whose hair was black and whose face he could not see. They stood by a giant throne of carnelian that burned with an internal glow. There were three others there: they were shadows before glowing fires, silhouettes in the flames.

Then the opening in the obsidian wall drew apart, and the whelt, screeching, leaped from his shoulder to disappear through the barred openings in the cave's roof.

Through that opening stepped three figures: one winged wehr-master; one brown-furred, wingless guardian; one woman robed in cobalt who was not Mahrlys-iis-Vahais.

This woman beckoned.

He looked at Laonan, who had turned his face away, pressed his forehead to the wall.

"Well met, prince of words," he chided softly as he rose to answer the woman's summons.

She had golden hair and half-lidded eyes he could not read. Her broad forehead was banded with gold; gold drew her robe tight at the waist and hemmed its edges.

"I am not ready," he blurted out, though it could surely make no difference to her, and he was as ready as he would ever be.

The woman smiled encouragingly, extending her arm. The ossasim behind her fluttered half-tumescent wings and drummed its taloned fingers on its hips. He shuddered under the gaze of those red-in-red eyes, and took the woman's arm. The cobalt material was the softest thing he had ever felt, excepting Mahrlys' hair.

And it was thoughts of Mahrlys that consumed

him as the golden-haired woman led him up steps like frozen seawater and the ossasim fell in behind.

He looked around once on the staircase, and saw that the outer side of the black wall of his prison was concealed with hangings depicting a convocation of Wehrdom near the Isanisa's bank. He wondered what the hangings concealed—if Laonan was right and they had been watching him. It would explain their timely entrance. The brown-furred one had taken up a seat by the entry to the cell.

The stairwell, and the landing, and the quiet rock-hewn halls floored with cracked and jagged blocks of the seafoam stone gave way to high-ceilinged corridors whose very walls were slabs of angled, tinted transparency. These walls through which light came were never perpendicular: all the corridors curved inward, toward that sanctuary that was Dey-Ceilneeth's heart.

When they deposited him with two guards at a huge wooden door with brass hinges, he had seen such oddities as left his head spinning. On the floor below this one, the outer wall had been removed, or broken. Women worked there, shaping bricks of mud and straw, and fitting this masonry into the frame which had once held the wonderful transparent wall. On the other side of the same corridor, the side made of the black material, bricklayers and painters were also at work. Set into one finished portion were torch sconces, filled and blazing. On the floor just below, all this work had been earlier completed, and temple scenes brooded there, in a darkened hall.

He had seen other doors like this: set into frames of gleaming metal; shimmed into place with the clumsy craft of the like that bricked the missing outer walls. And yet, such a door as the double one before him, carved with flowers intertwined, was no low item of woman's work. Only when viewed against the background of Dey-Ceilneeth did the efforts of her caretakers seem mean, tawdry, insufficient.

In spite of himself, he craned his neck and stared around as the guards led him into the Sanctuary of Mnemaat.

There was a handful of women in that tabernacle, and their number again in ossasim, who all crowded around a black-haired woman and an ossasim even blacker, whose fur shone blue in the diffused radiance entering through the varicolored towers which threw long streamers of tinted light about the hall. Where three or more rays intersected, misshapen figures seemed to stand, shimmering, so real that they moved as he moved, appearing to face him wherever he was. He held back in the guard's grasp, and the ossasim's wings snapped loudly as it pulled him along an aisle marked off in white stone.

Before the raised platform on which the fourteen waited, the guard released him, brushing at his tunic in disgust. He heard himself announced.

The back of his neck afire, he realized he was supposed to climb those stairs of his own will, to meekly ascend to take their . . . what? Judgment? He did not know.

So he climbed them, glad enough to get to the end of all things mysterious. As he ascended each of the twenty steps, he could see more of those atop them: sandals gave way to furred, booted legs or long clinging robes, to girded hips and armed ones, to a crowd that split to funnel him into place before Mahrlys-iis-Vahais and the black ossasim. Both were resplendent in black silk and silver; each item of his masculine attire finding its counterpart in her woman's wear. She even bore a slim dagger at her hip, tucked through a loop in her belt, its blade and hilt exposed. As he did.

Disconcerted, he looked around him. Six other pairings displayed themselves to his eyes. A growl issued from him. So deep was the animal response this state of affairs evoked in him, he did not even know he had made a sound until a woman tittered. Then he growled a second time, articulately, that there be no mistake.

He had wanted to seek her out. When things had been bleakest, when he had cheated death in the forest, he had determined to do so. He took another step toward her, and the black ossasim, whose right wing was pierced where it fringed his bicep by an encircling armlet of silver, stepped forward and laid hand on his chest.

A moment they stood so. Then Deilcrit retreated a pace, and the black-furred ossasim also stepped back.

He had wanted to seek her, to beg her aid with his soul's distress, to pour out all that had so confounded him and hear her wisdom make sense of it. He had held her of high spirit: she had proved herself less than his faith had pictured her: his piety was bitterly disappointed. And his stance echoed his thoughts so clearly that the black ossasim tossed back his forewing imperiously, and before Deilcrit's eyes the wings began to stiffen, rustling, until they framed his glistening form.

"Eviduey," said Mahrlys imploringly, and the black ossasim, with a toss of his thick-maned head, spoke:

"This is a formal review: let it be so written." Deilcrit found himself fascinated by the ossasim's black lips, framed in a manlike beard, through which red tongue and white teeth peeked with each word. A back of his mind noted a silent procession filing along the tabernacle's walls: priestesses and ossasim and the brown-furred ones and . . .

"Kirelli and Ashra, for Wehrdom." The announcement split silence, and like one being, all on the dais turned:

Through the double doors, before they had truly swung back, ambled a huge ptaiss the color of moonlight, who bore on her back Kirelli the whelt. A murmur followed them up onto the dais like a train of fine silk.

Eviduey bowed low, with exaggerated flourish, wings rigid.

The great ptaiss yawned, and sat upon its haunches in the middle of the aisle of dignitaries. Kirelli, with great aplomb, hopped from the ptaiss' back, took air, and, amid a growing rumble of conversation, alighted on Deilcrit's shoulder.

Slowly, so as not to unseat the whelt, he turned back to face the black-and-silver-silked pair. The ossasim's eyes gleamed like bloody slits in his face, and Mahrlys' visage was for a moment so contorted that he flinched, seeing what her beauty camouflaged. Then she smoothed it, with an obvious effort like the shooing of wrinkles from a gown. The whelt trembled, shifted weight, its talons piercing his jerkin to rest against his skin.

A scribe, brown-furred, scuttled to Eviduey's side and crouched there.

"With your permission, Kirelli?" queried the black ossasim Eviduey in a voice like velvet.

The whelt humped its wings.

"We are here," continued the wehr-master, reaching beneath the nightfall robe draped over his shoulders to bring forth a scroll which he unrolled, "to adjudicate the crimes of one Deilcrit, formerly iyl of the Spirit Gate, and determine suitable penance therefore.

"Deilcrit, before the convened wisdom of Dey-Ceilneeth, say truth only, on pain of dissolution. Do you agree?"

"I do," he replied, dry-mouthed, while recollect-

ing his determination to keep silent about what
had passed between him and the spirit power called
Chayin.

"Mahrlys-iis-Vahais will pose the allegations,"
intoned Eviduey. With yet another sweeping bow,
this time to Mahrlys, he stepped back a pace.

Her lips trembled. She took a breath that quivered her nostrils, and Deilcrit tried to squeeze from
his inner eyes' sight those moments he had spent
with her in the forest. But what lay under her silks
had been exposed to him, and a fury he did not
understand raised bile in his throat, that she had
so demeaned them both in advance of this moment.

"Allegations!" she spat at last, when all eyes
waited upon her words. "These are no allegations,
but a redundant exposition of facts!" By the shock
rippling Eviduey's wings, by the black-pelted arm
that reached out, cautionary, and then withdrew
without having touched her, Deilcrit understood
that these words were not those she had been
expected to speak.

"This is a farce, a joke!" she continued. "Imca-
Sorr-Aat demands this offender's life. Will you be
the one to deny him? You, Eviduey?" And she
spun on her consort, who looked then to his feet.
"Or you, whelt? Or you? Or you?"

When none of her court made answer to this,
somewhat calmed, she continued:

"Not I. Bring it in. Let us have done with this
game!" She spoke over her shoulder, to someone
out of his sight.

As two brown-furred ones wheeled in what
seemed to be a caldron, Eviduey whispered in
Mahrlys' ear, proffering the scroll. With an angry
shake of her head, she spat some answer to him in
a tongue Deilcrit did not know. Kirelli, on his
shoulder, cooed reassuringly, tugged at his hair
with his beak.

He was not invited to crowd around the Eye of Mnemaat, which had a rod or handle of brass protruding from it. Rather, the ossasim Eviduey himself attended him while the twelve paired jury members, and the ptaiss, and even Kirelli filed down the dais to join Mahrlys and the two servants by the wheeled basin.

"This is a rather sorry introduction to Wehrdom," said the ossasim, distinctly and very low, when all were intent upon the caldron's contents. Then, when Deilcrit made no reply: "Let us hope something in your intent may mitigate."

Try as he might, he could make nothing of those words, nor the black creature's expressionless face; nothing other than the hostility and wariness in those stiffened, ever-fluttering wings.

They filed back, up the far side of the dais they had descended, and every face he saw was thoughtful, worry-lined, guarded. The ptaiss fairly slunk, belly brushing the ground.

"Proceed, Eviduey," ordered Mahrlys, becalmed, glowing with a feral satisfaction.

Taking up once more his position at her side, the ossasim read from the scroll an itemization of Deilcrit's failures: his failure to stop the intruders from lighting fire; his failure to save the pregnant ptaiss; even his failure to die under the attacking wehrs' claws. And his sins of commission, also, were chronicled: his raising of arms against wehrs, his prostration before the "powers of Evil," his defilement at the hands of the sorcerous Estri; even his admission that he thought himself wehrchosen, which he had made only to his cellmate Laonan, was included, labeled as sedition, among his crimes.

"Do you deny that you did these things?" asked Eviduey finally.

"No," answered Deilcrit. "But I would have come

here. I would have come to you." It was to Mahrlys he spoke, in spite of his design against it. "You asked me for the swords. I gave them to you. Ask for my life, I will give you that. But I did not mean—"

"Deilcrit," interrupted Eviduey softly but firmly. "Your life is not yours to apportion. Whose it is, we will now determine."

There was a preemptory casting of lots, preceded by a huddle that included Eviduey and the ptaiss, but from which Kirelli and Mahrlys were excluded, as was he.

She stared the whole time with venomous eyes at him, and when the jury formed its twin lines again and their spokesman proceeded betwixt them to whisper in her ear, her face drained white as the ptaiss' pelt. Then she in turn whispered in Eviduey's ear. It was he who spoke to Dielcrit:

"The Vahais of Mnemaat has taken the measure of your transgressions, and its mercy proclaims sentencing as follows: Tomorrow you will take the Trial of Imca-Sorr-Aat. You will seek him out in Othdaliee and receive from him either absolution or death. Should it be absolution, you are free to return to within the Wall of Mnemaat. You may have whatever comfort and aid you can request before this length of silk touches the floor."

He had one moment of understanding before the ossasim reached skyward, let go the length of black silk, and it fluttered toward the seafoam stone. He saw Mahrlys' face, so suffused with fury that it seemed enshadowed. Kirelli screeched and flapped heavenward, and he blurted his answer, Kirelli's mind-picture clear within him:

"The man, Laonan. The green-metaled sword. Mahrlys, this night, to myself."

And as the jurors buzzed and Kirelli screeched, circling with dizzying speed around the tabernacle's dome, he caught her blank, then stricken, then tearful expression.

Though he did not comprehend, he felt elation, and more, as she stepped unsteadily backward, shaking her head, and the black ossasim followed, obscuring his sight of her. For a long moment there were only those inky spread wings, and the disconcerted mutterings of the crowd, and Kirelli's blaring caw.

From nowhere, brown-furred wingless ones converged upon him. As he was hustled away he caught scraps of converse from those who lined the walls.

"So much for her. She will never . . ."

"If I were Eviduey, I would kill him myself." This from an ossasim.

". . . so she did not win his heart to lay on Mnemaat's alter. If . . ."

". . . to subvert so eloquent an ally as Kirelli, he must be . . ."

". . . as dead as if Eviduey lopped his head off here and now. From the gardens of Othdaliee there is no returning. The question is, obviously, why she is not content with that. Did you see Eviduey's face? She'll have trouble . . ."

And when the double doors closed out the sounds, and he was alone with the brown-furred guards, he was glad of it.

They did not take him back to the cavern cell, but deposited him in a small, irregularly shaped chamber walled in the black, glossy stone on three sides. The fourth was an outer wall such as he had seen in the corridors. Through it, he was able to determine the time as near midday, even though vines and high branches crawled in profusion upon the outside of the green-tinted transparency that made a window twice his height in the otherwise featureless cubicle. He stood for a long time with his forehead pressed to the cool slick surface, staring out past the overgrowth at Dey-Ceilneeth's inner-most maze.

He tried not to think of those things he had overheard. He tried not to think of the tears he had seen in the eyes of Mahrlys-iis-Vahais. Or of the murderous snarl that came from Eviduey as he whirled to comfort her. He did not understand what he had done. She had not withheld her person in the forest. But that was not true: it was an instinctive vengeance he had levied upon her there in the tabernacle of Mnemaat, and no part of the whelt's counsel. The words had sprung of their own will from his mouth, spilling out just before the square of blacksilk made contact with the seafoam floor. Although much was a blur in his memory, this he recalled distinctly: Kirelli's raucous screeching, and the settling of the silk upon the stone.

He sat before the window and drew up his knees and rested his elbows upon them and kneaded his left arm with his right, staring unseeing out the window crafted by his most remote ancestor.

"Deilcrit," he said glumly, resting his chin on his crossed arms, "although I would not have believed it, you have managed to make a bad situation worse." His self made no retort. He snorted derisively. "Nothing to say? Othdaliee, is it? You have about as much business there as in the Temple of Mnemaat, defiled as you are. Or in the arms of Mnemaat's high priestess. You deserve all you get, spoiled one."

And though he fell silent, that part of him which hallowed Mnemaat urged him to renege, to beg the priestess's forgiveness, and permission to enter once more Mnemaat's sanctuary—this time to pray.

To which his emerging self replied that any god who would still hear him after all that had occurred deserved no man's homage, and that as for

Mahrlys' desserts, he himself was going to see that she got them. If he must set out on a hopeless journey with only death at its ending by her design, he would make sure that she, at least, carried a memory of him that would last the length of her soul's survival.

When two priestesses came to prepare him at the sun's set, he was still sitting there, listening to the dialogue yet raging within.

He let them lead him dumbly into baths and chambers filled with women who fussed about him, whispering scandalized incomprehensibles among themselves. He was docile while they cut his hair and picked the parasites from it, and redressed his arm with foul-smelling unguents and bound it up again with white gauze; and when they fed him, giggling, he ate as they demanded, carefully, so as not to despoil his anointments or the fine-woven robes they draped around him. The robes were cut for ossasim, with great slits where sleeves might have been, slits deep enough to accommodate a pair of fine-furred wings.

When he became impatient, demanding his right, the same blue-robed woman who had delivered him to the guards appeared, extended her arm to him as she had then, and led him to the chamber of Mahrlys-iis-Vahais.

Awaiting in that chamber was not Mahrlys, but the ossasim Eviduey, lounging with wings at rest on a caned platform, supported by two whelt-head full-breasted female statues as tall as he.

He hesitated at the threshold, but the cobalt-robed woman pushed him inside and closed the rushed doors behind his back.

He stood there in consternation, staring about for sight of Mahrlys. No Mahrlys did he see, but such grand and gilded lamps and benches and legged cushions as befitted a woman of rank. And man-size diorite statues, those of every god in Benegua's pantheon, as befitted Benegua's high priestess.

The ossasim beckoned him, and lit an oil lamp, then globed it with a translucent amber shade.

Self-consciously, holding his borrowed finery about him, he folded himself onto the stool Eviduey chose for him and accepted a goblet full of a dark, sweet juice.

The other studied his polished nails, retracting them nervously.

"You are not Mahrlys," said Deilcrit when he had gulped the drink, staring into the ruddy eyes of the ossasim.

It ran its long fingers through its mane and leaned forward.

"Deilcrit, I am not here because of Mahrlys, but in spite. When she arrives, I hope she will not find me. I would like to ask you some questions."

He tore his eyes away from those all-too-manlike lips.

"I have never seen a wehr-master with bearded lips," he replied. "Are you . . . ?" And then he could find no way to frame his query as to the ossasim's nature, preferred mate, or feelings for Mahrlys, and said instead: "Are you convinced of my guilt?"

The ossasim scratched its beard. "No, I am not. I am convinced of little. I would support an individual such as some ptaiss and whelts feel you to be. I will support anything that advances Wehrdom." Earnestly, gesticulating so that his limp wings rustled about his wrists, the wehr-master laid his case before him: "Consider my position. I have no allegiance but Wehrdom, no function other than the correlation of such factions as exist within our ranks. Some men are not wehrs. Some beasts are not wehrs. All ossasim are wehrs. I voted for the trial of Imca-Sorr-Aat, as did the majority of us.''

Deilcrit turned his goblet in his hands, inclined his head. "So?"

"It has been long since Imca-Sorr-Aat has asked anything of Wehrdom. It is long since anything has been heard from Othdaliee, exempting the wehr-rages, which grow further and further apart."

"You do not have to justify yourself to me. It is I who wish to justify myself before Mnemaat the Unseen," said Deilcrit softly.

"Mnemaat? Ah, Mnemaat. Better Imca-Sorr-Aat: he is the intermediary between mortals and the god. If indeed the god still lives. You are surprised?"

He had made the star sign before his face. "Mnemaat is not dead," he pronounced.

"You have not looked into his Eye, then."

"That is true," he conceded.

"Well, you saw me look into it, just today. And the others. And know you what we saw there? We saw what we wished to see. His Eye shows us whatever we choose. Once it commanded us, bade us match our actions to the scenes it displayed. His mouth has not spoken to us for generations. You stood upon it! Did the Mouth of Mnemaat speak to you?"

"No," he whispered, agonized, finally realizing that there was no love of the Unseen in Dey-Ceilneeth, as there was in the forests.

"Of course it did not. You have been in His most sacred sanctuary. There is nothing else. You have seen the unseeable. And, I hope, seen through it. Some say the god is dead. Some say another is on the way. Some say the three for whom the Spirit Gate opened are that very thing: new gods for a godless age. What say you, who have seen them face to face?" And he took Deilcrit's goblet, refilled it, handed it back.

"I asked them that," he said in answer. "I, too, was concerned that they might be gods. But they said that they were not, though one said that if I need him . . ." And he stopped, and thumped the full goblet down resoundingly on the stand, so that it slopped over and the red juice crawled along the cane and dropped to the stone.

He sat back, but very slowly, and tried to make his ears stop ringing so that he could decipher the ossasim's words.

Some while later, when the black-furred one took his leave, it occurred to him that he did not recall exactly what had passed between them, though they parted on good terms.

Standing by the door of tied rushes, it came to him that the drink had been stronger than he anticipated, and that he should drink no more. But when he went to pour out the remaining juice, he found no signs of the pitcher, or the goblets either, though a red stain on the caning and a wetness on the floor proved that he had not imagined it.

He was on his hands and knees by the bench, his finery forgotten, when she entered from a curtained doorway he had thought to be simply curtains, and drew him wordlessly within.

V

Step-sister's Embrace

We sat in the crotch of a gargantuan tree overlooking the maze surrounding Dey-Ceilneeth. The ancient titan was hoary with overgrowth but in places the crystal of her cathedrals still shone like jewels in the sun.

I shivered, and wriggled my back more firmly against the forest giant's bark. Sereth sat on a limb wide as I am long, his feet swinging, Chayin between us. The cahndor's arms were folded over his chest.

"You take nature's whim as a personal affront," he growled at Sereth, who had not spoken since we had seen the children in the forest the day before.

"What affronts me is my own concern."

"So be it!"

"Stop this!"

Sereth tossed me an indecipherable glance, and came in from the branch, to lounge against its parent trunk. "How long do you propose to sit here?"

I looked at Chayin, who studied the memnis' bark. I wished it could be otherwise between us. Especially now when we entered what could easily be a dangerous situation. So my forereading showed it. Chayin and Sereth were each keeping their own counsel. There had been entirely too much of that from all of us, but not even I would be the first one to stop it. No, I would not do that. I looked at Sereth, and at Chayin, who had not yet replied.

"You know we are going in there," I implored him. "You will go for Se'keroth. I will go for Deilcrit. He will go because he cannot stay away."

"You are wrong, Estri," said Chayin. "Sereth will go for Deilcrit. You go for him. And I in one sense for Wehrdom, and another for Mahrlys-iis-Vahais." The veil was heavy on him. Sereth, enmity wiped from his frame like dust by the wind, crouched down, leaning forward, intent on Chayin's face.

"When Deilcrit is no longer Deilcrit, and a blackened Se'keroth lies across the arms of a carnelian throne, we will depart this land. Not before; and failing that, not at all," came the cahndor's singsong from the far side of the abyss.

"Chayin," I said softly, "please—"

"Estri, you do not talk to Sereth of Wehrdom. Why? Because he will no more accept its hegemony than that his own skills wield over his actions. Truth?"

"Yes," I admitted, as much to keep him talking as anything else.

"Do not forget that. He is hase-enor, of all men: that, too, recollect."

"Chayin," said Sereth evenly. "See your way into the maze, and out safely. See the moment of entrance, and its perils."

"Surely," said the cahndor in that same bemused voice, and reeled off the turnings. After a time, his voice became more normal and his observations more tentative.

I studied Sereth covertly. He and Chayin were barely speaking, yet he had not wasted this opportunity to benefit us. Whether Chayin would deem what had just passed an invasion of his privacy, a use made of him while he was indisposed, I did not know. It seemed likely. They were more and more wary of each other, and as a consequence, more wary of me.

Chayin had spoken with me once of Benegua in genetic terms. It is a science of which I am not totally ignorant. What he had had to say disturbed me. But I had not mentioned it to Sereth. He would not like what Chayin's theory portended.

As of this sun's rising, we had been thrashing about in the forest for eighteen days. Eighteen days of their growling at each other, of shields snapped tight, eighteen days within the wall of Mnemaat. How long we lost in the obviation of space that spat us out at a cold campfire strewn with our carnage, I could not determine. Long enough for no Deilcrit, no Se'keroth, nor my blade either, to be lying there when we arrived.

We had expected nothing different, and so were not disappointed. We spent one uneasy night listening to the forest's mutters: Chayin got very drunk on a miraculously spared skin of kifra, and said a number of things better left unsaid, and he and Sereth did not speak except in monosyllables for three days. Hence their pace was hard, and I, too, turned surly trying to keep it.

On the morning of the fourth day since the obviation, which we undertook directly after a day-night vigil for Chayin's dead there by the sea, Sereth came to me as I wakened.

I had, since he overheard Chayin offer me asylum in Nemar, found it prudent to sleep with neither one of them. Prudent but difficult. Abstinence is for me a weighty yoke, and I was only too glad to slip into his arms when he extended them.

And I was heartened, lying in the grass with him

as of old, that so easily might I chink the breach growing between us. It had been a couching full of promise and promises, one of new beginnings. So I started to speak to him of Chayin and the strains I knew lay upon them both, but he rolled over onto his belly and said:

"Watch." And with a distant little smile on his face, he traced my name with his finger in the grass. As his nail moved along the blades they seemed to shrivel, then smoke, then the very ground beneath began to run together. Still with that faraway little grin, he laid his hand flat beside the letters of my name branded a finger's-joint deep into the earth.

"As easily can I destroy him. And I will, if owkahen serves me up your loss." Sereth always whispers death. "Is that clear?"

And I nodded, for he was watching me out of the corner of his eye.

"Good. Now, look." And he waved his flat palm over the letters singed deep into the turf. His forehead furrowed, and grass reappeared where my name had been. Or rather, other grass appeared: it was of a lighter green, and more densely packed, than that around it.

"What did you do?" I queried, hushed.

His eyes flickered sidelong at me; he tucked his chin in and stared at the lighter-green ESTRI written in sod among the darker grasses.

"I borrowed it. The first sod, that I burned away, became smoke and ash. This is from a year hence. I took it from the same spot."

"So my name is gouged in the ground a year from now, in this place?"

"Something like that. I thought the technique might help you with your time discrepancies. Do you want it?"

"Do I want it," I echoed dumbly, sufficiently chastised.

"There is a condition," he said, turning his narrowed eyes full upon me. "You will teach this to none else."

I knew whom he meant, but I agreed. So began the taking of sides.

And the nursing of the tension that crackled around us in the tree's crotch like owkahen's own lightning.

What can I say in excuse for myself? In retrospect one dredges up alternatives that seem more workable than those that have come to be. But only if I were other than myself, and they also some other folk, could it have gone differently. Chayin alone inherited from our progenitors that talent for existing always in the selection of consequences some call the sort. Sereth and I grit our teeth and wrestle with the moment, drawing (at the best times) a sufficiency of what we desire therefrom, so that with the aid of what we have already gained we can repeat the process. My forereading is a mass of tantalizing obscurity which like some diabolical instructor leads me into truth by way of error. From which I emerge, I hope the wiser, and with a wry understanding of what my visions earlier portended. The best I can say for myself is that I seldom make the same mistake twice. Seldom, but not never. . . .

The mistake I was then concerned with not making was of being the last so high above the ground in the crotch of the huge memnis, as I watched Sereth's head disappear between the branches. He would not wait for Chayin's indisposition to pass, but swung out and down like some sucker-footed tree-kepher, leaving me to talk Chayin back from the land of veils.

I sat and fumed and choked back curses, and

then, asudden very conscious of the winds that blew around the tree and shook its fronds so that they whispered, turned to the task at hand.

It had been long since Chayin spoke from beyond the abyss, long since the veils held him entrapped. Once he had been sorely afflicted by this manifestation, called by some forereader's disease, and I had used my skills to ease him out from its grasp. It was a measure of owkahen's tumultuousness I saw there in his inward-staring eyes, in his boneless form melted against the memnis' trunk.

I inched toward him, uncertain of my footing though it was more than ample, and made the error of peering out into space, where Sereth scrambled ever downward, far below.

Then I put concerted effort into returning the cahndor's attention to what we call the present.

It took some extensive laying-on of hands, there on the swaying branch.

"Dey-Ceilneeth awaits," I murmured, when his membranes snapped back and forth tentatively and he uncrossed his arms and at my urging slid inward to the safety of the memnis' cleft.

He looked, for a moment, all of his father's son, staring at me from across the abyss. Then he shook his head and rubbed his eyes with his palms, and said: "Now?"

"No time better," I affirmed.

"That is not strictly true, but"—and he yawned and stretched, and gathered his legs under him—"I am anxious to retrieve Se'keroth from that jungle boy of yours. . . . Where is . . . ?" And he himself peered between the memnis' uplifted arms to spy Sereth, descending.

"Se'keroth?" I wondered. "Then you do not recollect what you said?"

"No."

So I told him what he had said to us, and at the

retelling's end, with a wail I could not suppress, sought the shelter of his arms. "How has it come to this, that we use each other so ill?"

"Ssh, little one. Things are not as they appear. It is Wehrdom whose distrust we feel. It is the very air which divided us, the echoes of their converse which make us like strangers in our own minds."

I shivered, my face pressed to his leathers.

"It is as it was with the children: He thinks I obstruct him. But it is not me."

I nodded. I well recalled the children we had seen in the forest, strewn about like discarded rag dolls, their stuffing spilling out onto the ground. And the live ones, all huddled in a group that wandered helpless in the wilderness.

They had crossed the road, headed eastward. We had been thrice sickened by dead ones we had passed, and we followed. But no attempts to get near the children availed us. When we showed ourselves they screamed and the little group of thirteen flew apart and disappeared. Sereth had been determined to catch one, if only to offer aid. This he did above Chayin's mysterious and seemingly arbitrary protestations.

The child we cut from the herd and pursued was fleet. We chased it, circling, closing in on the little girl from three sides. When at last the tiny thing cringed with its back to a large boulder, weeping, its capture sure, we heard a snapping among the trees and something dark and winged swooped straight down. There came a moment of shadowed wings and whooshing air, and the child was gone, snatched into the air, only to reappear, hurtling groundward. Even as I lunged forward, it struck earth with a sickening crash.

We stood over that crushed and broken body, peering up into branches that seemed to seek eternity somewhere above our heads.

"I told you," Chayin growled, prodding the child's corpse with his foot. Indeed, he had told us that only death could come from our mixing in these affairs.

"If you had not obstructed me," spat Sereth, "the child would be alive."

The cahndor had thrown himself upon Sereth, dragging him to the ground, when the wehr's shadow first darkened the earth.

Chayin, breathing hard, grass in his black mane, rubbed a fresh bruise on the side of his temple.

"Sereth, I will not tell you again. We have entered the wehrs' domain. Our rules do not obtain here. A strong territoriality does. We have twice withstood wehr-rages; it is because of this that they no longer attack us. By their own ritual, we have won the right to walk these woods. But we stay not still, and this makes the wehr-folk uneasy. By the rules of their society, if *we* rage—if we start another bloodletting—they will fight us until either all of us or all of them lie dying. And there are very many of them. We have acted outside their conventions. The wehr-mind stretches to accommodate men who are more than men, wehrs who are less than wehrs, creatures who carry their territoriality with them."

"How do you know all this?" Sereth demanded, his fingers toying with knife sheathed at his hip.

"I have spoken with them. As might you, if you chose."

And he would say no more.

So we followed the children in their ragged band, and saw a thing even more strange: they came to a widening trail, at the end of which a mud-brick wall encircled a score of bent-branch huts on the Isanisa's bank.

It was getting on to day's end, and the light grew uncertain. We circled around the youngsters and concealed ourselves near the wall, within its very shadow in a clump of the silver-berried bushes.

Just when we had done this, two men slipped through a low door in the wall and scuttled to obscure themselves in the trees that lined the path.

Sereth laid hand on my shoulder, but I needed no warning. I held my breath and stayed very still.

I cannot recall what I expected to see, but it surely was not what passed before my eyes:

The group of children had broken ranks. Two came, almost together, pell-mell along the trail, out of sight of the others. One had hair as red as the sun.

The men in the bushes waited until the children were almost parallel to them. Then, as one man, they leaped upon the fleet little forms. The redhead, by some few feet the straggler, let out a strangled cry and wheeled to run back the way she had come. She could not elude her pursuer.

The men secreted the children's bodies in a pit I must assume they had dug there for that purpose, and took up once more their vigilance in the trees.

Sereth hissed articulately, and Chayin warned him, very low, that any overt attempt to interfere would bring weighty consequences, that Beneguan ways were not Silistran ways, nor his to adjudge.

For a moment I thought they would tear each other to pieces among the silver berries. Obviously they did not, but they did sit unspeaking while the rest of the children, still bunched together, passed unmolested by the two concealed men; sat there until the moon rose and the men, with grumbled laughter, forsook their concealment and pounded upon the gate that had opened to admit the balance of the children's band, and were themselves admitted.

It seemed that within the mud-bricked wall a celebration was under way, for the silence was eaten up by laughter and the thrumming of drums and the piping of eerie pipes.

On our way back to the great road we had quit to witness this odd and terrible scene, we stumbled over two more slain children.

"It is as it was with children," had said Chayin. "The very time divides us." I could feel in myself the detached patience I had felt then, that cool heedlessness that had saved me from some pointless attempt to intervene in what was none of my affair. But this time, my mind told me dryly, everything was very much my affair.

"Do not withhold your aid from him. For my sake," I dared to beg. And then he did not answer but only pushed me gently away. "Then, if not for me, for whatever you hold sacred."

"How cometh your obviation of space?" he queried bitterly, letting me know that he was aware of what Sereth had given me, and the price I had paid. I lowered my head. "What I will do is for his sake, not yours. I will get him through the maze and pick him up if he falls. But I will not let him die for his ignorance."

And with that, he made motion that I should descend the tree before him.

Which took most of my concentration. I am no tree-dweller, not like Sereth, who spent his youth in forests. My youth was spent upon silken covers, learning my womanhood and those joys it can give to a man. I begrudged the loss of those days, and the joyous ignorance I then possessed.

It seemed to me that as far as Sereth remained "ignorant," to that extent was he blessed; that we were both in that respect unlike Chayin, who sought knowledge for its own sake. And I caught my first glimpse of what Sereth had dubbed the "lack of compassion" in us Shapers' spawn, as I climbed slowly and painstakingly down the towering memnis and Chayin followed behind.

Another thing that occurred to me as I scratched and scraped and slid my way groundward was one which caused me to reach out under my shield, testing as a warrior might reach out beyond his shield arm's defense. I sought Wehrdom. I sought the touch that had brushed my sensing and withdrawn when we entered by the Spirit Gate; that had nearly drawn me down into its whirling tunnel when I destroyed the wehr-master. I had devalued that at the time. I had not wanted to think that Wehrdom might be a worthy foe, or even an intelligence whose wishes need be considered. A certain smugness comes with successes such as ours, and in that smugness is the most insidious of perils.

So, at the last possible moment, as I joined Sereth where he sat on a flat, moss-grown boulder, I considered Wehrdom, and took some care as to my armament before it.

It was a soft crowd in my mind, back behind my sensing, cautiously curious like untold pairs of round eyes, blinking. I saw it as a curtain through which Sereth and the day and Chayin's approach were not obscured, but intensified with a wonder that danced like a multitude of phosphorescent insects in all the air about, giving it volume that undulated in a pulsing dance.

I made some affirmative sound to Sereth's query as to my well-being, though it hung long moments in my ears bereft of meaning, as Wehrdom heard it, before my habituated understanding precipitated a response.

I know Sereth looked at me strangely, for the wehr presence about me made a space of two breaths stretch interminably and performed a minute investigation of his face therein.

I walked easily; I was aware of all that passed around me with a multiple perspective that showed me the wood as a magnificent palatial estate in which all things were about a perpetual reordering. There is a joy in wehr-thought that is equally from fury and ecstasy, ascendancy and suffering, birth and death. They are one and yet all, and from them I could separate the berceides who guard the maze whose every hungry mouth and yawning pit and sinksand dead end was as familiar to me as to the campt which awaited at the most hideous misturn of all; or to the wehr-master even now striding through the jicekak to intercept us.

I said this to Sereth and Chayin, and cautioned them to tread unerringly the very middle of the first corridor, on whose every side pink mouths waited gaping.

We did this, and I saw Sereth's heels before my downcast eyes. Both Chayin and I called the turn, together, and my mind slipped out from the wehr-knowing, startled, fearful, and I spent long awkward moments battening down the cracks in my shielding through which Wehrdom's song yet could be heard.

When I heard it not, I heard another thing: the hissing of the berceides as they reared upon their coils for a better view. And saw Sereth's doubtless instinctual reaction: like two popping gourds, the berceides' heads burst apart. The steaming ichor splattered, but we three kept very still. The pink mouths of the hedge writhed and slurped and strained forward. We stood unmoving, though the death throes of the coils whipped around us, safe within the neutral barrier we had earlier determined to employ. Neutral, but immobile, sunk into the very bedrock of the universe. If Sereth wished, he could have held that envelope of space inviolate before a force that would powder the planet. As it was, the lashing tails of the dead snakes merely rebounded from any point closer than an arm's length to our bodies.

"That settles that," growled Chayin, and spat disgustedly. "We are going in bloody: what else can follow but more of the same? It is rage for rage, here. *Why must you do this*?"

"Ask your forereading. It tells you all things. If it told you true, you would know that two snakes are a cheap price for such an introduction, and will save higher blood later on."

"You persist in this hierarchal prejudice! This is Wehrdom. No such—"

"*Silence!*"

And he got it. Total, complete, unbreathing absence of sound.

The hairs on my body rose up, waved in the air, returned to their normal rest. The barrier dismantled, we proceeded into the second maze.

I wondered if I would dare open my mind again to Wehrdom, after what Sereth had done, and then reflected that I, as he, might as well dare what I chose. There was precious little from which to choose; it would remain thus for a space. Such is owkahen's price to those who wish to lie with her: she denies us nothing, but rather designates that toward which we strive.

The wehr-master met us at the beginning of the innermost maze, though I had expected him long since. But when we turned that corner, I understood.

He blocked the aisle of silver-berried bushes, wings folded around him like some fabulous cape. His loins were bound in black silk as shiny as his coal-dark pelt. Behind him were ten of his kind, all colors, and these had their wings stiffened, akimbo.

Besides the tall black-maned wehr stood a woman whose face I had seen in Deilcrit's dreams, a woman whom Sereth yet thought to be a man: Mahrlys-iis-Vahais. Something prompted me to glance at Chayin, and the expression on his face was an odd mix of assessment and shock. I did not sufficiently mark it, for then the black-winged creature stepped forward.

"What in the name of Mnemaat," it growled throatily in a voice quite unexpectedly clear, "do you want here? What further sacrifice could you possibly demand? What brings you to war upon us, and from whence? Who are you? What is expected of us?" As he spoke, he came ever closer: by the time he had finished speaking, he was kneeling at my feet, peering up at me through totally red eyes described by two concentric black rings that seemed to be iris and pupil. I looked into those blazing fires.

I did not know what to say. I stared down at him, noting that as he waited, his wings began to rustle. Sereth, besides reaching behind my back to touch Chayin's arm when the thing approached me, made no move.

Before words came to me, while yet I stared into the red-on-red eyes of Wehrdom, the woman whirled on her heels. I heard the scramble of those behind her to move out of her way.

"Wait. You have not been dismissed," Sereth advised, so quietly that I thought perhaps the woman did not hear. She took two more steps between her winged guardians, then turned stiffly and proceeded to kneel beside the black-winged one at my feet. I had seen her eyes, and there was no doubt in me that it was Sereth's will, and not her own, holding her on her knees. And the tremors that coursed visibly over her flesh an instant later proved me right: such is the aftermath of flesh-lock.

I surreptitiously tugged on his tunic. Accidentally,

he jostled me. The winged creatures, each man-sized or larger, stood very still, watching through their red eyes. Some had head ruffs or manes; some had lips, and some did not. A few were thick, with wrestlers' muscles taut amid their wings, so massive that I wondered if they could truly fly. Most were lithe as shadows, pale as a young moon. But all were formidable, armed only with what nature had provided. I knew why they did not speak, but I was not about to open myself to Wehrdom's thousand throats.

"Most High," hissed the woman at my feet, "restrain your servants. I am iis of this place. Only reveal your desires to me, and they will be sated. But please"—and this an agonized whisper—"do not shame me before my wehr-masters."

I answered her in a deep and formal tone, that all of hers might hear:

"I want a man called Deilcrit, and those belongings of ours that he has upon him. And I want your sage counsel as to how you can make amends for the loss of our ship and men." This last was at Sereth's rather obvious urging.

The woman put her head in her hands, raised it, and said: "Might I rise?"

I nodded, and they both stood, and I saw from the flames in her green eyes that she played a part only, one forced upon her, and that she was concerned that I realize the fact.

"What in the name of Uritheria is going on here?" exploded Chayin in Parset. Sereth silenced him in the same language, while the woman, composed, suggested that we accompany her into Dey-Ceilneeth.

When Sereth asked her in her own language whether or not she would accede to our demands, the black-winged one answered for her that there would be difficulties in granting our requests, but all efforts would be made to satisfy us, if we would only follow, and allow them to explain.

The woman stood straight as a rod, as if she had not heard, as if men's converse, whether it be man or wehr-master, was beneath her ears' concern.

"This is Eviduey, follower of Mnemaat, Third Hand, His Austerity of Wehrdom," said the green-eyed woman. The creature made a deep bow, as if standing in some reception hall. I nodded, then introduced Chayin, giving all three of his titles; and Sereth, calling him the Ebvrasea, dharen; even ransacking his past for two additional honors. As I had expected, when I had announced my companions, she then spoke to me of herself:

"I am Mahrlys-iis-Vahais, Daughter of Mnemaat, Keeper of His Eye and Mouth, First in Dey-Ceilneeth, Most High."

That last was, of course, what all this had been leading up to. As she said it her proud carriage drew itself even taller, and with stately grace she extended her black-robed arm to me.

I took it and gave some small account of myself in a suitable tone: dhareness of all Silistra, high-couch, daughter of my father, etc. It was not important what I said: I could have called myself Keeper of the Offal of Apths, for all she knew of the western shore. But I observed the form, and took her proffered arm, saying sweetly: "And are you not also of Wehrdom, and bound to Imca-Sorr-Aat?"

I heard a strange rattling noise that could not have come from a human throat: Mahrlys' face drained pale; I spun on my heel.

They faced each other, Eviduey and Chayin, with Sereth, arms outstretched, a living barrier in between. As one woman, she screamed something in a sibilant tongue and I in my native one.

There came a rustle behind us from among the

creatures I would learn to call ossasim, and I dropped pretense and ran to Chayin's side. I flew against him. I shook him by the shoulders. He hardly noticed me, but stood there.

One part of my mind noted Mahrlys unintelligibly calming the stiff-winged wehr-master; another part felt Sereth press close, heard him whisper: "They just backed up and froze. What think you?"

"Some ritual taking of each other's measure? How would I know?"

"*Chayin!*"

And then: "Get back."

"No." But I did, and Sereth slapped the cahndor, flat-handed, so hard that he staggered. But he woke, and caught himself, and snarled something about the probable parentage of the wehr-master Eviduey.

Mahrlys leaned on Eviduey's arm, and from that distance asked me if I thought we might now proceed. I looked from her, to her reinforcements, to Sereth warily attending Chayin, and nodded. This fracasing in poisonous hedge served no one.

I said as much, and she turned upon her heel and with Eviduey marched through her own ranks. The corridor of furred forms stayed open.

We went into it three abreast, me in the middle between them, and when we were close upon Mahrlys' heels, the ossasim followed at a respectful distance, double file.

"Now what?" asked Sereth, most diffidently, in Parset. "Or should I say, 'Now what, Most High?'"

"I saw no reason to inform you afore the fact. Chayin knew. It was there in the sort, in Deilcrit's memories. Shall I be a Most High for them? Will you continue with this charade?" It was Sereth who, grasping all, had knelt Mahrlys at my feet rather than his own.

"If it makes them more comfortable. If it gets us

what we want. . . . I do not see any reason to disabuse them of their misconceptions."

"It might prove ticklish," cautioned Chayin.

"She just might be, at that."

Chayin did not find that amusing. "What are you implying?"

"Nothing. What was that with the birdman?"

Chayin, this time, said: "Nothing."

Sereth saw something in that ritual opposition of bodies. So did I. I saw it in the luxurious femininity of the woman whose black mane swayed before us, in her wide-set eyes that glistened like the ocean in the sun. I knew Chayin and Sereth well, knew their tastes: she was a woman neither would push from his couch. But I did not put enough concern into this observation: I did not know the difference between woman and wehr; or rather, knowing it, did not mark the significance of the fact nor how much influence it would come to have upon us all.

"I came to greet you myself," observed Mahrlys, acerbic now that the doors of tied rushes were closed and the curtains drawn over them. Beyond those doors awaited Sereth, and Chayin, with Eviduey and another black ossasim, in a long narrow hallway of pieced and colored glass.

"I came to you of myself, and you denigrated me before my own." All pretense cast aside, she glowered at me, regal among priceless antiquities in that chamber filled with towering plants and statues of stone carved into creatures part-woman, part-beast, who stared from their height down upon us through faceted brooding eyes.

I glowered back, and paced off the room in an inventory that was both peremptory and unabashed, saying: "You came to me tardy, in self-aggrandizement. You knelt before us at our will rather than yours, and this offends you? Perhaps you had better become accustomed to accepting such offense: if you do not quickly and completely meet our demands, you will find yourself in receipt of such chastisement the like of which this day's display is only a mild forewarning." And I took seat upon an offering table of black diorite held extended at the level of my waist by a muscular, whelt-headed deity.

Mahrlys' face paled as she strode toward me, her silk robe pulled close by tight fists. "Who are you? Who are they? What need was there to slay the berceides, and all the other creatures you have wantonly killed?"

"Who I am," I said softly, judging her ill temper sufficiently worsened, and therefore sliding off the statue, "I have already told you. But you do not understand. As for my companions, they are each regents in their own right, as well as my consorts, and they do not belong waiting in hallways while two women prattle over what such men have done."

"Indeed? And what makes these men qualified to take a hand in the affairs of nature, when all know what poison their ilk has perpetrated in the past?" Her lips trembled, and her fingers also, and her voice rose toward a shriek.

I threw her a mocking stare from under a slightly raised brow, and made my voice low and soft and full of composure, though what she said shook me to my core. "Have you no use for men, then? How do you survive?"

"We have use for them." And with that she pulled hard upon the reins of her temper, and ushered me with all decorum to a caned bench supported by two whelt-headed female figures carved from black stone. "We have use for all creatures. Men till our fields, they give us the craft of their hands, and children. But we keep them from the self-destruction that lies within their cleverness, and they do penance here for what they have done in the past: it is Wehrdom's way, and the way of nature, that all live together, no one variety of the forest's children ruling over all the rest. Is it not so in your domain?"

"No, it is not. There is a whole world out there, and beyond its expanse other worlds; and upon none of them does one sex count the other so low, instead favoring other creatures of diverse heritage."

It was the winged one to which I referred, and she knew it. "I am wehr first, and woman second. Ossasim come from such wombs as mine—speak not of that with which you are not familiar. How dare you adjudge nature's finest fruit, and find it lacking?"

I ran my fingers through my hair, found a knot, worried it in a search for some suitable answer. She waited upon me, those eyes through which Wehrdom peered expressionless fixed upon my face.

"I am only trying to save you grief: my companions are not like the men with whom you are familiar; treating them thus can only bring bloodshed and death to you all."

"Then they are just exactly like the men with whom I am familiar, only scandalously freed to work their evil wiles."

I almost lost my temper. "I am telling you, I cannot speak for them, nor make agreements in their behalf."

She looked at me in pity, and offered refreshment. I accepted, and while we awaited the menials that entered to the summons of her clapped hands, we spoke no words. When the wingless, furred creatures had set a tart juice before us and departed, I said:

"If all this is true, if men have little worth here, why will you not cede me this Deilcrit and let me depart, and save those subjects of yours that you may?"

"Why did you let your creatures slaughter my berceides? They were among the wisest, most valued of my—"

"Look you, we are not here to exchange insults, or detail our damages to each other, but to reach some kind of understanding between us."

"I will not treat with men! I would sooner make a bed partner of a guerm!"

"Are guerm, then, less sweet than ossasim? The distinctions, the niceties, escape me!"

"You are insufferable!"

"In truth," I agreed. "And if you continue to devalue my companions, you will suffer as you have never dreamed possible. Your only recourse, as I see it, is to quickly meet our demands and let us depart, lest you learn obedience knelt at their feet."

"Would that I could!" she spat with shaking voice, and bent her head away to pour us new drink and seek composure. "Am I expected to be terrified by that sorcery in the hedges? I am horrified, disgusted, appalled. I have powers," affirmed she, graciously proffering a full cup, "should I need to use them. I am no wanton, spilling blood enough to bathe in at my slightest whim. You have slaughtered whelt, ptaiss, quenel, guerm, campt, fhrefrasil, ossasim." She ticked them off upon her fingers, and when she looked up, her eyes were filled with tears: "Even the berceides of the second hedge. They counseled my mother and her mother and her mother before her. Do not threaten me with your men! It is you whom I hold responsible for this whole affair. Poor, despoiled Deilcrit! It is you with whom I will treat. If necessary, it is you with whom I will contend. And when I say 'I,' be assured that the whole of Wehrdom will stand behind my words."

Owkahen showed bright and clear the consequences if I dropped her to her knees in helpless flesh-lock, went to the doors and admitted Sereth and Chayin, consigned her to their mercies. The price was too dear, the repercussions too great. Instead I said:

"Mahrlys, if you feel the need of a test of strength with me, I shall not deny you. But first, hear me out."

She inclined her head. Assured of the royal permission, I continued:

"You have reason to be distressed, as have I. I and mine have been set upon by this Wehrdom of yours. We emerged unscathed. If you should again come against us, we would be forced not to simply beat back your attack, but to make an example such as will run your river red with wehr blood." I said this very calmly, leaning back against the sculptured stanchion's thigh. "Simply call the time." And when she did not call it:

"Then so be it: I will call Sereth and Chayin and we will enter into—"

"No!"

"Mahrlys . . ."

"I cannot suffer such a thing to be seen in Dey-Ceilneeth." She was very beautiful, flushed with her pent rage. "I petition you that we instead exchange attendants, as is meet."

I almost told her that I would not, even that I would not breed down, but it was an overture on her part, the only one, excepting pitched battle, she had made.

"Give me Deilcrit."

"I do not have him."

I rose up and circled the chamber, readying my stroke, but she continued: "He is gone on Imca-

Sorr-Aat's business." And my prowling mind told me she spoke the truth, that Deilcrit was not in the holding.

"Nor Se'keroth, either, then?"

"I do not understand," said she, uncertain as to what had gone awry.

"The green metal sword he had."

"When he left he took all with him."

"How came he," queried I, catching the thread, "to leave upon this errand?"

"Imca-Sorr-Aat requested it," she answered smoothly.

"Did he? And who is Imca-Sorr-Aat?"

At that her eyes widened, and she made a sign before her face. "From what bowel of ignorance do you come, woman? Imca-Sorr-Aat is His Spirit abroad upon the land. His call was the honor that saved the foul creature from the death he earned cavorting with you in the forest." She actually spat.

"What could there have been about what passed between me and Deilcrit to affront one in whose land children are slaughtered not only by beasts but by men, and none raise hand to help them?"

"Estri," said Mahrlys after a long pause, "you do not understand. And I do not understand. And I am beginning to doubt that I want to understand. Or should. I am sure there are many things as sensible and commonplace to you which would sicken me should I look upon them. In point of fact, you have brought two with you. If I am willing to accept such a creature, even in the search for peace between us, then take that as an article of my faith. I cannot give you Deilcrit unless you would wait here until his return. Which you are welcome to do."

I did not like the way she spoke that last part.

"I will tell you tomorrow. I repeat, I only speak

for myself." Though they had said to me that I
might play Mahrlys' game, I had been unable.
There was too much enmity, born of instinct, between me and this not-quite-woman who ruled the
shores of which none were empowered to speak.

"If I cannot give you Deilcrit"—Mahrlys smiled
warmly—"and I cannot give you the weapons you
have lost, is there anything I can give you?"

"Have you a ship that will sail an ocean, fit as
the one you destroyed?"

"No, I have no such ship."

"Do you have skilled labor with which to build
one?"

"No, I have not that either. Are you then
marooned here?" Her upper lip had a slight curl
to it which became more pronounced when she
was pleased, as she was then.

"No, only at a loss as to what might be fair
reparation for something you have not the skill to
replace. Can you direct us on the path Deilcrit
took?"

"If you wish, though it is no easy trail even for
one familiar, which you are not. Why not, better,
remain with us until he returns? That is, if you
can control your creatures." She smirked.

"I do not control them, and they are not creatures.
I will ask them, and let you know our joint
decision."

"Please do. The duties of a gracious host are
much lightened by knowledge of how long the
guest will abide. I could prepare some wondrous
entertainments—"

"I thank you, no."

"Will you not dine with me this meal, then?"

"I think not. We have had a surfeit of excitement.
A meal in our chambers and an early rest would
suit us all."

Her brows knitted. "If not a meal, then, we must

at least view the rising moon. It is customary when exchanging attendants."

"I am not sure—"

"Please, again I beg your indulgence in what is customary."

I sipped the drink she had long ago handed me, and turned the beaten bronze in my hands. "Is it that black ossasim you propose to send me?" I asked.

"Eviduey." Her tone caressed the name, and her arms drew together about her breasts. "I do you great honor. Do not reject it. He is more than Third Hand to me."

There was steel in her voice as deadly as the dagger she fingered beneath her robe. I had not previously marked it, and I found myself fussing about my boot tops, caressing the slender circles nestled there.

"It is the dark one I would prefer," she breathed on a sigh, and let her hand fall to her lap.

"I will ask him." And though she did not understand, she caught my sarcasm and gave me a quizzical look, head cocked, that reminded me that wehrs looked through her eyes, and I begged exhaustion.

Etiquette ruled in Dey-Ceilneeth. If I had foreseen the automatic response my soft inquiry as to the location of my rooms evoked, I would have done it much sooner. Happily, she profusely apologized and then seemed to lapse into the familiarity of her ritual. If I had understood the sanctity of form and demeanor in that society when first I challenged it, I would have fared better. As it was, I followed along dumbstruck as she pulled me to the doors and threw them open.

They were faced off in a triangle. By reading Sereth and Chayin's feigned ease, the fight readiness in Eviduey screamed at me.

Oblivious, Mahrlys strode down the corridor to, as she had said, examine the humble quarters her staff had prepared next to her own. Helplessly, drawn in her wake, I followed. Sereth and Chayin, and the black wehr-master, after a moment's mutual hesitation, joined us.

None spoke. Breathing sounded loud in my ears. Mahrlys' back as we proceeded along the corridor gradually stiffened until I wondered what such a rapid change in bearing might portend, but nothing showed when she threw open the door of rushes and with a flourish invited me to step in before her.

I thanked her, complimented her on the creamy carpets that lay like foam on the emerald stone. The pleasure in her face was not feigned, nor her pride. Only when she turned to leave and saw Chayin stripping off his filthy boots did her smile freeze stiff on her face.

I caught a glimpse of Eviduey's wing-cloaked arm wrapping around her shoulders as Sereth closed the doors of tied rushes and slid the crude bar across.

The chamber held two huge oblong wooden baskets, a bench or table of stone that matched the floor, caned platforms, low, with loose cushions. I sat on one, rested my elbows on my knees and chin in my hands.

I had hoped to hear, sitting there, jokes or banter between them, a query as to how I had fared— anything that smacked of normalcy, confederation, the three of us at work upon the problem at hand. But there were not three there. In that room of ancient and dilapidated splendor were three units of one each. Chayin pulled off his garments one by one, stuck the sword belt between his mud-caked boots, and stretched full out on the carpet with an explosive sigh. Hands under his head, eyes closed,

his regular breathing might have fooled a stranger:
to me it said "Do not disturb."

Neither did Sereth even so much as query me as
to my success with Mahrlys. He made a thorough
circuit of the room, barred a second door he found,
and leaned for a long time against a hanging pulled
back from an overgrown window, staring out between the leaves.

When nothing had changed but day to night, the
nearing of moon's rise made me speak. "Ask me
how I fared, Sereth," I suggested. I had hoped he
would join me on the cushioned platform. He had
not previously. He did not then.

"If you have something to say, say it." He did
not even turn from the window.

I wondered what I had done to elicit such censure from him. I can perform miraculous feats,
wreak carnage, trek continents and the space between the moments when in his company, or to
serve him, or to make him smile. Ousted so arbi-
trarily from his grace, I felt unworthy of grace.

My voice shook. "I ended up telling her the truth,
but she will have none of it. Woman to woman, or
not at all. With one exception: she wants Chayin
for the night."

That one, who had been pretending sleep, sat up
abruptly.

"And she sends me her black and winged friend,
in an equal gesture of trust and respect."

Sereth turned from the window, leaned back
against the wall, slid down it, and crossed his
arms. "No."

"Let me make my own decision, dharen," said
Chayin. There was no veil upon him then. "For the
good of all, for the equality, trust, and respect
between our two lands, I will take my chances
with Mahrlys-iis-Vahais."

This was the cahndor whole, decisive, as I had

once known him. He dug a pouch from his sword belt and touched it to his lips. It was small and held little, but that little was a potent drug, used by Parsets in moments of decision or stress.

Sereth tossed his head, stared up at the ceiling. "Chayin, things are less than they might be between us. We do a precipitous dance here with the unknowable. Owkahen serves itself only. Do not be foolhardy. We can ride out this time and things will be as they were before. Or we can act regardless of what might change. Do not pursue a course on whim, with no clear end in view. Too much depends on us."

I had thought I was beyond shock, but that from him left me speechless.

Chayin, too, looked long upon him before he answered: "Sereth, I appreciate your concern. I see what you see, and admit the risks. But from my point of view there is no other choice. Even Eviduey saw that."

"I like not this love affair of yours with Wehrdom."

"I know," said Chayin sadly.

I merely looked between them, castigating myself for my shallowness. Then Chayin asked me when he was to be summoned, and I explained about the assignation at moon's rising, and Sereth rose up and began pacing.

"Estri," he said as he came abreast of me, "just what would you like me to do about this Eviduey?"

"I . . . I do not know. Whatever you like." You may think that a coward's answer, but you did not hear the tone of his question.

He grunted, and began methodically to draw from me all that had been said about Deilcrit and Wehrdom's workings by Mahrlys-iis-Vahais.

He was still about it when a woman came to lead us to her mistress. He was his most ingratiating self, grinning out from under his hair at her, and asking about baths and fresh garments and laundry and what was planned for our meal. His eyes danced with humor at her consternation that he would speak to her at all. But she rose gamely to the moment, answering his every question, her face turned pointedly away and in my direction, as if indeed I had queried her of these things.

Now the word that Mahrlys used, that I have translated as "attendant," was not that at all, but "ipherim," which means literally "attendant of ipheri," which in turn means "radiant," "resplendent in the sun's rays." The word, as the entire language spoken of as Beneguan, is in reality much older than the Benegua, or Wehrdom; old as the Darsti tongue from which it devolved, old as the science the Darsti language evolved to service; older than Dey-Ceilneeth itself.

Once, in a time hazy in my great-great-grandmother's memory, the continent of Aehre-Kanoss was a great power, possessed of mighty sciences, bastion of the Laonan faith. Near the Fall of Man, at the onset of the mechanist wars, Dey-Ceilneeth was constructed, light in the eye of a great nation, to stand witness to what majesty had existed therein. Here was enshrined Se'keroth, symbol of the Laonan rise—until Khys and some few others stole it back. Those tempestuous days have been elsewhere chronicled, but allow me to remind you: it was the ideological incompatibilities of Silistra and Aehre-Kanoss that precipitated civilization's fall, and framed by its flaunting thereof the genetic policies that have since that time obtained on civilized Silistra. Staring around, awed, in the fabled tabernacle of Dey-Ceilneeth, I conjectured as to what mismatched recombination had created a climate in which such an all-pervasive mutation as the communcations gene shared by

Wehrdom could become dominant. I could think of no circumstance which would inculcate as bizarre a collection of strategies upon a society as had stabilized into the tableau before my eyes.

Chayin, himself born of a mother whose genetic strengths had been chosen by man and not owkahen, seemed to draw about him the very light that inundated the temple, though the moon only peaked the hedge. It was a soft light, thrown from the six crystal towers that pillared the hall; a light that threw holographic phantoms into each corner. They watched, those mindless light sculptures from Dey-Ceilneeth's past glory, eyes ever upon the viewer, facing always each observer as they had for thousands of years. Once hailed as the greatest art ever produced by the technocratic elite, they guarded the temple impassive, their nature forgotten, their countenances smooth and unruffled by the tragedies that had made of them deities before whom sacrifices were zealously and punctually laid, befitting their station as ipherim to Mnemaat the Unseen.

When these ipherim of light were pacified with offerings of fruit and oil and grain, two liver-brown ossasim swung their weight against a brass windlass and without even a single screech of metal a whole section of the temple's stamped metal ceiling drew back to admit the light of the rising moon.

Coincidental to this opening of the ceiling, the holographic figures dimmed, and into the square of moonlight was rolled a hemispherical basin on casters, from which a handle of brass rose a hand's height, then curved back toward the basin's surface.

It was this handle Mahrlys rubbed repeatedly with her palm after we had all filed down the dais to crowd around it. Into the depths of this caldron-like affair we stared: myself, Sereth, Chayin,

Eviduey, and an ossasim whose pure white fur and stooped hobbling gait denoted advanced age.

So we looked into the Eye of Mnemaat: in the basin, which seemed to be at least in part composed of a convexly ground crystal, a turbulence began. From Mahrlys' stroking palm, along the dully glowing brass, circling around and down the caldron's circumference, traveled a pale blue, pulsing light bright as an electric spark. Through squinted eyes I saw the basin's crystal seem to melt, to take chop like a restless sea. And then the glow burned so bright I turned my head away. But when Mahrlys breathed a command that we commune with Mnemaat, I turned back my head and saw within that frothing brightness a massive throne hewn of red stone, and a sword set across its arms, and that sword was Se'keroth. Then the vision was obscured as if by giant wings and the hook-beaked visage of a whelt glared at me from the basin's depths.

I squeezed my eyes shut. Mahrlys uttered a thin cry and snatched her palm from the handle as if burned.

"It is an evil omen," muttered the aged ossasim on my left, as he peremptorily gestured me away from the caldron's edge.

Not one of us in that hall supposed otherwise.

There was a time of staring around, shattered by the ossasim attending the windlass that rolled closed the ceiling to the night.

Mahrlys, white-faced, spoke a benediction in Mnemaat's name. Then the pale-furred one left by one door with his underlings, and we by the great carven ones. When they had shut behind us and we stood in the torchlit hall, Sereth brazenly demanded of Mahrlys how long Deilcrit had been gone.

This Eviduey answered smoothly, before Mahrlys

could retort, "A day and night and half a day again." His wings were half-raised, his eyes the brighter for the uncertain illumination, and he bade us accompany him in the same breath with which he answered Sereth.

Inscrutably, Sereth assented, taking me firmly by the arm. I had no idea what course he intended to pursue in this affair. Nor had I thought much about it: I had been watching Chayin. He in turn was intent upon Mahrlys, every muscle of his form dedicated to communicating to her his desire, his desirability, his magnificence, and his strength. I found it strange to see these introductory intimacies lavished upon another, the slight brushings of limbs and inclinations of head I had previously thought restricted to myself alone. I turned from it at Sereth's urging wearily, not pleased with the dismayed rustlings prowling my stomach. I deemed them jealousy, and jealousy they seemed to be, and I spent the walk back to our quarters sunk in a self-castigation the crueler for my error. It was not jealousy; it was owkahen's advice and assessment of what I saw between Chayin and Mahrlys, but I did not trust myself. Nor did I trust the Eye of Mnemaat, rather assuming that the psionic device had picked Chayin's prophecy from his mind and displayed it to us all.

How subtle owkahen is, to display before us a raging tornado that it may suck unheeded from our path the pearl of knowledge before we stumble upon it. And we see the tornado and battle the affront and congratulate ourselves afterward that we have triumphed, while we have truly suffered the most ignominious of defeats, uncomprehending.

What I could at that time not comprehend was what Sereth intended for me and for Eviduey, Third Hand, Follower of Mnemaat.

Upon our way to our sparsely furnished chamber,

the ossasim detailed with conciliating candor all that Sereth asked of the trail to Othdaliee, wings fluttering relaxed in an easy drape over his arms. I was more conscious than I had previously been of the ossasim's size: he was of Chayin's stature, carrying perhaps a sixth again Sereth's weight.

It was to be expected that this painstaking civility between them would wear thin, and we had barely chased out the torchlighters with their fire pots and closed the doors again when Sereth asked the ossasim point-blank if privacy was required to this satisfaction of local mores, and the ossasim answered:

"Yes. Yes, indeed it is, if you feel it is." He was a splotch of shadow upon the pale carpet, wings draped around him. He spoke cautiously, as he did all else, his every movement calculated to disarm, to present as little threat as possible. "Shall I add," said he, "that I can provide amply for your amusement, or include you herein, or whatever you—"

"Whatever I want is the freedom to travel this keep at will. It is an old and much-storied wonder, and I would explore it."

Rage, dismay, dumbstruck hurt, understanding, paraded through my mind.

"Sereth," I murmured, almost in tears.

He was accepting the silver armlet Eviduey unclasped from about his bicep. His thought, clear as speech, slit the shield I had long been keeping against Wehrdom as if it were a length of Galeshir silk. *"You orchestrated this. Bear some of the cost. I need this reconnaissance."*

He had spoken no word. The ossasim gave no sign that he had caught the exchange. I sat very still in the aftermath of his skills, making no reply as he clasped the armlet about his left arm and wished me tasa and departed, wrapped in his wiles.

Said Eviduey to me, as Sereth pulled the door shut: "Ask me anything."

I went and sat on the low platform, opposite him. I, too, have been long in the Parset Lands. There is something satisfyingly fit in opposing your enemy with every cell of your body.

"What are these powers of which Mahrlys boasts?"

"Open yourself to Wehrdom, as has Chayin, and see for yourself."

"You said ask anything."

"Who can say what power the wehr-spirit will direct us to employ?"

"Is Chayin such a prize, then, that Mahrlys courts him?"

"No more than you would be, to me."

"To you. . . . Is it not the whole of Wehrdom which acts through each? Are not your actions bent toward the greatest good of the whole?"

"You see your fears. Such shallowness is unworthy of you." He stretched out on his side, his bearing radiating a forceful composure divested of any threat.

The torch snapped and spit in its sconce. "I see what is."

"No," he denied. "It is the individual which serves itself. Wehrdom exists thereby; it serves all selves, and its self is complete in the weakest whelt fledgling, or in the meanest of campts."

"I do not understand," I said softly.

"Open yourself and seek understanding. Let me aid you." I could not take my eyes from him, from the slowly stiffening wings, from the grayish circle on his bicep where the armlet had worn away the black fur.

"I thank you, no," I demurred, beginning to realize the untenability of my position. "I am going to explain something to you, about how I feel, about Sereth, about what can and cannot pass between us." And I proceeded to detail his deficiencies in regard to any possible compatibility index, and my particular xenophobic reaction to creatures whose rating on that scale fell below 7.00000, which his most certainly did. I would not have bothered if I had understood the stiffening of his wings in the context of his prostrate, waiting form. There is with ossasim a ritual of stalking which presupposes a facing off: without this decorous commencement there can be no ossasim coupling. When his wings were fully erect, he rose from the mat and began slowly and inexorably to approach me, chest rising and falling deeply, red eyes so filled with black pupil that they seemed almost manlike.

I backed away and pressed against the wall, and, shivering uncontrollably, prepared to strike him down. Once I had boasted that there was in the universe no being capable of desiring me whom I could not fulfill. I had been Well-Keepress; I had given pleasure to thrice a thousand men, given it even to those who were not quite men, those from other stars. But this apparition from a geneticist's nightmare that backed me against the unyielding stone was anathema to my very flesh. I sought a turbulence of killing force as his taloned hand, nails protruding their entire length, sought my breast. I babbled wildly that he must let me bathe, that I could not couch anyone so begrimed. He would not hear me, and as he touched me all that would be forced awry by my application of hesting skills to this moment paraded before my inner eye, and I let the turbulence, now palpably glittering behind his bent head, disperse.

There are some couchings in which one can go elsewhere, if the reality does not suit. This was not one of those. I could not dream him another, not Sereth, not any of my kind. And I could not restrain my need to bite until I tasted his blood, nor to sob epithets in my native tongue; but I did not kill him, nor drop him in flesh-lock, nor open my mind to him and Wehrdom that I might do premature battle, which was what he desired, more even than my use.

They are creatures and they couch like creatures, with a rut that dissolves self and leaves them inarticulate, a mechanism for their own reproductive urge. That mechanism used me until I panted exhausted under it, well past the point where I could struggle against the strength in those slick, pelted shoulders.

I left him scars he will bear evermore on his hide. I came away with fur and flesh under my nails. And with a deep acknowledgment of my kinship to ossasim that my brain and my prejudice would not, indeed still cannot, accept.

"Now, leave me. I have fulfilled your chaldra."

"What?" growled he, not willing yet to remove his imprisoning weight.

"My apologies: a word from my own language. Get you back to your own kind. Your customs can surely demand no more of me!"

Those whiteless red eyes blinked, searched deep, withdrew into a coldness.

"No"—and he sighed and gently rose—"I can demand no more." He rubbed his lacerated shoulder, flapping his flaccid wing impatiently to one side. Then he put his fingers to his mouth, licked the nails free of blood. "I am ... sorry ... that this"—and he gestured aimlessly—"that I was not for you what I intended. Often, these things ... succeed. There is too much lost in time between us." The hurt in his tone metamorphosed, hardened as he spoke.

Unable to stop myself, I asked him again if he would depart. He did not move.

I could not resist it. If he had left when I asked

him, what other tale might I be telling now? But
he did not. My guts churned with horror long
restrained, and in one flashing moment I took that
precipitous leap in the abyss, knowing full well
what owkahen would pay me for my moment of
spite, and willing to bear all I could not dare to
accept when first his taloned nails touched my
breast. Then, I had not known him. Then, I had
not endured his use.

I threw off that blockade that battened down my
mind in the face of Wehrdom's storm. Into their
composite will I sent greetings, and even as he
backed away with stiffened wings, disbelief in his
eyes, I called back the greeting I had sent, and set
it spinning back upon itself with all of Wehrdom's
reply whipping in its wake.

How Wehrdom howled! The sound shook the
very walls of Dey-Ceilneeth as savagely as the arm-
long, spinning turbulence I wielded struck the
ossasim Eviduey. He flew sideways, as if thrown,
which indeed he was. I recollect standing over him
while he lay dazed and helpless, my skills reaching into his sensory network and twisting, until
his body doubled up at my feet and shuddered in
its pain. After a while, as the howls grew louder, I
regained my temper, put sleep upon him, and ran
from the chamber calling Sereth's name.

And collided with him, unseeing, in the torchlit
hall. I struggled wildly until his identity seeped
through my terror, by which time he had us before
Mahrlys' door.

"Stand back," he ordered loudly, for the keening
of the wehrs drew ever closer.

The door dissolved in a snowfall of splintered
rushes before Sereth's onslaught. But I had ceased
to wonder at Sereth's developing skills, and merely
leaped with him through the doorway as the tread

of Wehrdom became a thumping of many bodies running.

Perhaps if he had blasted the door to component atoms, or razed it with heat, we might have noticed the soft powder that drifted down on our heads as we crossed that threshold.

But Chayin lay motionless at Mahrlys' feet, and we skidded to a stop before the cahndor's still form and the black-silked woman who held a sword by the hilt. The blade of that sword lay across Chayin's throat.

"I thought," said she, "that this might be something you would understand." There was an infinite satisfaction in her voice, one not clear to me until everything else became unclear, until between breaths all the room undulated as if seen through deep water and my knees quaked beneath my weight and I slumped forward, my hand outstretched to Sereth, a warning unspeakable on my lips. As I fell groggy to my hands and knees, I heard her further remark: "Yes, you understand steel, and it seems you understand fahrass. Go, then, to the step-sisters' embrace."

I went, only at the last understanding the significance of the powder that had fallen upon our heads and made its way into our lungs, unnoticed, moments before.

VI

Nothrace By Night

"Let me assure you," grunted Laonan, swinging the sword scythelike, "that I appreciate ..." The fhrefrasil, squealing, fell, holding its entrails. Another manlike, agile combatant leaped toward Laonan, slavering jaws wide.

"... that I appreciate ..." Laonan grated again, kicking a severed arm from between his feet. "... your having freed me from Dey-Ceil ... My mother!" Another score of the shoulder-high, rust-pelted fhrefrasil dropped from the trees.

"Watch," advised Deilcrit, and slashed behind Laonan, even as he turned, to skewer a bludgeon-wielding beast who dropped silent from an overhanging branch.

Laonan sidestepped and grimly halved another as it charged. "Like I was saying," he rasped, paused on the balls of his feet while the howling fhrefrasil hopped up and down, brandishing staves and clubs and vine-tailed stones for throwing. "I do not mean to sound ungrateful, but how long do you think we can stand against these odds?"

Deilcrit grimly surveyed the thirty-two fhrefrasil, wiped his brow with a gory forearm. "I had not thought about it at all. You will doubtless outlast me. It is I who am in your debt, for leading you into this. If I were you, I would not appreciate me—."

"Death is better than bondage. Watch—they'll come now."

The fhrefrasil spread in a half-circle, two deep, about them. Some searched the ground and re-armed themselves. Others waited, yellow eyes blinking.

It was quite plain to both of them that they could not survive a rush by all that massed against them.

"One thing pleases," spat Laonan in a snarl as the fhrefrasil continued to hesitate, motionless, like a single being.

"What is that?" grunted Deilcrit, easing himself sideward, shifting the jeweled hilt in hands whose blisters had already bled.

"You're no wehr. Or wehr-pawn, either. That had me worried."

"And I . . ."

The fhrefrasil lunged forward in a wave. The green sword sang and thwacked, and blood spat-tered his eyes and he screamed words whose mean-ing he did not know as a stave caught him across the temple. Reeling into Laonan, he heard his own bellowed demand: "Stop!"

The ground rushed toward him. He grabbed Laonan's waist, expecting momentarily the rip of demon claws, the fire of teeth biting deep, the explosion of bludgeon shattering his skull.

He staggered, released Laonan, regained his feet.

The fhrefrasil, each and all, stood poised. From their midst came a whine, slow at first and then growing.

Laonan cast him a wary, wild-eyed look that brought them shoulder to shoulder, blades at ready.

The fhrefrasil, hunched and crying, backed step by step toward the trees.

He could feel the thrill run through his companion's flesh.

"What in the name of Fai Teraer-Moyhe . . . ?" hissed Laonan.

Deilcrit took one step, then another, in the direction of the retreating fhrefrasil. The whine changed to a hiss that susurrused among the trees.

"No! Stay still," pleaded Laonan. An iron grip closed on Deilcrit's shoulder. He shook it off, but he did not advance any farther toward the fhrefrasil disappearing among the trees.

He turned to Laonan, and with a voice naked and hopeless, in which rode all his tortures and his fears, said: "Tell me again that I am not a wehr." And he threw the green sword to the forest's floor, and knelt down, staring blankly at the inscription which slithered indecipherable along its cutting edge.

They were barely a half-day's journey north of Mnemaat's Wall.

He heard Laonan crouching beside, felt the rough pinch of the man's fingers once more on his arm. "Deilcrit, man, this is no time to get superstitious. It was great fortune we had, that was all." And, in response to Deilcrit's negation, "And if it was not that, we will figure upon it. By a nice fire in a good brick holding with some soup in our bellies. I have friends. It grows late. We should waste no light here, but strike out. If we leave now, we could be in Northrace by night."

"We? Have you not had enough of my troubles?"

"Boy, I would have sat in that damnable hole until my teeth fell out. I can spare you my sword arm on as hard a journey as Othdaliee. I've been twelve years in retirement; my own business is going to take a bit of resurrection. Come on. Nothrace awaits."

As Laonan shook his shoulder, something occurred to him: "I was born in Nothrace. Eviduey told me."

"Shan't be much of a homecoming. Those that live there now—if they still do . . . it's twelve years, remember—moved in after the wehr-rage killed the Nothrace to a man. How came you to escape it?" This was suddenly very cool, and slow, and as he spoke Laonan took his hands from Deilcrit's shoulders and began to trace the writing on the green sword's blade. Something flared in Deilcrit: outrage, indignity. It took great effort for him not to snatch the sword from under Laonan's hand. But he did not, only unconcernedly stretched out his raw palm to ease it up from the sod.

"How, I do not know, except that I was dedicated to Benegua and delivered there shortly before the Nothrace tragedy. I would not recognize kin there, if they all lived yet: I do not know my mother's name, I have no memories before Benegua. But I would still like to see it. . . ." Holding the sword, he felt somehow in command of more than a weapon. "No man has ever returned from Othdaliee. I am going to." Deilcrit rose and sheathed the blade in a single motion, jostling Laonan as he did so. "And when I return from there, do you know what I will do?" Their eyes locked, and each saw truth in the other's.

"No," said Laonan very softly. "What will you do?"

"I will put Mahrlys-iis-Vahais at my feet."

"Will you, now?" The voice was warm, thoughtful. Laonan stroked his burred beard. "I believe you just might. Eviduey, Third Hand, Follower of Mnemaat"—and he spat those words with a venom that made Deilcrit examine his companion anew—"will not like that at all. In fact, he might not live through it. . . . Deilcrit?"

"I care not for Eviduey. I will make a drum from

the stretched hide of his wings, and use it to call my children." That voice, choked with fury, he hardly knew as his own.

"Deilcrit," repeated Laonan. "If indeed that is what you are about, I can promise you my own sword and some few others. How few, I cannot say. But many I knew twelve years ago would have hewn their way through thrice that many fhrefrasil to win a place on such a battle line."

Deilcrit turned away, walked among the memnis, ran a hand over the silvery bark.

"Are you saying you could not use my aid?" demanded Laonan, behind him.

"No, I am not saying that. I am saying only this: you speak of blood to fill buckets, and it would be bloodier than even you can conceive. I spoke in haste, in battle heat. Let us first return from Othdaliee; then if you still wish to offer yourself further, offer. We may neither be in the position to offer anything to anyone."

"You will accept my sword, then, until we have quit Othdaliee?"

"I will welcome it. How not?" But he said it absently, for he heard again the whelt's words in his mind: *"Allow me to guide you, when that is past, to accompany you, when that, too, is gone, to follow."*

The trail to Nothrace is hard. She lies at Mt. Imnetosh's foot, in the splay between the giantess's big toe and her long one, on a coastal cliff so precipitous that she could never make use of the fingers encroaching from the sea. The tide is fierce and the spume breeds fog, and Nothrace's bare bones gleamed muzzily through her cold, wet shroud.

He was past wonder at his acceptance of Laonan's aid. He had added the man to his soul's burden. The matter was a fact, and by the law to which he yet subscribed, immutable. But the rest; his grandiose boasting; his communion with the jewel-hilted sword; his exhilaration in his slaughter! And worse: the creature he sensed himself becoming; he who yet stood at the horizon of his mental line of sight. It was *he* who had spoken of blood in overslopping panniers and of vengeance man must never dream.

He was wet and he was tired and he was hungry and he was numb from flogging himself with his crimes. He said: "And tomorrow you will accept them, as you did the ravishment of women, as you have all else. You are sinking, but into what?"

"I did not hear," said Laonan, relieved at what seemed the end of Deilcrit's long withdrawal.

"You were not meant to. I spoke to myself. I am used to being alone. What is that?" He pointed to a more brightly lit patch of fog than that about them.

"Nothrace." They saw each other by eye-white's flash and silvered shadow in the gibbous moon's glow. In that glow Laonan's teeth glimmered as he grinned and clapped Deilcrit on his left shoulder. Deilcrit winced, and growled at his companion to take care of the arm.

To which Laonan replied that it had not notice-ably impeded him in the fighting. "Where did you learn to use a sword like that? Not in Benegua, surely. I have heard and seen that none are al-lowed there." The implication was that this was the truth whose difficult lesson he had learned in the bowels of Dey-Ceilneeth.

"I do not know," said Deilcrit shortly, and an-swered no further query until Laonan bade him wait in the shelter of the undergrowth while Laonan alone knocked upon the planks of the hut's door, through which light streamed to slat the dark.

To this Deilcrit would not agree, and after a protracted quarrel in whispers as to whose responsibility to whom entailed what, the door opened on its own.

A hunched figure stood there, backlit, a poker or thin staff in its hand.

"Laonan?" she called softly, as if blessed with night vision.

"Laore's child. Do your ears hear?" Laonan replied in a singsong.

"I have cut them off and laid them upon the sand," she shot back without a hesitation.

He whom Deilcrit had known as Laonan heaved a mighty, satisfied sigh. "Blessed be He, some things never change. It's safe. We can go in."

"How do you know, after twelve years?" hissed Deilcrit, setting his heels like a recalcitrant draft beast, ready to take up the argument once more.

"She told me: Identification: response. Query for shelter; acceptance thereof."

He waited a time wherein Deilcrit only breathed and regarded him steadily.

"Come, now, Deilcrit. Two and two are four, so they say. You've surely got me figured out by now. I'm surprised you think I'm this stupid."

And with that he strode out into the square of light and stood talking with the woman on her threshold.

The two went in, leaving the doorway wide, and soon he smelled a savory broth on the fire, and his stomach pleaded in low churning rumbles.

He ignored his hunger as long as he could. For a while it was overpowered by his fear of the unknown, a fear that seeped back whenever the commanding assurance that more and more frequently swept him was gone. He had been less than thirty days out of his swath of forest near the Spirit Gate. He fought homesickness like quicksand. Almost, he tore headlong through the woods for his bower. But the impossibility of taking up that life ever again hit him like a cold slap of seawater and left him once more hungry, disfranchised, alone.

With a growl and a mumbled prayer that Parpis' ghost attend him, he walked into the hut of the woman of Nothrace.

Actually, it was women, for there were three. They were all of the same family, three generations of a beauty that slipped almost unchanged from granddam to mother to child. But the child was no child in fleshly measuring, and he steeled himself, lest the lust that had thrice overtaken him catch him up and he dishonor himself and spill his pollution on this house that succored him.

The girl's name was Heicrey. She had sunset hair and an aristocratic nose and thighs like a young memnis.

Her mother was Lohr-Ememna, and he truly believed the woman to be what her name declared: Vessel of Faith. She was enraptured, transfixed with hopeless hope fulfilled, there with Laonan beside her after an absence most had sworn meant death. The Spirit was in her and she hummed in a soft low voice as her mate told his tale to them, rocking back and forth at his feet, her head against his knee.

The third woman, Amnidia, was aged as Dey-Ceilneeth's towers, with a face that had been refolded by Mnemaat's artistry into a Wisdom Mask the glory of which none possessed in the most orthodox of temples. From hollows deep as the night sky her bright eyes peered out, missing nothing. She rocked back and forth by the hearth on the room's only padded stool, carding wool and subjecting Deilcrit to a straightforward scrutiny that made him sure to close his mouth as he ate, careful not to slurp.

The lithe Heicrey collected the meal's remains, preparing to take the bowls outside to wash. He rose to go with her, offering himself. She smiled, and let her eyes flicker against his.

"*You will not!*" aspirated the old woman for the first time that evening, in a voice firm and querulous and clipped. "Sit down, Deilcrit, and talk to me. Quendros, walk your daughter to the well." And the man whom Deilcrit had known as Laonan slid the bar back from the door and pulled it open. Then with a low bow and his daughter's answering giggle, the two melted into the night.

"Lohr-Ememna, see if you can card wool in the dark," commanded the hunched and ancient woman.

"Mother!" objected Quendros' woman, but she took from her dam the raw wool and the started card and pulled the door shut behind her.

"Deilcrit, come closer." He did, and sat upon the edge of the hearth with his back to the whispering coals, attentive.

Her skin was a chronicle of her days, and he found the settlings of her face majestic. In the dignity of her, he read wisdom. In the sharpness of her, he read knowledge. In the set of her words, he read revelation. And he did not like it.

"Deilcrit, lay hand upon my grandchild, and though you have saved Quendros, I will slit your throat with my own hands. I will . . ." And he stared at that gnarled and clawed curl of fingers that shook before his face.

"Old woman—"

"That is right!" She grabbed him by the tunic and pulled him against her sharp knee. "I am an old woman, and I was a Wise Woman once. Do you know what that means, heathen?"

He stammered that he did not.

"It means that I know about you. And I know what kind of living death you have granted my daughter's mate." She let go of him. He crumpled into a heap at her feet, stunned.

"Woman, why do you say these things to me?"

"Because you will feed my Quendros to Wehrdom, and plant its awful stigma in poor Heicrey's belly, if I let you."

"No!"

"I was *there* when Imca-Sorr ordered the destruction of every child, woman, and man in Nothrace. I was on Mt. Imnetosh with two others. I was a Wise Woman. I tried with all my might to save what hope we could. Do you know what hope I mean?"

"No."

"Imca-Sorr saw dire threat in Nothrace. We supposed it a human nemesis. We tried to save that child whose birth had been foretold, that changer of destinies, unheedful of the warnings that, as seeking became reality, the omens began to provide. But you see, we were very wrong in our interpretation." She rose, trembling visibly, and got wine from the sideboard.

She allowed him to pour it for her, and the normalcy of the action helped him ease the dizziness he felt. His mouth was very dry, and the wine slid down his aching throat like salvation. He took only a taste, remembering his previous faring with wine, but it warmed.

She, too, seemed bettered when she had drunk.

"Ah," she whistled and laid the diminutive cup on the hearth, "things will right themselves. To each comes one chance to erase an error, repair a fault, pay a debt." Her eyes seemed to wander, and her breathing quickened.

"Ipheri, explain to me how you were wrong, what interpretation I should see for these facts that yield no knowledge. Please." He pressed her hand, hearing the chatter of Heicrey and her father's maundering tones and the musical one of his mate.

"Please," he begged as the door scraped slowly, cautiously open.

"What interpretation, wehr? Even on the door-step of your death you jest with me? Do you not seek Othdaliee and the carnelian throne? I—"

"Mother, this is enough!" announced Lohr-Ememna, sticking head and shoulders through the doorway. "You are . . . Mother?"

Deilcrit, black lights obscuring his vision, tried to stop the old woman's body's insensible fall. Then he tried to stop his own. Then he only listened from a great distance.

"Quendros, that vial there, quickly!" Sobs. "What possessed her?"

"Hush your tears, Lohr. She felt no pain. She chose her own time. Be as brave. Here, open his mouth, quickly. He is breathing. He is large and strong." He felt his head lifted, something poured between his teeth, choking him with its dry powder. It was bitter. Water followed. He swallowed eagerly, glad to wash the salty sludge down.

When he could see again, the insect buzz in his ears resolved into a grieving Lohr-Ememna and Quendros' low service over a shrouded corpse that took up most of the hut's floor.

That was when it hit him: Quendros was not *Laonan*, but *a* Laonan; an infidel; devil-demon; a mage. But as the antidote took hold and he struggled erect in Heicrey's solicitous arms, he reasoned that the man was no more threat then he had been before. The Laonan sect was so long ago swallowed in the mists of time that even faced with a household of them, he could not recall its tenets.

The body was buried, in its own faith, out beside the hut.

He enjoyed the digging; it was thoughtless, healing work, good for his arm. In that thoughtlessness he felt elation that the woman was dead and he lived. He felt no sorrow, no distress over what she had done and said. She was a demented crone who sought suicide. Nor would he let Quendros—he struggled over attaching this new and foreign name to his cellmate—slip from his service. He coveted Quendros' usefulness too much to balk at the man's religion. Then he heard himself, that cold and utterly capable self with whom he battled, and grated aloud: "Quendros, I need help."

"I had thought you might," rejoined that one in a hoarsened voice from the pearly mist across the grave, "but I had not figured the cost this high."

Deilcrit did not immediately answer. He looked at the two women strewn like leaves upon the new-turned mound, weeping. "It is not fitting to grieve so for the dead," he said very softly.

"I will tell them," snapped Quendros, and threw down his pick. "You are at times a difficult man to like," he added, and motioned Deilcrit toward the hut.

"I am not in any way admirable," Deilcrit agreed.

"I would not say that," demurred Quendros. "You are an admirable tactician, a good fighter, charmed beyond belief. I said you are difficult to like."

"I am sorry."

"You would be."

"What of the women?"

"They have fended well enough for twelve years. Shall I now insult them with my pretense that their survival was only luck? Or are we expecting something, say, a wehr-rage?" He thrust his face toward Deilcrit's. Mist swirled between them, lit by the hut's door. "Are we?"

"No," said Deilcrit with utter and complete certainty. And: "Why do you not kill me?" The miserable bleat sprang out of him, unsummoned.

"Over Amnidia? Only one who has never been

espoused could ask such a question." Quendros chuckled, shoving the door closed until only a crack admitted the night's moist mist. He fussed with the fish-oil lamp, refilled it, then set to stirring the fire's embers. "Deilcrit, what did you mean? Just what kind of help do you think you need?" And when that elicited no reply, he twisted around, hunkered down on the balls of his feet, saying, "I can help you fight Wehrdom: I know that battle well. But sometimes you look to me to be fighting *for* it. In that I will not, indeed cannot, aid you. If in truth you are fighting to extricate your soul from Wehrdom's grasp . . . ?" And he let the question hang unfinished, as if, having voiced the horror, he regretted it.

Deilcrit picked a hangnail until it bled, and the blood ran along the course of dirt that blackened his cuticle. He sucked at it, pondering a way to begin, regretful that he had spoken of his distress. But once started, it poured out of him like a flash flood. Somewhere in that telling the two women entered and set about boiling a brew of steeped leaves. He hardly noticed them. He told of his youth in the forest: when about the Children's Trial, in his tenth year, he had been separated from the children's band and first to approach the gates of Nehedra to claim his manhood. As he had come tearing down the path, heart and lungs pounding, a huge form had jumped upon him from the trees. Rolling on the ground, he had found a rock. When he rose and realized that he had smashed the skull of a grown man, he had been terrified. Looking ever and again over his shoulder, alert for the pounding of feet that would be the balance of the children's band, he had rolled the body (for it was too weighty for his youngster's strength to lift or even drag) toward the leaves. When with a final breathless grunt he pushed it once more, it fell into the leaves and disappeared with a crash of broken sticks into a pit that the piled leaves had obscured. He stared at the body in the pit, long uncomprehending, until a growl signified ptaiss about, and he raised his tear-streaked face to his death.

But the ptaiss was growling over a man-size corpse which it worried in the brush, and he staggered backward, away from it, toward the trail, his eyes fastened on Nehedra's mud-brick wall, so close and yet so far. . . .

Then, when he had gained the road's middle, the group of which he was member broke from the thickets, all wild-eyed and running pell-mell toward Nehedra and the maturity that lay beyond the tight-shut gates. It was the only Children's Trial of which he had ever heard during which no children were struck dead by Mnemaat's henchmen.

"So what?" demanded Quendros. "With the exclusion of Beneguan children, all know how Mnemaat's culling takes place. There is nothing supernatural about it. So you killed a man who would have killed not only you but also the first three or four children to complete the course. Good luck and good riddance, is all."

"But you do not see: I was this big!" He laid his hand on the air at about his waist's height. "And the ptaiss killed the other man, while I struggled with the first. And meekly sat there gnawing while all of us ran by. . . . I have been saved from death six . . . no, seven times by wehrs; and that exempts all of this insanity that has come to pass since the Spirit Gate opened."

"What other evidence do you have of wehr-favor?"

Then he told all, and as he confessed his conjectures and his fears, his heart lightened. Somewhere in that exposition the women joined the exchange, first offering gourd cups asteam with a sweet infusion, then adding soundly thought postulations as to what Deilcrit's brushes with Wehrdom and its inarguable predisposition to him might portend. What might in the end be gained concerned them. What risk he ran, what could become of him if Wehrdom's soft touch in his mind became a strident command which he could not disobey, did not: they sighted his strength of character and his very nature as protection enough.

But Quendros did not add to this lighthearted comfort they offered. His former cellmate grew contemplative and somber. He picked his teeth with a charred splinter and scratched himself, and occasionally his mouth twitched in a grimace whose meaning Deilcrit could not read.

When his words grew bleary and the conversation dribbled to a halt, Quendros supposed that Deilcrit might have the just-departed Amnidia's bed, a straw heap under a blanket near the hearth. They, Quendros and Lohr-Ememna, made exit through a low, curtained doorway that was set in the hearthside wall, beyond which lay a shallow dormered eave.

Heicrey fussed over the low, banked blaze, her curtate brown robe gathered close, her unbound hair a cascade about her hips.

He looked at the curtain still swaying slightly, behind which her father and mother lay, and softly denied the cup she held out to him almost shyly. Her eyes were deep and dark as new-turned earth, like ancient Amnidia's.

He shifted uncomfortably and started to pull off the crude canvas boots given him in Dey-Ceilneeth. Astoundingly, she moved to aid him. Not knowing how to stop her, he allowed it, thinking of what the old woman had said to him in her dying breaths.

"Have I taken your bed?" he asked when he could stand the awkward silence no longer.

"No," breathed she, who scraped with her finger at the mud which caked his boots. "I sleep there." And she pointed to a second waist-high door, this one of ill-fitting planks, on the hearth's far side.

"Then you had better do so," he growled roughly.

With downcast eyes she turned and rose from her knees and banked the fire as suits for an easy rest, and rustled wraithlike past him in the gloom. There was a creak from the darkness as she pulled open her dormer's low door, and then nothing.

He sighed and lay back, hands under his head, and closed his eyes. After much tossing and turning, he sat bolt upright and stripped off the rough sword belt which insisted on jabbing him, and the binding, ill-fitting tunic, then took the rolled blanket at the pallet's head and spread it over himself.

He was at dream's elusive gate when a swishing noise resounded in that echo chamber on sleep's threshold.

He held very still, wishing the embers threw light. Then the blanket was lifted and her firm little breasts burned against his chest. He turned his head slightly and she froze immobile. So did he. After a dozen breaths she eased her length against him and glided one thigh over his own.

It occurred to him that she yet might leave if he pretended not to wake, but he could not suppress the smile that touched him. Unmoving, his hands under his head, lying on his back with her bent leg thrown over him, he awaited what would develop, his eyes wide to the darkness.

She was delicate, persuasive, her movements eloquent. After a time he drew his right hand from under him and wound it in her hair.

Later, he chased her back to her own straw, when the dawn birds whispered their sleepy tentative songs. He slept then deeply, dreamlessly, and

awakened to scents of boiling grain and Quendros'
homely banter.

He rose and pulled on his garments amid jibes
as to the lateness of the hour, all the while wondering how Quendros' rawboned, lumbering mass
could have spawned anything as delicate and supple as the girl-child Heicrey. Then, only, he remembered to be embarrassed by his near-nakedness
before that one's mother, and abashed at his cozen-
ing abuse of the pair's hospitality.

But it lasted only a moment before the well-
being he felt, and when Heicrey herself entered,
rubbing sleep from her eyes, it was as if a ray of
sun had struck him in the face.

Her discreetness shamed him, and he struggled
to emulate it, but his eyes repossessed her and he
resented with all his heart the knowledge of her
that darkness had veiled from him.

It was not long after the meal that he contrived
to speak with Quendros alone.

"Tell me about the Laonan faith," he began
awkwardly.

"Which facet?" Quendros teased. They were chop-
ping kindling. Deilcrit attributed the other's bared
teeth and squinting eyes to the sun's bright rays. In
the daylight the hovel was poor, flaking, cracked,
a three-humped overturned piece of pottery bak-
ing in the sun. *Thunk*! went Quendros' huge bronze
ax. "*Thunk!*" replied his own.

"What are your betrothal vows?" he blurted
out.

"Son," grunted Quendros between strokes that
would have felled whole trees, "you're a miserable
risk, not much in the way of temptation to a
woman's eye. What have you?" He leaned upon
the ax and wiped his sweat-soaked hair from his
eyes. "Not even your life's sure. You'd have her to
ask, y'know. 'Tis not my place to intervene. But

these battle-brink couplings are often born of
desperation. Nothing comes of them but grief. If I
were her, I'd not hear you till you're back from
Othdaliee. And then maybe I'd not." He snorted,
hawked. "But I'm no woman."

"And it would not anger you?"

Quendros regarded him narrowly, stroked his
just-shaven chin reflectively. "Now, that's up to
you, isn't it? What you make of it, I mean. If you're
not out to harm her, and if you'd be to her what a
woman requires of a man, who am I to object? But
if you're deceiving me ..." He leaned close, so
close Deilcrit could gauge the procession of rot in
his front tooth. "Then I would ... do whatever
seems just. I'm no Wise Woman, to read the future.
It's on you, to read your intent."

Deilcrit drew in the dust with his booted foot,
then met Quendros' glare once more. "I cannot say
what I will do. That is what I have been trying to
tell you.... Things are happening to me that I
cannot control. I want a thing, and it occurs and
brings great trials, and then I must want something else to survive the trial, and then I am in
worse straits than before. I cannot say...."

"Why not wait and see?"

"I cannot." It was wrenched from him through
clenched teeth. "I must either have her, or leave
this night."

"That bad, eh?"

Deilcrit grunted an affirmation.

"Well, ask her mother, boy, is all I can suggest...."
But Kirelli's abrupt descent wiped the rapine grin
from the big black-haired man as if it had never
been.

"Oh, Kirelli," Deilcrit pleaded silently, *"please,
not now."* And with a soft "Kreesh, breet," the
whelt circled once about his head and was gone
heavenward.

Filled with thanksgiving, he squinted after the receding dot until it was lost in the greening sky. Then he turned from Quendros, who again chopped wood with a fervor that spat chips, and hurried to the hut, that he might speak with Heicrey's mother before his courage left him or Quendros changed his mind.

Lohr-Ememna dashed his hopes into sharp, glittering shards, and as if she sensed this, she was excruciatingly careful as to where her words trod: "Deilcrit, I cannot, as a Wise Woman, condone this match. It is to be hoped that you will understand that Laonan vows are sacred vows, and that if you later care to take up the study, things might change."

They both knew this to be an excuse. Her tired countenance pleaded with him not to press the matter.

He retired to ponder whether Woman's Word could be binding upon him if the Woman herself was not bound by his laws.

Then, decided, he chased down Quendros, who wandered by the cliff's edge where crumbled Nothrace overlooked the sea.

There were tumbled buildings once tall as the maze around Dey-Ceilneeth, great ways of rubble among which quenel and roema, their smaller, scavenging cousins, hissed and spat and slunk. There was a spray salty in his nostrils, a drizzle blown inward from the sea that intensified as midday and its rain approached.

When Deilcrit came upon him, around the twisting of a hovel's one remaining angled wall, Quendros was seated on a heap of clay bricks, listening to the thunder of the waves as they sought to climb the cliff's face.

To his right and rear, Othdaliee squatted, as always enwrapped in mist and cloud. She is not high when judged from land's height, but at the Northrace ledge, where her skirts drop sheer to the sea, her true proportions are revealed.

He sat by Quendros' side. His face must have bespoken his disappointment.

"We will leave soon, then?" ventured Quendros, scanning the choppy waves far below.

"We, or I."

"We, lad. You have my word. But the day is half-spent. Rest another night."

He squeezed his eye shut upon hearing that, and knew he did not have the strength to refuse.

"If you must," he acquiesced without emotion, suddenly very tired.

Quendros clapped him upon the back and rubbed his shoulderblades. "That's a good one; it never pays to fight fate."

"Are you sure?" he retorted, somber.

"No," murmured Quendros, rising abruptly to stretch. "I am not sure. I am sure of less and less the longer I live. But of one thing I am sure: even one woman cannot flaunt another in matters of the heart. And speaking of matters of the heart, I have some deep matters to discuss with Lohr-Ememna before I take the trail. She is a difficult taskmistress, but her touch fortifies." And he stretched a stretch that creaked bone, and set off down the ruin-strewn street.

He spent the midday there wandering among Nothrace's ghosts, turning a chunk of rubble here, a bleached bone there, seeking some feeling that might tell him he was home. He peered in twice a score of empty doorways, even three which were not empty. In one of these the door was slammed in his face. At the lintel of two others he was forced to explain his presence. Each time, he used the Laonan/Laore exchange formula he had heard Quendros use with Amnidia.

Only later it occurred to him that he might have been endangered. At the time, he was calm and secure and unconcerned.

He unearthed a verdigris-eaten knife hilt in an empty, three-windowed hut of stones calked with clay. Its floor was three concentric sunken ledges, and it was in the bottommost of these that he was kneeling, scratching among the soft, loose dirt. The top half of a skull and some far-scattered human bones told him how the occupant had died: the skull casing was shattered, bones cracked for marrow. He lounged easy under its mournful stare, digging in the cool sand with the ancient knife.

Outside, the steady drum of afternoon rain commenced, and all around him the shadows lost definition. But he was dry and warm within the hut, which leaked in only four places. He spent a long time watching the water drip from among the ceiling stones, wondering how the rocks could have been cajoled into assuming the arch of an inverted bowl.

She tinkled: "Deilcrit, I have searched everywhere," and ran lightly down the stepped flooring.

Her red-gold hair was darkened, plastered to her head with rain. Water streamed from the end of her braid. She reminded him, in that moment, her face alight with joy and dappled with raindrops, of the spirit power Estri. He shook the specter aside, reached up, and sluiced a drop from her nose. "How dare you chase after me in the rain? Your mother will have both our hides."

She blinked at his severity, and crouched beside him, pressing her head to his chest. He took her tiny, icy hands, both of hers in one of his own.

"Please do not send me away," she pleaded, her lips finding his throat.

"In daylight? Never." He chuckled, and set about extricating her from her sopping robes.

She was not the fine-honed Estri, nor the soul-sating cup that was Mahrlys, but her slim thighs hugged him and her shapely arms wrapped him around and her hard little belly heaved with her abandon.

Mindful of his predicament, he sent her home and waited a suitable interval, hoping that she obeyed him and bathed before entering her mother's presence.

He was lying back, counting the moments' passage and enduring his arm's complaint of the dampness, when the whelt alighted in one of the three shutterless windows.

"I have been expecting you," he said, almost relieved. "Was it you who routed the fhrefrasil just beyond Mnemaat's Wall?" Three more whelts appeared in the window just left of Kirelli's perch.

Deilcrit ignored them. "Was it?" he demanded, and opened his mind to Kirelli as if he did it thrice a day before meals.

A whisper sounded within his inner ear, and though he looked upon the silver-beaked whelt in the window, a flowing mass of visions passed leisurely across his sight, each one somehow filled with enlightenment that came in great reams enwrapped in single words.

The whelt touch whispered "no" and he was inundated with a whelt's-eye view of what had transpired in the battle with the fhrefrasil. And the respect with which the whelt viewed him, the patience with which it awaited his awakening, told him more than a hundred parables.

He saw the Eye of Mnemaat, and the carnelian throne pictured therein. "Take it up, for yourself, for your destined conscription into Mnemaat's service, for us all," sighed Kirelli's thought astride a low twittering that filled his ears.

And he saw Mahrlys, and Eviduey, and what

else opposed him. And in an unreeling of the years gone by, he saw what factions dwelt in Wehrdom, what perversions of its strength the Dey-Ceilneeth coterie expounded; what Kirelli's folk decried and obstructed: "Such determination by the few for the good of the many only services the few. Wehrdom cracks asunder like a melon overripe, and only a digging out of the putrefaction will keep the whole fruit from rotting away." Thus did he hear the prince of wehrs; but it was what he saw chronicled of that long struggle which cried out to him that here was no choice but a duty.

Or was it the part of him that had been readying itself for this moment since his birth?

This final horror, the fear of losing self that had crippled him thus far in his journey, having gasped out its ultimate defense, slunk away before Kirelli's desperate fury.

The whelt hopped to the earthen floor and danced upon it, wings outstretched, kreeshing. Behind, others filled its vacated perch, and in the third window the paws and slitted eyes and tiny black fingers of quenel and roema and even a ptaiss' twitching ears could be seen.

But Deilcrit saw only the whelt Kirelli, who had so long sought his bond.

And through those squawks and squeaks and the mind-touch that deciphered them he heard the tenets of those of Wehrdom who sought him, and found them to be acceptable, conversant with his own. The blur that was Kirelli's wings aflutter showed him a great maw yawning amid the sharp-spired gardens of Othdaliee, and he heard tell of the wonderful creations housed within. And the danger. And the death that was not death, but a different sort of life.

And he shuddered then, and unconsciously drew his limbs about him, as the whelt danced the details of his days in the packed earth of a Nothrace ruin.

But the whelt's intelligence spoke on: of the shadowy unknowables, of might-be and must-not-be, of the unalterable limits within which all to follow must take place, or die stillborn.

"Some have flown by and seen that the portals are still open, but all haste! Soon Othdaliee will be impassable, closed up for a thousand years."

"And what if the doors should close?" He formed the wehr-thought hesitantly, discomfited by the easy proficiency his mind displayed.

"If the door should close," twittered the whelt, its head cocked, green eyes blinking, "then Mahrlys and Eviduey and theirs will triumph and you and I and all who oppose them shall perish in the greatest wehr-rage Aehre-Kanoss has ever suffered. Wehrdom shall be only one-sided, and that dedicated to the endurance of the group who will then rule her."

"And what," stormed Deilcrit's wehr-voice, ringing in all their inner ears so that Kirelli hopped backward and squawked in alarm, "of Imca-Sorr-Aat? Has not Mnemaat a hand to lend?"

"Mnemaat is no more. Imca-Sorr is an empty title, a vacant throne with no presence worthy of the honorific 'Aat' to guide it."

"I see," said the wehr-voice of Deilcrit, and he did.

There passed between them then some assessment of dangers awaiting, and all the while the wehrs gathered, until when at last he extended his arm to Kirelli and the whelt flapped to his right shoulder, the windows were black with them.

Careful of the whelt riding him, he walked up the ledges to the hovel's door. Around the stone hut they crowded, ptaiss and fhrefrasil and campt and berceide and even ossasim and guenel and roema. He heard the far-off wailing of fear from the hut whose door had been shut in his face, and he grinned without humor and reached up and smoothed Kirelli's raised crest.

He halted for a moment before those gathered to pay him homage, then made his way through them to the over-look where he had previously sat by Quendros and pondered questions whose answers had not been in man's ken.

Those adherents of Kirelli, those wehrs who were also his, followed after like the white wake of a bark.

At the very edge of the precipitous drop he halted. A thousand lengths below, guerm churned the water, phosphorescent, wriggling like snakes in a basket, slithering on one another's backs, leaping from the surf that they might better see what scanned them from the cliff's height.

After a time, he waved his hand and the sea subsided. He turned to the gathered wehrs, dismissed them, and they were gone.

Then he strode through the rubble of Nothrace, with Kirelli on his right shoulder, toward the hut wherein awaited his human ally, Quendros.

But when almost upon it, he slowed, and spoke gentle commands to Kirelli, and sent the whelt to wait in the trees that circled the hovel round.

The reason that he did this was a portent in the form of shrill and angry voices that split the air of the waning day.

It was Lohr-Ememna's voice that was the loudest, and hence her tirade which first made sense to him: "... And if *you* want to succor some red-eyed hairy bastard, you go ahead! But not in this house! I will not have it. The shame! I—"

Then Heicrey's falsetto bleat: "Father, do not let her make me do this. I beg you. Please!"

And Quendros at the same time: "Silence, the both! Let me think!"

And though there was not silence, there was moderation of tone, and he could make out no more words, just voices and Heicrey's sobbing wail.

With a curse upon the sharp noses of women and their power, he sneaked to the hut's door and flattened himself beside it, attempting to sort matters out in the light of what Wehrdom had revealed. Mahrlys' face came to him as if her very presence hovered beside. At length, not pleased with what he had discovered, and not knowing what he would do, he took advantage of a break in Lohr-Ememna's marginally lessened ranting and shoved open the door.

The three froze, Lohr-Ememna with her mouth open.

Heicrey's shivering form was huddled in a corner, her whole countenance red and swollen, hands balled into fists, hugging herself.

Lohr-Ememna wrung her fingers and closed her mouth.

Quendros looked very slowly over his shoulder, as if to make sure he in the doorway was really Deilcrit. Then, his lips twisted in disgust, he raked his hand through his hair, ordered Deilcrit to shut the door, and strode to the sideboard, where he uncorked a large clay rhyton and drank deeply from it.

Deilcrit leaned against the door he had closed, arms folded, his eyes flitting from Heicrey, who had her fist stuffed into her mouth in an effort to check her hysteria; to Lohr-Ememna, who seemed about to attack with tooth and nail; to Quendros, who had not yet fallen down dead from the stuff he had drunk.

Instead, Quendros drew near, pushing Lohr-Ememna roughly toward a corner. The woman, with a ptaisslike hiss, sank down there, her face covered by her hands.

Deilcrit shook his head mutely to the earthen vessel Quendros extended.

"Drink it, idiot. It's not poison. You're going to need it."

Deilcrit did that under the pitying, exasperated scrutiny of Quendros, whose great frame rocked with suppressed emotion. "Wise as a guerm's anus, aren't you?" he rumbled, low.

And when Deilcrit only returned his glare with a stricken blink, he ordered him to sit down and have another drink.

This, too, Deilcrit did, settling self-consciously down cross-legged before the hearth.

Quendros pulled the padded stool under him, and summoned his daughter with a resounding snarl. Hiccuping, the girl swayed before her father, at his order took seat on the cold hearth's edge.

Quenros looked from one to the other and rubbed his face with his palms. "Well, you two, you've done it for good and fair. Now I'm going to tell you both some things I maybe should have told you before, but—"

"Quendros, you cannot allow this disgrace—"

"Woman," snarled Quendros at his spouse, "I will shut you up if you make me. They don't understand. . . . He certainly didn't know, and you're deep in this yourself from having kept silent. Now, repeat the tactic, and you just might equalize things."

Deilcrit, amazed, twisted around to see what the woman would do. But she was no Beneguan woman: she muttered, only, and obeyed.

"Now, my spouse is not unjustly upset—"

"Father!"

"You, too, amorous one. If you had paid more attention to your studies and less to your puberty, you'd have had enough sense to know without being told, after all that has occurred."

The girl started to cry, fat tears racing down her cheeks.

"All right, that's not wholly fair, but—"

"Quendros," interrupted Deilcrit, fortified by the drink, which with each swallow eased him more, "you know how I feel ..." And he let it hang, because he did not really feel that way at all; not now.

But, even if a half-truth, it was the right thing to say.

Quendros smiled glumly. "Yes, son, I know. And it's a pity, but ... Look: did you know Amnidia was the woman who diapered you cross-country to Benegua? Neither did I. Lohr-Ememna knew, though, and to her that explains why Amnidia sought your death with her own."

Deilcrit had that piece of the puzzle: the Laonans esteemed the race of man above all others, and had misconstrued him as its instrument. But he did not say that, or anything. The creature he had been long becoming was wiser than that. It kept silent.

"Lohr-Ememna couldn't help overhearing what passed between you two: Amnidia called you wehr, and worse. Do you, as she accused, seek the carnelian throne?"

Only the day before, he would have been at a loss to answer. He said: "Yes."

Quendros hunched over on the stool, elbows on his knees, hands clasped. "You say that, understanding that no human, no man, can ever reign from Othdaliee?"

He shrugged.

"I told you!" screamed Lohr-Ememna, charging toward him.

As Deilcrit scrambled back, Quendros caught his

woman and held her until her struggles subsided and she leaned against him in a paroxysm of grief.

Heicrey, chin on her drawn-up knees, looked on Deilcrit from out of the shock of betrayal. "I thought she was wrong," the girl whispered, while he wondered where all the water that sprang from her eyes could have been stored.

"She is wrong," he mumbled helplessly, and spread his hands against the urge to hold the wounded girl close.

"Is she? Will I bear a baby, or a winged wehr?"

"I do not know that," he admitted gently.

She reacted as if she had been struck in the stomach. She doubled over and began in earnest to weep.

He got to his feet and went to where he had safed the makeshift sword belt in his straw and strapped it about his waist, staring at the wall's mud bricks.

Heicrey lunged at him and wrapped her arms around his legs, moaning his name.

He knelt down carefully and extricated himself, holding her by the arms, forcing her to look at him. But he could think of nothing to say to her, and they still huddled thus when Quendros stooped out from under the curtains that separated his sleeping chamber from the main room of the hut.

"Come on, you two," he said in a lowered voice from under raised brows. "Deilcrit, what's this about?" It was the binding on of sword that Quendros meant.

"I thought . . . I have to make Othdaliee before . . ." And he could not tell them more than that.

"Sit down, the both. Good. Now, Deilcrit, first, and to make matters most clear, I'm not sure I give a damn about all this"—and Quendros motioned around—"but I told you I would not fight for Wehrdom, and if you're seeking not only Imca-Sorr-Aat but other things there, I just don't know . . .

"One thing at a time. First, the question of the child."

"Is there to be one?" he wondered, not knowing how they could all be so sure.

"Yes, that's the question, but not the way you meant it. The question is whether man should suffer a wehr to live, most especially if it comes out of woman's belly. We'd been arguing that question so long after Wehrdom proved that we should have acted at the outset that it seems, to Laonans, academic. We don't tend to speak of it: it subsumes all we do."

"You mean you would kill the child?" he disbelieved, outraged.

"If it's an ossasim, most certainly. The question is whether to abort it in her womb."

Heicrey wailed, and tugged pathetically at his sleeve.

"What sets you up as executioner of unborn children?"

Quendros hawked and spit and growled for the drink to be passed him.

"Look, son. You're a Beneguan and I'm a Laonan, and there's no getting around that. Outside the Wall of Mnemaat, men don't farm fields expressly for campts to trample. We're hunters, gatherers—not draft beasts for Wehrdom. We eat what we can catch, and not just an occasional fish. And women don't call the shots, nor are we forbidden what tools our resources can provide. Understand? Those are the pathetic remnants of our old ways, the ways from which you and I and Heicrey and Eviduey and Mahrlys-iis-Vahais are sprung."

"So?" He feigned unconcern, reminding himself that he had eaten campt liver and the kills of Mahrlys' ptaiss.

"So, *those* are the ways of man, the ways such as built Dey-Ceilneeth and the gardens of Othdaliee in which you're so anxious to test your mettle."

"And those ways failed them, and they fail you," observed Deilcrit. "They almost wiped life from the world. If man is no longer the most successful, be comforted: some men are wehrs."

"You're really gone, now, aren't you?"

And Deilcrit wished he could speak to Quendros alone, of all Kirelli had revealed, but this was not the time or the place.

"I am Beneguan."

"That's right: a man who would not slay a ptaiss for its hide if he'd freeze to death without it but rather bend down with his head to the ground and let the ptaiss eat him."

Quendros stared long and piercingly at Deilcrit.

"Boy, I can't tell how much you're going to comprehend, but I think I'm beginning to see my part in this. If I'm wrong, that's my problem. But I ask you, by reason of all that has passed between us, to listen, and open your mind and try to understand."

In that pause cut to fit his assent, he allowed that he would do those things. Heicrey edged closer to him, and he put his arms around her and she laid her head in his lap.

"Once there was a man called Laore, and he taught wisdom and grace in a time so far gone as not to matter, except for the irrevocable changes that have come to pass from out of what he wrought. It was a light of learning, a way for man to become more godlike, that he taught my ancestors, and from him sprang a sect, and then another, whose revelations were scientific and whose blessings unto the race of man were material as well as spiritual.

"As with all sweeping changes, some acceded,

some obstructed, and some led revolution. It was a long and tumultuous reign that knowledge had, and then man proved himself too shortsighted to deal with the power he had come to wield."

Deilcrit saw the room anew. His awareness multiplied and came back on him from all sides, and he knew that Kirelli and some few others looked through his eyes.

"The green sword you got from these folk at the Spirit Gate: it comes from that age."

That startling bit of information jerked his attention back from the new perspective Wehrdom offered.

"It is said that the blade is unsheathed anew at every change of ages; long it was thought lost to us, the property of Mnemaat, who reclaimed it at the Fall of Man. But you have come to possess it, and for that reason alone I think I might have to aid you. . . . But I digress. I was trying to explain to you both why Heicrey's mother was so upset, and rightly.

"Just prior to the Fall, man could work some godlike wonders. Dey-Ceilneeth is one. The Eye of Mnemaat, which works by mind's power but without magic, is another. Even greater wonders did they create in the realm of medical science, and they turned their skills to the eradication of death itself, and to the perfection of the race of man. This is where the Laonan faith split in two." Quendros coughed.

Heicrey nodded. Deilcrit wondered what possible significance this might have upon the present.

"Who precipitated the war, we will never know: too much was lost. But in the aftermath, two things became increasingly clear: first, that war had so despoiled the land that man as he had evolved might not survive; and second: that many of his experimental creatures, once useful in the search for a stronger race of man, were not experimental anymore. Do you understand?"

"No," said Deilcrit, "I do not."

Quendros sighed. "I cannot teach you enough science to enable you to comprehend the process, but I can make it very simple: Wehrdom is man's creature. Man's and evolution's. Certain genetic predispositions were injected into the gene pool in the hopes that in the metamorphosis from the old evolutionarily stable niche, by then obviously untenable, to the new stable state that might obtain when nature sorted out which of her creatures might live and adjust, and which could not and would perish, man might win a place. And if not man, then his stepchild, the ossassim. . . .

"But none had reckoned on the communications ability mutating on its own among all the recombinants and artifically structured genes and the catalysts the added radioactivity provided. . . . Wehrdom began as a stopgap measure, in case man did not survive. Some say Imca-Sorr-Aat was Mnemaat's agent, oversaw Wehrdom's development. I'd like to ask him. . . ."

"The child, Father!" Heicrey sniffed impatiently.

"Right, the child. Well, what we now know as ossasim was a last-ditch attempt, and those who could work such miracles did not survive the birth of their last creation. So when it became clear that ossasim come in only one sex, and only from human wombs, it was too late. And when, even later, it became likely that man per se would also survive, the particular ability to produce ossasim either by breeding with one, or by breeding to a human whose grandparents had those particular latents in their history, was well-seated in the race. As my ancestors would have said: Ossasim have a set of evolutionarily stable strategies the highest paying of which is coupling across species lines."

"That is impossible. You cannot mate a ptaiss with a quenel."

"You can mate two varieties of any breed. And I'm not talking about what we can do; I'm talking about what our forebears could do. They could take apart the tiny particles, like beads strung on a string, that make you the person you are, and rearrange them in any order they pleased. They could even split each bead in half, and attach disparate halves. They had not only the choice of which bead lay next to which, but of what each bead itself was composed."

"But they could not make ossasim females?" Deilcrit disbelieved, hard-pressed to imagine beings that put other beings together with strings and beads.

"They might have erased the imperfection if they had survived. But they did not, and we are the people we appear as a result of what they did."

"You are telling me that Heicrey is a wehr?" Deilcrit hazarded.

"No, I am telling you that you are one, even though you do not look like one, and that a child resulting from your union with one of Heicrey's descent will have only one chance in three of being a true man or woman."

"You said that before you told me all this."

"I know, Deilcrit, but I thought it might help you if you understood *why* the child must die."

"I do not understand it yet. If it is lucky, by your standards, it will be human. If it is not, it will be an ossasim. What is its third choice?"

"It will be like you," said Quendros softly.

"I see nothing so terrible in that," Deilcrit replied.

Heicrey did, and she commenced weeping once more.

Try as he might, he could not understand why Quendros thought it better to be a "true man or woman" than a man of whatever kind he himself was, or than an ossasim.

But when Quendros stared steadily into him, he said: "I have listened, and I have tried to understand. If by calling me other than a man you feel you can absolve your obligation to attend me, I hope you have succeeded in your own sight. In mine, you need not have bothered. Stay or come as you please. These distinctions are too subtle, between kinds of men. There is a saying that man has not long to live in Wehrdom. Perhaps the truth of the saying is rooted somewhere in what you have just told me." He stood, hitched the sword belt up on his hips. "You may keep the sword of white metal. Stay here with your family and adjudicate these weighty decisions. You neither want nor need my interference." He reached down and ruffled Heicrey's hair as she pressed against him, arms thrown around his waist. "I offered to be whatever your customs demanded, but what I lack is suitable blood, and I cannot change that. So I will leave you to do as your conscience thinks best." The wehr-call was strong in him, so strong he heard his words over its cooing.

"I do not understand how you can be so dense," snarled Quendros, snapping to his feet. "I told you, I'm coming. And I told you, I just wanted you to understand Lohr-Ememna's grief, and Heicrey's decision, when she makes it. It is not up to you or me, but the two women, and I'm damn ready to be quit of women's troubles myself." With that he went and got the white-metaled blade, mumbling: "Be thrice cursed if I were fool enough to stay here when I have a chance of laying eyes of the bearers of Se'keroth, or even regaining her."

But Deilcrit heard no more over Heicrey's heart-broken snuffling. Even if he had, he did not know the name of the green-bladed weapon he bore, over which so many before him had died.

It was no easy leavetaking. He promised a multitude of promises which he doubted his ability to fulfill, even if he had so intended, in order to ease Heicrey's pain.

When they were quit of the hut and Lohr-Ememna's imprecations upon both their heads, he heaved a sigh of relief that made Quendros chuckle, and that one remarked that he, himself, felt rather like he had when they first stood beyond the Wall of Mnemaat and watched the Northern Gate close slowly amid the creak of winches, and knew freedom once more.

Deilcrit took a deep breath, and agreed that there was no freedom that he could see within Quendros' hut.

Quendros advised him to take his own wisdom to heart, and stay out from between the clutches of the ladies from that moment on.

Then Kirelli joined them, flapping with one small joyous cry to land on Deilcrit's right shoulder.

"Kirelli, this is Quendros, my ally among men," said Deilcrit.

Kirelli's polite "Breet" was not answered by Quendros, who became of a sudden immersed in a study of the ground they trod and the vagaries of the trail ahead. When pressed, the Laonan muttered about whelts' legendary treachery.

Deilcrit, as the wehr pressed its beak against his cheek, found that he had become possessed of a thousand eyes through which his progress could be seen: from above; from every side; even from so great a height and distance that he was only a possibility sliding through the dark, as if he stood on the pinnacle of Othdaliee and awaited himself.

Quendros indicated a right-hand turning, and as they took the fork, Deilcrit queried the whelt of ossasim. Some short while later he said to Quendros, "You are not wholly right about Wehrdom. Kirelli says that you are wrong about ossasim. Those women who look human, but are wehrs, are ossasim, not women."

Quendros shook his head, saying, "Go on."

"Ossasim have no interest in the blind, deaf-and-dumb females we call truly human. But between the manlike wehr and the ossasim wehr there is competition for human wehr females. Ossasim can become, if they wish and if there is a need, female for a season, and procreate. Human wehrs cannot."

He waited to see if Quendros would speak. Deilcrit wanted him very much to speak. But he did not, and Deilcrit said: "From the wombs of both ossasim and human wehr females have begun to come spawn which are wingless and oftimes infertile, but some show themselves capable of playing female to a winged ossasim."

"It is long overdue." Quendros grunted. "Nature heals all wounds."

"Does she? I think that the end of the ossasim's dependence upon mankind is an awful omen. Once there is no need for man, then what? We receive from ossasim a certain favoritism: most ossasim suckle at woman's breast. Though the competition for females between man wehr and ossasim is strong, Kirelli says it is a mere foreshadowing of doom. Once ossasim are secure as a species, the man who is not a wehr will perish."

"And the man who is?" growled Quendros in an uneasy tone.

"Ah," said Deilcrit, "now, that is what remains to be seen."

Both fell then into their own thoughts. All that could be heard was the cough of ptaiss and the slither of berceide and the low bark of the quenel who were also a part of the unseen entourage ranged around them in the wood. So did they trek untroubled out of Nothrace by night, in the safe-keeping of the prince of wehrs.

VII

The Bowels of Dey-Ceilneeth

I recall a number of their miscalculations: occasions on which I was too besotted by the drug to even realize that the man strung by his manacled wrists before me was Sereth; occasions upon which they would remind me of that fact, and of who I myself was. And I would strive to hold some elusive significance that I might attach to his identity and my own, succeed therein; but by that time have forgotten why I struggled so against blind existence; and fall into the difficulties of recollecting myself once more. I have thought that if they had known me, known my history and what previous experience I had had with living bereft of self, they might have tried some other tack. As it happened, I was the wrong woman on which to try that sort of interrogation, and they got nothing from me in that manner.

Which I suppose led them to gradually decrease the amount of drug in my system, a process which I recall as a gradually coalescing dream which slid into reality so subtly that I cannot remember exactly when I lay in the straw of our cell and realized that I was deep in some soporific's embrace. There was a long period of struggle with this concept during which I seemed to sit within my body's cavity, my own ribs a white framework sprung amid orange-brown, pulsing flesh. And I wrote thereupon my plight in huge red letters that glowed when I looked at them. Which I did, bereft of relevance so completely that I would spell out the letters slowly, puzzlingly, but by the time I had reached the last, forgetful of what letter the first had been.

I was starting once more at the first letter of the first word scrawled on my inner eye's lid when I felt rough hands lift me up, and a sharp liquid forced down my throat, and an interminable journeying that must have covered all of three manlengths.

They snapped my wrists into close fetters high above my head, and I dangled, slowly swinging. Whether it was the dank liquid or the kiss of metal bracelets that brought me to, I would not wager. I tried to lift my head. That first time, it fell back against my raised arm, but I had realized that I was chained, strung, and I began a desperate search for the present and cognizance that yielded adrenaline which buoyed me further until I could force open my eyes. I did that, and sought more. I called up my mind's skills but could not marshal them—the effort of raising head cost too much.

So I waited, and held my eyelids apart and tried to make sense of the blurs I was seeing.

It was Mahrlys' figure I first discerned, robed in black, her green eyes swimming above in a pale oval face.

"So, we have you at last conscious. How does it feel to hang helpless in Dey-Ceilneeth knowing that your sorcery will not avail you?" And she leaned so close her spittle sprayed my cheek. "You see, we have had experience with sorcery before. I told you I had powers. . . ."

And she nodded to someone I did not yet see.

But I recognized Eviduey's touch as he spun me around. And I saw Sereth, head lolling, strung as was I on a chain from the ceiling.

"What think you now of your most formidable companion?" Mahrlys hissed from beside my ear.

"I think," I croaked, then spoke clearly, "that you had best kill us both quickly."

"Kill you?" She chortled. "I have promised you to Eviduey. And besides, I have only started amusing myself with him."

I squinted through the drug's haze and saw what amusement she meant. And the fury and doubt that assailed me brought me new clarity: "You have disastrously overreached yourself, saiisa," I snarled, not caring that she could not know the word's meaning. "If he should wake, even as much as I, he will bring this dungeon down upon your head."

She laughed a barbed laugh, and even Eviduey chuckled.

"Do you think"—she leered—"I did that to him while he slept? What satisfaction, if he had not the sense to struggle? What value pain, if its recipient is not conscious to endure it?"

It was then I realized that Mahrlys was not woman, but wehr. No woman would have ordered those weals and bruises, not upon such as Sereth.

"Wake him, Eviduey." And the winged one, like a shadow, did as she bid. Then I realized what had ravaged Sereth: the like of the ossasim standing beside. There came from Sereth, as Eviduey's claws raked out, in answer to Mahrlys' command, a low groan. A shudder racked him, and his head swung slowly upward.

I watched him swim up through the drug, as I had done, and sort the sights before him.

"Again," spat Mahrlys.

His eyes shut momentarily, his nostrils flared,

and he leaned his head against his upstretched arm. Only that.

We hung there, for an interminable moment alone, our antagonists forgotten, staring across the man's-length gulf that separated us, through the miasmic mist the drug threw out.

"Estri. Good," he whispered.

I tried to make him know, with my eyes, that I also was heartened that he lived, for my voice would never have held. When he fell limp in his chains, as the undertow of the drug reclaimed him, I hissed a prayer to my father, Estrazi, that I would endure long enough to see Dey-Ceilneeth a smoking pile of rubble in which no thing lived.

This from me caused Mahrlys to command Eviduey's violence upon Sereth anew. The pain woke him, and sweat broke on his brow and dripped down his corded frame.

She asked me many questions, most concerned with Chayin and our respective origins, all of which I answered with some degree of truth that I might save Sereth what I could.

Once when Eviduey came close, I spat upon him, and he, rather than strike me, took vengeance upon my couchmate. I did not again show temper, but answered numbly all that Mahrlys asked. In me was the surety that if indeed Wehrdom could triumph over us three, the fate of Silistra was sealed. I cared little. The kindness I did Sereth mattered more to me than the fate of a thousand worlds.

When Mahrlys tired of the sport of posing questions, she departed, and there were only Eviduey, and Sereth, who seemed barely conscious, and I, in that small cavelike prison cell.

He studied me in the torchlight, walking around me where I dangled, suspended. Then he gave Sereth a drink of the bitter liquid, holding his head up by the hair. And me also he watered, gifting me with the slight increase in the clarity of perception the drink provided.

I found I could almost taste his thoughts, almost gather my wits, almost seek action upon the time. But hesting, that alteration of what exists by mind's command, eluded me in the thick drug mist, and after a while I realized Eviduey yet loitered, limp wings draping him like a cloak, long-taloned nails gleaming against his biceps, and that our chains had been winched downward so that my feet rested upon the straw.

It was a dangerous game he played, restoring me sufficiently that I might understand what he did and be responsive to him before Sereth's eyes. But he seemed not to care, and I was not the one to caution him.

I begged him to release me from my fetters, when all else was passed.

He laughed softly in answer, ran his sharp nail down me from throat to belly, took the torch, and left us in the darkness.

"Sereth?"

"Ci'ves, try to rest," he advised, his voice low as straw rustle in the utter blackness of the cell.

"Sereth . . ."

"When I have decided on a moment, little one, you will be the first to know." I could hear his pain.

"What of Chayin?" I blurted.

"If we live, and he lives, we will . . ." He stopped midway, and I heard the chain rattle, and a grating as of teeth. ". . . consider ourselves anew. Now, let me gather my wits, and you try the same."

I was a long time doing his bidding. I was close, so close that I was on the verge of speaking of it, when a wingless ossasim shone a blinding torch in our dark-accustomed eyes and pried apart my clenched teeth and thrust something chalky and gagging into my mouth and I lost all I had gained.

How many days passed thus, I can only vaguely calculate. Once Sereth hissed an oath at Eviduey, and I thought he would die as the consequence thereof. Once Mahrlys tortured us both. Once, when Sereth could not respond to her, she flew into a rage that brought me for the first time truly under the claws and teeth of an ossasim. They must toy with their kill in the wild; they are cruel beyond mortal conception and inventive beyond mere human skill.

I fastened my eyes upon those red fires that were Eviduey's, and at first my silent pleading weakened him, but the heat of the game won him back. I was not so brave as Sereth: the fiery scourging of my flesh, coming ever dreaded from behind, from my side, from before me, divested me of all pride.

It was my lesson at the ossasim's hands that raised my pulse and sharpened my mind so that I could again, as I had not since my first recollection in the cell, plunge through the stepsisters' mists in search of my skills.

When I had found them, and begun to test the time, the hinges had not yet creaked, the cell had not yet flooded with torchlight as it did once "nightly" when some one of Mahrlys' servitors appeared to give us our food and then more of the drug.

"Estri," he said to me, just as I was about to speak, "I want you to try to reach Chayin's mind."

"And you?" I talked to the dark.

"I am going to see what might be done to unlock these fetters." In his tone I could hear that grim humor which signifies a chancy venture. But previously, I had heard only drawled queries as to my faring, and softer comforts when I whimpered in the night.

I wondered if my arms would still function if indeed he was successful, if they could ever recollect their former function. They had been held above my head so long that they had ceased to ache.

Then, as he requested, I fixed my attention inward and sought Chayin's thoughts through the corridors of Dey-Ceilneeth ranged above my head.

It was not long until I located him, and thus verified what I had not wholeheartedly believed: that he lived and had not moved to aid us. My mind sniffed around the chamber first, in search of evidence of incarceration; then around the edges of the cahndor's awareness. I had thought that if he lived he might be sedated, as were we. Even when first I caught his accents upon the wehrwind, I presumed that he was acting under pressure, constrained. With a troubled mind, I withdrew, and said only, "I have him. What would you like me to say?" into the utter darkness of our cell.

It was a moment before he husked an answer, long enough for my heart to leap and thump about my ribs. But he was not dead or unconscious, only deeply absorbed: "Determine his location, his condition. Do not let him sense you. More, do not let Wehrdom catch your thoughts."

I nodded, and tried once more for Chayin. Then I told Sereth what I had seen there.

Even as I did so there was a blaze of agonizing heat at my wrists, and I was falling. Arms caught me in the pitch dark, eased me to the straw.

I gibbered against Sereth's chest, hysterical with relief, entreating him to leave then with me and forget Chayin and Se'keroth and all else but ourselves.

"Ci'ves, quiet, be quiet. It is all over. I was not

about to go through that again." He made reference to an earlier captivity we had shared. "It was just awaiting the moment. Now it is here." And I could feel his probing attention invading me, aiding my system's attempt to throw off the effects of the fahrass.

When I felt more myself, I felt pain. He moved to untangle us, but I gripped him tight, lips pressed to his throat in the darkness. "I did this," I confessed dully. "I could not control my temper. Wehrdom . . ." And I shivered, then started again: "I saw the result, but I did not care. Please, do not hate me."

"Estri . . ." His fingers gripped my shoulders, pushing me back. I knew what look he must bear, beyond the dark. "Why do you always gather up everyone's blame and try to heft it? I was on the brink of something similar myself. It might have happened from my slaying her berceides. Better thus . . ." And he fell silent.

And continued again: "Wehrdom makes my guts crawl, and I cannot deny it. See to your body, as I must to mine. There is much to do."

"Chayin?"

"At the very least. I cannot do less than confront him, after all we have shared. There is a testing in this for him. We must be most tolerant."

"Ebvrasea, however you want it," I whispered, and he drew me against him and we shared strength further, until he tossed his head and whispered: "Someone comes. Be ready to relocate to Mnemaat's hall."

"Sereth . . ."

"I will do it. Just allow me." His fingers explored the lacerations on my back.

"You?"

"If we need it. The flaw in your method might complicate things. We cannot afford to be separated by time. I am untried, but conversant with the procedure." And I heard in his voice that determination before which no words have worth.

"If we do not need it?"

"Then we are going to walk Dey-Ceilneeth and gather up a little satisfaction on the way."

"Restrictions?" I queried him, beginning to feel the agony in my arms.

"None at all, although I may ask you for some snychronization."

"None at all?"

"That is right. We are going to kill some wehrs."

I must confess I felt nothing but eagerness, and a weary, wise joy that adversity had built a bridge over the growing chasm between us. I sought his hand in the dark. He enclosed my fingers in his fist and I drew it to my lips and kissed it, even as the door opened in a blinding spill of light.

When I could see, I saw the wingless ossasim, choking, torch in mid-drop toward the floor. Its hands were around its throat and it gagged and heaved, falling to its knees and then to the straw, retching blood.

"What did you do?" I gasped, lunging upright. Staggering, I almost fell. I had a difficult time making my limbs obey me, and only half-heard his reply:

"I threw an envelope around it and sucked out all the air. No one argues long with a vacuum." He said it in a clipped, hard way that made me know that he considered any weapon meet, and everything he had a weapon.

The torch was guttering. He knelt to retrieve it: slowly, very cautiously, weaving on his feet. His scabbed, scored back betrayed little of the peculiar alert ease with which his body responds to battle. And when he turned, one hand on the stones to steady himself, I knew that the drug still held him in its fervent embrace; that he, as I, was in little shape for what lay before us. And I saw how much the simple envelope he had cast about the ossasim had cost him. But I saw a thing I had not expected, also: that inward, death-dealing laughter behind his eyes that had been the last earthly sight of so many adversaires.

"You will bear some scars this time, ci'ves," he assessed, half-staggering to his feet, torch in hand, and leaned against the wall for support.

I think I said: "It is no matter," but the drug lay like new snowfall in my ears, and I am not sure. I recollect realizing that he was right, that I had not the energy to spare upon the half-healed wounds Eviduey's claws had dealt me. I sought his side over a distance that was mere lengths, but seemed to stretch ever longer with each step I took to close it. I noted the wingless ossasim, for I stepped carefully over its outstretched arm; but I gave it little more importance than my own befouled state, or Sereth's, or the two chains that hung swinging from the cell's high ceiling. The manacles that had once depended from them were no more: their molecular structure, by Sereth's will, had become volatile in the air about them: they no longer existed. All that remained was a slagged link at the end of the chain; and long, risen blisters encircling my wrists, and his.

He took me under his arm, and though he was greatly weakened, I felt a share of his strength come into me.

"Chayin," he muttered. His body was stiff against mine as we sought the corridor. There he threw the bar on our prison's door, that door like a score of others in the vault.

Even while he hesitated before the cell next to ours, as if he might open it and free the occupant, a low growling rose in the back of my mind. My ears did not hear it, for it was Wehrdom's growl: they acknowledged their dead.

All the hairs on my body stood away from my skin. My heart pounded loudly, and by its efforts chased back the drug mist until it was a shroud wrapped about owkahen's disclosures. Under my shield, awkwardly, I reached out and tried to disperse the mist. I had foreseen this moment: the stone like frozen ocean deeps and the straw-strewn corridor and the two of us, naked, weaponless hips brushing, his arm about my shoulders as we assayed the climb out of the bowels of Dey-Ceilneeth. But I had not seen the "how" of it: owkahen shows me only fragments of what is coming to be, not always how the thing takes shape. What it showed me then by way of the wraithlike mist wrapped around the schematic of my days caused me to shiver and pull him closer.

"The wehr-rage. Sereth, do you feel it?"

He nodded. "It is a pity the guard had no weapon. I would rather fight my battles with sword. It is less taxing. Perhaps the next. . . ."

The next was not long coming, but yielded no weapons to us, for the ossasim and their wingless siblings are well-armed by nature and only strap blades about them when in ceremonies concerning their human kin. Three ossasim, two wingless, skidded down the tall, narrow staircase, to fall lifeless at our feet.

It had been so smoothly done that I had not noted them until they had started to tumble, but Sereth sank down on the stairs, shaking his head savagely. His chest was heaving, and the hand that held the torch shook. "Curse this drug, and these . . . things," he muttered.

I blinked back tears.

"Sereth, there must be hundreds of wehrs in Dey-Ceilneeth. We cannot fight them all. Please . . ."

He glared up at me. "Please what, Estri? Leave Chayin sunk in Wehrdom's slime? We owe him more than that, no matter what he has come to feel about us. If by our actions we have driven him to seek elsewhere for what comfort we could not provide, then whose fault is that? I told you, long ago, that we would one day come to contest over you."

"Over me? Sereth, you do not understand."

"I understand what he wants with Mahrlys, what he sought in her arms."

"It is not just that." I stepped over the tangled corpses and sat beside him on the narrow stair, though every nerve in my body pleaded with me to flee, though my hands shook and my mouth was dry as the Parset Desert.

"Sereth, you lump us together, Chayin and me, and call us lacking in compassion and ascribe that trait to the Shapers who sired us; but when it counts, you do not see. He is his father's son: Raet was a . . . being to whom Wherdom would have been irresistible. He and I are cousins, it is true, but my father's folk would not condone such as this."

He snorted, and pushed to his feet. "Estri, some intelligence has been at work here, and what it has wrought sickens me. I could not care less whose hand was turned to the task, but you can be sure your father and my predecessor did not raise a hand against it."

"And you will?"

"Watch me." His breathing was regular. His eyes were clear. I did not doubt him, but only matched him up that odd staircase, which could be best climbed diagonally, for the height of each step was uncomfortable to the stride and the breadth would not support a human foot other than lengthwise.

"Sereth . . ."

"Estri, I know what I can do and what I cannot. I am not unaware of what the time will and will not provide. *Down!*"

And I threw myself upon the stairs as a wind ruffled my tangles and with a rushing noise a winged wehr dived feet first, talons gleaming, at Sereth from the vaulted dark above. He cast the torch. It rolled down a dozen steps, the light from it dancing crazily.

He had no footing there, on those stairs barely the width of my hand. He pressed back against the wall, and the dark shadow whirled and dived again, but he was rolling upon the steps when the wehr struck the wall, and on the thing's back before it recovered from the concussion of striking unyielding stone.

Mind skills take a moment, or two, or three, to bring to bear. He had not had them. They grappled, rolling down the sheer staircase. I heard the whooshing sound, even as I leaped to follow, and reached without looking up into the wehr-awareness that hunted me, not caring that all of Wehrdom might enter into battle with me through that door I had opened. No, I did not care, only assayed my descent, searching my pursuer's nature. Then I saw through its eyes, saw my flight, sensed its dive, talons extended ready to plunge into my back and dash me against the wall. I felt its urge to gut me. Then I severed its optic nerves, and threw myself left.

My shoulder hit the leftward wall of the stairwell with a crunch, echoed almost immediately by the thud of the blind wehr striking the stair headfirst.

I rubbed my shoulder, shaking, deep in the wehr-thought, and threw a blast of outrage into that buzzing network that stopped the wehr-converse as if it had never been. In that silence, I could not promulgate the deafening effect I had used previously.

So I withdrew from the quiet, disturbed that Wehrdom had so easily come upon a counter-measure.

"Estri," rasped Sereth, reclaiming the torch, "you are going to have to kill swiftly. There is no sub-tlety in war. There is sometimes quarter, but not this day."

"Have we declared war?" I panted, taking his hand and by it gaining my feet.

"We are considering it." He grinned, a grim and momentary flashing of teeth.

It was then, while still the edges of my mind brushed Wehrdom, that I heard the other sound, the trumpeting that echoed through Wehrdom's ranks, but I knew not what to make of it, and had many other more pressing concerns. . . .

When we had gained the entrance to Dey-Ceilneeth proper, eleven ossasim and fifteen of their wing-less kin lay dead in the lower dark.

"This way," grunted Sereth, and I recalled that while I lay with Eviduey he had walked Dey-Ceilneeth.

We did not speak upon the way to Chayin, did not exchange even conjectures as to where he might be found. That was as clear to Sereth as to myself. Owkahen offered up that information with a glib smile and unmistakable anticipation.

Upon the way to Mahrlys' chamber we killed a black ossasim, but it was not Eviduey. That was all, though Wehrdom growled so deep and loud I felt it through all my shields, as one might feel a motor humming beneath one's feet.

What we did see, however, was two groups of ossasim fighting among themselves.

"What think you?" I hissed the query.

"Quiet!" said Sereth, flattened against the wall

where the corridor branched. Then: "Now." And we slid past the corridor's entrance unseen.

"I would give this whole continent for a sharp blade," he grated, glowering back the way he had come, at the corridor down whose length lay those quarters we had been assigned.

I wondered what the chances were of our belongings remaining in that chamber, then dismissed it, thinking that I could soon attempt to shape him a blade—manifest one from its molecular constituents. But in my heart I knew I would not, that this was no battle to be won by steel or stra, the green metal from which Se'keroth had been forged. And suddenly I saw the blade, and its bearer, and the blade exploded into light, and fell spinning down a sheer cliff face. Then a whelt's visage peered at me, silver beak aclack, and I snapped my mind shut and faced what lay before us: the rushed door leading to the keep of Mahrlys-iis-Vahais. We had been immured long enough for it to be replaced.

I touched his arm, cautioning. Under his shadowed cheekbones, a muscle twitched. The sound of his teeth grinding whispered in the corridor.

With his hand upon the wood frame of the door, he hesitated, and drew back, and stood very still, his eyes upon his feet. Then he ran his hand over his brow, and tossed his hair back from it, and turned upon me a look of such self-consuming agony that tears filled my eyes and my vision swam.

"Ci'ves, you are free with advice. Give me some now."

I thought of what lay before him. I searched for encouragement, but my mind was as empty as a tidal pool when its sea has become only a memory scoured on the rocks.

They had been of one flesh for years. Between them lay such blood debts as could hardly be counted. I said only: "I, too, love Chayin."

And he nodded and tried the door, which gave to his touch.

The cahndor lay with a red robe draped over his shoulders, and Mahrlys-iis-Vahais hunkered down between his legs, her head on his thigh. About lay the remains of a feast, the silver dishes glowing soft in the oil lamp's light.

As we slid within and closed the door behind us, he looked up, his hand on Mahrlys' black-haired head.

Sereth slammed the wooden bar into place.

Mahrlys-iis-Vahais sobbed, raised her head, bared her teeth, and growled, her eyes rolling.

My flesh-lock froze her. I could not take a chance that through her linkage Wehrdom might converge upon us before we were ready. In her terror at finding herself imprisoned in her own body, unable even to blink her eyes, was a warning for Wehrdom which I wished them to receive. I gambled that her plight would stay them. But I wondered, as Chayin unsteadily rose and faced Sereth, who leaned, arms folded, against the door, whether danger to any individual might constrain such a whole as Wehrdom showed itself to be. Up from the floors below, and through the windows and riding the air and by way of my sensing, I chronicled the wehr-rage. From all about I sensed things dying: within the forests and in the maze and in the sky and all through Dey-Ceilneeth the ineluctable massacre we had triggered by slaying the guard wehrs waxed, screeching. Once started, the wehr-rage would continue until the wehrs lay exhausted. This I knew. Chayin had eloquently warned us previously. But we had not heeded him. Behind my eyes hung a film of blood lust that threatened, even though I was its quarry, to enlist me. I looked at the cahndor through that red haze, and all traces of compassion, of love, were burned from my heart.

I only noted his uncertain steps and his faraway, inward sight as he struggled to make sense of what he saw in the face of the wehr-wind.

The membranes cloaked his eye, unmoving, protective. He looked at us, at our bruises, our lacerations, Weaponless, naked, befouled, we faced him, and he blinked, and rubbed his right shoulder, and croaked:

"Sereth. I thought . . . She said . . ." Then he ceased, and his fingers found his chald belt and toyed there, and he seemed to shrink smaller.

The silence made my ears ache. They measured each other.

"Release her," growled the cahndor at last, of Mahrlys.

"Chayin," Sereth murmured. "Tell me what you thought. Say something, anything, that will absolve you of blame." He was calm, laconic. I found need to sit, and sank to the floor. My legs would not hold me.

"Release her. She is mine." Chayin glowered.

"Chayin, I would hear what owkahen has been whispering in your ear, and what you make of it."

"Then release her. I have taken her in couchbond. You have Estri. . . ." And he blinked, and looked away, and it seemed that he shuddered.

"Estri, do it," said Sereth to me, pushing away from the door to ease his way warily toward Chayin.

I did, but only after I crawled over to her and made it very clear in a whisper what I would do to her if she so much as coughed.

"Where were you?" Chayin roared suddenly. "Why do you not bear Se'keroth if you went to reclaim it?"

"I come to you dressed only in my own filth, bearing heavy wounds, and you talk to me of fantasy. How is it that your sensing has so utterly failed you? Or is it that you would prefer not

to believe that your couch-mate has deceived you?"
Sereth spat that term, which is one not bandied
lightly about on our western shore. "Your couch-
mate," he continued, while, amazingly, from
Mahrlys' huge green eyes silent tears ran in a steady
stream, "drugged us, immured us in those dun-
geons beneath, and worked this art upon us."

And very slowly, arms held away from his body,
Sereth turned full around. When he again faced
Chayin, he added: "Is Wehrdom's wine so heady,
are her thighs so soft, that you and I will enter the
circle over it?"

It is a rhetorical cirlce, that of which he spoke,
and its meaning is a flight to the death.

"Say something, wehr," I hissed. But she only
sat with those silent tears.

Chayin wheeled on his heels and strode to the
wall and slammed his fist into the ruby hangings
there. From without came a howl, and then another,
and the sounds of flight and pursuit.

"Do you not realize what you obstruct?" came
Chayin's tortured query. The bunched muscles slid
on his back, his hands crumpled the hanging, and
with a vicious yank and he wrenched it from its
hooks, unveiling a window that overlooked Dey-
Ceilneeth's maze.

"No, I do not," said Sereth and I together.

Mahrlys then attempted to rise. I cautioned her
as to the inadvisiability of such a move, and she
sank back.

But Chayin had seen, and he strode to stand
between us.

"No, you do not," he mimicked savagely. "What
powers here contest, what might be gained, does
not at all concern you. The wehrs offend you. That
is enough for you both. I can smell the death on
you. You have judged and now would mete out
their fate. Little is it to you that this culture, as

old as that we call Silistran, fights its own battle
to survive.

"We came here, we upset a balance, we must
restore it."

"Are you telling me," said Sereth, "that you can
excuse what your . . . creature has done to us with
her own hands? On what scales are you weighing
us, that after all we have shared, Estri and I sum
less than this saiisa whose legs you will split a few
times and then discard her as you have all others?"

"No, by Uritheria, under whose wing I yet stand,
no! Sereth"—and he stepped close, and I saw tears
of frustration there—"I tried to tell you. Sereth,
there is a thing here that must be done, and that
thing has determinedly sought me. There is a schism
in Wehrdom. Curse your unwillingness to hear what
does not suit you: there is a struggle here, and
it is one best viewed from the distance of evolution,
and you will not hear that! Wehrdom seeks renewal
before the doors of Othdaliee close for a thousand
years. It was that reason that Wehrdom courted
me—"

"You are right, I will not hear that," said Sereth.
"Not because I do not believe it, because it does
not matter."

"But it is all that does matter," decried Chayin.
"I was approached, and I accepted. And certain
things I will do for them, as will we all—"

Sereth spat a word I have never heard him use.
His hands were on his hips, and though his fists
were clenched, they shook.

It was then that Mahrlys spoke, when I thought
they would summarily destroy each other while
Wehrdom howled about us:

"No, Chayin, you will do no more. Or you will
do little else than what you have done." With a
fluid grace she rose. I allowed it. She sought the
cahndor's side, and he took her in under his arm.

"You did not abrade me for deceiving you, and I thank you," she said to him, and then to us: "Chayin knew nothing of what I did. And I do not regret it. I sought to kill.you in such a way as he might never know. I failed in that, and then was wooed by what you might be able to tell me.... and I lost. But only partly. I needed time, and time I gained." She bit her lip, and took a deep breath. I knew she held back still additional tears. "All gamble; sometimes, the best of us lose."

Chayin growled.

"No, beloved, I *have* lost. You can hear them: Wehrdom fights Wehrdom, and it will not cease until one faction or the other no longer exists. Our only hope now is what might occur at Othdaliee."

"I could—" started the cahndor hesitantly, but she cut him off.

"No, brave one, the time is both too late and too early for that." Sereth looked at me, but I only shrugged. I could make no more than he from that exchange. "I have lost, and I must flee Dey-Ceilneeth. I am unfit to guide her; what you will see when the run rises will attest to that. Nor would I be allowed. Death is my society's answer for what misjudgments I have made, and death is the only flight at whose end I might find amnesty. I . . ."

Chayin whispered in her ear, and she sagged against him and began weeping in earnest.

He looked at Sereth with such an abject plea for understanding that I rose and sought the dharen and ran my hand along his back. His thought touched mine, and it was a thought of what could be lost here and what might be saved.

Sereth said: "Keep your life, woman. Give us our clothes and our weapons and we will go our way. Chayin, you can come or stay, as you please."

The cahndor's brow furrowed. "It is to Othdaliee we must go."

"No!"

"For Se'keroth, Sereth. And for Deilcrit, and for an easy night's sleep at the Lake of Horns. Owkahen shows it clearly. You do not have to believe me. Look yourself."

And Sereth squeezed his eyes shut and expelled a deep breath and said: "Estri?"

"Your will, as ever," I replied.

"Chayin, if I must, I will accompany you to death's door in search of an explanation for what you are doing." The flat, cold words hit the cahndor like a backhanded slap. "But I will have one. And I will have it before either of us sleeps again. I have had about all the temporization and forereader's gibberish that I am willing to take. Now, get us our belongings, and out of here."

Chayin, in a thick voice, mumbled to Mahrlys to return us our things if she had them. Which she did, in that very chamber. And that led me to ponder how Chayin could have been so completely fooled by her, and even if he *was* fooled. And consideration of foolishness led me to mark the abrupt change in Mahrlys-iis-Vahais since last she and I had talked, when she had so demeaned such men as Chayin and everything for which they stood.

We used her bath and excused ourselves from her ministrations. I would rather bear my scars than chance some new acquaintance with the drugs of Benegua.

During that time Chayin announced that Mahrlys must accompany us. Sereth objected, and I thought they would, after all, end their lives trying each other's strength when the black-haired girl herself entered the conversation.

"I cannot go through the forest. The whelts are supreme there right now, and may hold it indefinitely. My enemies—Kirelli—would spend a thousand lives to make me spend mine. I cannot, should not leave Dey-Ceilneeth. My death awaits me here."

So I glimpsed what forces Mahrlys found herself ranged against, or thought I did, as she pulled a white robe about her and girded it with a child's dagger and slipped her feet into rope sandals.

"You must go through there," she said, and pointed to a hanging that could have concealed a doorway. "It is the quickest way to Othdaliee. Indeed, the only way you might survive the journey. And thence, there is no returning." And she took a slow and wistful tour of her chamber, stroking the bosom of the whelt-headed deity on whose tray I had once sat.

"*You* must go," repeated Chayin. Mahrlys made a motion of denial.

"My very thought," agreed Sereth. "If nothing else, she will make a good hostage."

At this Mahrlys, whose circuit of the chambers had drawn her near the outer door, dashed for it. Sereth, who was closer, dived after her, and I heard a muffled scream and in a moment she was stumbling toward the cahndor, lips drawn back from clenched teeth.

"You want her. She is your problem," said Sereth, giving Mahrlys a final push that sent her sprawling against Chayin's chest.

We withdrew then, to arm ourselves in what we had reclaimed and leave them to their muttered argument.

I was much strengthened by the simple act of pulling on my boots, in whose tops eight razor-moons nestled, and my belt, which held, beside the empty scabbard, a knife in sheath. Sereth had the twin of it. We have had them a very long time. They are talismans, the manifestation of our bond, and though occasionally we have lost them, each time they have been returned to us. Stroking the single red jewel set in the knife's hilt, I was greatly eased.

There are many truths that elude me, but the truths of that day, life or death, are those with which I am most comfortable. It is the decision to do battle which is hard. The battle, seemingly, would come to us, which suited me. I readied myself and took stock of my internal strengths as the drug residue faded away.

I was not wrong. Neither was I so innocent as to imagine that Sereth did not know what approached while we lingered there, dressing at our ease, and Mahrlys engaged Chayin in an interminable altercation. If Sereth had wanted to avoid what then occurred, we would have forced an earlier exit. As it was, he leaned against the jamb of the arch that divided Mahrlys' inner, less formal chamber from the outer, statued room of ruby and purple while Mahrlys detained Chayin most artfully. He even went so far as to whisper me to silence when I proposed to him that we hurry them. It is possible that he wanted Mahrlys to reveal herself, or that he sought to determine how deeply enwrapped in Wehrdom's mists Chayin really was, or even only whether Chayin was a party to this delaying action. Sereth keeps his own counsel, still, upon those affairs.

Then, he only stiffened slightly against the jamb as the wehr-howl rose and the door, battered, reverberated and burst inward, sending debris flying, and Mahrlys in a wondrous imitation of surprise froze as Chayin dived for his sword.

Inward burst the slavering throng, and Sereth grunted and the oncoming wave of fang and claw and six-fingered hand flowed around the edges of the hemispherical barrier that they could not see, but against which they bludgeoned and clawed and bit and butted in vain.

I heard a moan within Sereth's periphery's silent center, and I saw Mahrlys: no longer did she dissemble calm. She took upon her knees. Her nails clawed the carpet. Her eyes rolled.

She spat and hissed in some sibilant tongue and threw her head savagely. I almost softened to her then, as she fought so valiantly to shake off the wehr-rage all around. Louder and louder ululated the shrieks of the wehr-wind. She held her ears. Sereth dragged her rudely to her feet and slapped her thrice, and shoved her stumbling before him toward the hanging-obscured wall she had earlier indicated. The noise of the frustrated wehrs was deafening, half a thousand throats crying. And suddenly I was alone, facing a crowd of creatures who climbed the invisible barrier, their bodies describing its dimensions. Mouths pressed against it, distorted as if by glass. I turned once, full circle, and then fled to Chayin, who was himself swaying, transfixed, near the inner door.

I pulled him by the arm, and he snarled. I dropped my grip and stepped back.

"Chayin?"

Slowly, from a long distance, his taut stance loosened and he unclenched his fists. Behind his back a red-eyed ossasim leered at me.

And fell inward, along with a score of others, as Sereth's barrier flickered. And died in that instant, severed exactly in half, as Sereth regained his hold upon the molecular construct that served him.

Chayin and I stumbled through a rain of appendages and body fluids, and then we saw why Sereth's field had flickered:

The hanging at the chamber's back wall concealed a featureless door of black metal, which even as we spied it drew up into itself.

Sereth held a key of black metal in one hand and Mahrlys-iis-Vahais at arm's length with the other. She struggled vainly, furiously, and I made sense of their interchange only briefly above the wehr-rage. It seemed Mahrlys had succumbed to her fellow creatures' influence at last.

And then Chayin urged me within and Sereth dragged Mahrlys by the hair. With a soft hum the metal slab began its descent. When it was half down, the wehrs surged inward, no longer impeded by Sereth's will. But none reached the descending iron slab but one, and he left his hand within, only.

I saw the ossasim hand severed, heard the scream, and then all was silent and dark as the space between the worlds.

I picked out Mahrlys' ragged breathing, heard a rustle that clanked and by that identified Chayin. I was on the verge of speech, having decided that we must make our own light, when Mahrlys' laugh, throaty, triumphant, rang in the dark space.

"Now it is done," she chortled. "There is no way out of here, save Othdaliee. I have died, but Dey-Ceilneeth might yet live."

I reflected that had we not been able to obviate space we might indeed be concerned by whatever unknown danger lay ahead.

There came to me in the dark a feral snarl, and a scratching sound like chalk on slate, followed by the sound of bodies grappling.

I did not ask, but closed my eyes and concentrated on enclosing some suitable constituents of the air in a circular pocket I conceived above my head. In making a miniature sun such as the one I constructed there, one utilizes emotion, almost as if thought were the catalyst for the controlled incandescence which technically is achieved by splitting a paired particle and not allowing the halves to form another pair by the spinning motion that the particle-pair conceives as balance. Instead, the halved particle rotates more and more frantically in its space, striving in vain to throw off a replacement twin. But instead of allowing the recreative force to culminate, we drain it off, and use the energy we thus milk for our purposes. This is the Shaper way.

The miniature sun, bobbing calmly above my head, twinkled brightly in the square, regular tunnel whose angle led downward and whose end was not in sight.

Mahrlys, crouched against the wall, had her face buried in her hands.

Chayin stood over her, nursing a bloody arm.

Sereth looked at them, shook his head, and gestured that we should continue down the corridor.

Chayin started to speak, thought better of it, and raised the girl. The corners of her mouth were dotted with froth.

I sidled past them in that corridor barely wide enough for three to stand abreast. My minuscule inferno bobbed behind me, throwing long distorted shadows down that rectangular channel driven deep into the earth.

I was just about to say that it seemed not a fearsome place to me, only dull, when on Chayin's very heels a second rectangular slab thundered downward. When it hit the stone, the ground quivered.

Mahrlys, leaning heavily on Chayin's arms, giggled.

"Cahndor, before I walk another step into this, I would hear some answers," said Sereth. In his anger, he seemed to loom huge against the green-black stone. The tiny sun drifted toward him and rose to the ceiling behind his head.

"As you wish, Sereth," said Chayin stiffly, distracted, his attention and concern upon Mahrlys, who drew away from him and turned her face to the stone.

"Wehrdom," said Chayin, "is a society whose price of admission is first the ability to perform as a wehr, and second the severance of all other ties. A wehr who is a ptaiss has no kin altruism for other ptaiss, but for Wehrkin."

"Chayin," Sereth said warningly. "I am no supporter of Khys's catalysis genetics."

"Nor of Wehrdom. I can excuse the one no more than the other. You *are* catalysis genetics. Estri called you an atavist. That is true, in part. You are an altruistic atavist, so admixed that kin altruism predisposes you to all men, since few hold stronger relatedness to you than a total stranger. But you are deaf to truth. The catalysis cycle hinges upon the concept that man becomes progressively more gregarious until he has outstripped evolution's ability to suit him for living with the restriction of such an altruistic overload. Then he either destroys that culture or leaves it by means of more accelerated technology that he may satisfy his mounting xenophobia, his territoriality, and the need to own and dominate which is ever paired with the genes which predispose to creativity. In a society of warriors, the pacifist may become for a time successful, for he will not be killed by the warrior by reason of his very reluctance to fight. Thus he will be evolutionarily successful in that he will reproduce. More and more the pacifists enter that society, until they outnumber the warriors and begin to constrain the very making of war. But when this happens, the warriors resurge, because in any fight they will triumph over the pacifist, who is neither disposed to fight nor very good at it. When the warrior is threatened, he fights; in fighting, he culls the pacifists. Only the most ata-

vistically oriented, war-capable pacifists remain.
The warriors become dominant in the gene pool,
and the cycle starts again. It is vastly more com-
plicated, of course. One must take into account what
predispositions each group has in breeding, and
the individuals capable of deception to the extent
that they can for a short time triumph and themselves become dominant, until they are found out,
at which time they recede—"

"*Chayin!*"

"Learning lessens no man," retorted the cahndor,
to Sereth's exasperation.

"I want to know why you were willing to let us
rot in Dey-Ceilneeth and why you are dragging us
to Othdaliee. I could care less about what offal you
learned from those old ladies at the Lake of Horns."

I had learned the same offal. Though I thought
Chayin had not studied Sereth's inversions, in my
opinion he was not too far off in the rest of it. So I
said:

"He is trying to tell you that Wehrdom is in a
strategic flux; it is experiencing something akin to
the passing of power that occurred when you took
the Lake of Horns. There is sometimes a violent
flipping between opposite-seeming but equally stable hierarchies. Violent when viewed in evolution-
ary time. But what exactly does that have to do
with us?"

"It is the Curse of Imca-Sorr-Aat." Chayin grinned.
Sereth stared.

"No, truly. Once in a thousand years the interface called Imca-Sorr-Aat changes. Which creature
holds that position determines how the next millenium will develop; what strategies, even what
factions of Wehrdom will be dominant. Man has
done poorly here this last thousand years. In fact,
he is nearly extinct. He is merely food for Wehrdom,
and his artifacts are but curiosities. In another

Imca-Sorr-Aat's rule they might have provided him a secure place. The manlike wehrs, because of a drastically limited gene pool, make fewer and fewer appearances. And the ossasim, who provided the last Imca-Sorr-Aat, have almost succeeded in establishing themselves as a species. If an ossasim should again hold the interface known as Imca-Sorr-Aat, the man-wehr will certainly become extinct.

"What men are left will be like those we saw when we watched adults kill their own children. That place is called Nehedra, and its folk provide not only fields to be grazed and stores of grain for droughts, but fresh meat and a good chase. And they cull not only their weakest in those forest trials the children take, but their strongest as well: any child who precedes the bulk of them, and all who reach the town's gates before sunset, are slain. So it has been under the last Imca-Sorr-Aat, and so it will be under the next, if he be ossasim, or ptaiss, or any other creature but man himself. You see, the creature of Wehrdom recall what man did to them, and they would not risk a recurrence. Their methods are, I suppose, resonable coming from species who witnessed the pinnacle of technological man, and fear his works." And the cahndor leaned forward and wet his lips.

"But it does not sit well with me. And I was given a chance to better the fortunes of those whom I call kin here. Could you, Sereth have resisted such a call?"

Sereth blew out his breath, and did not answer, but instead crouched down before Mahrlys.

"He has told us what he thinks is happening, and how you enlisted him. Now you tell me the truth. You think you have us trapped; it should not matter to you if we know your designs."

"Aah, you are a quick one, manling," she said on

a shuddering breath. Her eyes were no longer wild, though triumph gleamed therein. "All he thinks is true, as far as it goes. It is a difficult thing to lie in the wehr-wind."

"But it can be done."

"Indeed, Sereth crill Tyris, it can be done. But there was no need to lie, only to be circumspect with what information we made available. I did not tell him that Imca-Sorr-Aat decreed this flight of yours to Othdaliee, if I could not kill you. Die here, die there, it is no different to me."

"Mahrlys!" exploded Chayin.

"Chayin, I told you they would die chasing that stupid sword, and they will. And you will live to make Wehrdom safe for another thousand years."

There was something in the way she said it which made me know that what Chayin expected to do and what she had in mind for him to do were two different things. The key and the answer were there, in what she said, but they did not see. Perhaps only another woman could have marked it. And yet, even knowing, I could not pierce the wehr-veil and determine how the thing would fall out. I saw what I had seen in the Eye of Mnemaat, and tried a wild guess: "What has Deilcrit to do with all this?"

"Nothing, nothing at all," said Mahrlys sweetly. "He was given the trial of Imca-Sorr-Aat that he might die mercifully. You will doubtless reclaim your sticker from his corpse. In all the days of my reign, none have ever completed the trial and returned." We have a creature, in the west, like a ptaiss but winged. It is called a hulion, and with her green eyes shining yellow in the miniature sun's glow and that puff-cheeked smirk on her face, she reminded me of one, when the kill is sure and the hulion can take time to batter its prey.

"You predict, then, that I might live long enough to see Othdaliee," I replied in the same sweet tone.

She shrugged delicately. "Let me rephrase that: *Chayin* will reclaim it."

"You would do well as a forereader, with that tongue," said Sereth. His fingers toyed with the hilt of his knife. His eyes measured Chayin's concern. Then he rose and stretched and said, "I gave you your life once. Do not make me take it back."

And he motioned that Mahrlys and Chayin should precede us down the featureless, sloping corridor into the dark.

"What think you?" Sereth subvocalized, while in front of us Chayin took up a low dialogue with Mahrlys and their backs receded before us down the steady incline of green stone.

"I think," I replied, my lips at his ear, "that things are not so simple as the 'man-wehr-facing-extinction' story. How does Chayin's visit to Othdaliee make Wehrdom safe for a thousand years? And why is Mahrlys so anxious to help the reins of power change hands when she stands so high in the present hierarchy? And if kin altruism is in effect between those sharing the communications gene, why is there strife in Wehrdom?"

The miniature sun sent dizzying shadows dancing across the low ceiling. I steadied it.

Sereth's gaze searched the crannies in the stone. "I know nothing of communications genes and kin altruism, and care less. But I know women. Her plan was that we enter this passage without her. She objected quite strongly to being dragged down here. If she could have convinced me that her own creatures sought her death, so that I left her to their mercies, she would have been much pleased. She says she is dead, yet she walks before us. She celebrates our demise—I feel very much alive. And

I intend to stay that way. She calls on Chayin to make Wehrdom safe for a thousand years; he could not keep himself safe from her clutches.

"I will hazard that she has not yet drawn back for the kill. All this has been foreplay."

"She fought realistically enough when we changed her plan."

"And yet she did not break. She is too haughty for one who faces death. Real satisfaction is a difficult emotion to conceal."

"My reading of her agrees with that."

He looked at me askance. "What do you draw from Wehrdom? All I can dredge out of those mists are wordless songs and clicks and whistles and the taste of warm blood. I come away feeling like I want to eat something raw."

"The Stoth priests maintained that all of time, owkahen's entire extent, is but a function of volitional consciousnesses. Wehrdom is a multifaceted *unit*: one consciousness. Thus Wehrdom is not really volitional *individuals* interacting in owkahen as possible futures."

"Which means you get nothing from it either."

"That is what I just said."

"Estri, does all this lead you to conjecture anything?"

"What?"

"I read Wehrdom only when it brushes events in which I am physically concerned. The same must be true of you. And yet it is out there, wrapped around the time-coming-to-be. The woman flaunts us, admits she has lied, chortles over the fact that her attempts to kill us have, to her mind, succeeded. And my reading gives me nothing but some splinters floating on the top of Wehrdom's fog."

"You see those? Deilcrit, and Se'keroth, and Chayin?"

"Yes, but over what, I cannot ascertain. It is not

knowing enough to deduce a motive from a displayed moment of culmination that is the problem. Wehrdom is there, but its methods of symbolizing and its concerns are different from ours. It makes them dangerous. Their machinations do not show on owkahen's face."

"As if they were not creatures of time. The Shapers and the Mi'ysten race have that exemption. But Wehrdom is composed of time-space creatures. They, too, must inhabit owkahen."

"Our owkahen? Or a part of it not natural to our use? Wehrdom is concerned with things that do not concern owkahen as we know it. They have not yet the capacity to inject their will into that arena in which all intelligent beings contest. Which means, obviously, that they are a greater threat than they would otherwise be because we cannot preguess them; and, not so obviously, that they may be a self-extinguishing threat. If owkahen does not acknowledge them, it may be that they will not survive long enough to be acknowledged."

I murmured a noncommittal reply, thinking that Sereth was reading his preference into the time; that he, himself, was the most likely reason Wehrdom might not survive long enough to be acknowledged by owkahen. It rode his words, sat behind his tight jaw. I knew then that if he lost Chayin to Wehrdom it would not be Chayin whom Sereth would blame. Wehrdom would feel for his grief in a rage the like of which they had never dreamed.

I was about to comment that even Khys, who had ruled previous to Sereth, had had the grace to let this shore go its own way, when Mahrlys and Chayin, with an exclamation of surprise, suddenly dropped from sight. The cahndor's grunt hung momentarily in the air; then it too disappeared.

Slowly, cautiously, we approached the edge,

wholly invisible in the uncertain light, over which they had plunged.

Sereth crouched down, a hand on my arm. "I should not have let them go so far ahead. Send your sun down there."

And I did, into that sudden fifty-five-degree angle of descent. Sereth, most carefully, for the floor on which we squatted was itself angled downward, called Chayin's name, leaning over the steepened incline. When no anser drifted up from the dark, he ran his palm along the stone floor where it abruptly changed to a black glassy material. "Frictionless," he pronounced. "The Beneguans no more built this than Dey-Ceilneeth. See if you can drop the light lower."

So I did, and my little fireball hovered ever farther down that corridor that plummeted into the depths of the earth. We saw the walls and floor and ceiling converge in a trick of perspective. All we could determine was that the passage kept the same relative dimensions but for the steepening of its angle.

"Well?" I asked when he had been long silent.

"Take my hand."

I did that.

"We are just going to slide down it. Under no circumstances tense up. Try to keep your head uppermost, but do not stiffen your legs. It should be a fast descent, and if at the bottom the rock continues, you could break a limb on impact if you are not very careful."

"Sereth!"

"Now, you are not afraid of a little slide like that, are you?"

And his tone told me that there was no arguing, so I said that I was not afraid and sat back on my haunches and extended my legs and muttered a quick prayer to my father, who had certainly not put me on Silistra to have me end in a pulped mass of flesh and bone in the well-forgotten belly of Dey-Ceilneeth.

Then I thrust my little sun downward, and Sereth said "ready?" and I nodded and we slipped down into Dey-Ceilneeth's well.

There was a rising of my stomach, a hissing of wind in my ears. My eyes watered and burned and saw only a blur of stone. Then blackness: we passed the miniature sun as if it were hovering unmoving, and plummeted on into the darkness.

The feel of the black, frictionless material was like liquid ice, a strip of cold under me, and yet there was no sensation of weight, as if our speed had outstripped gravity itself.

Sereth, drawing me closer by his arm wrapped around my waist, shouted in my ear: "Get your light down here."

I closed my tearing eyes and called it, trying not to think of how long we had been falling, nor how fast we must be traveling to have so quickly overtaken the little sun.

"I used to kite-jump off the Nin-Sihaen ridge," he confided loudly, as my hair whipped around me and the rushing pursuit by my miniature star made it seem that we were rising and my stomach threatened to leap out of my mouth.

I was still thinking of a reply when Sereth rumbled: "Look!"

And I did, and remedied myself for whatever glowed with its own light up through the dark beneath us.

Closer and closer came the other light, until the glow rushing toward us showed itself white water and the light of the little star was swallowed in a dull luminescence and I braced for the concussion.

"Relax," he ordered as we began perceptibly to slow. I looked at his face in the bleaching light that seeped up from below, and knew from his expression that he sought to break our fall with mind.

So I relaxed and concerned myself with aiding him, and when we hit the white frothing water it only knocked my breath away for a moment.

Then the warmish water closed over my head and I concerned myself with not drowning in my entangling hair and kicking my way surfaceward.

Gasping, I broke into the air. My little star hovered, uncertain, where the stone chute's ceiling arched up into a cavern from whose dome hung gigantic stalactites that glowed whitish, and silver, and green.

Sereth's head erupted from the choppy water on my right. He surveyed the ceiling, and the ledges that edged the fast-rushing subterranean river. Then he indicated Mahrlys and Chayin, huddled drenched and exhausted and tiny at a stalagmite's base, and bade me swim toward a promontory jutting out into the stream. His shout, swallowed in the echoing river roar, did not reach the cahndor's ears.

Spitting out the tepid, mineral-tasting water, I swam until my stroke brought me close enough to grabe the iregular rock and cling to it. Still, my feet had not touched bottom.

Sereth hauled himself along the froth-slicked jetty, hand over hand, to my side, and boosted me roughly upward.

We lay there a time, facedown on the half-submerged ledge, listening to the muted cacophony of the water's slap and our own breathing. The rock under me was not cold, but tepid, as the water had been. I wondered how deep into the earth we were, and my geological knowledge told me that this particular kind of cave, at this depth, with such a river whose course was so rapid, was as anomalous as the fact that fresh air brushed my cheek and dried the droplets on it.

Sereth tousled my drenched locks, and motioned me up, and we emptied our boots and took stock of our weapons, which had, by reason of sheath guards, not been lost in the river. Then, with a grin and a tucking in of his chin, he suggested we join Chayin and Mahrlys, somewhere downstream to our left amid the forest of stone.

We wandered between spires that were thick as Benegua's memnis, and some taller, and came after a time upon Mahrlys and Chayin, who leaned back against the bone-white stone, eyes closed, in a pool of his drippings.

She had disrobed and spread her garment on the stone to dry. She watched us approach, with a widening smirk.

When we stood above her, she touched Chayin, rose, and said: "Welcome to the outer gardens of Othdaliee. Beyond this cavern"—and she gestured upstream—"ends Nothrace and begin the gardens proper. In them we shall find my triumph and your demise."

Chayin grabbed her ankle, and she fell roughly. His face was so contorted that I stepped backward and Sereth drew a sibilant breath. But Mahrlys only laughed a laugh that ripped her belly. It multiplied in the cavern, coming back on us from all sides. She reached for her robe, slipped it about her.

I followed her gaze and hissed Sereth's name, and he, too, turned to look at what Mahrlys-iis-Vahais had found so amusing.

Up from the depths of the river rose the majestic heads of two of the most gargantuan guerm I had ever seen. They looked about them, blinking coal-black eyes and tossing their creamy, streamered manes, and made directly for us.

"No!" wailed Mahrlys, as from Sereth's stance and mine she divined our intent. "These are not such guerm as you slew at the bayside. They will bear us into Othdaliee! They are elder creatures, with great—"

"Fangs," Sereth interrupted. "If you think I am going to get on the back of one those poisonous monsters, you have been taking too many of your own drugs."

I was very glad he had said that. I hugged him and nuzzled his neck.

"Those streamers are not poisonous. These are the creatures from which the savage ocean guerm evolved. They are not . . . ah, I care not. Walk!"

That seemed like a perfectly good idea to me. Another good idea seemed to me to be halting the sea beasts who slithered toward us through the white water. I was about this, only flesh-locking them that they would drown on their own, when Sereth bade me cease.

I looked at him, unbelieving. Chayin had whispered something in his ear while I had been busy ascertaining the mammalian nature of the guerm and exploring their nervous systems. I did not immediately release my hold on the guerm. Water flooded their lungs.

They stood closer together, Mahrlys hanging on Chayin's arm, Sereth with my miniature sun bobbling behind his right shoulder, illuminating his displeasure.

I dropped the flesh-lock, and the water before me erupted in coughing, writhing paroxysms as the guerm sought to save themselves.

"You certainly are not going to change your mind," I pleaded, backing away from them. "Sereth, I am not going to get on one of those things. . . ."

I knew better than that. One does not say "I will not" to Sereth.

Dismally, as the huge snakelike, finned monster came abreast of the promonotory, I mounted. Awkwardly clasping my knees around its muscular barrel, I wondered if guerm held grudges. Sereth slipped on behind me, and the guerm with an undulating surge headed off upstream. I wound my hands in the streamers of my beast's crest, and Sereth put his arms around my waist. And I reflected, as the beast moved easily beneath me and the waves lapped my hips and the stalagmites whipped by in a blur, that if we were not killed this manner of conveyance had much to say for itself.

VIII

The Carnelian Throne

Deilcrit, in hopes of shaking the burning cold away
with movement, crawled to the edge of the ledge
and stared down the way he had come. He crouched
there, slapping himself, his breath streaming white
as the mantle that draped the Isanisa River far
below.

Kirelli, stiff-legged on the cold, joined him.
Together, to the rhythmic buzz of Quendros' snor-
ing, they stared down at the cloud mantle through
which they fought their way the day before.

He could not see Dey-Ceilneeth, nestled in the
shelter of Benegua's northern gate. Nor the Wall of
Mnemaat, occluded by the forest and the mists
and the thick icy clouds that girdled Mt. Imnetosh's
hips.

Winter or no, it was too cold. The savage chill
had ridden the white clouds down the mountain to
plague them. It had frosted the rocks with ice and
numbed their fingers and slowed their sword arms,
as if in league with the wehrs who had harried
them. From out of those clouds the wehr-rage had
come, while they stumbled, climbing blindly upward. It had been Deilcrit's bad footing that sent
him skidding into the shallow cave. He had not
seen it, only the ice mist swirling around.

And they had made a stand there, their backs against the lichen-covered mountainside. Long into the night they had hewn and cleaved and rived what came out of the mists at them. Even in the weak morning light the corpses were easily chronicled: at his feet lay two ossasim; a fhrefrasil, gutted, made a pillow for Quendros' head; whelt feathers decorated the shallow ledge, glittering with frost; and below on the jagged slope sprawled a score of unmoving black shapes, casualties of the wehr-rage.

Squinting at the leaden sky which lowered ever blacker, he wondered if the wehrs would come again, out of the rain the sky promised.

He had never heard of a wehr-rage lasting so long.

His left arm ached, and he rubbed it, knowing he should wake the exhausted Quendros, but unwilling.

Kirelli butted his side, hopping about from foot to foot. The whelt was shivering. He squirmed back from the rocky shelf's edge and offered the whelt his right arm. Gladly, with a little squawk, Kirelli took perch on his shoulder, and then moved higher, so that a clawed foot clung either side of his neck. The whelt's breast pressed against the back of his head and its pulse and its tremors came clear to him. He reached up and stroked the half-raised crest, trying to share his warmth.

They had shared many things since leaving Quendros' hut. They had shared even the wehr-rage. He muttered to himself, trying to push the memory away, but it displayed itself stubbornly to his mind's eye:

They had been climbing the slope of Imnetosh where the trees begin to thin and the shale lies treacherous on the Nothrace ridge.

It was the rage itself that first came over him, so that his heart beat fast and his mouth turned dry, and he had been hard-put to conceal it from Quendros.

Then Kirelli took flight, screaming, from his shoulder, leaving him to wrestle with the whelt's message and its implications:

"Eviduey's flock and mine do battle, manling. Choose what side you may."

And then there was no choice, nor need to conceal his lust for blood from Quendros, for the wherrage overtook them in a tidal wave.

First came the non-wehrs: animals of every species fleeing blindly, screeching and trampling one another in their fear. He saw a wild-eyed berceide swallow a quenel whole, and head straight for him.

In the loose shale they had no footing, could not have hoped to elude the oncoming stampede.

Quendros shouted a farewell, and wagered as to how many beasts he might take with him out of life, and then the great berceide, to avoid the feel of the shale or Kirelli's screeching dive, veered eastward, dragging the non-wehrs in its wake. Straight for far Kanoss rampaged the non-wehrs.

Quendros muttered a prayer and chuckled uncertainly, and the pointed, openmouthed, upward: the sky was black with whelts.

Kirelli, among his own, wheeled and dived and squawked.

And then he had no more attention for that. From out the forest crashed the first wave of wehrs.

Not until it was all around him and the cloud of whelts dived screeching into the fray did he make sense of what he saw: wehr fought wehr, ptaiss tore ptaiss, berceide enwrapped ossasim in its coils. Death rattles from every throat in Benegua's nature filled the air. Creatures he had never even seen before churned around him.

And he found himself hewing about him with

the green-metaled sword, knowing with certainty who was friend and who was foe as easily as did the battling wehrs themselves.

Ossasim shadows filled the sky. Manlike bodies dived, howling war cries, taloned feet extended. He thrust upward without thought. And freed his blade just soon enough to behead a campt who charged with lowered tusks, upon whose hide was a breast-wide slash that only a sword could have made.

So did he come to realize that Quendros fought beside him, striking dead all that entered the range of the white metal sword.

Kirelli's soft voice rang in his inner ear, and he worked his way toward Quendros, who did not know enemy from ally, but hacked, grunting and heaving, at any creature that came near.

It was as he was attempting to close the distance between them, his feet sliding in the treacherous shale, that a whelt dived at him. He threw himself down to avoid it, and rolled to his back in time to see Eviduey's black form hovering above the dust cloud in which the wehrs battled.

Then that one was gone, and he gained his knees and then Quendros' side, and shouted to the man to have a care as to what he slew.

But Quendros only growled and lay more determinedly about him, lips drawn back from his teeth, eyes wild in a blood-splattered face.

So Deilcrit stayed with him, and fought there, until the wehrs that were Kirelli's encircled them completely, a buffer through which the battle could not penetrate. Then, as Quendros sank to his knees in that bloodbath's peaceful center, Deilcrit, with an animal noise he could not suppress, turned himself full over to his Wehrkin. He leaped, screaming wordlessly, to the battle's outer edge, where combatants yet clawed and charged and gutted and gnawed one another, and there he stayed until nothing moved on the field but Kirelli's wehrs; until he lay unable to raise his leaden sword arm one more time, sprawled across the long, warm corpse of a campt who in turn lay upon an ossasim's crushed form.

Paralyzed with exhaustion, lungs burning, through sweat-stung eyes he watched Kirelli dance his dance upon the shale carpeted with Wehrdom's dead. He knew that the triumph was his also, that all who licked wounds and limped slowly forestward were his.

And when Kirelli alighted beside him, a long chunk of some beast's heart in its beak, he received the offering without qualm.

It was as he feasted there with Kirelli's wehrs among the vanquished that Quendros limped over to him and sat heavily upon the campt's carcass and buried his head in his hands.

"Deilcrit," he said, "what in the name of Laore is going on here?"

Deilcrit licked his fingers and looked up at Quendros' face, hidden behind his fists, and said: "I am a wehr. You know all about wehrs. And wehr-rages. What you do not know is that Kirelli's wehrs and Eviduey's wehrs have a bone to pick."

"And what is that?" Slowly his eyes appeared over his hands.

"Me. I am Kirelli's candidate for the carnelian throne. Eviduey's wehrs will do all they can to stop us."

"Thanks for telling me."

"I did not know of this. I catch little wehr-thought."

"Well, all I can say is, when Mahrlys said 'trial,' she was not jesting."

"Did you think then that I could pursue the carnelian throne without obstruction?"

"No, I suppose I did not think that. But I did not

think that you were so much a wehr as to wade knee-deep in gore with them long after a man would have fallen dead from the effort."

"You yourself said to me that wehrs were very successful individuals." He grinned at Quendros. But Quendros did not grin back.

"Deilcrit, I'm getting worried. Before, I was just disquieted. You don't have any idea what you're doing. You don't really know what the carnelian throne is, or what you might have to do to sit in it. All you know is what the whelt has been telling you. Whelts are not the most trustworthy of creatures. What if this Imca-Sorr-Aat does not want to be superseded?"

"Eviduey said to me, when I was awaiting Mahryls in her chamber the night before we left Benegua by the Northern Gate, that Imca-Sorr-Aat is the intermediary between mortals and the god. If the god still lives. And Kirelli said to me that Mnemaat is no more; that Imca-Sorr is an empty title, a vacant throne with no presence worthy of the name 'Aat' to guide it. Kirelli says that we can change all that, together. I am inclined to believe him. At the very least, I should find out if Mnemaat is truly alive or dead. And that is something I need to know."

"Damn pious Beneguan, for one who just slew half an ecology."

"Quendros, you have known since we spoke in your hut that I sought the carnelain throne."

"But how do you know you'll want it when you get it? You don't know what it means, what responsibilities are entailed."

"What choice have I?" demanded Deilcrit hotly, all facade falling away. "I am so much a wehr that I had no choice this day. I hardly remembered that you existed until Kirelli reminded me. Yes, I did this. . . ." And he waved a hand around the battlefield. "And I am eating of my kill and I like it. It feels good. I could no more turn from Kirelli than I could reenter Benegua without having been absolved by Imca-Sorr-Aat. The wehrs would certainly kill me."

"We could try," said Quendros, looking behind him for Kirelli. "Or not reenter—"

"I do not want to try. This is what I am supposed to do. I know it. Are you so afraid? We have the wehrs. Their strength is ours until we enter the gardens. And Kirelli—"

"I am not afraid!" bellowed Quendros.

"Well, then, let us fill our bellies, and seek a high spot for the night, and when all this is over and I have Mahrlys at my feet, I will share her with you."

"I would rather beat the drum you plan to make of Eviduey's hide," Quendros quipped. Then he hawked and took his white-bladed sword and cut himself a thick strip of campt haunch.

"I will give the drum to you!" cried Deilcrit, glad that he had found something that might please Quendros.

"Let's get it first, man-wehr," said Quendros around a mouthful. "This thing looks to me to be one more easily said than done."

And so, when they had eaten their fill, they began to scale Imnetosh in earnest. When the day was nearly spent, the clouds had begun to roll down from the mountain's peak. All until the attack on the ledge that night was a blur in his memory. There was climbing, and the cold like knives in his lungs, and Kirelli's warm breast against his neck.

Until they had found the ledge, until the wehrs of Eviduey had attacked once more. Well into the dawn they had fought them. And now Quendros slept like a baby.

He peered into the darkening thunderheads, surveyed the carcass-strewn ledge, and shooed Kirelli from his shoulder. Then he busied himself rolling the dead from their refuge, in case the wehrs came again to besiege them.

The noise woke Quendros, who groaned and staggered erect and emptied his waterskin, casting it aside in disgust.

Deilcrit wished that he too had water, and then wished it no more as the icy rain began.

Hailstones pelted him as the sky came alight with jagged brightness; thunder clapped its palms over his ears so that they rang.

Kirelli squawked into the rising wind that drove the sleet and hail into their eyes, and scuttled into a cranny in the shallow cave's rear.

Quendros, with a bellow about folk that had not the sense to seek shelter in the rain, followed suit.

They sat long, shivering, in the dreary dark. Kirelli's feathers were dotted with icy balls, and his own teeth were chattering, when the whelt screeched and humped its wings and took flight, bursting out of the cave.

He jerked to his feet, slid on the icy stone, and skidded nearly to ledge's lip, over which peeked the red-in-red eyes of three ossasim.

One grabbed him by the ankle before he could stop himself. Together they tumbled into space.

He grabbed the wehr's wings, hugging it to him, and when they landed on an outcropping of rock it was the ossasim who was underneath.

He disengaged himself from the corpse, staggering to his feet just in time to draw his blade as the two other ossasim plummeted down toward him through the fiercely gusting rain.

Lightning exploded in the sky. He raised the blade. The ossasim pair folded their wings and dived after him.

He swung the sword blindly above his head, catching one ossasim's wing and slicing it through. There was a scream, a rush of air as the ossasim lost control and crashed into the mountainside. Then the other ossasim hit him, feet first, in the chest. As its talons raked him and he went down beneath its onslaught, the blade flew spinning from his grasp. Lightning blew the sky apart once more, caught the spinning sword in its blue-white fingers, caressed it. Its length enflamed, it tumbled groundward.

Then the ossasin's fangs snapped near his throat and the rock came up under him with concussive force and he wrapped his legs around the ossasim's trunk and shoved back on that mighty jaw with both hands. Grimly, red lights crowding his vision, he dug his fingers into the spittly chin, thrusting forward with his arms while pulling inward with his legs. There was a loud snap, and the ossasim lay quiet on him.

It was some time before he pushed it off. It was even longer before his lungs ceased gulping air. Then he sat, shakily, to consider his wounds. Through the coarsely woven jerkin his chest and belly were scored in twelve diagonal lines. But for his clothing's protection, the thing would have laid open his belly.

Something within his right hip twinged. His left arm was badly scratched where it had only been half-healed, and the sleeve of the tunic was torn away. He ripped off the rest of the flap in disgust, and used it to bind up the arm.

Then he assayed the climb down to where the sword lay in a narrow crevice ringed with ice.

He squatted down there, studying the blade that lay in a pool of slush. The metal shone dull, grayish, but otherwise seemed intact. The gemstone hilt was not even scratched. Even as he watched, the

slush that had been melted by the hot metal began
to crust. Satisfied that any heat the blade retained
must by now be dissipated, he picked it up, dried
it as well as he could in the continuing sleet, and
thrust it in the makeshift scabbard.

He was just rising, cautiously, intent upon the
throbbing twinge in his hip, when Quendros joined
him, blowing loudly.

"You are by far the most charmed man I have
ever met. That lightning was meant for you. I
yelled. Did you hear me? No. Well, I did. Lightning
loves nothing like the taste of metal. You are be-
witched. Anyone else would have been fried."

"Is that why you climbed all the way down here,
to tell me that?" He kneaded his hip tenderly with
his fingers, but found no spot where external pressure caused pain.

"No," said Quendros brusquely. "How'd the blade
fare?"

"Well enough," he replied, looking curiously at
Quendros' drenched face, which bore an expression he could not name.

"Well, son. Let's go get you installed in that
carnelian throne of yours. Nothing is going to stop
us now."

"That is not wholly true. Kirelli says we must
fear Wehrdom until we make that first ridge." And
he pointed upward, to where he thought that ridge
might be, hiding behind the storm.

"Ignorant savage," Quendros chided, offering
Deilcrit a countenance pursed like a closed fist and
kicking desultorily at the dead ossasim. "Se'keroth
is like a weathervane. It does not create a climatic
change, but it does indicate one."

It took Deilcrit a moment to realize that Se'keroth
was the name Quendros had given to the sword he
bore. Then he gave Quendros a blank stare.

Quendros, upon recept of this, grumbled that

they had best be making for the ridge hidden behind the midday dark, if they would face the real
dark safely.

Deilcrit craned his neck in vain for sight of Kirelli,
then agreed that they had better start climbing.
Hitching himself up between two rocks, he asked
Quendros what he meant about the sword being a
weathervane.

Quendros asked him if he could read. To which
he answered no, and Quendros pronounced that in
that case it was no use trying to explain.

But he knew that something in the morning's
occurrences had greatly heartened Quendros, and
if it was the dunking of the sword in a slushy
puddle that had caused the change in Quendros'
manner (and he strongly suspected that it was),
the change was still to his benefit. And he respected Quendros' knowledge. So he decided that
if the sword would in some way aid him, he would
let it, though he did not believe in material things
such as swords having desires or goals or significance
of the like with which Quendros seemed to credit
the strange blade.

When they had gained the ledge once more,
Deilcrit asked Quendros if he did not believe in
Mnemaat the Unseen. And Quendros replied quite
solemnly: "Not only do I believe in him, I have
seen him."

At which Deilcrit made a sign to ward off blasphemy, and Quendros laughed and said, "It is true.
Fifteen, no, sixteen years ago. I can't tell you on
what errand—gave my word, y'know—but he's
magnificent, a great golden thing with the face
everyone's father should have had."

"In the flesh?" said Deilcrit as Kirelli's wings beat
around his head, and with a deep sigh he extended
his arm to the whelt.

"In the flesh; clasped his hand."

"But Mnemaat is the Unseen!"

"Now he is, and that's a fact. Look, Deilcrit, when you're in a position, you hire me and I'll tutor you in history."

"Do you know something about Imca-Sorr-Aat that I do not?" asked Deilcrit, bending his head away from Kirelli's insistent attempts to give him a message.

"Nothing that will help you. If I were to think of something, you would be the very person I'd tell." There was something icy and deliberating in his tone that Deilcrit had never before heard there.

His feelings hurt by he knew not what, he took the message from Kirelli, who urged all speed, and with a curt word to Quendros started up the boulder-strewn ridge.

The rock and dirt and weeds blurred by. He climbed mechanically, surely, though he had never before been on Mt. Imnetosh, did not know her. When he had climbed with great attention, in the beginning, he had been dizzied and fearful. So he rested his attention elsewhere, and Kirelli sometimes rode his shoulder and sometimes flew around his head, and he thought of Mahrlys-iis-Vahais and what had passed between them.

The swoop of her white throat, her soft curves along which the light rode as he stripped her of her veils, the surrender he had not expected, that which his lengthy exploration of her had precipitated, all proceeded before his inner sight as he climbed. The dreams of her that had tortured his youth had not prepared him for the reality. Nor for the questions she had asked, or the rare pleasures, of which he had been previously ignorant, she demanded from him. And she had bade him kneel down before her, saying "Do you not show respect before her to whom you are sworn?"

A cold had chilled him then, causing his passion

to shrink and then blow away on the wind of her words. It was while she interrogated him that he determined that the day would come when their positions would reverse. She had cheated him of his dream, cheapened it. She had drained from him his strength. He grunted and pulled himself by the arms over a chasm between two boulders, and up onto the shelf above.

There he rested, swinging his legs, while he awaited Quendros, looking into the receding storm clouds pushed eastward by the ocean winds. It was because of Mahrlys, more than any other thing, that he had accepted Kirelli's proposal. All his life, those above him had asked him to do nothing, to be quiet, to be passive and follow orders and live the life he had stolen from Mnemaat's henchman without letting on that he truly should have died in Nehedra's dirt. Within him burned proscribed fires, needs which his station in life could not fill. Kirelli had held out to him a purpose, a striving, something more than the spitting of an occasional guerm. Kirelli had something to gain that was not yet revealed, he was sure; but the whelt had proposed that they *do* something, that thing for which, said Kirelli, only Deilcrit was fit. He mattered to the whelt. He had never mattered to anyone but Parpis, and to Parpis he had been a child to be protected, even when he stood twice the old man's height.

He did not matter to Mahrlys yet.

Then he thought of Mahrlys' tears, and Heicrey's, and reflected that his touch always seemed to bring women tears. All but the spirit power Estri, who was not a woman.

And thinking of women brought him to Amnidia, and her pronouncement that he would feed Quendros to Wehrdom if she let him. The ancient crone's face hovered before him. He shook it away and extended his hand to Quendros, just levering himself over the canted boulders.

He had thought Quendros might care for him. Now he was not so sure. But he resolved that the older man would not end in a wehr's belly upon his account.

"Why so solemn, Deilcrit? Lose your whelt? Sun's about due. We'll both feel better with the ice melted off our bones."

"Did you see Eviduey leading the wehrs who attacked us on the shale?"

"No," grunted Quendros, shifting until his legs, too, dangled off the shelf's overhung edge. "But I don't doubt that he's about." Quendros peered upward, around his head. "Most wehr-masters who've become high as the Third Hand tend to stay pretty much in council. Eviduey has always been out in the field, himself. He likes it, I guess. The Byeks—the human ones, that is—all met in Bachryse the year before Nothrace was razed, and they put a price on his black head that would set a man and his children and their children free from drudgery."

"Are the human rulers of the outer provinces those for whom you work?"

"On occasion. I try to stay self-employed, on the whole. There's plenty for a man to do, if injustice concerns him." Quendros gave Deilcrit a sidelong glance.

"It is revolution, then, that you are about."

"Survival, more truly. There are not enough men left to launch a successful revolt."

The way he said it made Deilcrit know that he had well studied the question, and also that he did not believe the answer.

He said slowly, "If I am successful . . . I would do what I could for your folk."

At that Quendros did not laugh, but only locked eyes with him and nodded gravely, telling Deilcrit more than he wanted to know about Quendros thereby.

Then the soft touch of Kirelli's wehr-thought brushed him, and without another word he scrambled to his feet and began the difficult ascent to the ridge top.

The boulders were loose and the vegetation sparse and the rock iced slippery. When he could finally lie prone upon the ridge's summit, he rested, eyes closed, until Quendros' muttered exclamation made him lift his head and peer through his tangles at what lay enfolded in Imnetosh's skirts.

Othdaliee gleamed sullenly in the thin air. She was hewn into the V where Imnetosh's final sheer ascent met the ridge's lee. Through her middle a river ran silver, and in the middle of the river was a gigantic amber bubble, dark-centered, like the eye of a dead fish. Around this bubble, on either side of the river, rose squat rectangular towers of shiny black, like the glassy stuff he had seen in Dey-Ceilneeth. Each of the twelve towers was connected by an elevated, enclosed span that arched over the river and the amber bubble set into it.

In the whole city of Othdaliee, nothing moved.

"By Laore's eyeteeth," said Quendros on an indrawn breath. "All men should see this before they die." The reverence that choked his voice was incomprehensible to Deilcrit, for it was a reverence of man's art.

They descended the ledge in a shower of tumbling rocks until they reached a staircase, invisible from above, cut into the stone. The stairs were very wide and fanned out from the mountain. The steps were worn round and slick with the years, and in their corners fat black spiders spun elegant webs.

The wind with its icy chill howled over the ridge,

but its claws could not touch them in the sheltered ravine.

Where the green rock stopped and the black slick stuff began, Kirelli waited. He sat upon the head of a statue whose whelt's visage rested upon a woman's body. It was one of the first pair of many enshadowed by the overhanging staircase by way of which they had descended.

When they walked between them and Deilcrit extended his arm for Kirelli, a humming sound cut through the faraway whine of the wind over the ridge, and sent Deilcrit hastily retreating, until he was stopped by Quendros' arm.

"What's the matter, boy? Don't like your palace?"

Deilcrit was struck speechless by what he saw between the two statues, and did not answer.

The apparition stood in a bath of light converging from the eyes of the whelt-headed statues.

Then Quendros' arm was on his shoulders, and the older man's reassuring voice whispered in his ear that the thing that approached them, through which the black paves could be dimly seen, whose head was like a whelt and whose body was like a woman's, was a projection of light, a thing of man's elder science, and told him not to be afraid. His mind heard, but his body did not. It shook like a leaf, until Kirelli straddled his shoulders and pressed cheek to his and gave him wehr-comfort.

So fortified by the confidence of both his allies, he neither fainted nor dropped to his knees before the glowing, flesh-toned apparition with its silver beak and cobalt crest.

This vision, which in Benegua's mythology was that of Imca-Sorr-Aat's female attribute, beckoned them, whelt-head cocked. Then it turned and floated down the middle of the black way along which sixteen identical statues stood guard.

Deilcrit's teeth chattered loudly, and he clamped

his jaws together until they ached. Quendros, beside him, gawked right and left, but when Deilcrit asked him how the light-thing could move away from the statues that Quendros said created it, the older man opened his mouth, closed it, and said: "Never mind."

Before a gaping portal thrice his height and wide enough to hold the men standing abreast, the image flickered, faded, and from within another, seemingly identical, beckoned out of the dim.

Quendros strode across the threshold. Deilcrit's legs were rooted to the back steps. Kirelli nudged him, cooed softly, then tugged at his hair.

Quendros, within, shouted: "Look, Deilcrit," and thrust his hand through the substance of the whelt-headed deity and waved the hand around.

Deilcrit squinted above, at the sky, at the last pair of black whelt-headed statues with their beaks turned toward him, staring down reproachfully; at the huge obsidian tower within which Quendros already stood.

There was a soft kissing sound. Kirelli squawked, took leave of his shoulder, and darted through the mighty portal. Deilcrit hesitated another moment, realized that the portal was indeed closing, and bounded through in three leaps. To find himself pulled up short by the slamming together of the glassy slabs upon the tail of his ragged shirt.

He lunged against the thing that restrained him, unthinking, and the ill-used tunic ripped from his shoulders and he stumbled into Quendros' arms.

"Easy there, Deilcrit, it's only a door. You made it. We made it. We're *in* Othdaliee."

Embarrassed, Deilcrit pulled away and stared at the glassy black portal from whose mouth dangled his garment, and at the patiently waiting apparition. Then he craned his neck and followed the black walls up into the dark. At about eye level on one of the walls was a large oval in which bricks of colored light were stacked. As he watched, the bricks flickered, changed color, ceased to exist. Quendros was peering intently at the oval. So, apparently, was the apparition, which stood by Quendros with raised arm.

As he joined them and Kirelli alighted on his shoulder, he realized that the apparition would point to a brick and then Quendros would touch it and then the color would change and they would repeat the process.

When Quendros did not answer his query as to what he was doing, Deilcrit turned around and stared at the black doors, closed up for a thousand years.

Then Kirelli nudged him and he turned back to where a rainbow display now filled the oval and the wall was drawing back into itself to expose a corridor lit with a dancing red glow. The whelt shivered and made an agitated little noise.

So he thought calm thoughts to it, reminding the whelt that soon they would both have their freedom, one way or the other, while he hissed at Quendros: "What did you do?" once again.

"Pressed what buttons were indicated. You want to go home, this is a little late." And he bowed low and sweepingly to Deilcrit, and indicated the corridor wherein danced the red light.

Then Kirelli humped up his wings and shook off his fear and flew first into the corridor of reddish mist. He could do no other than to follow. He was just turning to reassure Quendros when the wall through which he had entered closed upon itself.

He pounded on the wall and yelled Quendros' name until he realized the futility of what he did, then sat at its foot and closed his eyes and took stock of himself, searching out that purpose which he had thought he had here.

Even through his closed eyelids he was dizzied by the lights pulsing. He fingered the hilt of the sword he bore, and spoke harshly to himself and dredged up Mahrlys' face. But it was a long while before his legs would hold him and he rose up in the narrow, low corridor to take Kirelli onto his shoulder and walk the length of it, looking betimes at his feet, which seemed to sink into webs of flame that splashed and clung to his ankles. The farther he proceeded down the corridor, the deeper the sticky webs became, until he slogged through them rather than raising his feet so that he could see them between steps. By the time the strangely liquid filaments had reached his thighs, both he and the whelt knew that this was what they had come so far to find, and their cheeks were pressed together and their minds embraced more tightly than ever he had allowed himself to be enfolded by Wehrdom's caress. So tightly that Kirelli heard his every fear and he himself was inundated with wheltly trepidation, and all of Kirelli's conjecture as to what strength they might throw into that consuming red glitter that threatened to wipe from them all cognizance of individuality came clear to him.

Tightly held the whelt to his mind. Brightly burned its claws in his shoulder, and he was glad of the pain as the red stuff through which he walked congealed thicker and lapped about his chest. He felt little stingings, like insect bites, from the filaments the stuff threw up, but once his skin was immersed in it he felt nothing. It was not a physical danger, in truth, he faced there, but one of mind. When Kirelli's claws and his chin were beneath the surface and the salty taste of it lapped against his lips, he felt terror that even their combined strengths would not be enough; that the inundation of knowledge to which their linked minds were being subjected would prove too great; that their conjectures were unfounded and they would lose remembrance of their purpose before the moment at which they must act to save themselves came. And then the sparkling red mist was in his mouth and his eyes and he felt Kirelli shiver against him and closed his lips and lids and tried to breathe the stuff in and his lungs exploded and he did indeed forget who he was.

But Kirelli did not, and he was conscious of raising his arm slowly through the viscous stuff around him to steady the whelt on his shoulder. He wanted to stop, to cease the senseless pushing, but the whelt urged him on. He plodded sightless through the blood-warm sea for eternity. Eternity consisted of Kirelli's wehr-voice cooing his name and the whelt's claws in his shoulder and at its end lay the dreaming mind of Imca-Sorr-Aat.

"Deilcrit."

"Kirelli ... I cannot think. ... What is it I must not forget?"

"Imca-Sorr-Aat lives in dreams. He kills for dreams. We must not let him. ... Deilcrit, do not sleep. ... If you cannot hold, open your mind to Wehrdom. ..."

And then he heard the whelt no more, but only faced that which rose out of the mist at him: a muscular ossasim thrice the size of any he had seen, talons extended. He tensed to throw himself aside, upon the boulder-strewn ground, then recalled there were no boulders in the corridor of red mist. There was red mist: it seemed that the whole ossasim was comprised of red mist, and when he grappled with it his arms would not obey him and his hands closed upon empty air. Yet he felt its teeth in his neck and then its great weight pinning him down as it poured into his defenseless mind all of the burden of knowledge that had been Imca-Sorr-Aat's for twenty-five thousand years. And he screamed, and gurgled, and drowned in what no man should hear. Insanity beckoned, mindlessness a cool dark refuge with a lovely woman at its gate, yet he could not even surrender, for he lay helpless in the clutches of Imca-Sorr-Aat. The mad red eyes burned into him every knowledge forgotten and damned, and the lives of the billions it held chronicled within were his lives, and he lived them each and all. And at the end of them trailed his own, and he recognized all that he had been, and recollected his purpose, and tasted of his own strength. Then did he open his mind to Wehrdom and let the crushing weight of the years flood through him and out into the mind of every wehr who lived. And there came a great sighing, and a wailing shook the ground under him, and it cracked asunder, and the red mist that was Imca-Sorr-Aat began to discorporate before his eyes.

A terrible urgency filled him, that Imca-Sorr-Aat might escape and leave him trapped in the shuddering dreamscape. With all his determination he called on those wails as his own, willing the most palpable. Slowly, the thing that was Imca-Sorr-Aat took shape once more, and as it did, he grabbed its neck in both his hands and dug in his thumbs. For a score of heartbeats there existed only his straining fingers and the jaws seeking his throat.

Then he was coughing paroxysmatically, on his hands and knees, before an open doorway. Kirelli the whelt lay motionless by his right hand. By his left glittered oasasim feet through which the floor could be seen. Still choking, his eyes streaming tears, he gathered up the whelt and held it to his ear. A heart beat, weak but clear, within the feathered breast. He pressed the whelt against him and rocked slowly back and forth on his knees, not knowing what else to do for it, though within him rustled something which knew more than he ever dreamed possible. He did not prod that nightmare, quiescent. What lapped around the edges of his conscious mind told him more than enough. He knew for what the whelt-headed attendant waited, knew what yet lay between him and the carnelian throne.

But he sang wordlessly to the whelt, limp in his arms, content to wait.

This was their journey, together. He thought, inundated by grief, that though it was but a few steps more, he could not make it alone.

"You promised me, whelt, that you would follow me one day. That day has not come. Live!" And he pressed his head to the whelt's, and sent himself within its mind.

A soft, frightened thing curled there, whimpering. He reached with comfort, with success, with love, into the whelt mind. But the crying thing would not come forth.

Wordlessly he entered his despair, his own fear, his need, into that empty space, and Kirelli came to fill it.

The limp whelt body stirred, fluttered, grew animated in his arms. He sat back on his haunches and laid Kirelli on his thighs and stroked the cobalt crest. There was an explosion of wings, and an irritable "Breet," and the whelt stood uncertainly on the floor by his knee, shifting from foot to foot.

Deilcrit rubbed his eyes and snorted and growled menacingly to the whelt that their host awaited them. Then, trying hard not to grin, he extended his arm.

As the age-old guardian of light preceded them down innumerable corridors that lit when they entered and darkened when they left, he allowed himself the first small thrill of triumph. He had not been consumed by the trial of Imca-Sorr-Aat.

The corridor had not judged him fit only to end as fodder for Othdaliee's fire. And his mind had not turned to curd. . . .

But then the light figure winked out abruptly, and all about him the illumination dimmed, and the walls drew back to admit him into the presence of Imca-Sorr-Aat.

Here were corporeal attendants, ossasim in resplendent cinnabar robes who stood rigid about the octagonal chamber's walls, staring straight ahead of them. These were the servants of Imca-Sorr-Aat's flesh, deployed around their master, who slumped as if sleeping in his carnelian throne.

With a whisper to Kirelli to take wing, Deilcrit approached the throne alone.

None among the ossasim lining the walls moved. Their eyes did not follow him. It was possible those eyes did not see, that they saw only Imca-Sorr-Aat, that they had seen nothing else for a thousand years. He did not fear them. They would not move to stop him. They were disfrancished with their sleeping regent.

He climbed the three steps slowly, heavily. He had won this right, and none would stop him, but as he faced his last grisly task, he faltered.

He looked down into the peaceful, sleeping face of the snow-white ossasim whose dreams had ruled Wehrdom for the last millenium. His hands clenched convulsively on the sword he bore at his hip. For a thousand years the interface that coordinated Wehrdom had been this ossasim, kept alive by Othdaliee's elder knowledge. Yet and still did the burden of that correlative function lay upon the brain whose projection had battled him in a dreamland of its construction. What would be left of Deilcrit as he knew himself when he alone bore Wehrdom's weight? Not for ten thousand years had he who bore the title Imca-Sorr-Aat been more than an idiot-savant. This the thing which lay in the back of his mind told him smugly.

Upon an instant, before the thing that dwelt in him could weaken him further, he drew the sword and mounted the final step and lopped off the head of the ossasim who had been Imca-Sorr-Aat.

Then did he feel the full weight of what resided in Othdaliee.

IX

Gardens of Othdaliee

Twice since entering the gardens of Othdaliee had we been beset by creatures intent on turning Mahrlys' prophecy of our deaths into truth. First, the guerm attacked upon putting us ashore at a flight of hand-hewn steps leading toward a crevice from which spilled amber light. And we had killed the guerm, and Mahrlys had wept, and Chayin had growled, and Sereth warned them both that he was near the end of his patience.

The second time had been at the stairs' head as we peered about us into a silent, petrified forest under an arching dome. From their perches in those leafless giants whose wood had ages ago been replaced with scintillant silicates they attacked: strange creatures, angular and gnarled as the limbs from which they descended on us. The sandy ground was littered with them, as if with dead branches after an electrical storm.

Sereth leaned against one of the great tree bolls. His chest was heaving and sweat gleamed on him. Through the trees at his back I could see the curve of the amber dome riverward, toward the place where the narrow island met the water.

"Chayin, I would speak with you alone," he said, wiping his eyes with the back of his hand. I, too, was perspiring freely. The air within the dome was close and moist and stale.

Chayin left Mahrlys' side and approached him.

For prudence's sake, I sidled close to her. She was staring, back turned to the men, through the trees of stone toward the little isle's center, where something gleamed as warmly as the dome above, as if a second hemisphere of amber rested there.

I said, "What is that?"

And she answered: "The heart of this garden's rarest flower: the recollections of Othdaliee."

And then she shuddered as if struck from behind, raked her fingers through her black hair, uttered a little scream, and fainted dead away.

I heard: "How dare you vent your wrath on her?" And whirled in time to see Sereth push Chayin from him with the flat of his hand. The cahndor staggered back a pace, then another, then slipped in some white slime puddled near a tree-thing's corpse.

Sereth, a smile on him, waited patiently while the cahndor recovered.

The two cirlced each other.

Numbly I sank down beside Mahrlys, and closed my eyes: owkahen sprang clear and bright into my sensing, all wraiths of the wehr-mist ripped away.

And I screamed: "Chayin, Sereth did not do this. Look. Look at owkahen," and by then I found myself between them, my fists pounding the cahndor's chest.

Chayin imprisoned my wrists in one hand, snarled, and by that grip pulled me from between them. Then he hesitated, asking Sereth: "Is this true?" And his membranes snapped as he sought conformation from the time.

"It is. You did not ask me. I think you and I need wait upon excuses no longer. One reason is as good as another."

"No, Sereth, no," I blurted. "Please, seek owkahen. Something has happened. Wehrdom stands clear and revealed." And then Chayin shoved me toward Mahrlys and I crouched there, shaking, staring sightlessly at her chest rising and falling under the thin white robe.

I did not watch: I read death in that silence broken only by a foot sliding in the sand and a rustle as they circled each other. No, I did not look, only shuffled through the enlightenment the time held out. And then moaned, struck my forehead with the flat of my hand, and shouldered my way into Mahrlys' unconscious mind.

Ah, I could not have done it sooner, no more than I could refrain from it then. Therein I found the nature of her designs, the awful fate she had orchestrated for Chayin. I saw what reality was called Imca-Sorr-Aat. And I saw what had dropped her senseless and chased her mind into the corner where it cowered: Imca-Sorr-Aat no longer dreamed. Thereupon I did not need her further, for owkahen showed me why: It showed me what responsibility was Chayin's, in what way he had betrayed us. But I cared not, for all else was shown me, and in that larger context all things are fit.

So I turned from her, opening my eyes, and watched carefully as they closed, grappled, fell together in a heap. For a moment I thought I could do no good, that they would never break apart; but Chayin's grip on Sereth's neck slipped. They separated. I found an opening in that tangle of limbs and I flesh-locked them both so neatly that my father, were he watching, would have been proud of me.

I knew what I did, how great the risk of applying physical force to Sereth, but I did not really consider it.

Unsteadily, my steps slow and careful, I went

and knelt down between them, my eyes on my own knees that I not see Sereth's face and lose hold on them. Then I said: "Give me long enough to explain, and do what you will," and dropped the hold, far becoming untenable as Sereth's fury sought to breach my defenses.

I had a few moments, while the tremors attendant on flesh-lock rolled over them, and I used them well:

I told Chayin what life Mahrlys had planned for him, that of a semisentient vegetable who would dream Wehrdom's dreams a thousand years and never wake; and I remanded him to owkahen for instructions as to what punishment might fit such crimes as hers.

And I told Sereth to look there also: for Chayin's crimes, if crimes Sereth judged them after seeking counsel in the time, were no more than hesting Se'keroth's legend into fact without heed to consequence. And then I brought both their attention to the designs of Wehrdom newly etched on owkahen's face, and said:

"It is not any of us whose minds will be turned to jelly by Wehrdom. Though it seems to me late, it might be fit of us to attend him who took Chayin's place on Wehrdom's altar. Perhaps we can offer him an easy death."

I broke it off, eyes still lowered, waiting for Sereth's revenge: I had raised Shaper skills against him. But it did not come. When I looked up I saw that they sat regarding each other, as if they had not heard.

"Chayin, you promised Deilcrit your aid. Mahrlys lies unconscious in but the reflection of his need. Can you sit and pick an old bone with Sereth, knowing that Deilcrit suffers the very agonies she meant for you?"

"If Sereth agrees," said Chayin stiffly, "we will continue this at a later date."

"Gladly. But on one condition: I will do what I please to that saiisa of yours, and we will worry about reparations later."

Chayin's mouth tightened. He looked at me pleadingly. I only shook my head. Even if I wanted to use it, I had not enough influence on Sereth to lift the murder from his demeanor. And I did not want to. I almost asked Chayin whether he would have slain Deilcrit for Mahrlys, but bit my tongue, and rose stiffly and brushed the sand from my knees instead.

Chayin gathered up the unconscious Mahrlys in his arms and brought her to where Sereth quietly explained to me how we were going to obviate four people into a place we had never been, on the strength of the image of that room owkahen held out to us. I did not disbelieve him, only followed his terse instructions and added my strength to his own, while a part of me ruffled all the pages of owkahen seeking some probability in which Deilcrit was not a mindless hulk, sacrificed to the time. And I thought I might have found one, in the very presence of Wehrdom's web about owkahen, when Sereth said, "Ready?" and I nodded and took his hand and Chayin's and the three of us put our combined strengths into the obviation of space for the first time.

There was the golden glow of nonspace, and the cold that nibbled at my substance; but there was no pain, only a gathering as if to spring, and a sucking in of the flow we rode. And when I let go Sereth's hand and blinked away the vertigo as my substance repaired to its accustomed form, I saw the carnelian throne I had viewed in the Eye of Mnemaat, and upon owkahen's face.

It centered a featureless octagonal chamber of

black glass, bathed in a pool of amber light of the same sort as poured in through the wide-open door at our backs.

In it slumped a battered figure, one rag wrapped about its loins and another about its left arm. His belly and shoulders were scored with clawmarks, his chin rested on his chest. And above, perched on the throne's unornamented back, poised a huge whelt. Across the throne's arms rested a gray-bladed sword with a jeweled hilt.

The battered chest rose and fell very slowly. He did not stir. The whelt humped its wings and gave a forlorn cry.

I looked at the figure, and tears blurred my vision. I whispered Deilcrit's name, and Sereth gave me shelter under his arm. Without a look at Chayin or Mahrlys we approached the throne and what rested therein.

"There must be something we can do," I quavered to Sereth as the whelt took screeching flight and from behind us came a bellow:

"Stop right there."

As one we turned, looking past Chayin, who crouched over Mahrlys' just-stirring form, and saw a huge, blackhaired, ragged man striding toward us brandishing a steel sword. As he came upon us I recognized it as the sword I had lost in the forest, and whispered that to Sereth.

"Who are you?" demanded the man. Giving us a wide berth, he circled until he stood between us and the motionless figure on the carnelian throne.

The whelt, squawling loudly, dived toward us, veered at the last instant, to take perch again on the throne's back.

The man waggled my sword, repeating his query. His eyes were red and his cheeks bore clean white tracks among the dirt and stubble.

"Perhaps we should ask the questions," Sereth

said, letting go his grip on me and stepping a pace closer to the man. "That weapon you hold—"

"Quendros, stand aside," came a voice, deep and distant, from behind the hulking giant. That one, with a grunt of surprise, stumbled backward down the steps.

"Deilcrit!" I cried, and ran toward him. Sereth caught my arm roughly and pulled me up short.

The face looking down on me was sheened with strain. Under sheltering brows, long brown eyes flickered back and forth across us; touched Chayin, and Mahrlys, and Quendros, and then returned to me. The chiseled, ascetic features remained unmarred by emotion. The luminous eyes held no hint of recognition.

"Imca-Sorr-Aat," he corrected, and then leaned back and seemed to fall asleep. The whelt bent its head to his, and cooed softly.

X

Imca-Sorr-Aat

He dreamed a dream of life behind locked lids whose key he had misplaced. In the dream the presence called Imca-Sorr-Aat spoke through his mouth, and the growling sound echoed back in his emptiness and disturbed him. So he went to the pool of recollection and stared long therein, listening to the lullaby Imca-Sorr-Aat sang in his inner ear, that he might dream of man-wehrs undisturbed while that which dwelt within him held audience with what dwelt without.

But they were his eyes which Imca-Sorr-Aat opened, and what they saw belonged to him also. Three creatures like shadows before flame, the eyes had seen, and the vision triggered another vision that had been Deilcrit's when he alone commanded the flesh in which he rode. In the vision there had been himself, and the three combusting silhouettes, and a black-haired woman and a man. Such was the ladder of recollection Deilcrit climbed while Imca-Sorr-Aat hung to his legs and whispered sweet songs. And when he had pulled himself up that great distance he had no strength left to say whatever it was he had wanted to say.

So Imca-Sorr-Aat, who had held a hundred thousand audiences and partaken of the strength of those who had come to him, spoke through his mouth as it had through a quarter-hundred mouths before. The ritual of audience was one of the oldest of Imca-Sorr-Aat's memories. It prepared to lure the creatures it saw into the chamber of its desires, where it might, as it had countless times, claim the memories of those before it and add them to its own, strengthening Wehrdom thereby.

But Deilcrit had heard and seen and stood helplessly by in his own temple while a foreign priest oblated therein. When his eyes opened by Imca-Sorr-Aat's will and that name came from lips which were once his own, he screamed and thrashed in the tiny prison left to him and battered his identity like a great pointed stake against the walls Imca-Sorr-Aat had constructed to hold him.

Wehrdom dreams the dreams of all its children. Through the child whose flesh becomes both terminal and interface to that biologic correlative function fashioned by the sum of knowledge within it, Imca-Sorr-Aat rules Wehrdom. Had it been otherwise once? The Imca-Sorr-Aat presence recollected, reluctantly, that it had.

And Deilcrit, dangling from his life's visions over the dreamscape which sang so softly songs of enchantment, drove his identity like a wedge into that hesitation and reclaimed the volition of the body in which they both dwelt.

And for the fourth time since he had stumbled over the slain ossasim and sunk into the carnelian throne, his eyes opened.

The first time had been in the shock of inundation, when every light in Othdaliee had blinked on and every way but the way out had opened wide, and he had sent the disfrancísed ossasim with their decapitated lord on their last journey: by now servants and the past-master trod the sands of Othdaliee's heart; soon they would exist in the kiss of memory only, their substance gone to make broader the recollections of Imca-Sorr-Aat.

The second time had been at the moment the flame-figures disturbed Imca-Sorr-Aat's cogitations and called traces of Deilcrit up from where he languished imbound.

The third time he had watched in horror as Imca-Sorr-Aat made use of him, and felt Kirelli's mourning mind's touch, and even supplied the presence with Quendros' name. And therein lay the key to his success—there and in the fate Imca-Sorr-Aat held out to those who sought wisdom in Othdaliee. For Imca-Sorr-Aat sought wisdom also, and any receptacle thereof was to its ever-ravenous belly the most delectable of morsels.

Deilcrit, through waves of nausea, forced the numbness from his limbs and pushed away the bricks Imca-Sorr-Aat had placed upon his lids and upon his shoulders and mortared like a sarcophagus around his limbs, and thrust his body upward with all his might as sight came to him. Not because of him would Quendros end in Wehrdom's belly! Nor Mahrlys!

That which was Imca-Sorr-Aat sighed, commenced a dirge within his inner ear.

But he stood upright, on trembling knees, braced on the arms of the carnelian throne. His ears heard the sound as Se'keroth clattered to the steps at his feet.

Having heard it, he sought the sight. When the sword swam on the step before his eyes and he was sure that he did not yet dream, he raised his head to those who awaited him.

The cords stood out in his neck and perspiration rolled like rain down him, but he managed to retrieve the blade. Legs braced wide apart, swaying, he turned his head slowly from figure to figure, waiting until each one bore a name in his mind.

Then, heavily, he descended the steps until he was eye to eye with those who stood on the bottom one, and held out the blade to the dark power Chayin, beside whom was Mahrlys-iis-Vahais, her hand pressed to her mouth and her eyes wide above it.

He was conscious of Quendros, suddenly at his side, offering aid.

With a savage shake of his head, he refused. Not before Mahrlys would he be supported by another man.

There was an unbearable interval within which he chased the gift of speech, while they waited, the spirit powers and Quendros and Mahrlys. Shame flooded him, that he could not speak but only stare dumbly, and upon its heels came rage that he would be cheated of even this small triumph, and then Kirelli landed upon his shoulder and he almost fell.

The whelt's claws dug into him, its head pressed against his. With a wracking sob that echoed through the great hall, he gave over the blade to the dark power Chayin, and called that one's name, as he had been instructed, in his need.

He knew that he was falling forward, felt Chayin's arms about him, and a sharp light like a length of steel pierced the shroud through which he saw the world.

Those filmed eyes searched deep in his, and when he pulled back, the skin against which his own had rested glittered with moisture.

"Deilcrit?" said Chayin.

Deilcrit? "Yes," he said, and heard "yesssss."

Fortified by that success and what seemed like a great light coming from the spirit powers, he said to Mahrlys what he had long wanted to say, what he had longed to say since she had told him there was no place for such as he in the world, what he had needed to say since she had stolen from him the beauty in which his mind had long enwrapped her. He said:

"Mahrlys-iis-Vahais. You are my priestess and my betrothed. Do you not kneel before that power to which you are sworn?"

She seemed to melt rather than kneel. He stared at the black cascade of her hair upon the steps, and thought that now he might sleep content.

"No!" came an irresistible command like dry twigs rustling in his mind, forcing the presence of Imca-Sorr-Aat which had crept up on him disguised as his own will to shrink back. "Speak," commanded that voice, this time in his ears. He turned his head to follow the sound and beheld the scarred countenance of the spirit power Sereth. Those slitted eyes impaled him where he stood, holding him upright. At the periphery of his vision he glimpsed Quendros' agitated attempts to get his attention. But he could not turn from the power's grasp.

"I . . . we . . . Kirelli and I . . . though that together . . . we sent the truth throughout . . . all the minds . . . . If the remembrances that lurk under the amber dome . . . could be . . . silenced . . . it would be as it was meant. . . ."

"Thank you," said the spirit power Sereth, nodding.

He had done well. The spirit had asked him questions, and he had answered them. He, Deilcrit, had answered, against all of Imca-Sorr-Aat's protestations.

Within him, Imca-Sorr-Aat wailed, and took thought to its own safety, a thought it had never had to think in all the years of its cogitation. Desperately it struggled to retake the instrument through which it affected life, for without the mind's will to which it was bound, it could not initiate any action.

But Deilcrit was leaning upon the spirit power Sereth. That one held Deilcrit's arm across his own broad shoulders, and his whispered queries ripped answers Deilcrit did not understand from the memories of Imca-Sorr-Aat.

Out through the gaping portal into that hallway where the great doors still clamped shut upon the shirt Mahrlys had given him in Dey-Ceilneeth, Sereth propelled him, while Imca-Sorr-Aat babbled to him of Mnemaat and what glories for manwehrs they might together attain.

And they stopped before the glowing oval within which rested colored bricks. But they were not colored bricks. With Imca-Sorr-Aat looking out through his eyes, screaming in horror a hundred bribes and offers and imprecations, he gritted out the sequence long ago entered into the organic memory, discorporate, that was Imca-Sorr-Aat. And that intelligence faced oblivion, as for the first time in all that time the biophysical interface programmed itself: by invoking its own accession, it remanded Imca-Sorr-Aat into the prison of eternal dreaming whence it had come.

It was Sereth's fingers which did the work, for Deilcrit claimed only half those moments as his own, and when Imca-Sorr-Aat spoke through him he murmured and pleaded and cried ancient tears and toward the last both Quendros and Chayin held him.

There was a pride in him, a joy though he expected death, that Kirelli had sat on his shoulder, that at last they had managed to complete what it was that they had started. And a pleasure, too, that Mahrlys was not there to hear Imca-Sorr-Aat squealing through his mouth nor see them wrestle him to the ground.

The oval before his eyes swam close, brightening unbearably. Across its face shot red lines, then yellow, the white, while under his body, pinned by Chayin and Quendros to the stone, the whole universe heaved and quaked.

He saw blackness, unutterably complete, heard the screaming recede from his inner ear. After a time he felt emptied and crawled around within himself seeking any traces of the red mist, but there were none.

Deilcrit opened his eyes. Chayin's, and Quendros', peered into him.

"Deilcrit?" demanded Chayin.

"Deilcrit," he said, a hoarse rasp, hardly intelligible. But Chayin removed his weight, and Quendros also.

He sat, rubbing his left arm, and felt his skin pimple as the sweat began to dry. Chilled, he rose to his knees. Dizziness assailed him. But they only waited, to see what he would do.

In his mind was a soreness and an ache and a rubbish pile of knowledge he knew would take him a lifetime to sort and arrange.

It was Kirelli who attended him, while he huddled there, head hanging, seeking the strengh to rise.

The whelt alighted before him, thrust its beak into his face, and inspected him closely. Then it cooed and tugged on his hair.

A hand was extended. He ignored it. Clumsily but under his own power he gained his feet and held out his arm to Kirelli.

As the whelt sidled up to his shoulder, he surveyed the entrance hall of Othdaliee: The light, soft amber, still came from the arched ceiling. The outer doors were still locked tight. The oval still gleamed, but with three pinkish bricks only.

Otherwise, everything was changed.

The corridor in which he had taken the trial, where the red mist had inundated the substance of his body, lay open, and there was no mist therein. All along the hall's expanse were similar passages, each attended by two whelt-headed creatures spun from light.

Sereth obscured his view. The assessing look upon the spirit power faded. He extended his hand, palm up, to Deilcrit.

Wishing that his limbs did not shake so, he met it with his own.

"This had needed doing a long time. Errors of copying fidelity in any organic system cannot be avoided. You have not lost. You are still Imca-Sorr-Aat; what that one was supposed to be. Rule well, and stay out of dreamscapes." He was grinning.

Deilcrit felt his face pull up in an echo of Sereth's grimace. It felt strange and stiff and the muscles in his face hurt.

"I know," he said. "When we sent the call of Imca-Sorr-Aat throughout Wehrdom, we ensured that nothing would be lost. I think we all know. And for some, it was the first time that such knowledge was presented. You might say Wehrdom has been introduced to itself, at last."

"To its *selves*," corrected the spirit power Sereth.

From out of the pile of years in his mind came an understanding, a surety based upon the audience Imca-Sorr-Aat had once held with a glowing creature whose strength was unassailable and who had arrived, like this one, in a shadow form black before flame.

"You are Mnemaat's successor, are you not?" he asked of Sereth, and that one, suddenly unsmiling, inclined his head.

"If you will refrain from called me Mnemaat, I will refrain from calling you Imca-Sorr-Aat. And I promise you, I will be Unseen soon enough. I am not one to take a hand in others' affairs unless invited. Or forced."

There was a remonstration there that Deilcrit did not misconstrue. But also there was a confirmation, a promise of aid should the occasion arise.

"Imca-Sorr-Aat means 'he who came into being out of many,'" replied Deilcrit. "I would not be that, even in name. I will be Aat-Deilcrit, the self-begotten, for I am he who came into being out of Deilcrit."

Sereth laughed softly. "Then might we not be Aat-Sereth, Aat-Chayin, and Aat-Estri? It suits me better than Mnemaat. I am not so holy as all that."

Kirelli leaned forward and rubbed his cheek. He sensed the whelt's concern, and fingered its banded leg. "Kirelli wants to know if this means that you will not, after all, remain Unseen? The whelts liked not the banded servitude that the ossasim Imca-Sorr-Aat imposed on them."

"You tell your co-regent that it is a long journey to the Lake of Horns, and that neither I, nor any of mine will again make this trek unless you or he should call upon us for aid. I am not in favor of opening these shores to my own kind."

Kirelli made a small and regently "Breet" and inclined his beak majestically.

"I must go collect my woman: the time for me to become Unseen fast approaches. Chayin?"

But neither Aat-Chayin nor Quendros followed Aat-Sereth into the octagonal chamber where waited Mahrlys and Estri in the crowd of light-forms who attend the wants of the master of Othdaliee.

Chayin had the grayed blade in his hands, scraping at it with a fingernail. Where his nail scratched, the gray came away, and the green metal shone through.

Quendros, a little behind him, merely stared after Sereth's retreating back, incredulity doubling the size of his eyes, which seemed to want to hop from his head and follow the successor of Mnemaat.

"How did Se'keroth get like this?" asked Chayin without preamble. Quendros jumped as if struck, and turned his gaze upon the cahndor's massive litheness as if seeing it for the first time.

"Aat-Chayin, I beg your forgiveness. I was fighting ossasim, and it flew from my grasp, and lightning struck it, and it fell down the slope," said Deilcrit.

The cahndor's right eyebrow lifted high. He squinted at the sword, once more digging at it with his nail.

"Go on, you . . ." And then Quendros seemed to remember to whom he was speaking. "Go on, Aat-Deilcrit, finish it: the blade fell down the mountainside and landed in a pocket of ice."

A shrill ululating cry pierced his ears and echoed around the hall. Sereth came running to the doorway. The whelt screeched and beat the air, claws digging his shoulder.

Chayin held the sword high, and again the Parset victory cry blared from him.

Sereth advised something in a tongue even Imca-Sorr-Aat had not known, and Chayin lowered the sword and slipped it through a loop on his belt and studied Deilcrit for a time, during which Quendros fidgeted around with pursed lips as if what he waited to say would burst from him against his will.

Deilcrit stroked Kirelli's crest and shifted from foot to foot, wishing one of them would speak of what concerned them.

He was about to seek Mahrlys in the throne room when they both blurted out, together: "I would speak with you alone."

"Cannot the spirit power Aat-Chayin speak freely before the Minister of Histories, Third Hand of Othdaliee?" asked Deilcrit somberly, and then could not suppress his own grin at Quendros' shocked expression.

Chayin took no notice of Quendros' shy shuffling of feet, ludicrous as it was on a man of such bulk, but ground out: "What would you say if I asked you for Mahrlys' life?"

Deilcrit, misunderstanding, said: "She is in no danger from me. I have loved her in my dreams for years. All who erred under the sway of Imca-Sorr-Aat's nightmares will receive absolution. We have all learned a great deal. We may have even learned how to be ourselves. But were I not giving mercy as it was given to me, I would still spare her. It will be a wondrous thing to have her at my feet. In a sense she is what I have achieved."

He spied Quendros' troubled face, and thought of Heicrey, and quickly added: "Surely Imca-Sorr-Aat's successor may have more than one consort, after so many Imca-Sorr-Aats have been abstinent. I will bring Heicrey here too. They will learn to love each other."

"Boy, you know nothing of women," Quendros burst out. "They will kill each other."

"It is true that I know nothing of women, but there is only one way to learn. And Kirelli well knows Mahrlys. . . ."

Then he looked at Chayin's face, whose expression he could not name, whose hand clenched, unclenched upon Se'keroth's hilt. There was a snapping of membranes and behind them, a drawing back.

"You have done me great services. You quenched Se'keroth in ice for me, something perhaps only you could have done. You preceded me into the maw of Imca-Sorr-Aat. You invoked my word upon me when Mahrlys urged me to slay you, and thus kept me from a folly I would later have regretted. But I wonder if I do you any service? I, myself, know more of women than most men, and she worked such wiles upon me as I have never before seen but for Estri's."

"She is mine," said Deilcrit, folding his arms over his chest, wincing as they pressed against the deep scores Eviduey's ossasim had dealt him.

Aat-Chayin growled, and spat upon the tile. "She is that. But if you find you cannot handle her, bring her to Nemar, and I will instruct you." From the thickening of Aat-Chayin's voice, by the dignity of his bearing as he wheeled and strode toward the carnelian throne, did Deilcrit at last understand that Chayin, too, felt love for Mahrlys.

And he inspected his feet, thinking that he had two women and the splendorous spirit power had none, until Quendros clapped him square upon his bandaged left arm and he yelped.

"Remember, you're going to share her with me," Quendros grinned lasciviously. Deilcrit, recollecting the boast he had made to Quendros, nodded rather stiffly.

"And another thing? Recall when you said we'd make a drum of Eviduey's hide? Come on, I've a thing to show to you."

He and Kirelli went where Quendros dragged them, down a corridor that had, Quendros said, materialized with all else that now was opened wide in Othdaliee soon after the maw of red mist had swallowed them up.

"You should have been here. It was amazing. Those big doors to the throne room opened up and out came these sleepwalking ossasim with a dead one and its severed head and they went down there." Quendros pointed to the corridor across the hall from the one which they traveled. "So I slipped in *here* that they might not see me, and

stumbled over this ossasim passed out full length
in the corridor. Must have been the same thing
that knocked Mahrlys senseless.

"Anyhow, I'm not the one to turn down an
unexpected gift, so I wrapped him for you...."
And they turned a bend in the corridor.

There lay Eviduey, trussed with strips of Quendros
tunic, propped against the glassy black wall. Kirelli
humped his wings and uttered a soft cry.

The red-in-red eyes stared defiantly at them.

Quendros halted. Deilcrit did not, but strode to
stand over the huge ossasim, whose muscles swelled
in vain against the stout bindings.

"You said once that you would support anything
that bettered Wehrdom. I have bettered Wehrdom,"
said Deilcrit very quietly, as he had heard Aat
Sereth do. "And you said that you might support a
creature such as Kirelli and some others though
me to be. I have proved myself that thing. I claim
the function that was Imca-Sorr-Aat's. I am Aat
Deilcrit and I will rule from Othdaliee. And I will
do it with Mahrlys at my side. Will you support
me?" Quendros, behind him, growled.

The ossasim hissed and took a deep breath and
closed its eyes. He knew what considerations went
through Eviduey's mind by way of wehr-thought,
but he did not probe there.

After a time the ossasim opened its eye and said,
"Aat-Deilcrit, you leave me little choice. Kirelli
prince of wehrs, you have acknowledgment from
me. But let me leave Aehre-Kanoss, and roam where
I will. I cannot in any conscience serve you. There
are too many conflicts in my heart."

"As you will, Eviduey. Under those terms, keep
your life. Enter my domain thereafter, however,
and you will lose it."

And he motioned to Quendros to unbind the

ossasim and made hurriedly from the scene, before the Laonan could protest.

As he wandered among the whelt-headed women and the newly opened corridors, he reflected that he had broken one promise to Quendros, and would possibly break a second—he had no intention of lending out Mahrlys. But the other, that of aid to the Laonans—that, he would keep.

He felt his ordeal. It weighed down the aching muscles of his arms and shoulders; cuts and bruises stiffened his walk. But he hummed to himself, stroking Kirelli's crest, and did not hurry back to the carnelian throne. It would await him as long as he pleased. He peered into a chamber that was unmistakably one for sleeping, and reflected that he would have to recruit real attendants, the kind who could not be seen through. Those ossasim who served that function had gone into the memories of Imca-Sorr-Aat, with their master's flesh. And he smiled to himslef, leaning against the doorjamb, looking at the richly adorned pallet with its legs of wrought gold, and thought what a pleasure it would be to have Mahrlys tend his wounds. "What, what, what?" he sang to himself, but he knew the answer. Parpis would have been proud to see how far the guerm-tender had come. Mahrlys had been wrong—there had been a place for him in the world, after all.

Thereupon the master of Othdaliee put aside his weariness, and passed with new surety through his halls, stopping only briefly to query his whelt-headed women of light as to how he might best make welcome the first guests of his reign.

This he did by means of his voice, not Wehrdom's network, which to his mind's eye lay greatly changed. He did not fear the whelt-headed ones: their nature lay clear among the mountain of knowledge he had received from Imca-Sorr-Aat. Nor did the splendors so long locked away in a quiescent Othdaliee amaze him. They had waited, with all else, for one to come and call them up to life by vanquishing the monitoring system called Imca-Sorr-Aat. So had the creators of Othdaliee designed it, and so had it come to pass. Othdaliee was open to him, all her power and her beauty. The black glass walls had forsaken the shadows of sleep: Othdaliee was alive with color and masterworks of forgotten art.

Before one he paused, and stared into golden eyes so real-seeming that he shivered. Kirelli touched him through the altered wehr-thought, no longer wraithlike, but a multitude of varicolored points of light, each marking an intelligence active in the circuit.

"Deilcrit," said Kirelli's thought, "do not fear."

But he did fear. Warped or no, Imca-Sorr-Aat had guided Wehrdom for thousands of years. "Who am I to aspire to such a role?" he answered the whelt.

"Who are *we*? We are the best that could be had. We are sufficient by our success. Mnemaat's chosen acknowledge us. We will do better for Wehrdom than even they might, for we are of it."

"Kirelli, I am so tired. . . ."

And the wehr-thought showed him Mahrlys and the spirit powers who awaited by the carnelian throne. He grunted, and they made their way into his throne room.

All eyes followed him across that threshold. Their touch made walking a treacherous undertaking.

The whelt-headed light-forms hovered unobtrusively in the octagonal hall's angles. Three angles were no longer black, but clear, open to the ridge side. One looked over its spine, westward toward the sea.

As he sought the nature of his domain's view, Kirelli forsook him for the throne.

He joined Aat-Estri there, though Mahrlys still knelt in a puddle before the carnelian dais, Sereth and Chayin on either side. He took the spirit power's copper hands in his own and kissed them, and said: "Most High, allow me to serve you."

Her hair glistened like melted bronze. She stood on her tiptoes to kiss him, and laughing, replied: "Lift from me the curse of Imca-Sorr-Aat."

He felt Mahrlys' eyes boring into his back, and Sereth's also. He released her, taking his hands from the cascade of silken hair on her hips. The pressure of her breasts was gone from against him, and he could only look, and remember that time she had touched him in the forest, and grin.

When Aat-Sereth joined them, Deilcrit offered the hospitality of Othdaliee to Mnemaat's successor, who accepted without a smile, on the condition that Deilcrit view the rising moon with him, and then said:

"Chayin feels I have taken too much on myself in what I have done here. He says that we have interfered, and that you have lost more than you have gained. Do you feel this?"

"Oh, no," he said, and whirled to where Chayin sat lowering upon one of his throne's steps. And then he understood how such a one might think that, if looking through Mahrlys' eyes. Her Wehrdom was largely decimated. She found no friends among the remaining wehrs. Kirelli, with a derisive caw, took flight and soared in circles near the chamber's roof.

"It was my solution, one I could not implement, that Sereth aided me with. You saw—you held me—you heard Imca-Sorr-Aat speak through my mouth. Seek Wehrdom's flow; it is different, weakened; but it is not decimated. And if I am not much, Kirelli is more, and together I am sure we will manage."

Aat-Chayin's face showed him that what he had guessed concerning the spirit power's feelings was not far from the truth. And he added, very low: "I had some doubts myself. But I have put them away. If, as you said before, I have aided you, do me the honor of the benefit of your doubt."

And the spirit power muttered someting, and looked away, and allowed that he would give any man that.

It was then Quendros returned from setting Eviduey upon his freedom, while still Deilcrit pondered a way to delicately extricate himself and Màhrlys from their guests. He had things to say to her that could not be said in others' presence.

So he called to Quendros, intending to assign him the task of seeing to the spirit powers, and began to introduce each power by name.

But Quendros interrupted, saying: "I am Laonan," and holding out his hand to Aat-Estri.

"Indeed?" murmured she. "Laore's child?"

"Once and always," stammered Quendros, making a sign with his outstretched hand, which she echoed. Sereth leaned back against the wall, arms folded over his chest. Chayin strode toward Quendros and clapped him upon the back.

"It is good to know that something of civilized man remains here," the spirit power boomed.

"Truth." Estri smiled warmly. "Priest, were we not needed here? Did we merely snatch from you the moment of your triumph?"

"No, no." The Laonan Quendros scowled. "I was, I am afraid, insufficient to the task. But as Minister of Histories and Third Hand of Othdaliee"—and here he moved away from her to Deilcrit, and clasped the youth warmly about the shoulders—"I am sure I can put my small familiarity with all that has gone before to good use."

There was something Deilcrit did not like in the relief he saw upon all their faces, something that chiseled away at the foundations of his triumph. But he said only what he had intended, asking Quendros to take charge of his guests and see what could be found among the ossasim's stores to eat. Kirelli swooped low, showing the way out. And then, magically, they were alone.

He stared out through the wall that had once been blackened glass, but now showed him the cruel, icy ridge slope and the sun blazing low over the western sea.

He did not move, but bespoke the doors. He heard the hiss as they closed, and knew satisfaction: he could command what he willed in Othdaliee.

He said, still watching the sun drip flame upon the ocean, "I would have preferred that you come to me willingly, but we all take what we can get. I spared Eviduey, if it is any comfort to you, though he tried determinedly to slay me."

"Thank you," she said evenly.

"I will try my best to make you content," he said, while before his eyes a tiny bird chased a whelt who soared on the air currents, caught it, and rode its back.

"I would not bother, were I you," she replied.

His hands played with the thong that bound the empty scabbard he had made so long ago from Aat-Estri's discarded tunic, that she had used to clean the mucus from the newborn ptaissling. He would see about the ptaissling, perhaps invite it to Othdaliee. And he would see about carting up some small trees that thrived in shade. It was not only Kirelli who would be uncomfortable living in this bare and unyielding forest of glass and stone, which smelled of metal. And the whelt had few places to perch in the throne room, and none at all in the empty corridors. He looked up at the domed ceiling, measuring it with his eye. A sizable memnis could be moved in, were its pot ample enough.

"This place will be better with some green around. You will come to like it. It is not dead like Dey-Ceilneeth. The very walls will do your bidding." Then he heard her sob, and he did turn around.

She huddled before his throne in her ragged robe, once white, elegant, but now ripped away at mid-thigh and begrimed. Her face was buried in her hands. Her shoulders shook. He longed to go to her. He said, instead:

"You always cry. You cried when I claimed you in Dey-Ceilneeth. I command you to cease."

And when she did not, he did go to her and take her by the shoulders and shake her, very gently, while the thrill of touching her once more threatened to consume his sense. *Not yet* he told himself fiercely.

"Why did you cry then, Mahrlys? Why do you cry now?"

"Mine have died by the thousands, and you ask me why I cry," she said, her green eyes swimming in tears. "I cried in Dey-Ceilneeth when I realized what you were, and saw all tumbling about me in ruins. And now it has tumbled. Let me go and join my dead, where I belong."

"No," he said, and then it *was* time. He set about convincing her, there on the steps of the carnelian throne, that she might find life under his rule preferable to death.

At length he lay exhausted and unsure that he had done so, but when he pushed up and regarded her, and saw the sweat beading her upper lip and the smile that tugged at it, he was greatly eased. She ran a finger down his cheek and touched his lips with it, and said: "Man-wehr, if you can keep that whelt of yours from clawing out my eyes, I might bear you an heir."

And he wondered, then, if the spawn of their union would be winged, with red-in-red eyes, but did not have the heart to ask her. He said, instead: "Not yet, woman. Do what you must, but see to it."

And she lowered her eyes and said, "Yes, my lord," and pressed her forehead against his shoulder, and he had not the heart to tell her of Heicrey, either.

He sat full upright and peered at the sky, dull green and darkening, and pulled her onto his lap. She did not resist. He looked at the softness that resided in her face, a softness he had never before seen, and regretted that his next words would drive it from her green eyes like night drove color from the sea.

"We must go attend our guests, and see why it is Aat-Sereth required our presence at the rising of the moon."

"Deilcrit, I have a confession to make," she breathed, pulling the torn robe so pitifully around her that he cast about his new memories frantically for something in which to clothe her.

"So?" he prompted, and lifted her to her feet.

"I saw you kill the henchman of Mnemaat when we took the children's trial in Nehedra."

He had never dreamed she even recollected him. He blinked, and mumbled a wordless sound, and bade the doors make way for them.

The spirit powers were housed in the chamber Mnemaat had used when he rested in Othdaliee, the one whose pallet stood on golden legs and whose hangings were all shades of gray, like polished slate.

Quendros' raid on the kitchens of Othdaliee had yielded up a sideboard full of carnivore's delights.

Deilcrit squeezed his eyes shut, then opened them, reminding himself of the grisly feast he and Kirelli had shared on the shale of Mt. Imnetosh's slopes. As he had then, the great whelt flew from his perch on a haunch of meat toward Deilcrit, a bloody strip in his beak.

Mahrlys hid her head in his armpit and pressed her body to his.

"Kirelli," said Deilcrit aloud, "tell Mahrlys you mean her no ill."

But Kirelli only squawked, dropping the meat by Deilcrit's foot, and raced about the plushly appointed chamber.

He urged Mahrlys forward, finally realizing the tension that held the spirit powers all wordless.

Aat-Estri lay upon the silken coverlet, her boots kicked off, toying with her hair, her eyes on the pattern worked into the spread.

The dark power leaned against a chest bespangled with inlays of bone. Beside him lounged Quendros, his ragged tunic discarded, wet hair dripping.

Sereth sat half upon the massive table that centered the room, cleaning his nails with a knife. He, too, was stripped down to breech, his hair and skin gleaming wetly. As Deilcrit and Mahrlys entered he put the weapon by Se'keroth, amid his gear which strewed the tabletop, and came to meet him.

"You should not have waited for us to eat," Deilcrit said mechanically, trying to pinpoint what was wrong in the room.

"We find ourselves concerned with things other than our bellies," said Sereth. As Mahrlys quavered Chayin's name, stiffened in Deilcrit's graps, he looked more closely and saw the dark power's foreboding demeanor. Then he looked back at Aat-Sereth and said that he did not understand.

"It is customary here, as we learned in Dey-

Ceilneeth," said Sereth easily, disarmingly, with a comradely smile, "to exchange ipherim. So we thought, Estri and I, how fitting it would be to celebrate your accession in that manner."

Mahrlys' whole form quaked, and she moaned. Deilcrit looked from her to the spirit power Estri, and then at Aaat-Sereth. He dropped his arms from Harlys' shoulders.

"So be it," said Deilcrit, watching Mahrlys closely.

She stood like a statue.

But the cahndor pushed himself away from the inlaid chest and struck an eloquently threatening pose.

"As you can see," continued Sereth blithely. "Chayin has some small objection to this, which if we ignore I am sure—"

"Sereth," growled Chayin.

"Yes, cahndor?" Sereth grinned, sliding off the table.

"There can be only one ending to this."

"So I, myself, have surmised. Let us commence. The food grows cold."

"You need not worry. You are not going to be eating it, but will be instead cold as any carcass on that sideboard."

Deilcrit flicked a glance at Quendros, whose hand scratched his new beard and whose eyes were hooded.

Then Sereth asked for Deilcrit's help with the table, and they moved it to the side of the room.

Exposed thus was a circular rug the color of mist.

Estri had taken leave of the couch. She sauntered leisurely to the center of the gray circle and said, "Well, is this not apt? I see only one problem."

"What is that?" asked Deilcrit, when no one else

did, as he instructed the doors to close and took Mahrlys under his arm.

Quendros, upon Chayin's request, unstrapped the white-bladed sword and handed it to him.

"The problem is," said Estri quite calmly, running her toe through the fleece of the rug and watching the track it made, "that there are not two chalded witnesses. Not even the Laonan priest would be acceptable to our authorities as witness in a death match when both men's holdings comprise a continent." And she wet her lips, and expelled a shuddering breath, and continued less calmly: "So, since we cannot have a death within the circle, even though we have a circle, both of you put those weapons down! I will not stand for it! As the only ranking neutral party, I demand hands only, full conventions, permanent injury penalized."

Eyes flashing, she tossed her head. "Deilcrit!"

"Most High?"

"You are going to see something few have witnessed: the dharen of Silistra and the cahndor of Nemar scuffling on the mat like apprentice Slayers! So goes it with these highly skilled, intelligent scions of the most evolved race yet produced among all the worlds of creations. So goes it with a Mi'ysten child whose father was a god before whom Mnemaat quailed; and with Hase-Enor, our long-awaited pinnacle of genetics, he who is kin to all men. I tell you, Deilcrit," she continued in a slightly lowered tone, "my father would not—"

"That is enough, Estri," snapped Sereth. "You are right about convention, but I need no lectures from you. Get out of the way and keep quiet."

She did that, and Deilcrit was glad that Mahrlys watched.

"Chayin, what would you fight for?"

"For the love of seeing you at my feet."

"Estri, do we have your august permission to fight with no prize?"

"No," said Estri, "Use Se'keroth, and all that accompanies it. I have had, as you say, about all of this I am willing to take."

And Deilcrit was then not glad at all that Mahrlys' head swayed from side to side as she followed the discussion. He pulled her nails from between her teeth, and wondered as he held her wrist what lay between her and the cahndor.

The two spirit powers stepped onto the gray, fluffy mat and Estri came around it to stand by Deilcrit's side. Her arms were crossed over her breasts. He could see her pulse jump in her throat.

"The cahndor," said Estri quietly, "will take the offensive, try to get Sereth in close, if . . ." And then she fell silent as the dark power, crouched over, suddenly unwound and his long arms lashed out.

Sereth ducked under them, his hands moving in toward the darker man's throat, and at the last moment dropping down.

Chayin straightened suddenly, throwing his torso back, and Sereth, from out of Chayin's reach, stepped one step in and his hands left his hips to deliver two simultaneous blows to Chayin's neck with the inner sides of his hands. Struck a nerve-debilitating blow by the short bones below Sereth's thumbs, Chayin dropped to the rug without even a groan.

Estri expelled a breath, muttered a curse, and took a step forward.

"That is a four on the pain chart. You could have killed him," she said very softly.

Sereth stirred Chayin's crumpled form with his toe. "You underestimate me, Estri. Chayin did the same. You see the results. Now, call it!"

"You have it: Se'keroth and a new enemy, and twice the trouble you had before."

"Thank you, neutral witness."

Flushed, Estri bit her lip. He heard her mutter something about knowing better. Then she went up to Sereth and said soft things and he took her in his arms and Deilcrit was reminded that he, too, held such a woman, and pulled close Mahrlys.

After a time he heard Kirelli's raucous squawking, the thunder of wings above his head, but he did not look up.

When later he walked them to the ridgetop, alone, he marveled at the clearness of the night air, at the tiny crescent of a moon, and at the dimmed amber dome that had once housed the memories of Imca-Sorr-Aat.

The cahndor, as the spirit powers called him, had taken his defeat better than Deilcrit could imagine he might have done, were the positions reversed.

Doubtless Chayin would have acquitted himself better with Aat-Estri if he had been included in the spirit powers' version of the exchanging of ipherim. Which he was not. He was in another chamber, under Quendros' care.

This had been of great concern to Deilcrit, for he knew himself no match for even the loser of the contest he had beheld.

So he had bid Quendros minister to the dark power, while he himself was taken deeper into Estri and Sereth's company than he had ever expected to be.

And it had greatly constrained him, to use a woman with another man.

He felt like a thief, a masquerader, an impersonator about to be unmasked. He still felt so, carrying visions in his head which shattered the Beneguan law into fragments too tiny ever to be reclaimed. He recollected the softenss of Estri, and stole a sidelong glance in the moonlight.

As if hearing his thoughts, she turned to him and said that if ever he found the sheath of Se'keroth, which Sereth had cast into the bay, he should return it to her.

He promised that he would look for it.

Long after they had disappeared, leaving behind little wisps of flame that danced in the air, he sat on the ridgetop and stared down at Othdaliee, at the browned globe on the little island in the stream, at the twelve black towers waiting for him to explore. Mahrlys was down there. He conjured sight of her ivory throat, arched back in passion. Quendros awaited him with all the education and guidance he could desire. Kirelli swooped along the corridors, gloating, his "Kreesh, breet, kreesh" echoing in the halls of their freedom.

Why was it, then, that he felt so lonely?

He rested his elbow on his knee and his chin in his palm, and thought that he would look very hard for the green sword's sheath.

Estri's Epilogue

Chayin left us; courteously and with a small show of affection, at the Lake of Horns. It had been Sereth's obviation. He had asked me the date on which I would like to return, and I had told him what my own estimate of the actual date was, and he had brought us all into the seven-cornered hall without even a shiver of cold touching my sensing.

Which startled our faithful Carth, who was holding a meeting there.

Of Carth we asked the date and found it to be Cai first first, which pleased Sereth, so that the corner of his mouth, where the scar runs by it, pulled inward.

The cahndor went to Carth, and pulled him away abruptly; and Sereth sought a tatooed Menetpher, gathered him up.

While I played hostess to the high dhareners of Silistra, smelly and ragged in Chayin's undertunic and hardworn leathers, Sereth and Chayin bespoke their unification agreement to Carth and to the ranking dharener of the Parset Lands, who was also there, he whose cheeks bear green bolts of lightning, three on a side.

So, it was done. I watched them together and breathed a sigh that caused one of the lakeborn dhareners to raise a golden eyebrow. I ignored him, staring above me at the ceiling with its ruddy gold scales, then down at my feet where the Shapers' Seal, sign of my father's people, glows eternally up from the floor. It is that of a universal order not completed, but one in which each of us have a part.

We have come a long way since joining forces. They will mend their differences. Or they will not. What matters is that for a time they shared love, and during that time they created out of their love a lasting monument to those times. My whole world will benefit from what union the cahndor and dharen have bestowed on Silistra: a change in the viewpoint of a few individuals that indeed affects the fortunes of all the individuals who consider themselves part of the whole called Silistra; a succinct summation of catalysis genetics; a monument to Khys, Sereth's predecessor, that he built in spite of his own intent, by acting according to his sense of fitness.

I remember the thrill that went through me as I watched Carth and the Menetpher witness Sereth and Chayin's pact. And all that had almost been lost on the shores of Aehre-Kanoss paraded by my sensing, and I wondered why Chayin had risked it.

I thought of how early he had been intent on his course, recalling that it was he who was first through the gate, and he who bound us to Deilcrit by his word. And when it was done and Chayin came toward me, I knew that he would leave.

He hugged me, and kissed my neck, and told me to come with Sereth in summer to Nemar North and look over the yearling threx, and I found myself near tears, though I saw his father's stamp on him, and it chilled me.

As I told him how much I regretted what had come to pass, my voice betrayed me, and he and I stood awhile unheedful of all else. When he released me and wished me tasa and strode away through the dhareners into the outer hall, Sereth was nowhere in sight.

So I bade Carth have a meal placed in the dharen's keep, and sought my couch-mate in the baths.

Glossary

(B) = Beneguan
(P) = Parset
(S) = Silistran
(St) = Stothric
(M) = Mi'ysten

Aat: (B) To come into being.

Aehre: (B) The eastermost country that comprises half of the continental aggregate termed Aehre-Kanoss; the city-state Aehre, on the inland Imaen Sea. Continental Aehre contains Benegua, Nehedra, Bachryse, Fhrelatiadek, Aehre proper, and Othdaliee. It is bordered on the north by the Rosharkand Mountains and Fai Teraer-Moyhe; on the east by the Valsima River, Piyah-Ptesh, and the Imaen Sea; on the south by Kanoss and the Embrodming Sea; on the west by the tip of the Rosharkands and the Embrodming.

Aehre-Kanoss: (B) Designation for the inhabited areas of the continent that dominates Silistra's eastern hemisphere, including the islands east of Kanoss, whose shores none were empowered to speak of; the lands ruled over by Wehrdom.

Bachryse: (B) A Laonan town on the Isanisa River in the Rosharkand Valley; one of the six remaining

strongholds of man in continental Aehre-Kanoss,
Bachryse is administrated by an elected male
Byek.

Benegua: (B) Those lands within the Wall of
Mnemaat; the stronghold of the Vahais of Mnemaat, Aehre-Kanoss' ruling body; the spiritual
sanctuary of Wehrdom.

berceide: (B) Large, constrictor-type serpent.

Byek: (B) Any of the local administrators of
Aehre-Kanoss; a Byek may be male or female,
man or wehr, though this is regulated by the
traditions of each city-state. All Byeks are subject to the Vahais of Mnemaat, but to no secular
authority. They rule supreme and unmolested in
their various preserves, subject only to the
Beneguan mandate, the whims of Wehrdom, and
the aggressions of their fellow Byeks.

cahndor: (P) "Will of the sand"; warlord of a
Parset tribe; in usage, one who commands the
speaker's allegiance and respect.

campt: (B) A long-bodied, tusked carnivore whose
average length and weight are thrice a large
man's; the campt has four legs, a tail one thrid
its own length, a hairless hide usually russet in
color.

catalysis genetics: (St) The catalysis cycle (see
the writings of the dharen Khys, Silistra, hide-
years sixty-three through sixty-five); the reference formulae upon which the science of societal
engineering was based. In outline: a proposed
genetic cycle based in sociogenetics stating that
atavism resurges at intervals made opportune
by the manifestation of psychosocial triggers provided by inbreeding individuals with strong pre
dispositions for agricultural gregariousness, cre
ating a technological burst which undermines
any existing feudal power structure and allows
for the reassertion of individual aggressiveness

This balance, sought repeatedly in rising civilizations, must be exact, or collapse of civilization follows. Hence the *cycle*: gregarious strategies create agricultural societies at the beginning of technological surges, curve produces progressively more altruistic, then atavistic individuals at moments of technological ascendancy; culling between groups commences; precipitates a fall back to basic agricultural grouping; cycle proceeds in increasingly pronounced curves until unstable level of advanced technology triggers manipulations of societal stable strategies in an attempt to preserve the race as atavism physically assaults existing morality and survival rate lowers. Prevalent correlates on Aehre-Kanoss show an attempt to hold to a pretechnological culture by culling both the most and the least survival-suited individuals, in an obvious ploy to show the progress of the genetic curve and hold it at agri-man, against evolution's ever-more-energetic efforts to inject atavistic catalysts into a gene pool so stagnant that it, of itself, demands and produces them.

ci'ves: (S) A small, furred predator common in the Sihaen-Istet hills.

couch-mate: (S) Persons bound together by love and/or issue; in usage, those in extended couchbond, those who consider their relationship more binding than simple couchbond.

couchbond: (S) A companionship agreement between two consenting adults.

Dey-Ceilneeth: (B) The Brinjiiri Laonan Museum, once a part of the Laonan cult's capital city, around which was built the Wall of Mnemaat, later appropriated by Wehrdom.

dharen: (St) The spiritual and secular ruler of civilized Silistra; the supreme authority of the Day-Keeper hierarchy; planetary potentate.

dhareness: (St) A word coined for Estri Hadrath diet Estrazi when she became couch-mate of the dharen Khys; this position has no formal duties or dignities attached to it as yet.

Fai Teraer-Moyhe: (St) The derivation of "Fai Teraer-Mohye" is Strothric; this brings us to the problem of crediting words as "Beneguan" or "Darsti," when both languages devolved from Stothric. In Strothric the term means "Cove o Resurrection." In modern Beneguan its has come to mean the "Dark Land." Fai Teraer-Moyhe is the fabled spot upon which the adept Laore was disembowled after being convicted of necromancy, heresy, and sedition; and from which he rose whole of form seven days later to begin the dialogues with his waiting adherents which were to form the bases of Stothric thought in the ages to come. (*See* Laonan.) In present Beneguan society it is a land of banishment, of death, from which no living being returns.

fahrass: (B) A highly poisonous silver-berried plant; the berries are called stepsisters by Beneguans. The ingestion of one fingernail-sized berry may cause death by oversedation of the autonomic nervous system.

fhrefrasil: (B) A large, carnivorous primate with opposing thumbs, generally manlike, but possessed of a prehensile tail and long, silky sorrel fur.

guerm: (B) An amphibious mammal found along the shores of Aehre-Kanoss. There seem to be a number of varieties of guerm, and as all else in this glossary, any definition I might give is limited to what I learned in our short reconnaissance and what matches I can make with knowledge I already possess. In this case I have very little, and leave the detailing of the spawning, feeding, and mating habits of guerm to those who will give Benegua the detailed biological study it deserves.

hase-enor: (St) Of all flesh; the purported goal of Silistra's long-standing policy of genetic mixing; one whose genealogy includes all bloodlines; a thoroughly admixed individual.

hest: (S) To bend or twist natural law to serve the will; to command by mind; to cause a probability not inherent in the time to manifest.

high-couch: (S) A Well-Keepress; any woman able to demand over thirty gold pieces per couching; formally: the hereditary head of Silistra's Well System.

hulion: (S) A large, ptaisslike, highly intelligent winged carnivore prevalent on continental Silistra.

iis: (B) Priestess; literally: "austere." In use with another title, as iis-Vahais, it denotes ascendancy: high priestess of the Vahais.

Imca-Sorr-Aat: (B) "One who came into being out of many"; Wehrdom's organic memory storage; the corporeal interface which implements the cogitations of that memory.

Imnetosh: (B) The mountain upon whose slope lies Othdaliee.

ipheri: (B) Literally: "resplendent in the sun's rays"; an honorific address.

ipherim: (B) Attendant of ipheri; a consort or couchmate.

Isanisa: (B) The Isanisa River, whose sources are both the subterranean river that winds through Othdaliee and down Imnetosh's slope, and the Bachryse Falls in the Rosharkand Valley.

iyl: (B) Literally: "eyes." A male honorific restricted to those employed by the Vahais of Mnemaat.

jicekak: (B) A thorned, lanceolate bush ubiquitous in the Beneguan valley's rain forests; the itching, weeping syndrome resulting from jicekak scratches in allergic individuals ranges widely in severity, though some irritant effect is visible on any skin scratched by jicekak thorns.

Khys: (St) The dharen Khys, now deceased. Let me refer you to *Wind from The Abyss*, wherein Khys is well-delineated, both by myself and by Carth; or, better, to his own writings: *Ors Yris-Tera; Se'keroth, the Motif of Catalysis; Hesting, the Primal Prerogative*; to name but a few. Khys Enmies, molecular biologist, genetic and societal engineer, Stoth adept, Laonan priest, Shaper's son, dharen of Silistra, can hardly be reduced to a dozen lines in anyone's glossary. What might be most pertinent to say about him here is that, in good Darsti fashion, having experimented extensively with western Silistra, he let the east go its own way. The lands of Aehre-Kanoss were those shores of which none were empowered to speak by his command. However, the longevity of humans and wehrs seems to indicate either the introduction of Silistran serums into the gene pool of evolution's commensurate action: although those of Aehre-Kanoss are not long-lived by Silistran standards, we saw no evidence of later-life lethals such as debilitating diseases in the mature, and this has led me to conjecture that though Khys' hand is not in evidence, it nevertheless has touched Aehre-Kanoss.

Laonan: (St) The Laonan faith; proselytizers of Laore's life and work; precursor to the Stothric church; the mystical society founded by Laore and based upon his life's teachings, most notably the two-volume *Forewarnings* and *Se'keroth, Sword of Severence*, a four-volume prophetic allegory; anyone practicing Laore's disciplines.

Laore: (St) The founder of the Laonan faith, from which sprang the Stoth disciplines and later the Day-Keepers' hierarchy that yet holds sway over civilized Silistra.

Lake of Horns: (S) The Day-Keepers' city, capital of the dharen Sereth, located at the Lake of Horns, from which it takes it name.

memnis: (B) A large, white-barked tree that prefers a riparian environment, the memnis has long frondlike leaves that may depend to touch the ground, of a yellow or yellow-greenish color; its inner bark is ascribed great medicinal power and is the main ingredient of most Beneguan poultices.

Menetph: (P) The southernmost of the Parset Lands; a desert principality recently come under the co-regency of Jaheil of Dordassa and Chayin of Nemar; one of the Taken Lands, Menetph has the best seaport and shipwrights of any state in the new Parset conglomerate and is also the site of the co-cahndors' winter capital.

Mi'ysten: (M) The world Mi'ysten; the race of the same name; experimental sphere of the Shapers.

Mnemaat: (St) The corruption of Laore's postulated "Differentiating Unfixed"; the personalization of the Unseen into which the Laonans fell in the Late Mechanist Age. Some factions believe that the creation of the Wall of Mnemaat around the Laonan Museum was a contributing factor to the schism that split the Loanan faith in twain and spawned the Stoths as we now conceive them. That Khys encouraged the use of that nomer for himself in the minds of Wehrdom must, I feel, be an expression of his humor; and not, as Sereth has postulated, an indicator by which we may judge the depth and strength of his hatred for his ancient enemy, Aehre-Kanoss, and the Laonans who once ruled supreme there.

Mnemaat's henchemen: (B)   Those who implement the strict culling of over- and undersuccessful individuals during the Children's Trial.

Nehedra: (B)   A town within the Wall of Mnemaat, Nehedra lies on a small tributary of the Isanisa just east of Dey-Ceilneeth Road. She is concerned primarily with the maintenance of the Beneguan preserve, and takes charge of all children consecrated into Wehrdom's service. From all of Aehre are the children gathered into Nehedra, some once in their lives to take the Children's Trial, some for long periods of time to study the parables of Beneguan law and become fit to serve Wehrdom. Whether consecrated to Mnemaat the Unseen, Imca-Sorr-Aat, or directly to Wehrdom, all children's instruction and all Benegua's commerce is handled in Nehedra.

Nemar: (P)   One of western Silistra's Parset Desert Lands; birthplace of Chayin rendi Inekte, and his hereditary kingdom; now the winter capital of the co-cahndor's reign.

Nothrace: (B)   The razed town on Nothrace ridge; the shelflike ridge at Mt. Imnetosh's foot. Nothrace, like most of the eastern coast of Aehre, has no slope gentle enough to provide a harbor, but rises in a sheer cliff face to more than ten thousand (B.S. Standard) feet above the sea; the purported birthplace of Aat-Deilcrit.

obviation of space: (S)   The Shaper mode of travel, only now coming into use on Silistra; the transportation of matter *around* distance by making use of the nonsequential circuits that exist out of time: it is said that from the place called the domain of the Seventh Sorter all destinations are equidistant in that they exist coeval with the point of immutable now.

ossasim: (B) The man-derived, winged creatures to whose advantage Wehrdom was designed and has since evolved.

Othdaliee: (B) The capital "city" of Imca-Sorr-Aat, Othdaliee is a living relic from Aehre-Kanoss' Mechanist past. I can find no mention of it in any of our records and must assume that it was, even then, of a most secret nature, to have housed such experiments as Imca-Sorr-Aat.

owkahen: (St) "The time coming to be"; those probabilities among all the available futures that will manifest as reality.

Parset: (P) An individual of any one of the five Parset Lands, the desert regions held by the co-cahndors. The Parset Lands still maintain their autonomy, notwithstanding the alliance formed between the co-cahndors and the dharen of Silistra.

peona: (B) A pink-fleshed, black-skinned melon that grows wild in the Isanisa river valley.

Port Astrin: (S) Well Astria's dependent city; the Liaison's Port, that is, the only facility on Silistra for starships. Estri diet Hadrath Estrazi's hereditary holdings included both Port Astrin and Well Astria; the port from which the expedition to Aehre-Kanoss was mounted.

ptaiss: (B) An eight- to twelve-hundred-pound, wedge-headed carnivorous mammal with slit-pupiled eyes and a tufted tail, in size and shape resembling the Silistran dorkat, but with the mental skills and intelligence of a hulion.

quenel: (B) A small, bushy-tailed carnivore, with a long, tapering snout, markedly rounded cranium, and paws with opposing-thumbed, five-digited "fingers."

razor-moon: (S) A sharpened disk of steel or the green metal stra; a casting weapon with several varieties; the boot-sheathed razor-moons I favor are the one-way, nonreturning sort whose diameter is about that of a woman's hand.

roema: (B) A smaller cousin, seemingly, of the quenel, with the difference that while the quenel's eyes are round-pupiled, the roema's are slit. It is a burrower and a stalker, and makes no sound other than a sibilant hiss.

saiisa: (S) A Silistran term of disrespect usually applied to coin girls of questionable cleanliness.

Se'keroth: (St) The legendary blade of which Laore wrote, and with which, by all accounts, he was slain. "The blade itself, Se'keroth of the fire-gemmed hilt, was reclaimed by Khys at great personal peril in the last pass before the onset of the Fall of Man. With six lesser priests he crossed the Embrodming and liberated the sword from the Brinjiiri Loanan Museum, in the midst of that enemy's capital. . . ." ". . . Se'keroth's magical nature ensures its possession by those catalytic personalities that shape each ensuing age, all of whom undergo rigorous purification before the sword falls into their hands. . . ." "He who wields Se'keroth is himself that weapon, is himself wielded by that same which transmutes the gross into fine. . . ." —the dharener Carth. ". . . The legend inscribed on the blade, 'Se'keroth, direel b'estet Se'keroth,' literally: 'Se'keroth, light from out of darkness by the sword of severance,' is ostensibly a simplification of the aphorism 'reduction/resolution' that pervaded early Stothric attempts to deduce the relationship of substance to matter."—E.H.d.E., *Wind from the Abyss*.

Shaper: (S) One who can control the constituents of matter and form them to his will; Shaper designates not so much a race or bloodline as an ability; Estrazi, forebear to many races, is a Shaper, as are those he calls brothers, though even in that small circle not all actually shape;

Chayin carries Shaper blood through his Mi'ysten father, Raet, though not all Mi'ystens shape. Khys had the skill from his father, Kystrai, who was Chayin's grandsire; and Sereth has come to his ability through a series of genetic inversions which brought his own traces of Shaper heritage into contact with the beneficial mutations Silistran evolution so frequently provides, causing totally new configurations of interacting predispositions to appear than have been previously encountered.

sort: (S)   (n.) The probabilities inherent in a specific moment of time; those alternate future available to one trained to seek them; the display mode of probability.

sort: (S)   (v.) To "sort" probability; to determine in advance the resultant probabilities from postulated actions.

stepsisters: (B)   A colloquialism for fahrass berries.

telsodas: (B)   A pinkish, carnivorous plant with reddish-brown leaves that depends upon flesh to stave off indehiscence.

threx: (S)   The preferred riding beast of western Silistra.

Uritheria: (P)   A beast from the Parsets' Tar-Kesian mythology, said to have ignited the sun in the sky; a gigantic winged and clawed serpent-like beast that is the cahndor of Nemar's traditional protector.

vabillia: (B)   A strongly revivifying root when taken in small doses, vabillia grows submerged around the edges of shallow pools.

wehr: (B)   Any mind capable of entering into the community of minds called Wehrdom; an individual possessing the pan-species communication gene.

Wehrdom: (B)   The hierarchal organizations of wehrs.

wehr-master: (B) Colloquial phylum name for ossasim; any coordinator of wehrs for the benefit of Wehrdom.

wehr-wind: (B) The circuit by which Wehrdom communicates; the network of joined minds of Wehrdom; any communication by way of that network.

Wisdom Mask: (B) A mask like that of an aged woman, used in Beneguan mystical rites.